CITY DOGS

Also by William Brashler

THE BINGO LONG TRAVELING ALL-STARS
AND MOTOR KINGS

CITY DOGS

A NOVEL BY

William Brashler

Harper & Row, Publishers
New York, Evanston,
San Francisco, London

First Edition

Designed by Janice Stern

LIBRARY OF CONGRESS CATALOGING IN PUBLICATION DATA

Brashler, William.
  City dogs.
  I. Title.
PZ4.B82273Ci   [PS3552.R33]   813'.5'4   75–9350
ISBN 0–06–010448–1

76 77 78 79 10 9 8 7 6 5 4 3 2 1

For my Mother
and Father

CITY DOGS

1

He sat in the upper corner of the bleachers. Alone, with acres of empty benches around him, early September. A wind coming off the lake ripped into the stadium flags, and he pulled his knees to his chin, his teeth chattering uncontrollably. In front of him were the green grass and the vines of Wrigley Field, and against the green the Cubs and the Cardinals going through the motions. He shook and rubbed his clenched fists together, so rapidly that he could hardly make out what was happening. Still, he didn't move, the lone holdout in the bleachers, underdressed in a thin, gray jacket and a pair of baggy work pants, leather shoes but no socks.

Near a tunnel below him, he spotted a vendor, the peanut and popcorn man, a graying black wearing a plastic Cub hat and a heavy coat. The vendor's peanuts lay cold and unprofitable in front of him, the box swinging freely around his shoulders as he warmed his hands in his pockets. Were it eighty degrees and the middle of August, with the Cubs still close and the kids jamming the bleachers with their tee-shirts and yellow hardhats, the peanut man would be strolling and singing, laughing and throwing out the bags, snapping quarters in midair.

But today he wasn't singing and wasn't selling. He loitered in the aisle, watched a few pitches, then he met the stare of the hunched, emaciated figure sitting high up in the stands.

The vendor turned and began the ascent into the bleachers, the wind hissing and snaking inside his coat. He turned his back to it and moved laterally along the benches until he stood half facing the solitary fan.

"Damn Cubs," the man said, his eyes glued to the field.

"Weather ain't fit for no Eskimo," the vendor said. He bounced on the balls of his feet to keep warm, pumping his body up and down, jiggling what coins he had in his belt.

"If they was winnin' there'd be forty thousand here."

"Seems summer come hot one day and turn ice the next," the vendor said.

"I saw 'em win, you better believe it. Thirty-two, thirty-five, and thirty-eight."

They both followed a curving, line-drive double down the left-field line. A Cardinal, not a Cub, and the team went three runs down. The wind gusted, the vendor lurched offbalance then regained his stance.

"What you got today?" he said.

"Stone. Good one."

"Blue? My man likes blue."

"Yeah."

"How 'bout timepieces? Gonna snag some more a those?"

"Dunno."

The vendor went into his box and grabbed a bag of peanuts. Inside his palm he cupped a fin, wrapped it around the cellophane, and handed the package to the man. Instead of a quarter, the man returned a gold ring set with a gleaming baby-blue zircon. With a glance the vendor inspected and okayed it, then slipped it into his pocket. By nightfall it would be across town, on Maxwell Street or Comiskey Park when the Sox came back to town.

The vendor swiveled and headed back down the aisle.

"Some weather, ain't it, Harry?" he called back. "Deathly."

Soon he was down and out of the wind, disappearing into the tunnel below.

2

The figure in the bleachers didn't follow him, but kept his eyes on the field. He shivered and trembled, only his pocket warm with the fin. He was nothing but a dwarf beneath the scoreboard, a spot of gray in the gray. And through his teeth, through reddened cheeks and a two-day beard, he spat out the words, "Thirty-two, thirty-five, and thirty-eight."

He had wedged himself between the bed and the wall, a fish, this fish breathing through his mouth in a rasping, sucking rhythm that he called sleep. He would have stayed that way, bent and uncomfortable, circulation in the one leg which he'd pulled under him ebbing, purple, had not his stomach rung the bell in his brain. It was his personal, portable, built-in alarm, his thirst alarm, and it told him once again that his stomach was an empty reservoir that needed filling.

He rolled to his left, away from the cold plaster, and his once-dead, bent leg shot pinpricks of surprise to his shanks. He rolled like a fish, into the center of the mattress turned hammock, and through the funk of his mind he realized he had been sleeping with his clothes on again.

Gently, without craning his neck or twisting his eggshell of a head, he pulled his shoes on. Light poked holes through the shade like spears, a sure sign that it was daytime, unquestionably, even morning. He tried to swallow, first things first, and he felt only the carpeted folds in his throat. With his left hand he wiped his mouth, the crud on his lips, a slight turn of his wrist and the letters faced him: L-U-M. Tattooed in purple across the back of his hand, personal neon over the tendons and under the knuckles. It was him all right, Harry Lum, all fifty-seven skinny years, and looking straight into the fat-faced innocence of another Sunday morning.

In a moment he was hustling down Wilson Avenue, no socks on, his heel-sloped leather shoes untied, the tee-shirt and pants he had slept in pulled up underneath a thin, gray jacket. The three blocks between his room and Liberty Bell Liquors he knew by heart, even on his nose when he crawled

3

it, usually walked it, weaving against the winds off the lake, now long blocks since his mouth was dry and sour. The shoelaces whipped wildly against his white-hollow ankles. He was 135 pounds, with a stomach twice as deep, twice as empty as the night before last when it was Death Valley. It was five minutes before noon and his Chicago Cubs were out of town.

Within a block of the Liberty Bell, he saw the crowd. Two regulars and a beefy blimp of a woman, standing in a triangle staring at the sidewalk. One of the men, in a fluorescent orange Naugahyde cap, leaned against a parking meter, his terrier winding its clothesline leash around his leg and the meter. The other chewed on a plastic cigar holder. The woman, whose face was puffy and flushed pink to match her housecoat, watched the terrier and absently jerked the leash of her whining German shepherd. Harry pulled up with a stumble and waited with them, grumbling while the balding Jew owner of the Liberty Bell bubbled rancid cigar smoke and pulled back the iron grating from the windows and door.

Standing there, the bottoms of Harry's feet began to absorb the dampness that oozed from the sidewalk, the gray soup that at dawn worked its way through the pores of the cement like a sweat. It was still September, not that cold, but damn if every day in this town didn't have something cold in it, with a clammy sky that wouldn't let the sun come through to dry things out. The dirt, the hot-dog papers and the Lloyd J. Harris pie tins lay in soggy heaps against the curbs, occasionally blowing like weeds against Harry's leg.

He shifted his weight. The lousy Jew opened late to spite him cause he was a Polack. Lum. Harry Lum. Short for Lumakowski. The fat lady's German shepherd sniffed at Harry's mealy shoes. He kicked at the dog's licorice nose and it growled; the woman jerked the leash and glared at Harry as if to say that he'd do for just about half the beast's lunch. So shit, dogs were shit, city dogs, emaciated worm-ridden hounds that ate garbage and mounted bitches in intersec-

4

tions without regard for race, color, or size. Or cop dogs, one-half nut better than alley mutts, that would swim to Milwaukee if the copper told them, the ones that pinned Harry in the alleys and sliced through his cuffs with teeth that looked like they belonged on a piano. Cop dogs weren't dogs anymore, not like the old neighborhood mutts that fetched sticks. But they were dogs, dogs that had to be fed and fixed and clipped and pushed out the door so they could shit and then ten-to-one they did it on the sidewalk where human beings who paid for the damn dog food stepped in it. He, Harry Lum, had done that enough, and with his shoe leather not thick enough for a pancake it was a rotten thing. Then the Jew opened the door, the Bell's neon came alive, and Harry's head smelled home.

The fat woman pushed in front of him, like the fat kids in the hot-dog lines at the ball park, and Harry lost his breath against the door frame. Finally he panned sixty-three cents for a bottle of white port, smelling the shiny aluminum cap, turning it off with his tongue. The Jew took Harry's coins, jingled them in his hand, put some of that Star of David grease on them, then tossed them into the drawer. The G. Heileman Brewing Company Chicago Cub calendar looked down at them like an eye chart, 165 chances for the Cubbies to throw it to the tubes, the '69 season becoming a tragedy that Harry lived, and he reached down to pick up the pint from the counter where the Jew had slapped it. Harry tucked the brown bag into his waist, his port in the storm, he always said, and drew his jacket over it.

He ran his hand through his hair as he barreled on home. Three reverse blocks. He tried to swallow, itched for the port. He would drink it with a hamburger bun and some jelly back in the room. Then he would count up his money, rummage for it through the underwear and the sheets, the cigarette packs, the empties, and decide what to do for the day. He was sure he had a sawbuck in a pair of pants, somewhere

5

on earth, laying there crinkled up like good news, enough for another bottle, an elderberry, an Amigo, and watch them Cubs on the telly.

He stepped around a pile of shit heaped high in the middle of the sidewalk—no dog had done that one—and admired his footwork. He was clear now, the fuzz off the inside of his eyeballs. Only his belly talked back and he would have to do something about that. For a time he had been buying a bottle of Maalox with every two bottles of port and that helped some, like Three-in-One oil. But he was fifty-seven, nineteen and twelve, and he hadn't let a doctor shine a flashlight up his ass in years. He was skinny except for the sunken balloon gut of a stomach, and his white, blue-veined skin clung to his bones like soggy canvas over tent wires. At times he had trouble catching his breath, dug for it out of his lungs, then looked down and saw the veins in his hands bulging and pulsing, the river in his temple gone mad, his fingers shaking uncontrollably. Then he would panic, try to get his appetite back, swig Maalox and order greasy chicken and kielbasa at the diners. But he would throw that up, like sauerkraut through a strainer, get the drinker's shakes, and decide that the wine was worth it, worth the morning cotton mouth, breath that could start fires or put them out. His blood was wine, not red but pale white and dry. He would get by from day to day, like the Cubs, like the dogs, like the days.

He turned away from a paddy wagon, the blue-and-white paddy that rattled and grunted over chuck holes, and he glued his eyes to the sidewalk. Cops were part of the scenery in this neighborhood, City of Chicago, State of Police, just blue belching assholes in their hats with the checkered bands that made them look like cabbies. Cops were nothing special in a landscape of winos, hustlers, hillbillies, Indians, niggers, spics, and any other assortment of jagoffs who came to Wilson Avenue because their cars had broken down, or because they'd gotten off at the wrong CTA stop, or who stumbled and fell, all of them staying for the rest of their lives. They moved in and out and across each other, pecking, bitching, ratting, slicing, shooting, spitting, ignoring one another. Which is what Harry wanted to do just now, a Polack in a Sunday wasteland, the promise of port in his belly button, looking as if he had no secrets. He was almost home and in no mood to be toyed with. The paddy wagon passed. The two patrolmen inside picked their teeth and didn't bother to look at him. He felt for the bottle in his waist, the glass lump that would take care of things until he figured out what he was going to do.

The port went down like milk. It was lukewarm and bitter, running over his teeth like rain over moss, and he shook himself. He found a rumpled pack of Camels on the bed and lit up the last scurvied survivor. A speck of tobacco clung to his lip and he tried to spit it out, like a nagging booger; he failed, then left it hang there like a fly on flypaper. The darkness of the room, the shade drawn shut, door closed, the single light bulb and the picture tube dark, brought back the bleariness, gummed with new wine, of the night before. He leaned back and stung the knob of his shoulder bone on the curved iron bar of the bed. He rubbed it and sank into the depths of his mind, his eyes closed, trying to see himself in Wrigley Field, where he always had dreamt of being, all in green and sunshine, gamboling in the outfield with Hack Wilson, losing himself in the vines after a screaming liner, the leaves and the cheers and the uniform all in him and of him, Harry Lumakowski of Milwaukee Avenue and the National League.

If he could have frozen his life at any point, it would have been in 1932. Not that life was particularly good then; in fact, it was the thick of the Depression and Harry was lucky to find work unloading groceries from trucks at a food store. But life for Harry in 1932, and it was etched in his memory, was the Cubs, the fighting, scratching, winning Cubs. Harry virtually camped out in Wrigley Field, usually after only a few hours'

7

sleep after work, sitting in the grandstands or the bleachers and rooting like a maniac, more fervent than if he were at a religious revival, with his gods wearing blue pin stripes and baggy pants.

He was devoted to the likes of Riggs Stephenson and KiKi Cuyler, Charley Grimm, and Billy Jurges, and he knew the weaknesses and the tritest characteristics of Gabby Hartnett and Babe Herman. Yet his real hero, his alter ego, his do-no-wrong tower of strength and glory was the Arkansas Humming Bird, the tall, gangling right-handed pitcher Lon Warneke. Harry saw most of Warneke's twenty-two victories and agonized through the few times Lon lost that year. It was an awesome, overpowering spectacle, Warneke going through lineups as if they were highballs at a Polish wedding, and Harry cheering him past every batter; even if he was sitting alone and curling his program he yelled as if he were leading the crowd. Or if he went with Billy Mrozsinski, the two of them would bet on how many strikeouts Warneke would get, or the counts he would run, the hits he'd give up. With each victory, not Harry's or Billy's, but always Warneke's, the two of them would stand up and beat each other on the back, hollering, whistling, catcalling. And during the show, as Lon whiffed through batters and fooled power hitters, Harry alone or Harry and Billy would sit back and smile smugly, purring with satisfaction over their personal lefthander who was the cream of the league.

At midseason Harry was so starstruck with Warneke that he began to use him, to flaunt him, to ward off his enemies with him. If Pittsburgh or St. Louis or Philadelphia got uppity while the Arkansas Humming Bird was on the bench, while Pat Malone or Burleigh Grimes or Charlie Root was throwing, then Harry would cup his hands around his mouth and hex the enemy with the specter of Warneke. It was a long, rolling catcall, three syllables usually bellowed in the silences of the game, not *War*-neke, like everyone else said it, but with the emphasis on the second syllable: War-*nek*-i! That way the Arkansas Humming Bird acquired a distinctly Polish heritage, War-*nek*-i, with all the gristle and *kapusta* and snort of Milwaukee Avenue, or at least as much of it as Harry could give him.

After a while it became a part of his vocabulary, a word he used as a threat in almost any situation. It ran through his mind, gaining speed and power like an overhand fastball: War-*nek*-i! as if it could somehow put out the fire of the moment, the impending danger, the uncertainty. He said it so much and in such odd circumstances that people began to look at him sideways, wondering if they heard right, not bothering to ask. Only Billy Mrozsinski really knew, for he had seen Harry lean forward countless times, tighten his eyes, and croon it like a midnight owl: War-*nek*-i.

But it was a fleeting memory that danced out as quickly as it had sashayed in, and left him in his stupor. Soon it faded, his mind drifted onto other things, images of what had happened only last night, bringing Harry back to reality. He replayed last night's travesty, a clown act on the street. Winthrop Street.

Winthrop. He leaned out from the dim light of the gangway, the narrow walk between two apartment buildings, scanning the opposite ends of the street. In the darkness and the cool bite of the night, Saturday night, he drew long drags from the Camel cupped inside his bony fist and waited. The block was quiet, eerie in the night shadows of the boxy brick buildings, turn-of-the-century giants with wide windows and cornices, built so close to one another that they blotted out much of the light and clatter of Broadway and Wilson.

He waited in a crouch, Peanuts Lowrey in the coaching box at third, waiting for a clothesline, a runner he could wave on home. He played the angles, glanced quickly to his rear at the walk which led into the darkness of the alley. He had already broken out the single gangway light, cracked it off at the base and left only the thin glass core to hang like an icicle, so he could wait in darkness. The black to his rear was escape,

9

a fence and a row of trash barrels arranged so that even he, arthritic legs, varicose veins, calcium knees and all, could jump over it like some kind of geriatric rabbit and get his old ass on out.

Winthrop curved slightly southeast, a natural shortcut to Wilson from the smoky shot-and-beer bars on Lawrence. From one-thirty to three in the morning, he knew, Winthrop was the Oregon Trail for the inmates of the jelly-ass halfway houses, the bins that lined Uptown like retarded mushrooms in a dog run. In the cool, hazy silence of the city, those muddle-headed, middle-aged deadheads whose ears never stopped popping, weaved and stumbled along the sidewalk as if it were made of noodles and they were the sauce, with nothing but vague instincts and dumb luck to guide them through the cheap booze and the goblins back to their cubicles.

But first, tonight, slap those palms on the shiny seat of his ass, they would have to get past be-nimbled Harry Lum. If he was lucky, one of them would have a remnant of his public-aid check, or gilt-edged sawbucks from a far-off and far-out relative still tucked in the folds of a purse. And Harry would set them free, shifting the weight to his heels, his back aching, reaching in his waist for the octane, the juice. But only a nip, nip in time saves wine, he thought, for he had to retain some edge over his victims, keep one stumble ahead of them. He stubbed his Camel against the brick and flicked it behind him. With his left hand he took a swallow—he was good with both hands, a natural glove man—and flashed the letters on his fist across his eyes, out of focus but never out of mind: L-U-M.

Maybe a few years ago he would have cornered all the angles, thinking all the time, but last night it had gone past him. He tasted the port, a little more for jazz, felt for another cigarette, and let his mind wander. Money, five, ten bucks maybe, he wasn't no damn financier, a relief check would do but his caseworker was too lazy to get him another one, the

10

Cubs against Cincinnati trying to salvage the series, Bill Hands trying to pitch and if the Mets won Sunday they'd be only three and a half behind with ten to play. The thoughts ran through his head like a newsreel; he was going dingy. He shivered, the scale in the washroom said 135, some fish went more than that, a lot of fish. He tucked the bottle into his waist like a good friend, that damn Durocher, and he finally thought of how he hadn't seen a squad car all night. Maybe years back it would have hit him like a fastball in the nuts, but now it slipped by, washing through like a breeze. He was getting thick.

He should have seen it, should have bombed inside of his eyeballs like a message from heaven, but he missed it. Parked behind the abandoned van, as obvious as a pimple on the Mayor's nose, was the unmarked car, the dicks, smelling like cop and Aqua Velva, waiting, like he was, the sweat running down their necks. They would follow the lurches bouncing down the sidewalk as if it had walls and they were rubber balls, watching the half-wits as if they were grandchildren, hoping their eyes weren't the only ones peering out of the dark on the limp legs and the rubber arms of the loonies and the alkies and the ne'er-do-wells and the few coins which clung to their pockets.

And one of them came, ambling, pigeon-toed and droop-kneed, a bleached-out bag of rolls and globs, about forty-five, nicely puttied over with boilermakers, the pocket of her dress torn and her makeup smeared from the beer she'd patted on her face like so much Saturday-night Chanel. Harry spotted her, like an old condor laying eyes on a prospector, meat on the bone, and knew he was home. He tucked the pint in his belt, spat on his claws, glanced at his escape route, and suddenly his feet, like delinquents on the make, were out from under him and hustling across the sidewalk. He would take her.

The two dicks were out of their car and operating on pure, uncut adrenalin by the time Harry spun her around and

11

yanked her purse. She stumbled and weaved, her legs crumbling caissons beneath a seiche of fat, lost her balance, then fell in a heap as Harry the vulture turned hawk, with his mind a clear snapshot of grab and go, jerked the strap on the purse and took off.

The two detectives panted and puffed a short fifty yards away by the time Harry firmed his grip on the vinyl and reached out for his first step. In full stride they motioned wildly at each other, then split up, one taking the street and the other heading through a gangway into the alley. As they pivoted they heard the woman let loose a hoarse, drunken bellow, a moose call that echoed through the canyon of Winthrop Street. One of the dicks again turned and shot up a gangway, the image of Harry's fleeting frame vivid; the other headed across the alley, over a fence, toward the elevated tracks.

Harry bobbed and weaved, dodged trash cans, then felt his legs and his stomach and his lungs calling out his age to him, and he glanced around to see one of the two dicks, like Rick Casares off tackle, hurdle a burnt-out car seat in a vacant lot to his right. The cop was young, hairy, Harry knew, and suddenly Harry's exhaustion, his wheezing gut took second chair to the fright of seeing that snub-nosed .38 service revolver, there as certain as the guy had a head on his pecker, strapped beneath the dick's armpit but in a second an oversized barrel digging for grunge between Harry's nose hairs.

The chase had really been short, a sprint, the best Harry could muster, under the tracks for a distance then over to a five-foot fence adjoining rear yards. Harry decided to change from a vulture and a hawk to a hare, make that one last jump and hope the dicks would lose him or give up or pull up with charley horses so stiff their legs would numb up like sticks of beef jerky. So he clutched the purse and hit the fence with an outstretched foot, not sure of just what, when the impact hit him like a punch in the gut and he lost the one thing closest to him. His bottle fell from his belt and crashed to smithereens against a concrete track foundation. The noise of it was deafening, Civil Defense, the fire alarms when the Sox won the pennant in 1959 and Harry jumped around in the middle of Damen Avenue with a beer sausage in his hand and Billy Pierce on his lips. The explosion of the bottle stopped him cold, pulled his pants down, white against the black and green of the elevated's iron legs. He froze, feeling the invisible zap of two guns drawn, leveled by four cop hands, fingers sweaty, shaking, puffing, two coppers who'd just as soon wing him or ventilate him or just play the carom. And Harry, in his wise old age, his criminoid perspective on life beneath the elevated tracks, knew the chase was over.

One of the dicks approached him, breathing like a leaky compressor, and yanked Harry's leg from the fence. Harry lost his grip and flopped down onto the hard, flat earth. His knee ached from the knock, or maybe from when he hit the fence, or from the strain the night had put on him, his bones brittle, dry, and he rubbed the kneecap and writhed in the dirt like an old skinny bird with tar-stained feathers.

"Shit on a royal bun." The detective spat as he pulled Harry up. "Harry Lum."

He kicked the jagged stem of Harry's bottle against the fence.

"Bust my ass. Almost get de-balled under the tracks and it's for Lum."

His partner pulled up, beefy and breathing, a navy nylon windbreaker breaking wind between his arms and flapping out back of him like a tail. He was short and stocky, a mustache that stopped on the corners of his lips, and slicked hair. He stopped, then heaved, "Aw, Christ."

They didn't put cuffs on him, didn't threaten or spreadeagle him or rap him in the nuts or the ribs or the Adam's apple like they would have any nigger kid in the same situation. They just walked him back to the street, still breathing and tasting their lungs, thinking how someone besides old man Lum had been goddamn stupid, and they began scheming excuses, shrugs.

They reached the woman where she was planted on the sidewalk, her legs spread like a turtle, wailing and carrying on and drawing a crowd and tearing her hair as if it had no roots. The first detective, with one hand strangling Harry's withered bicep, handed the purse to the woman. He shoved Harry's nose down toward the sidewalk, next to the woman, who was being lifted to her feet by a uniformed patrolman. Harry stood about chin-high next to her, a barnacle against a beached whale, with no desire to look into her crossed, bleary, leaky eyes. He could taste the blood in his own throat, his lungs stretched and thin, stomach in ribbons, the balm of Gilead shattered and drying against the elevated, and he rubbed his kisser with his free hand.

"He ain't the one," the woman mumbled. "Not this old prick. It was some nigger done it. Some nigger with hair."

"It's your purse, ain't it?" the second dick said.

The woman took it, ripped it open and stuck her hand inside. She grabbed a brown envelope, the government's return requested. "Sure are right. It's mine, all mine. How'd this old prick get it?"

"Ah, shit," the detective said. He shook his head at the uniformed patrolman and the officer steered the woman over to an idling patrol car.

"C'mon, Lum," the first dick said, pinching his steel fingers almost through Harry's arm, the only left one he had, and shoving him down the street toward their unmarked car. "Let's you and us go for a ride."

They bounced him into the back seat as if he were a medicine ball in the Mayor's Athletic Club. The dick who'd grabbed him at the fence was Angelo Marrietta, a young, muscled robbery cop Harry had run into around Wilson Avenue when Marrietta was trying to buy information. He'd even given Harry his card, like a damn vacuum-cleaner sales-

14

man, never asking if Harry could read anything but Polish, or decipher numbers. And Harry had laughed the hollow laugh that came from the pits of his jaws and squibbed through his good teeth, then threw the card into the gutter with the rest of the trash. But when Marrietta had walked off, sauntering like a dumb cop in toyland, Harry went and dug the card out of the crap and stuffed it into his pocket, a little insurance in case of hard times.

Marrietta's partner was Fleck, just Fleck as far as Harry knew, always with the slicked-back hair and the nylon jacket, looking like an off-duty umpire. Fleck repeated a lot of what Marrietta said, sat shotgun, and draped his hand over the seat like he was after a feel, which Harry didn't give, or hadn't for quite some time. Fleck was still learning.

For fifteen minutes they circled the neighborhood.

"We could get you for a gun and put on robbery armed," Marrietta said. He was driving slowly, making cars wait for him at lights, then wading through reds.

Fleck leered at Harry. Harry, knowing his lessons well, sat in the middle of the back seat.

"How 'bout dope, Harry? We could run you down with shit and set you up in court as a pusher."

Harry caught himself, forgot about his thirst, his aches. He wasn't going to let any coppers bait him, play him for a monkey.

"I don't shoot dope," he said.

"What *do* you do? Huh, Harry? What do you do when we ain't nailin' ya?" Marrietta said. He turned onto Broadway from Lawrence.

"Thief. I'm a thief."

"Hey. We finally met one," Fleck said.

"You ain't the shitter, are ya? We got a burglar around here, hitting all over, I mean like a blanket, and I'll be damned if he ain't a shitter. We go in and sift through the joints, guy throws stuff all over, for a half hour and damn if we ain't got to walk around his pile. Right on the dining-room

15

table. Curled like a damn Dairy Queen," Marrietta said.

"Yeah, and what's a couple a hotshot robbery coppers like yuse doing on burglary?" Harry snapped.

"Jeez, fucker knows the department better 'an we do."

"Yeah, well I know a lot of guys pretty sick of the shitter. Gonna make him eat his jobs when they get him. Take a collection in the station around National Diarrhea Week and make him dig in," Fleck said. He pushed a grin over his face but his partner ignored it. Harry looked out the window.

They drove around for another few minutes, time for the dicks to waste, without anyone saying anything. Harry saw they weren't getting to him, weren't going to book him, saw the picture, had seen it before.

"What's the rap?" he said.

"Could be a sheetful. Armed robbery. Battery. Petty theft. Resisting arrest . . ." Marrietta trailed off.

"So what's the rap?" Harry repeated. He could feel his stomach biting, nipping like a wife at the door, but more painful.

"Disorderly," said Marrietta.

"Disorderly. That's twenty-five, ain't it? Twenty-five and I walk?"

"Yeah."

"Good thing it ain't no murder rap."

"You been drinking, Harry?"

"Had a few."

"That what crashed back there on the fence?"

"Was my pecker, copper. Got within a foot of the wall."

"Yeah," Fleck said. "But it always drops off at your age, don't it, Harry?"

"Jeeezus," sighed Marrietta. "Yer mind's going, Harry. Why don't you find yourself a rest home somewhere and fall in love?"

The car turned off of Wilson onto Hazel, pulling up in front of a six-story public housing project which was a hooker high rise, a concrete claptrap that owed its mortgage to penicillin.

16

It glowered over the dark, dead-end street, a garbage-clogged strip of smashed-out Plymouths and glossy, spade-spangled pimp wagons with Kewpie dolls and lamb's wool. Harry rubbed his hands through his hair, under his armpits.

"This is where you get off," Marrietta said.

"I'll say hello to your old ladies for you," Harry mumbled. He could have bought and sold coppers like these once upon a time. He sat on the seat, then slid over. Marrietta got out and opened the door.

"We'll ignore that, asshole. See you at the ballgame, Harry."

"Box seats," Harry said.

It all came back to him as he lay there, in the back-up of his room, the morning after, his gut full and bubbling, gas leaking silently, warming his ass. All on Winthrop Street. Uptown Saturday night. His Camel burned into his thumb, the bruise on his knee where he had hit the fence now alive, stinging and yellow-purple, the dull throb of age. He leaned back and closed his eyes; his Camel dropped and began to burn itself into a brown, caramel blotch in the linoleum. His belly began to rise and fall, rise and fall, slower, more deliberate, rise and fall.

By four he awoke and kicked the bottle, which was empty and a memory. The black-and-white television hadn't seen a Cub all day—he'd slept right through it and them. He sat with his head against the wall, saw stuffed cabbage and sour cream, then the gray of the wall, the peeling paint over wallpaper. He needed a shave; the wine on his breath began to ferment, as if his mouth had been trampled by dirty feet. The *National Exploiter* leered at him from the floor, the best of a blonde's black pubic hair smeared with grape jelly, and Harry rubbed his crotch, pulled up his pants, and couldn't decide on which. He wondered about the ball scores.

He wondered about what he would do tonight. A repeat of the Winthrop bust was out, no chance, and he considered

17

some trunks, tools, or walking the alleys looking for an open door, not on a trash barrel, a real open door, a burglary, the word, Harry could say the word. Or he could forget about things and go to the Mission, the Holy Soup of Salvation, which was slop because the bums who made it spit in it or peed in it or committed all manner of ugly crimes against it as long as it came out brown or green and lumpy. He thought of getting up at 5 A.M., at the bare ass of dawn, and getting his dogs down to daily pay for a dishwashing gig or a kitchen job or anything at all. His thoughts drifted, like the mush in the soup, floating, turning over, sliding through and dripping out his ear, maybe something big, something headline, catch Yaras and Caputo, the old boys, the mavericks, get in on a vending truck, pull a genuine heist, a drugstore. He dozed then awakened, trying to peel back the layers of his thoughts, his daydreams, his reality, the area between his pants and his leg. It was getting dark outside. The sawbuck in his other pants wasn't there, or it wasn't his pants. He was broke. Harry Lum. What would he do, he wondered. Then, in the dull mist of the room, with the drone of a voice heard by no one, he said it aloud.

As Harry bobbed in and out of sleep, like a walrus flopping his head in the surf, Alicia Morris wiped her smooth, illicit self with a wet washcloth in the bedroom of her apartment on the sixteenth floor of the project on North Hazel. She sprayed deodorant under her arms, in her crotch, plucked at the snarls, then whisked along her thighs. She pinned a fireburst platinum wig over her short, mean, matted natural and slipped into an orange body shirt that snapped between her legs, snapped like teeth, snapped at the well-oiled micro-mini white vinyl skirt that whistled up her flanks. She stretched a pair of orange, screaming, knee-length boots, paper-thin and pliant, over her calves, then jammed a cigarette into a glass of dead Scotch. For a warm September evening, Alicia was devastating, ball-twitching, looking good, and sure as she was sure of the heft of her ass that she would score well tonight.

Alicia would wear the same outfit except for a pair of white, silken panty hose as Ronald Farkins, but Ronald would pat pancake makeup over his beard, his shaved chest, smooth and rippled like a cake of marble, and cruise the bars. With his soft, thin, satin cheekbones and his flawless skin, he would beguile and bewitch three men with his charms, three men who would ask no questions and pay him well.

Ronald Farkins would seduce them in a bar near the fleabag apartment of Donald Ray Burl, who, late that Sunday afternoon, was checking out his chromed, clicking .25-caliber Titan FIE revolver and feeling the cravings, the wrenching, tightening jones of his habit. In a few hours, Donald Ray would go after not less than $300 in small bills and whatever capsules he could grab. He would be aided and abetted by Jimmy Del Corso, screaming Jimmy the Dago, who would be driving a stiff, stolen 1970 Maverick with red plaid seat covers and a pair of white-fuzz dice dangling from the mirror. Jimmy had spent the afternoon lining up the car, drooling over it like a sixteen-year-old with his learner's permit, preparing for the moment he would jam the coathanger through the rubber and make the steal. He would show up with it for half of Donald Ray Burl's take.

Jimmy the Dago expected that and what his old lady could hustle in the roach-running Vicklen Hotel. She had been living with Jimmy, swimming in his green peppers and olive oil, for five months, was nineteen years old, smeared with Woolworth lip balm, named Deborah Cortez. She worked the rooms of the Vicklen, servicing the hillbillies and hoods and dried-up pensioners who wanted it rubbed, in a not-too-complicated arrangement with the downstairs room clerk.

But tonight, this lazy, itchy Uptown night, while Harry Lum lingered and belched through another bottle of white mountain port, while Alicia Morris flagged down cars on Hazel Street with a twist of her hips and Ronald Farkins creamily fellated an insurance broker in the front seat of a 1969 Oldsmobile, while Donald Ray Burl and Jimmy Del Corso nervously held up a Rogers Park drugstore, Deborah Cortez would thump her skull on the red Depression-laid brick of the alley behind the Vicklen, feel the blood rise in her throat, the blackness covering like a cloud, and pass out.

She would be found the next morning by a ragpicker, who would cut short his whistled arpeggios at the first sight of the blood on the brick. He would not see the three stab wounds like slots in her chest, but would notice with a touch of wonder that Deborah Cortez's cheek was pressed against the brick as if it were a pillow. And the ragpicker would run and shout unintelligibly, mumbling through his gums and his chewing tobacco, out of the alley into the middle of the dawn's quiet street.

And Harry Lum, lying downhill, would awaken, wipe the glaze out of his eyes, and get on down to the Liberty Bell.

2

Harry took one look at the crowd in the alley and couldn't resist. He'd always been a crowd lover, right in the middle of them, with a beer and mustard smeared on his chin, bellowing catcalls that came out of his head like poetry. Put him in Wrigley Field in a sellout and he was in crowd heaven, singing the Polish national anthem, pinching the girls, baring his ass to the umpires, eating Fudgsickles. So this crowd, with two wagons, three squads, unmarked dicks' cars—and Harry knew them all—double-parked like flies, and the neighborhood hangers-on, some leaning from second- and third-story windows throwing french fries on the cops, drew Harry like the scent of reduced-price port. He pushed through, grumbling, "Stand back, duh Mayor's here, hizzoner," until he was hip-on-hip with a patrolman, staring into the rumpled, curled body of Deborah Cortez.

"Suicide?" he asked the patrolman. "Girl do it to herself right here?"

The cop didn't answer, stood like stone.

"Well, I think it prolly was, if you ask me, which you didn't," Harry went on. He was feeling good, a little greased from his elderberry breakfast. "Dumb girlees think they can jump out of them windows and go up instead of down. Then they find out, you better believe it, that it wasn't no swimmin' pool they was jumpin' into." ·

21

He rubbed his mouth and looked around the alley at the half-dozen plain-clothes homicide dicks who picked and scraped and nosed through the trash and the dirt. They milled over and around each other's tracks, sniffing like terriers, clutching clipboards and taking notes with ball-point pens. One of them passed in front of Harry.

"Hey, who was she?" Harry said to him.

"Raquel Welch," the dick said.

"I know who did it to her then," he cackled. "Yessiree bob." He laughed harder. "Hey, copper, got a smoke?"

The patrolman shook his head.

"What got her, huh?" Harry said to a short, pudgy dick with a crew cut and coffee stains on his yellow tie.

"You tell me," the dick said. He looked at Harry and exhaled smoke through his nostrils.

"Wasn't the Mayor," Harry said. "He's too busy killin' us."

The dick took another drag of cigarette, holding it with two fingers and his thumb.

"Wasn't Willie Mays. He's too busy killin' the Cubs."

Harry was hot. The dicks nodded at each other, the two of them stopping to look at Harry. Harry pulled, then cranked up another.

"Wasn't Marilyn Monroe. She's too busy killin' herself."

The two dicks smirked; the shorter one threw his cigarette away.

"Guy's a million laughs."

They moved away from Harry toward the corpse as a thick, red-faced sergeant puffed and groaned and bent down to draw chalk slashes around the body, a rough outline of how it lay tucked against the base of the building, on its back with legs slightly curled, soft but lifeless, the upper torso twisted around as if she wanted to change her mind and crawl away. Then two patrolmen lifted the body onto a stretcher, draped a sheet over the top, and slid it into a wagon.

Harry tried to bum a cigarette off the smaller dick when

he lit up. The detective ignored him. "C'mon, I pay taxes, gimme a break," he chattered.

"A break anytime," the dick said. "But buy your own butts."

Harry persisted, didn't mind the brushoff. He could put up with homicide dicks; they were cops, smelled like them, drooped their trousers like only cops could, but homicide dicks were a piss-pot better than the rest. He knew hundreds of coppers, from the young, greasy beat men looking for handouts and phone numbers to the beer-bellied desk sergeants who tried to shove him around because they hadn't been on the street in seventeen years and didn't know a pinch from a salami. He'd made deals with them all, the fat general-assignment dicks who needed a pinch for the month, the young coppers just out of the army whom he paid off to keep them from cuffing him around in the men's room, making him flush the johns with his nose, sit in the pissers. But he knew the murder dicks, thought he did, the little Mick chained to his Pall Malls, the red-haired Polack like a dozen orange heads he'd seen grow up in the old neighborhood. They weren't petty shits like other coppers, wouldn't try to dump phony charges on you, even had memories, kept track of their I.O.U.s.

He figured that they would get pretty close to the other end of the knife that had cut into the girl on the alley. Murder was big leagues, Harry knew that right off, something you didn't mess with if you were a serious thief, something that would drag on you, cement you to a date in Joliet where they closed the door with a ten-year slam. So the dicks took down all the details, the three stab wounds in the chest, not small punctures like a suicide, where the knife probes and pokes and pricks while the courage builds if it is to build at all. But wide, jagged slits that severed muscle and artery and bone. The cuts were quick and deep, at least a six-inch knife, a long, midnight pocket knife, used well and probably often, tapping the veins like gushers until her thin pink short-sleeved

23

sweater was a field of scarlet which soaked everything, a pond, then draining into a congealed puddle on the asphalt. Her face, the expression, the mild eyes tempered with the blue, cold decomposition, even so soon, told the dicks that she had left the world about five hours before they stood there. And the same homicide dicks, grim, cynical, dogged, turned off by Harry's chatter, intuited that she had probably been cut by someone who knew her, someone who, at this very moment, was trying to put the moment out of the camera of his mind, crowding it out even as the handle of the knife rubbed against his thigh.

As the car doors slammed, the crowd broke up, the chalk slashes remained to be washed away by the rain, Harry sauntered off toward Wilson Avenue to bum a smoke, a cup of coffee, a few minutes of talk.

"You get that cocksucker," he said to the short, dark-haired dick as the cop slid into his unmarked car.

Johnny McMahon, the Irishman from the South Side, the nine-year homicide detective, nodded and held out a solitary cigarette. "Yeah, old-timer, we get all the cocksuckers," he said as Harry latched onto the smoke. "Shove it to them and break it off, bub."

"You betcha, and keep it greased, bub," Harry said, grinned a row of brown, then started looking for a match.

In an hour, as the dicks' car wound through the neighborhood, then over to the Foster Avenue station, Johnny McMahon ran through every resource he could muster in his book on Uptown. He saw the contorted face of Deborah Cortez, pale as it hugged the alley, serene like a doll, a face that shoveled up everything he had ever known about this asshole neighborhood, the North Side's Garbageville. A place close to McMahon because he picked through it every day like a dentist through gums, knowing the people who lived here, the hillbillies who poured out of Kentucky and West Virginia and came to Wilson Avenue, with rotten teeth and no jobs and no money, the Indians, the ignoble red men, who

24

flopped out of the reservations with their mean, dark faces and ponytails and affinity for straight whiskey, the spades who shot dope and hustled, the bums who stumbled up from Clark Street or Madison Avenue because a bulldozer flattened their favorite fifty-cent chicken coops, the politicians who bought votes from dead men or half-dead ones with muscatel or a chicken, the leeches, gloms, pickers, organizers —loud-mouthed and self-righteous, then gone when the money ran out—picketers, radicals, thieves, hookers, ministers, sheeny landlords, palm readers, gypsies, faggots, worms, spics, perverts, junkies.

McMahon knew them all, knew their talk, their silences, their rat-filled, roach-filled, lice-filled furnished rooms. He collected his informants, his Harry Lums, piling up barbed favors from them. He didn't justify or fink on Uptown, didn't try to change it or hold hope inside his Irish heart for it. He just worked with the odds, dodged the people and stepped livelier than they did, realizing most of the way that what they did to each other they did for simple, stupid, paper-thin reasons, without schemes or convoluted emotions, layered relationships, or complicated plots. People were killed on McMahon's beat with Saturday-night specials, shotguns, knives, icepicks, shovels, baseball bats, beer bottles, broom handles, two-by-fours, and shock absorbers. They died in brawls, arguments, and fist fights, usually because of lies or the suggestion of lying, for sleeping with other people's wives, daughters, or queens, for stealing televisions, spare tires, bottles of cheap beer, food stamps, or hair ribbons.

And McMahon climbed stairs and knocked on doors trying to run them down, putting them in jail, scaring them back to West Virginia or New Mexico or simply into a hole somewhere. It was part of something he did after he shaved in the morning, this morning, when the back end of the Vicklen Hotel became another Scene. In that hour that followed he and his red-haired partner named Eugene Farber found out about Deborah Cortez' arrangement with the night

25

manager, about how many tricks and with how much zeal she turned them in a night, and what kind of customers she serviced. From that, they began to piece together her dime-store life, find who and what, get names scribbled on their clipboards, matching them with living, breathing faces. Shortly after, they stared into the sweaty mug of Jimmy the Dago Del Corso.

"Whattaya mean, where was I?" Jimmy said. He sat in a wooden chair that creaked when he squirmed, in a narrow side room at the Foster Avenue station. He ran his hands through his thick, greased black hair, strong, ballsy Italian hair that curled at his neck.

"She was your old lady, right?" McMahon said.

"So what?"

"So maybe you might a talked to her once in a while. That happens with married people, you know," McMahon said.

"We wasn't married."

"Yeah, yeah, who is nowdays?"

"What's that supposed to mean, man?"

"It means let's quit shittin' around, Jimmy. Your old lady is found like a piece of meat loaf and you're giving us the dumb act." McMahon kicked a chair as he dropped his foot to the floor. He took a pack of cigarettes from his shirt pocket and fumbled with the cellophane.

"I don't know nothing, man. I been around minding my own business and I don't know nothing about what Debbie is doing at the hotel until she is found this morning," Jimmy said. He talked hurriedly, through his nose, then slowed and tried to get back his cool. "You got to find who did that, copper."

"So what'd you think when she wasn't in the sack last night? She was out eating tacos with the boys?"

"She might a been working. Who knows. She don't come home alla time."

McMahon exhaled loudly and struck a match. The end of

his cigarette flamed for a second before he released a cloud of smoke.

"Wanna smoke, Jimmy? That what you want?"

Jimmy turned his head and stared blankly into a corner.

"Okay, so why don't you come up with something? We got a sheet on you as long as your arm. Cars, punching trunks, parts. Ain't held a job since you got sick of your paper route. Now yer shacking up with some house dolly taking tricks for makeup money that we find on the wrong end of one of them dago specials people like you been known to carry in your socks. And one of our guys seen you yesterday making google eyes on some parked car. He figures you're up to your calling in life. And you look at us like we were from another planet."

McMahon stopped and leaned over Jimmy. He took the cigarette from his mouth and shook off an ash. It dropped on the edge of Del Corso's black patent-leather loafers. Jimmy scowled, tried to muster a leer, went for his hair, despising the detective, but keeping his eyes on the corner. He was sweating just above the collar of his knit, seven-dollar purple-and-black shirt.

"I don't know nothing, cop."

"You better learn, Jimmy. I'm gonna lean on you for this one." And McMahon turned his back on him and sat at his desk, shuffled through reports written up by beat men on the scene. Moments later he went through his drawer for a file on the Vicklen Hotel, a personal history of clientele and services. The sounds of the station seeped into the room. The district house had been renamed a few years earlier—then it was known as the Summerdale District—in an attempt to cleanse it of a scandal that scalded the entire department. It happened casually enough, when a burglar named Dickie Morrison started telling people that his partners were patrolmen, hard-working beat stiffs who helped him on the tough jobs, even to the point of taking goods home in their squads. McMahon loved those jagoffs, coppers who were lousy po-

27

licemen and even worse burglars, who ended up in the can, cost a few fat-assed superiors their jobs, even booted the Superintendent into retirement. And through it all McMahon still had to work the district, the eastern, lake half of the North Side, keeping his own files on buildings, hangouts, punks, hoods, contacts, sources, taking the shit people dealt him because he was a cop and coppers were crooks. But he plowed through it, just as he thumbed through his cards on the Vicklen, ashes falling, his tie cheap and stained, short sleeves. Jimmy chafed in his seat, his ass a worry of time and circumstance; he'd kill Deborah if he could, realized he couldn't but nursed the urge. He realized also that he was being ignored, crossed his legs and kicked a locker door.

"Get outta here," McMahon said without looking up from his desk.

Harry Lum knew Deborah Cortez like he knew a hundred floozies panting and sniffing and whining and working in Uptown. She was a straggly, whip-mouthed high school runaway with long nails, turned part-time hooker, part-time junkie, full-time leech. She hung around the flat during the day, the ripped couch, pillows on the floor, watching the soap operas, painting her claws, reading comics. Pregnant at sixteen after a roof-top job from some supercharged Puerto Rican fly who yelped in Spanish when he shot his load of bubbling chorizo, she ran away and met Jimmy Del Corso in a park when he tried to sell her $3 worth of mescaline and a $250 botch-job abortion performed by a male nurse with lacquered fingernails which left her bleeding and dizzy for a day and a half. But her groaning agony under an army blanket in his furnished hotel room left her with a blind attachment for the skinny, illiterate Italian. She tried to claw his eyes out only months after, ambushed him with a scissors after that, cried, screamed, tore her beautiful, ratted, oily Hispanic hair, even moved out and pawned his television on her eighteenth birthday. But it never lasted. She pulled herself together, shampooed that lush head of chocolate fantasy, oiled her irresistible caramel skin, the feather down that swept over her arms and smoothed and swirled down the canal of her back, dumped the string of one-room apartments and move-ins with customers, put on a few pounds, toned her makeup, the white-iced lips, turned enough tricks to get her a fistful of money, bought an electric wrist watch and a pair of patent-leather shoes, and went back to Jimmy.

In the last year the relationship floated. Deborah stayed busy, perfected her style, worked out the john set up with the Vicklen night clerk while Jimmy went out after cars and what he called "arrangements." They slept until two in the afternoon, she pouted, they screwed once in a while, usually rough when they were drunk or high, ate in restaurants. Gradually she felt as if she were married to him, tied to the skinny wop with blood, and she decided to take on his last name. He objected, ranted that it would give the cops one more hook in him, one more way to nail him, that her spic name was good enough, but she kept Del Corso tacked onto it anyway. It was a part of the bond she felt within her, part of what she clung to when she thought to herself on the street, felt her hair getting stringy, her crotch loose and wet. He was a bitchy, bony Italian prick who treated her as if she wasn't there most of the time, or all of the time. He had gotten her into hooking, played the hubby pimp routine, then egged her into dope to firm up his grip, then into petty theft. And, though she knew all along that she would get into such shit sooner or later, because she was made of the street, smelled it, saw it in her heritage, she could always blame him. It was important to blame someone, to bitch at them, to feel something more than blank unconcern. There was that attachment, and when she awoke in the middle of the morning, to his garlic smell and the sight of him sleeping with his mouth open, agape like an eel, she sniffed and itched and said to herself, so that nobody in the entire world but Deborah Cortez Del Corso could hear, that it was important.

She met Harry Lum unknowingly, the hollow-eyed old fart who tried to sell her a clock radio. She laughed when he said it was a Polish radio, picked up all the Polish stations and broadcast them in American or spic or whatever you wanted, she saw the crazy thin smile in the corners of his mouth, smelled his booze, then told him she could buy *him* for less than what the radio was worth, and that that wasn't much. He told her that she was just a cheap spic whore and that he didn't want to sell anything to her anyway, then lost his balance and took a punch at her. She side-stepped him then kicked him in the leg, square with the point of her shoe in what flesh he had on his lower thigh, choice, leaving a bruise that throbbed and looked like a soft prune for the next two weeks. Harry remembered the welt, like a sore, even after he sold the radio to a pawn shop for two bucks, and tried to get even. He watched the johns drive up to the Vicklen when she was working, saw the room lights pop on, and hawked their cars. He checked for open doors, pried open a few hardtops with a hanger, still with an amount of finesse, and got off with four boxes of Kleenex, a briefcase full of insurance policies, six golf balls. Then he lost interest, didn't really have a notion in hell if his efforts were cutting down on her business or just pissing people off. His nerves began to flutter when he found out that she was hooked onto Jimmy Del Corso, remembered that Jimmy used a gun and was a mad, fulminating asshole, rubbed his bruise one last time, and said to hell with it. She was a lousy whore junkie. He could care less if one day they found her lying face down in an alley, remembered shortly after he walked away, dragging on his cop-glommed cigarette, that the stiff, the little crumpled girl in the puddle that morning, looked vaguely familiar.

McMahon and his partner, Gene Farber, picked through the Vicklen Hotel, getting a list of every tenant, every guest, every serviceman, every bookie, every transient, every hooker who had ever set one cheek inside the place. They went from floor to floor, banging on doors, talking to women in pin curlers and bathrobes, bare-backed old men in baggy, beltless trousers and falling guts, from apartment to apartment down each hallway, jotting down room numbers, names, the responses of everyone, those who didn't answer and who would get a call the next day, the next night, the next week until they were home and opened up to explain where they were that Sunday night in September, who they were with, and what they heard.

The two detectives talked to the janitor, the maids, the boys who ran errands for tenants. Finally, they rang up robbery and burglary dicks who worked the area and tapped them for informants: bartenders, fences, ex-cons, pimps, fanning out on either side of the Vicklen for someone who might know something, or had heard a rumor, or, for a small mention of cash, might suddenly regain his memory of a certain slugfest and swan dive he'd seen that night.

But they found nothing, learned only that a few neighbors had heard muffled cries, a slammed door, perhaps a struggle, but nothing else. No running footsteps, no furtive glances from someone who didn't belong, not even a person who heard the thump of a girl's body against the brick. Aside from that, aside from the blank segment of collective memory which seemed to have gripped the Vicklen's clientele, they found a lot of faces who admitted to knowing of Deborah Cortez, or of seeing her around, vaguely assuming a knowledge of what she was up to and how well she did it.

The following night they met the night clerk as he came to work at 11:30. He was a paunchy middle-aged Greek named Gus Koutsos, a name found in the records of the Chicago Police Department and a mug prominently placed in its files.

From the start Farber wanted him. The red-haired detective was convinced that Koutsos knew of and perhaps had a finger on every movement in the fleabag hotel once the little hand passed midnight. Farber had done his homework on

31

Koutsos, an immigrant first arrested for torching a restaurant in the old Greektown strip on Halsted, no conviction, but later one for robbery, then petty theft, then possession and sale of stolen property the police believed he got from small-time Mafia types. For those reasons, and for others he didn't specify, Farber didn't like the night clerk and didn't trust him.

"Gus, let's start from the beginning," Farber said. He leaned over the counter and watched Koutsos as he scribbled on a stack of notecards.

"Look, you can save it and all the questions because I'm gonna tell you everything I know about everything," Koutsos said. "Just wait a second while I go through this mess here. I just got on, ya know."

"Sure, we know," Farber said. He eyed the Greek's toupee, a pitch-black piece that merged unevenly with graying hair above his ears. It would have commanded attention had not Koutsos had a habit of wearing bright orange and purple shirts, screamers that he bought at fire sales but never seemed to wear out.

"Seems like I'm always talking to coppers. My brother's joint has a little fire in the kitchen and they come talking to me."

"Can't understand that, Gus," Farber said. He reached out and took a cigarette from the pack McMahon had just opened.

"That was a long time ago. I was a kid back then and that should be off the books," Koutsos said. He stood up straight and it suddenly became apparent to Farber that the Greek was good-sized, short but broad and muscular, the kind of muscle necessary to overpower petulant hookers.

"C'mon, c'mon. We know what's to you, Gus, and we wanna know the whole bit behind the girl who went out the window the other night—"

"Now that was a tragedy, a tragedy kind of thing—"

"—the whole thing, not your bullshit now, but the girl's name and who her customers were, what she charged and how she collected, and who was the bastard, excluding yourself, of course, that killed her."

"Now hold it, hold it a minute," Koutsos said. He was beginning to sweat, beginning to get agitated beneath the hot light of the office and the rapid fire of Farber. "I aim to cooperate on this one. I'll show you what you want. Here. Here are the keys to the room she was in. Here are the keys to all of the rooms. You go and come how you like.

"But listen, and listen good to me, coppers, 'cuz this ain't like the old days. I got a job here and I done it good for a few years now. My family and me we had our problems. Sure I got a past that I don't talk about. But that don't apply to what happened the other night. I want to find who done it worse than you."

"Bullshit," said Farber. He raised his voice and became irritated at the Greek. McMahon turned and prepared to jump in should his partner get carried away.

"We know you work girls," Farber went on, "because our guys have taken you in for it. Not ten years ago but last month. We know you work a lot of things here right now. So don't be giving us the 'I'm clean, I got a family' crap. We wanna know who and what and how much and if you were in on it. If we find your fingerprints on that broad's neck we'll call your game, Gus, and your family will see you for the rest of your life on visiting days."

"Here! Here, so help me. Take the keys and look everywhere. Talk to anyone and see what they tell ya. I don't mess with girls no more. It's off. I keep my job and collect my paycheck and keep clean. That's it."

He held out his hand with a fat ring of keys on it.

"Go ahead. Go ahead. Take 'em all," he repeated.

McMahon suddenly stepped near the two of them and lightly patted Farber's sleeve with his clipboard.

33

"We'll be in touch, Gus. You know where to find us," he said. "And make sure that you keep thinking about the family and all that."

He said the last few words as the two of them headed for the single-door exit to the hotel. McMahon knew that they had gone past the point where they could have pried anything from the Greek, that he was a pro and would know how to cover his tracks and contain his outbursts. He also knew that Farber, his hair as crimson as ever, had come down too hard on the clerk this time around even though it was an understandable temptation, that Farber had taken an acid dislike for the Greek, and wondered out loud if he had killed her, or could have, or perhaps once in his crummy hotel-clerk life even considered it.

Beyond the Greek, McMahon knew he would have to dig. It was obvious to him that with this case there would be no one who wanted willingly to be the eyes and the ears that could crack it. Uptown was like that, a wide-open, brawling place where you could hear the cracking of gunfire on a good night, but also a place where people were suddenly struck dumb, or extremely deaf, a bit blind, saddled with memories that failed them at the most opportune occasions. He had walked into taverns that were wall-to-wall people before a shooting, then empty of anyone who heard or saw a thing once he showed up. It wasn't a protective or particularly secretive society, it was just a calculating one. Anyone who openly blabbered to cops might find himself on the smoking end of the gun of an uncle, or a brother, or just a friend of the person the witness helped put in jail. So nobody put anybody in jail without a reason, or a little coaxing, a deal, a nicely placed sheaf of dollar bills—some kind, any kind of leverage against the comparative safety of keeping silent.

McMahon decided he would go to his bag, his friends on the street who would tell him what nobody else would. He had long ago learned what any halfway decent cop had to learn: that his sources were his lifeblood when it came right down to the guts of a crime. He needed people who were on the street all the time, people who knew people and which ones belonged, those who heard the rumors and were able to sort them out. Without such individuals, without a network of eyes and ears that would deliver when he needed them, McMahon knew that he wasn't much more than a tourist in Uptown, and a hated one at that.

As a cop he had the leverage, a little money when times were hard for his people, a favor or two when another copper came down on them for pursuing their trades, a lunch, a lump of information, a detour from the County Jail. It was that way with the whores, the street tramps who lived with one leg in a paddy wagon and the other around a john. McMahon knew them and coexisted with them, aware that few if any hookers were killers, or lovers for that matter, but that they depended on their freedom for their livelihood. And a homicide cop was part of that freedom.

It wasn't that way with the thieves, the pimps, the con men. They had victims in their crimes, usually were too dirty themselves to talk, and knew, as every homicide cop knew, that at any time a jackroll artist might be confronted with a problem that would turn him into a killer. So they didn't trade, didn't fink, didn't engage in much stool-pigeoning unless the money was good and they were flat. Then they were sweet meat for any copper who wanted to take the risk.

So he asked Farber to drop him off and swing back in an hour. He wanted to make his contact alone, a relationship he had cultivated and used many times before. Farber swung over to Lawrence. He was a seasoned detective, a partner for four years, and he knew what McMahon had going. He had similar sources himself, for other cases, other situations. He dropped McMahon off and nodded; the car swung out and silently back into traffic.

McMahon walked a block on Lawrence. His cigarette trailed smoke over his shoulder. He looked very much like a

cop, a short, unspectacular one, but a cop. That, or a business-
man who didn't dress very well and smoked a lot, who wasn't
choosy about the neighborhoods he walked, or, as he turned
into the Black Bottle Lounge, the company he kept.

Alicia Morris crossed her legs and jiggled a chartreuse vinyl boot in the aisle. She was yellow hot pants under a black,
see-through blouse, a black brassière, a straight-haired black
wig curling on her shoulders. She was alone in the wooden
booth, the rear of the Black Bottle.

She waved through the smoke curling in front of her face
and smiled like a schoolgirl. "Hey, there, Big Johnnie . . ." she
cooed slowly through the vamp of the jukebox. "My one and
only *po*-lice man."

McMahon swung into the booth and sat across from her.
She inhaled a thick drag of smoke and lifted her hand across
the table, held it limply, and giggled when McMahon
wrapped his paw around it and squeezed.

"Big killer, you," Alicia said. "What you doin' here?"

"Ain't seen this girl for a long time. We're still friends,
right?" he said.

"Right as righteous. You big cop."

The bartender was over before he had to motion, standing
with a full bottle of champagne in his hand.

"A friend of mine, Bobby. Set up regular." Alicia said.

The bartender looked away, then shot her a snarl, but left
with the bottle.

"Fuckers. Always leaning. Push your ass until you half
crazy. That's why I don't make this place a habit."

"Haven't seen you much," said McMahon. "You moving
around?"

"I changes my scene once in a while, yeah. But I ain't seen
you either. In here tonight 'cause I can't get an attitude for
the places. I put up with this hustle here, this back-booth shit,
you know, until I'm in the mood."

The bartender returned with a whiskey and water and a
vodka gimlet. McMahon laid down a five-dollar bill.

"How's business?" he said.

"Ain't shit, that's how," she said and drank half the glass in a single gulp. "Yuh! Good for the breath."

She smiled and ground her cigarette in the tray; her fingers touched the cleavage of her bra and pulled at it slightly.

"So what you want?"

"Just around to keep in touch, see if you're getting along."

She finished her drink with a second draught and looked straight at McMahon. She had a wide, flat face with an upturned nose, a nasty smile. She was heavily made up with white eye shadow brushed like clouds up to her eyebrows.

"Don't get me wrong, me bein' here. I just do this when I'm down. You know. I got my places and my customers like always and I don't need this jive suckin' guys in the booths for the twenty bucks and the bottle of water champagne. Shee-it. I'm just lazy today."

"Thought you were going down South or Vegas and hit the big time."

"Oh, man! What you saying? I got two kids at home so what I want to be going down South for? I'd like to, yeah, on second thought. Make me some big money. Not this shit."

"It ain't the big leagues back here, Alicia," McMahon said. He was babying his drink.

"Good for when I want to save my body. Dudes come in here want a see a little titty on the stage then get it off. They don't want no part of screwing. Just in the boof and off wif the roof."

She stopped and winced when a new number blared out of the jukebox.

"So before the boss starts on me, what does Johnny the big cop want tonight?"

"Okay, Alicia. I'm interested in that girl in the alley. Hear about her?"

"You damn right I did," she said quickly.

"What?"

"Nothing much. Just that she was beat up bad, right?"

"Stabbed."

"Yeah, but beat up before that. Boy told me she had a jaw busted in four places before she hit the ground."

"Uh-huh, and three of her fingers broken."

"Yeah, I know. This girl, she knows."

"Anything else?"

"Nope. Just that she was a nothin'. Teenager doing it part time. Don't think nobody big did it. How 'bout her boyfriend?"

"We're on him. Just wanted to check and see if there was any word out on the street about this."

"Not yet, but there will be if somebody else goes. Nobody won't be trusting nobody no more. 'Cept you, Johnny. You just like the Bible with me."

Alicia laughed and threw her head back. She nodded at the rear of the joint and milked her hand up and down. McMahon rolled his eyes and bit on his cigarette. Alicia laughed even harder.

She hummed along with the jukebox.

"Just something else before I cut in on too much of your finances. You seen a guy named Jimmy Del Corso around?"

"Jimmy what, baby?" she asked.

"Del Corso."

"Don't know him if I did."

"Okay, one more."

"Yeah, well hurry up. This ain't no damn quiz show, ya know."

"The clerk at the Vicklen. You got any kind of book on him?"

"Big dude wears all them crazy purple shirts? And that hairpiece?"

"That's him."

"Yuh!" Alicia exclaimed, from her throat in a guttural burst. She picked up her glass and downed half of her drink.

"And I don't even like this shit," she added with a grimace and a sneer at the glass.

McMahon smiled slightly but let her go on.

"No offense, Johnny, but I ain't sayin' nothin' about that man."

"Well, anything, whattaya hear? What's the word on him?"

"I'll just say for the record, just between you and me 'cuz you done me a few favors, Johnny, that whatever you think about this dude, whatever you think in your cop head that he up to, well then, just let me say that as a person who's got an inside track that you'd probably be right. I mean dead center correct. Take it from me."

She stopped and checked around the lounge, trying to gauge the traffic and detect whether or not she was pushing her luck tying up the booth for so long. Then she turned and looked McMahon in the eye, her white, shadowy eyes lazily telling the story behind the lines in her face, the exaggerated rouge burning her cheeks.

"Yeah," she said, low, soft, definite.

McMahon slid from the booth and brushed her fingers as he passed.

"Thanks," he said.

She picked up on what he meant, how he meant it.

"Yeah," she repeated, with the same satin.

McMahon hit the door without glancing at the bartender or the bouncer sitting on a stool though they both eyed him. He stepped down onto the sidewalk and was jostled by a tall, nicely built man in a tee-shirt and jeans, a light jacket, long wavy hair dipping down over his forehead.

"Whoop," the man said when he was confronted with McMahon's cigarette. Then he smiled a tipsy grin and turned into the Black Bottle. McMahon smelled the beer on the guy's breath and made his conclusions, then he walked the other way.

Sliding into a booth, the guy in the tee-shirt belched.

"Whoop," he said again. Then he looked up at Alicia, who had not moved. "Howdy."

"Do I know you?" Alicia said.

"Name's Donald Ray, you know me now," he said and slapped a sawbuck on the table.

Alicia nodded at Bobby the bartender and he walked over with a bottle of champagne.

Donald Ray smiled and watched the sawbuck vanish. His head drooped suddenly, stopping about four inches from the table top.

"Don't fall asleep, honey," Alicia said.

3

Harry headed for the Ron-Ric Café for a cup of coffee, the worst drip in Uptown, or all of town, black and filmy, bitter because the pots were never cleaned. It settled in his cup, the steam swirling, reminding him of the gasoline rainbows he used to see in the puddles on the street.

"Raaaaa-haaaa," he spat, echoing his phlegm-coated distaste throughout the place.

Sully, the counter man, the white-aproned hash clerk with no upper teeth, rammed Harry's dime into the cash register.

"You don't like it, pour it in yer nose."

"I'll drink it, don't you worry about that. But sure does remind me of something I ate yesterday," Harry said into the cup. The coffee burned his tongue, awakened the buds, scalded the layer of wine dew.

He held the cup with both hands to keep it from shaking, letting the steam curl around his eyelids. Sully walked by with a plate of eggs rimmed with a range of sodden hash brown potatoes.

"Hey, how's about that Billy Williams?" Harry barked, but Sully ignored him, sauntered back to scrape the grill, tip his paper hat on the rear of his head.

"The sonofabitch could hit a fruit fly in a hurricane."

Harry felt his pockets, a bit of change, his roll now down to three dollars, green and crinkled but capable of smiling if he wanted, and sixty-five slippery cents. That would have to do, have to be morning, noon, and night, the salad and the dessert, until October, days away, when he would hound and chew out and bug his welfare worker for his $171.05 of general assistance, in this case most generally and generously accepted by Harry Lum. But he had to do something until then to get some money. Something. The coffee dripped over the cup and down his chin, a drop held on his stubble, then he wiped it into the patch of leather on the back of his hand. He looked through the haze of his thoughts and saw Leo across the counter, good old Leo, plowing through the hash browns and sunny-side-ups like a thresher through wheat. Harry stuck a finger through the thick handle of his cup and slid off the stool.

Leo looked up, stared over his lower lids, the reddish-pink, glistening lower lids, saw Harry, twitched, a stream of egg yolk winding a river through the cactus of his chin. He grabbed his fork with all five fingers and shook it at Harry like a cleaver.

"Away. Get off 'cuz I ain't got nothin' here," Leo growled. He stuffed a piece of bread in his cheeks, muffling his baritone rasp. His fork continued to waver, his head cocked at an angle, bobbing slightly and shaking the stiff hairs of a reddish-green toupee he wore on the top of his own hair like a hat. The wig came from one of the trash bins he picked through each day, lying there like a ratted, wild lily, and he took it and wiped it off and kept it as a treasure even though it was stained and matted and minus clods of hair, like a fairway sand traps dotting his head.

"Where'd ya get the money for the meal?" Harry asked.

"Girl gave it to me from a car," he mumbled, smearing the egg into his face like yellow dye. "A dollar."

"Jesus, brought your appetite up from the dead, it sure did. You ain't ate like that since Christmas."

"Not since Christmas," said Leo. A meal to him was like a bath, something he didn't expect and had learned not to look

42

for, working the streets, stumbling around all day for quarters, grinning blankly, trying to get the words out before windows cranked shut and he was breathing exhaust. When he was desperate he pounded car windows, drubbing and jabbering a hoarse, thunder-gibberish at cars captive at red lights, until a squad car came along and chased him off. Leo was somewhere in his fifties but wrinkled like lettuce, bleary, pink-faced, with sphincter muscles that had died and gone on to their reward and left him with a soaked crotch at the mere sight of a drinking fountain. He had to hide his mossy inseams if he wanted to sit at a diner, or hope a waiter like Sully didn't know, or didn't remember, or just didn't have the nose to smell it or see the steam rise from the stool.

"What you got, Harry?" Leo said. "You got something up?"

"Something big alla time. The roof, the sky's the limit, yessiree bob," Harry said.

Leo shook his head, as if he understood, a bulge in his cheek, then he choked on the potatoes and coughed into his plate, lunged at it as if it were the only thing keeping him from spitting up his throat. Harry sucked on his coffee.

"Clobber the bum, will ya!" Sully yelled from the hot counter.

Harry reached around and swatted Leo on the back, clopping him a couple of good ones, but Leo coughed until he began to gag. Then he suddenly stopped, looked up with a googly-eyed expression on his face, as if the blood had drained into his eyeballs, then went back to the slop on his plate.

"Somebody got it last night," he said.

"Yup," Harry said.

"Over at the hotel on Vicklen."

"How you know?" Harry hardly heard him, knew the wino's mind was as alert as his liver. The silt at the bottom of Harry's coffee cup came at him.

"I seen it," Leo said.

Harry put his cup to the counter, thunking it so that Sully

looked up, and watched Leo chase the last bit of yolk around his plate with his fork. Failing, watching the yellow glop paint a streamer in the grease of the plate, Leo put the fork down and finished the job with his two fingers, both black with dirt caked into the pores, one with no nail on it, pushing them around the plate like tugboats, then sucking them. He did it over and over again until the plate was smeared with the finger grime, each time sucking them as if he wanted to eat them too, two bungy, egg-flavored lollipops.

Harry got up and left.

He jaywalked across Wilson over to Broadway. The sun was out, a ball-playing sun, flat and warm, the Cubbies not around to enjoy it, and Harry opened his coat and let it beat into his wool plaid shirt. He walked with both hands in his pockets, part of the motion of Broadway, the wide sidewalks, the open doors of the daily pay halls. He ran his fingers over the change and the three dollar bills in his left pocket. Monday, he thought, the dog day, and he was almost broke, dragging his ass on the concrete. He thought about hounding his caseworker for an emergency check, he was an emergency, Harry Lum, right now, you can sit there and give me guff but I got to eat, I'm a human being and I pay taxes and I'm hungry, right now, not yesterday. But they would make him wait in the goddamn office for three hours just to tell him to get lost, wait until the first of the month, didn't have to be a genius to know that himself. They didn't tell Harry nothing new.

At Cullom he stopped in front of the Archway Liquors, a circus of blinking bulbs, windows boarded over and covered with hand-painted specials, sub-buck six-packs, Guckenheimer, Amigo wine. Regulars passing pints huddled in clusters, jabbering like politicians in caucus rooms, swigging the sting of the juice in noisy gulps, belching. Maybe another, a pint, Harry thought, a burgundy to chase the coffee out of his gut. He took a step toward the door; joints like this seemed

44

to have tilted sidewalks, so much so that Harry for years had lost his balance, as if caught in a thirsty undertow, until he was slack-jawed at the counter. But he caught himself, what the hell, mouthed the words as he thought, I ain't no wet-pants Leo, ain't no goddamned alky wino on the street smiling for quarters. Not your Polish Pride Harry Lum, with a heritage stronger than any one of these bums, yessiree, feeling those vines in Wrigley Field, passing the sour cream, and he turned around and ambled past the Archway. It was will power, you better believe it, he said to himself, will power two winos tucked into the foundation sucking muscatel just didn't have. He kicked rocks and empties across the vacant lot.

I got to get something up, he told himself. Got to.

On Winthrop, he walked a block until he came to a large red-brick rooming house with a four-by-five hand-painted sign advertising transient rates. He followed a concrete walk around the side and down to a basement door, kicked it three times, waited. Then he kicked it again, three dull thuds with the side of his foot. But the door didn't crack, no music, and he scratched his elbow bone and looked up the street. The apartment belonged to Frank Tulka, a squatty booster who wore pouch-lined sport coats that could absorb watches and pizzas, radios and pork chops. Once in a while he let Harry fence for him, hawk a zircon on the street for a few bucks, hop a bus to Maxwell Street and bargain with the niggers, or pass it off to his vendor at Wrigley Field. He hadn't seen Frank for a couple of weeks, no one had, but Frank couldn't have skipped, he wasn't that hot, wasn't that much of an operator. The cops had his address, nagged him, but didn't lay on him.

It was a good idea, Harry thought. The middle man, it appealed to his sense of merchandising, a salesman who could swap the ass of a hooker. Maybe he should wait for Frank; the two of them could pull something off. Like before.

But it was no good to hang around somebody's place. Like

45

hanging crepe paper on the joint, bullhorns, inviting the cops and their wives. He would find Frank somewhere around; he had his ways, Harry knew. He felt for his cigarettes but they were a memory, like the morning. He had no bottle, he had only the change and the three bills, which were crumpled and smothered with his fingerprints because he was mussing and pulling and wadding them in his pockets. Things were loose; he tried to yawn but couldn't, felt the thirst, his stomach, then twitched, shook his fingers, saw them shaking.

Then he spotted two heads in a car parked along Winthrop, not coppers but skinny, greased heads, and he walked toward them. He picked up the pace when he recognized Donald Ray Burl and Jimmy Del Corso slouched in the front seat of a '61 Chevy. He got to the curb on Burl's side, about a foot away from Burl's hand, which flopped limply on the car door. Burl was a hillbilly, still young, about a dozen lean years out of Kentucky and looked it, citified but still a shit kicker, his thick, hill-country brown hair combed around the sides of his head like Elvis Presley, a glop of curl hanging against his forehead like a hook. Burl had two lower front teeth missing, one left on the floor of a bar in Kentucky when he'd gone home for a visit, one he lost in a bar in Chicago. But, to take attention away from his pink gums, he had a pair of eyes with lids that drooped, lazy lids that made him appear tired or hung-over or strung-out even when he was sober as a stone.

"Got something up, Don?" Harry asked.

"Get the livin' hell outta here. We're busy," Donald Ray said.

"Don't give me the brush. I want in."

"The only thing yer gettin' in is my foot when I smash you one good."

"Gotta big mouth for a hillbilly. If you was thinkin' you'd know I could help yuse. Keep you out of the can."

"Shit on a bun. You ain't never done nothing. Talk like yer some gangster and you ain't nothin' but an ol' winehead." Donald Ray twanged the words out of the side of his mouth, coating them with beer and barbecue.

"Never drink when I work. One of my rules of order," Harry said.

"Never work, either," Donald Ray said.

Harry stood there, staring at the car, shifting his weight, not wanting to lean over the roof to give Burl a poke at him. He put his hands on his hips and spat on the curb.

"Shut up now, fucker, and mow your ass outta here. Corso got his old lady run through this morning and we ain't in the mood for you."

"I'm around if you need me. On top of things," Harry said. He shook his head and looked seriously at Burl.

"Bums like you are always around," Donald Ray said.

That night Harry succumbed to the tilt of the Archway and paid for his pint of elderberry. He stuck it in his waist, not wishing to share it with anyone, wanting to drink in peace and quiet, maybe with a cake. He turned and went for the vacant lot, but just outside the door, from the shadows beyond the blipping of the Archway's obnoxious bulbs, someone called to him.

"Hey, winehead. Move yer ass. We got something for ya."

For days they had cased the jewelry store, eying it from above and below, through the glass of a laundromat across the street, from a car, once from the platform of the elevated train a half block down the street. They watched and timed, drooling as the jeweler leaned into his window every morning and night picking and plucking his wares like children off stools. But on the third day, as they watched and bored themselves, trying to figure how much they knew and how much they had to learn, they were given an opening that whapped them in the face like a shaving-cream pie. They chided themselves for not thinking of it sooner, for not scraping their heads for television tricks. It was the plates that first hit them, white on maroon from Michigan, Water Wonderland, then

47

they saw the case, the lovely leather, smooth-grained, unfillable samples case. It lit up in front of them like a cashier's drawer, yet so much more real, so much more accessible.

Donald Ray saw it from the bar, threw back his stool as if he'd seen his woman rubbing up against a pair of strange thighs, and hustled down the street. He breathed it to Jimmy as Del Corso sat in the car, then both in the front seat, and they pulled from the curb as the Michigan plates passed them.

The salesman was a good one, patient, smiling like an undertaker, the bands, the casings reflecting in the lenses of his eyeglasses. He made four stops a day, returned to his car with the bag swinging, his keys, hat on the seat, made some notes on a sales pad and drove off. He was doing well, metal is forever, diamonds longer, and it didn't dawn on him to check out the '61 Chevy with Bondo on the fenders which was shadowing him at a religious three car lengths to the rear. Jimmy drove. Donald Ray sat with his fingers drumming against the dashboard, Nashville lovin' sounds in his head, trinkets for the baby.

They followed the Michigan plates and their light-blue '69 Ford sedan company car over to Lincoln Avenue. It was late afternoon and the sun bit into the windshield from the west, over the treetops from where it would sit in some cornfield. The car turned north on Lincoln and followed the diagonal route through the neighborhoods, the crowded shopping districts with their kids and paper vendors, until he hit the strip of motels on the edge of the city. It turned into Quality Courts, bumping over the high drive, jiggling the samples after a hard day. The '61 Chevy continued past on Lincoln, two pairs of eyes cutting swaths into the motel lot, then doubled back and around the rear of the motel.

They chugged up a side street about to hit another entrance, to swing through and around to cover the angles, when Donald Ray sat up and slapped Jimmy on the arm.

"No sir!" he shouted, then hurriedly, "Keep on! Go on!"

48

The look on his face was dull and scared and expedient, his eyes tightening, hands furtively slicking back a loose strand of hair, looking down at the trash and scuz on the rubber floor mats. For a while it hadn't registered, the short time that it took Jimmy to prepare for the crank of the wheel, the turn into the lot, then it hit him like a stab in the armpits, as if his daddy had cashed in a Dr. Pepper on his skull, and his mind clicked the shutter and he told Jimmy to hit it. He alone knew that private moment of panic, cooped inside the front seat, blessed, that's what I am, he said to himself, and he told Jimmy to drive on, get out and keep on going.

The next day Donald Ray Burl, in his best criminal intentions, decided to call upon the dimming, cirrhotic abilities of Harry Lum.

"Listen here, now. Listen, you old fuckin' winehead. We got this here thing all set up like you wouldn't believe. Me and Jimmy been working on this for a long time but we got to lay low on account of me being on probation and Jimmy just at the cops on account of his old lady. So we're gonna give you a little trial and see if yer really worth a puddle of piss or if yer just an old winehead who's worthless as shit.

"Now listen here. We got this here salesman, see. We got his whole route mapped out better 'an he knows it hisself. He's in town right now, see. Works the North Side, especially around Lincoln. Now we ain't gonna touch him, you know. We got enough shit for guns last time and this is gonna be simpler, anyhow. He's got this case, see. It's full of watches and rings, and bracelets and shit. About ten grand worth, I figure it. He don't sell it; he shows it and takes orders.

"So we been follering him, right. Driving all to hell watching him show that shit. But he always comes out with that case, see. And it's always full up. Good stuff with no numbers, no wear or nothing. Get rid of it in a hour.

"But here's the thing. Listen to this. He stays in this motel on Lincoln Avenue. He takes the case with him inside and

49

sleeps on it. That is, *sometimes* he sleeps on it. Sometimes he gets juiced up and is leavin' it in the car trunk right out there in the middle of the parking lot.

"Now yer saying why didn't we go and grab it when we sees him do that, and I admit we should a done it. But we had some trouble and couldn't get to it, and the next time we tried it weren't there and he had it with him.

"Now this is where you come in. We knowed you used to be a hotshot at punching trunks and things. We watch him, see, and when he leaves it in his car we come and picks you up. We drop you off about a block away from the joint on a back street at about two in the morning and you get on over there and punch it. If yer any good it'll be like breaking into a candy bar. We pick you up in back on the run and get on out. Split it twenty-forty-forty on account of we set this thing up and this is your first time in.

"Maybe some other jobs you'll get more. Shit, this is more dough 'an you seen in a year on welfare. Keep you in wine for a year.

"That's the way it's gonna be. He's got a '69 Ford, light blue, parks it near the side of the building in a corner. Dumb shit thinks it's safer there. You can't miss it cause it's got Michigan plates on. You can read something besides them wine labels, can't you?

"Now don't give me no shit on this, 'cause we got it set up and that's it. We'll be by every night by that store where you buy your juice at about one. If you ain't there you ain't going and you just blowed your chance for good. Could be tomorrow, could be the day after next. We don't know.

"And don't be gettin' loaded up and shouting all this to yer winehead friends on Wilson Avenue or in the Salvation Army or wherever yer shakin' out yer ass nowadays. You blow this, Lum, and we'll take care of you good. I ain't got nothing to lose no more because I done time and the fuckin' cops know me on sight. Some old winehead iced out here or there don't

50

mean nothing to me. I'll just blow your fuckin' head off and go back to Kentucky."

Harry shook his head up and down, up and down, like a kid on a gofer, feeling the linings of his pockets and the itch on the ends of his fingers. He'd go through a month of cold turkey to stay straight on this one, this one time, even as Donald Ray Burl, the hillbilly kid who hadn't shaved and smelled like rotten Old Spice, mapped it out for him as if it was Fort Knox and he was Yellow Kid Weil. He sat in the back seat of the Chevy, parked in an alley off Magnolia, nodding his head up and down, up and down.

Donald Ray's words were like the supplications of a priest, words that called him home.

4

The Chevy headed west on Wilson, Jimmy driving slowly, cautiously, trying to be a gentleman, not attract attention. They had picked up Harry in front of the Archway, where he stood in the shadows waiting like a kid for a bus to the ballgame. It was 1:30 A.M. when he swung into the back seat and Donald Ray checked him over for a bottle and smelled his breath to see if he had been nipping. But Harry hadn't had a drink since five that afternoon, a sacrifice as devout as any he'd made lately, and filled in the gap with a Polish sausage and three cups of coffee. To Donald Ray's random whiff, Harry reeked of heartburn instead of port.

He had prepared himself for this, prepared like he had not done for some time, flexing the fingers, training the concentration. If you were going to get back into it, get back into it seriously, like a calling, you had to do it right, start thinking about the job, like a ballplayer thinks about nothing but the game, getting up for it, eating right, laying off the bottle. It could be like a few years ago when he'd run with Yaras and Caputo, two tough bastards who picked locks and cased big joints, who listened to the right people and followed the leads. They pulled early-morning jobs, lots of planning, class when they came off. The time they relieved an office building of its cash boxes and adding machines, jumping from partition to partition after the alarms had been circumvented, driving off as if they were repairmen, and the office just repaired. It didn't matter that Harry was only their driver, only the guy on the outside, and it didn't matter that Yaras and Caputo blew down to Florida with most of the money and left Harry with a dead phone in his two-room flat on Grand Avenue. What counted was that he had been in on it, real big jobs, a craft you could tell kids about, and the really important guys knew him and called him even if it only meant being a driver.

It wasn't that long ago, at least he thought it wasn't. Not that long ago.

The memory was enough to force him to take a shave, pick up a new shirt from the Mission store, a pair of respectable shoes. He stopped sleeping in his pants, laying them out on the radiator instead after he had splashed them with water and tried to fold a crease down the front. That way he could walk down the street in most any neighborhood and look like he belonged, a grandfather, a landlord, someone the mailman talked to. The cops couldn't so easily drive alongside the curb and shout at him, telling him to get on, asshole, get on back to your block, which meant Uptown, and herd him like some kind of dumb alky back to Wilson Avenue. No, he didn't look like that, wouldn't, a job was up.

In the back seat of the Chevy he smoothed his hair down around his ears and zipped his jacket. Donald Ray had turned around and no longer leered at him as they drove. The car crossed Ashland, direct, with a mission, no cruising to attract cops, and left Uptown, past plain brick apartment buildings, Ravenswood, some small houses and lawns, new cars parked on the street.

Donald Ray turned toward Harry. "How much a what I told ya you forgit?"

"Nuttin'."

"You got a piece?"

"Don't shoot guns."

"Good, this ain't no gun job. Old fuckers shouldn't have

53

guns anyway. Kill somebody."

Donald Ray turned back and looked out the windshield. He was wearing a tee-shirt, stained beige in the armpits, smoking a cigarette that curled smoke through his fingers. Still the same droopy, evil eyes. The car turned right onto Lincoln and swerved slightly around an overdressed couple getting into a Thunderbird.

"Oooooo-hhh, momma, right here, right in here," Jimmy whined as he shook his head and rubbed his crotch, then craned his neck to watch the woman bend and lift her leg, the fabric tightening against her ass, then slide into the car.

"Shut up!" Donald Ray yelled and slapped him. "Stupid fucker! You'll bring on cops, actin' like some dumb clown!"

Jimmy coiled and turned to face off, lost the car and it swerved, then grabbed the wheel and scowled an open-mouthed oval, his tongue running along the inside of his lower lip. He hated Burl's guts, green guts, a goddamn hillbilly always giving orders. But he didn't say anything, breathed loudly over his teeth, stepped on the gas.

They drove in agitated silence for ten minutes. Harry sat still in the back seat, a cherub of obedience, nervous, thinking. He felt for the tools he'd tucked in his pants, tools of the trade: a hammer, a heavy-duty awl he called his punch prick, a sharply-filed screwdriver. Used to be there wasn't anything he couldn't get into with these, like an artist, a dentist in a jungle of wires. But three nights earlier, to practice up, to lubricate the old fingers, he'd gone out into the alleys and vacant lots on Clifton and punched open the trunks and doors of the junkers, the Ramblers with a door lock still on them. It came slowly at first, metal that wouldn't budge, new locks with crazy holes. But after a while, though he was noisy and a little sloppy, Harry found himself punching through the chrome and the steel until he was home. It was damn nice to be doing it again.

Suddenly the car slowed and pulled over to the side of the street.

54

"I got five minutes to two. In ten, we'll start for the alley side of the lot. You better be finished up then and looking like a treasure chest," Donald Ray said. He was looking directly at Harry, talking through smoke that obscured his teeth, the gap, and his heavy-boned farm face. Jimmy stared straight ahead, still mad, yet under control.

"I'll be there like the plan," Harry said. "I got ya."

He pulled up on the door handle and stuck a foot out.

Donald Ray put his hand on Harry's shoulder, stopping him short. "And, winehead, don't you be fuckin' up."

Harry walked slowly, casually, looking in store windows as he went. He wanted to look like an old man who couldn't sleep, minding his own business, that was all. As Donald Ray had said, don't bring on attention, blend in with the brick. The motel was within view, its Christmas-tree sign still flipping lights up and down in a curling, yellow arrow, advertising to the night. There was nothing complicated about the job as far as Harry could figure it, nothing he hadn't handled or couldn't handle. Just a tune-up for bigger things, a test Burl and Del Corso had found for him, as they watched and covered him, out of sight while an experienced hand, and whose but Harry Lum's, pulled off the act.

He subconsciously felt again for the tools in his belt, much slicker than a bottle, much more dangerous, and he zipped his jacket a bit more. He carried only his room key, no papers, no identification, only his fist and the L-U-M in indigo; there was a story behind that, but now he was interested only in covering himself, a hanky to wipe things off. Prints, he knew, it was damn important to think about prints.

In front of the motel, stepping into the syncopated shadows as if he were again under the shelter of the Archway, his heart began to beat into his throat. Cripes, the old nerves, he thought, something he hadn't anticipated, but something that strangely thrilled him, as if he had come alive once again, now on a real job. He did not look in the motel's wide windows for a porter or a room clerk, he didn't want to see them, or have them see him looking in, he didn't gawk at the cars which passed infrequently along Lincoln Avenue. He could hear the hum of the neons, the click of the bulbs, his ears buzzed. There was light on each side of the street, another motel, a drugstore, a grocery, lights blipping at each other, competing because time clocks told them to. Yet, in the light and shadows, the street, Harry could feel the stillness and the silence, his own solitary figure, and he turned into the parking lot.

He walked faster now, his eyes darting slightly to see if anyone was watching or standing, or just around. Between cars, across aisles, the yellow markers on the asphalt, and he made his way to the rear of the lot near the building where they said the salesman's car was parked. In his haste, his jerky motions, looking behind as well as ahead, he turned a corner too quick and caught his knee on a bumper. The pain ripped into his leg, a trumpet blast of fire into the bone, not cutting the flesh, but the sharp edge of the metal jabbing into the hollow of his kneecap, as if it had been shot there, screaming.

He sucked in his breath with a whoosh, bit his lower lip. "Holy Jesus and Mary!" he hissed and bent down to grab the knee with his hands. As he did, the awl and the screwdriver in his belt pricked his abdomen, jabbing with sudden pain. He grunted with the new jabs, nursed himself, then stopped and stood up to regain his composure. He looked to see if Burl and Del Corso had parked and watched the whole thing, him acting like a clod, a lush falling through a parking lot, and knew he was through if they were.

"Fuck 'em," he said to himself. "I'll take the crummy case myself."

Then he cleared his head and crept on, though limping, his bones reminding him that they were thin and brittle and old, toward the car. He spotted it right off, the color, the plates; Burl and Jimmy had been right about it. In moments he was squatting behind the license, his hammer and his awl in his hands, suddenly forgetting about the pain in his knee, and the first thunk of the hammer resounded bluntly, discordantly, across the lot.

He hit the lock again, three times, driving the awl into the tumblers.

Then lights went on.

"Right there! Drop it!" a voice shouted.

The sound of running footsteps, crashing through the lot like a rush of water through a dam, and Harry looked up to see figures heaving toward him, from all directions, like some kind of drill, but more like a bust. He froze, his hammer and awl in his hands as if he were a sculptor contemplating his next cut.

"Hit that fucking thing once more and I'll blow your eyes in!" the voice repeated. It rushed at him, among the herd, and Harry knew he'd been collared.

He dropped his tools and raised his hands, plopping them on top of his head, and froze in a kneeling position. He was too dumb-struck to think, then felt the hands under his arms raising him to his feet and pushing him against the trunk of the Ford. They frisked him, relieving him of his screwdriver; he grunted when they patted the tender spot on his knee, then cursed himself, began to realize he'd been taken.

Four plain-clothes dicks surrounded him, each with a flashlight, snub-nosed revolver, one clamping cuffs on him then pulling him back up and twisting him around. Three flashlights shone in his face even though the lot was well lit, his mug onstage.

"Sonofabitch!" exclaimed a short, dark-haired dick, and Harry suddenly recognized a familiar navy nylon jacket. The dick scowled and turned in disgust. "Fuckin' old bastard."

Harry placed the voice, the same fat, thick face of Fleck, the dick who had chased him under the tracks a few nights back.

"You're kidding me!" groaned another as he pushed through the crowd. Harry registered the form of Marrietta, dressed in the same shirt, the same flared, checked pants as he'd worn in the chase off Winthrop Street.

Marrietta turned and punched the hood of a parked car.

"I should a recognized the prick when he killed himself on that bumper back there," Marrietta said to no one in particular. Then he leaned toward Harry.

"What the hell you doing out of your neighborhood, Lum? Take the bus up here or something?"

Harry bit his lip and tried to swallow. He was in for a swan dive now, choking on the realization that his nose had been rubbed in the dirt from Wilson Avenue to the ass end of this Ford, with Burl and Del Corso pulling the string. His throat was dry as cotton again, his head clear, thoughts raining on him, and he chafed against the cuffs. He did not hear anything Marrietta said, for in the confusion and the surprise, with the flashlights in his eyes and his tools lying useless on the pavement, Harry saw that he had been made into a monkey, a sitting duck, a pigeon, he didn't want to name it. The cops had the place staked out like a museum before he even walked into the lot, watching his every move, his stumble, his contrived nonchalance, waiting to pounce. And Burl and Del Corso must have known, or set it up to cash a cop's double sawbuck, give them the old winehead, and then drive on without a care in the wide world. He tried to spit, but with the desert in his pipes, he could only spit out his stale breath.

"You must take us for real jagoffs, Lum. We plant ourselves in a parking lot for three hours and you think we're going to get excited about pinching your bum ass. We could go into your neighborhood and grab thirty of you bums. Don't think my boss don't know that and don't think we don't look like shit turning in a sheet with you on it."

Marrietta paced as he talked, his stomach more noticeable, falling, his shoulder holster tight across his back. Harry sat on a wooden chair in the middle of a small room in the Damen Avenue station, the detective house, second floor, lockers

58

and a ladder leaning against the wall, the smell of fresh paint.

"So," Marrietta went on, his voice a full bass as if he had been the neighborhood bully and enjoyed it. "Not to underestimate your exquisite skills as a thief, I'm gonna say that you didn't set up that by yourself. It's too big a jump from jack-rolling half-wit broads on Montrose Avenue. That car was tagged onto a stone salesman and you knew it. We know it too, and we know you didn't do it by yourself."

Harry shook his head, buried his chin in his throat and tried to put things together. He could have talked Marrietta's ear off, made deals, thrown him a line and walked out the door like W. Clement Stone. He was a thief and coppers were natural hazards of the trade, like bad weather. But not now. He had been pimped by Burl and Del Corso and in an old con that he should have checked out, but he was anxious, hot to get back to work, and he was forgetting things. Burl and his mouth, too loud, too sure, using him. He looked at his hand, his name, not saying a word.

"So what you got, Harry, who you got with you? A neighborhood job, right? Maybe you and Frank Tulka? Sure, we know about that, Harry. We're your goddamn conscience staring you right in the face. You and all the bums ready to clean this peddler out."

With his finger and his thumb, hungry, Harry began to dig in his nose.

"Jesus, Harry, cut that out," Marrietta said. "Here I am grilling you on the biggest job you done in ten years and you're more interested in the crap growing in your beak."

"Got anything to eat, copper?"

"Not enough for you in there?"

"Go chew on your banana, flatfoot."

"Jesus," Marrietta said. "I ain't been called that in years."

He shook his head and walked out the door.

They left him in the room for more than an hour, alone, the door open, a view of Marrietta's littered desk. They had taken Harry's cuffs off, left him to chafe and feel his knee, which he knew was beginning to go green. For the first half hour he sat, trying to see things, the mug of Burl, and he was too angry to doze. He needed a drink, rubbed his wrists; his hands began to tremble. Then he got up and walked around the room, looked into a locker, empty, and finally started to compromise. He had been in fixes like this before, all the time, in the old days when the coppers took him to the Wood Street station on sight. They would talk bullshit and take Harry's money and push him around. There was Pootas and Sergeant Lewandowski, always with their hands in his pocket, but he dealt with them because they were cops who needed the dough like he did. They were all the same, hadn't changed, now just younger with mustaches so the girls wouldn't know, but they all had their angles. He reminded himself, chided himself to keep cool and think of how the old guys would have done it, like Caputo who could talk himself out of anything. He had to think like a thief, not be getting the shakes and caving in and thinking about how to square up with the bums who put him there. He couldn't let the coppers treat him like they were shaking down rag-ass winos on Wilson or they would climb all over him. He had to think like a thief. Like in the old days. Like a thief. Like Caputo.

As he thought, he ran his hand instinctively over his shirt in search of cigarettes that weren't there. At fifteen minutes before 4 A.M., he went over and kicked the door.

Fleck opened it. He was alone, the only one in the office though it was bright from the overhead fluorescent tubes.

"Don't shit around with the property," Fleck said. He was drinking a cup of coffee.

"I got something to say. Where's the other copper?"

"Gone. You can talk to me."

"All right. I don't give a shit."

Fleck put one leg over the corner of a table, looking down at Harry.

"What you guys got me for? What rap?"

60

"Attempted burglary auto, damage to property, possession of burglar tools. And we just started thinking."

"Maybe a year, maybe eight months, and I walk?"

"Got a lawyer?"

"Piss on 'em," Harry said. "What you guys want?"

"Whattaya got?"

"Don't play around wit' me," Harry growled. "Don't be a jagoff."

"Look, asshole. We don't want you but you're here. We'll can you if we can't do better. Some nights you can't win for losing."

Harry shook his head. The cop was a jagoff, like he'd said. He wouldn't set up anything with the prick, wouldn't be safe.

Then Marrietta came around the corner.

"Hi ya, Harry. Feeling sociable again?"

"So what you want from me?"

Marrietta pulled a chair in from another desk and sat down on it backward, his arms crossed and leaning against the chair's back.

"Give us a few names, that's all. Who're your friends?"

Harry stuck his hands into his pockets. He looked away.

"I was alone on this one. Took it alone."

"Bullshit," said Marrietta. "The only thing you can take alone is Medicare. That lot's been hit three times in the last month. And never by you."

That crashed in on Harry, explained things as if a blackboard had been set up. Burl and Del Corso smelled on this one, all the way, and didn't want to hang around in the first place. Jesus, he'd been suckered, but never realized until just now the degree.

Marrietta held out a cigarette, then lit it for him.

"No deal on this job," Harry said.

"Then fuck you. We'll see you in court in eight months," Marrietta said. "It's the least we can do after you ran our nuts off under the tracks."

Marrietta stood up and threw the chair away from him.

61

Harry turned his eyes upward, took a breath.

"How about a hit job?" he said.

"What?"

"That girl was killed by the hotel. You know about it?"

Marrietta turned and put his hands on his hips, his cigarette pointing upward.

Harry stepped on his cigarette, still long, still alive.

"I know who done it."

5

Harry now, walking in the rain on Montrose after getting out of McMahon's car. McMahon, the shrimpy murder cop who wasn't really devoted to Harry, not to thieves like him, or junkies, or whores, con artists, burglars, but to all of them if they got careless with a cue stick, the automatic in the purse, a linoleum knife wedged in the belt. But McMahon got to know Harry, remembered him from the murder scene that morning when he'd pulled out a cigarette for the skinny old fart with the big mouth, now pulling the cigarette back because Harry was eyes and ears in the street. McMahon didn't ask Harry about his jobs, about his bungling in the lot, what he was into, with whom, but he played off Harry's sense of survival, that the pooch, for all of his shortcomings, wasn't a killer.

Marrietta had called, caught McMahon on the street with the radio, and in minutes Harry had a pass. He had waited for McMahon to come down Damen Avenue, the rain pouring down on the sidewalk, splashing angrily in puddles, soaking Harry's jacket, then had slid into the front seat of McMahon's unmarked squad. They had talked and set up the conditions. It was a string of freedom, take it, the copper said, and he talked quite clearly when he had the odds, or take the rap with Marrietta. As the car pulled over, he had been about to say thanks to McMahon, ask him what he thought of the

Cubs, the damn stretch drive and all, the bullpen, then he caught himself and got out of the car, without a word, into the rain, which had eased but was still falling steadily.

He went three steps, then ducked inside a phone booth to get out of the rain. The dampness and the cold, which stuck to his skin with the wet of his underwear, made him shiver, his hands shaking from a chill that worked its way into his shoulders and chest, the signs of the grippe that he knew one day would get him, low-bridge him, take his breath. One of the booth's top windows was smashed out, letting the rain blow against Harry's face, drops clinging to the hollows, the pores, the covering of his blood and his bones. It was not yet 4:30, the morning, A.M.

He began to think about Leo and where to find the old wino. That was the memory, the click that had given him the string in the station house, the yolk-slobbering crumb who'd said he'd seen the woman get killed, Harry was certain of it. And he would follow it up, Leo and his falling-down friends were always someplace, lying unnoticed, sleeping or nodding or knocked out in a wine-soaked stupor. Harry knew because they were always going to the cops for a payoff, information in exchange for wine money, ten bucks for a killer or a torch, which meant a dozen pints of juice. But now it was raining and that would make it harder. Harry didn't want to poke through the alleys and the trash heaps looking for Leo, lifting up newspapers and cartons, old coats with someone in them. It would have to be daylight before he would search the gutted buildings with their bad floors and rotting stairways, before he would check the walls and the newspaper heaps and the carpet scraps looking for the bum with his green wig. He would prefer to wait for Leo to show himself on his own, in the lots by the wine stores, the alley, on the street sponging quarters, Leo, still staving off the odds, stumbling and mumbling and peeing in his pants.

McMahon hadn't given him that much time: a phone call in twenty-four hours, a name in seventy-two. Otherwise Marrietta would get him back, time in the can, a court date. McMahon had been friendly enough at first, saying things like "Harry, we're friends, ain't we? We help out each other best we can?" And all the time smoking his cigarettes, chained to them but letting Harry bum them freely, smiling, checking the streets because cops are always checking the street. Then he'd gotten rough, whipped the butt out of his mouth like he was some kind of hoodlum and said, "Don't fuck around, Harry. You're too smart to try and work me for a pooch."

Back in his room Harry peeled off his shirt and pants and laid them on the radiator. He was exhausted, shaking from the damp, wet cold, then saw the steam begin to rise, a sodden, blank odor of wet clothes drying. He stripped and tried to towel off with a dishrag from under the sink, but it was streaked with coffee and pork and bean sauce. He threw the rag into the sink, on top of half-opened bean and tuna cans, and finished the job with the gray top sheet from his bed. The cigarette he'd gotten from McMahon lay soaked and limp in his shirt pocket. He reached under the bed and found an open tin of Copenhagen and pushed a wad inside his lower lip.

In the darkness, after he'd pulled the chain on the single light bulb overhead and sunk slowly into the mattress, he could see the figure of Leo, gurgling and grunting, over his egg plate. He saw it until a flood of exhaustion surged over him and he rasped in sleep.

He checked the lots by the Archway, the Liberty Bell, the Broadway, the Four Star, Augie's, and not one of the red-eyed, blue-veined bums in the tattered jackets and the greasy sportcoats was Leo. They stared up at Harry and hid the bottles, eyes barely focusing, scratching sores which poked through stubble and full-grown beards. Some pointed and said they'd seen him over there, over here, down the street.

"Who?" Harry repeated.

"Who?"

"Yeah, who?"

"Don't you know?"

"Leo."

"Yeah."

"The guy wit' the green hair."

"Yeah."

"Where?"

"Down here or over there."

"Who?"

They made him sick; they had nothing left, no honor, no pride, no ambition. None of them had any stories, nothing going for them. People liked to say that here were tragedies, all these men destroying themselves, human carcasses. Bullshit, Harry would reply. They were nothing in the first place. They made him sick. He had the decency to drink in his room, which he paid for each week. I ain't no bum, he said to himself.

By noon he began to hustle, turning over every face along Wilson, Racine, Clifton. At the Ron-Ric he stuffed a Polish sausage down and the greasy, smart-ass Sully said he didn't pay no attention to the bums as long as they showed money before they sat down. Harry called him a cocksucker and Sully pointed at him with a long fork, from the other side of the counter, shouting that he'd break Harry's ass if he ever set foot in the joint again.

Harry left, cursing under his breath, where was goddamn Leo, the leech you couldn't get rid of when you wanted to, his precious, bleary face lost in the gray ooze of the street when you needed him.

He wasn't Whitey, the one-eyed hillbilly who stood on the corners in his sweatshirt and tuxedo pants shaking and chanting: The-kingdom-of-God-is-at-hand-the-kingdom-of-God-is-at-hand.

He wasn't Stu, the old white-haired bum who grew his

beard as bushy as possible to cover up the fact that he had no lower jaw and because of it could not even negotiate the lumps in his pea soup.

He wasn't Blue Fox, the Indian who drank his pint bottles in a single draught, or Mrs. Loony, who sat in the diners marking off the shows in the *TV Guide*, or Roger Pointree, the weeper who cried tears for nickels from the ladies, or Skinny Red, who was only thirty-four but looked fifty and spent his afternoons licking the ketchup and mustard from the plastic packets in the Burger King trash barrels.

He was just green-haired Leo. And Harry couldn't find him anywhere.

He checked the missions, the daily pay halls, the Model Cities office, the Urban Progress Center, the ward office. In late afternoon he spotted Sylvia Lablow, an old, toothy, wide-assed hooker walking for cigarettes, her hair in pink pin curlers, her toes poking through a pair of silver, sequined house slippers.

"Who? Some bum with the wig?" Sylvia said. "Think I care?"

"I don't say you care about nuttin'. I say did you see him?"

"Wouldn't know if I did," she said, and lit up and began to walk away.

Harry hurried to keep up.

"Gotta cigarette on ya?" he said.

"Goin' to get some, ya mooch. Say, why you got to find a lousy wino anyway?"

"Important. Something important."

"Yeah, you in the cops for something?"

"C'mon. I ain't in with no one."

Sylvia hit the front door of a grocery and was gone.

The hookers never helped him anymore, now that he didn't have the dough, down on his luck and skinny. They would know, too. They knew where everyone was if they had to. Especially Sylvia, who was ugly and mean but smart.

He cut down Clifton, then over to Kenmore. He would

67

check the lots again and hit the junked cars. He searched a Rambler, a Ford Falcon, a '62 Cadillac. Nothing but newspapers and cans, a few beer bottles from kids, flattened tubes of glue.

Across the lot he saw a Ford station wagon, yellow with white trim, the windows still in, a green, greasy tarpaulin draped over the rear half. Harry walked over to it, saw the tarp was drenched and heavy from the rain, and with two hands pulled it up and off the car, exposing a smashed-out rear window. Three young faces suddenly peered up at him, kids about twelve or thirteen sprawled out on newspapers, pale, scraggly-haired, one with a face full of pimples and his pants pulled down to his knees.

They were momentarily surprised by Harry's presence, staring at him like mongrels in a cage. Then the pimply-faced kid grabbed madly for his pants, trying to pull them up as he sat on them.

"Perverted cocksuckers," Harry growled. He went for the tarp to pull it back over the car, then decided it was too drenched and heavy.

Harry turned away and walked back across the lot mumbling and bitching and counting his troubles. The faggots, he knew, eagerly corraled school kids for service in their apartments on Saturday mornings, showed them movies, paid them each two dollars, then did what they did. It made Harry want to puke at the thought of it; all queers did.

He put his mind back on Leo, started to run, stumbled over the weeds, felt himself getting cold. The sky had cleared in the morning but was now overcast again, probably to rain still more. He thought of the buildings on Kenmore and decided he would have to go through them. But not before he checked with Lennie Blankenship.

Lennie was a runner, about fourteen, an Appalachian hillbilly who ran the neighborhood, sometimes legitimately, usually not, on a fat-wheeled bicycle with a wide wire basket in front. He had been a lookout for Harry back when Harry

68

could afford to pay him, but he laid off Lennie when he figured the kid might be in with the cops, playing both sides for the money. But Harry still liked him, liked that the kid was always around, always ready to do something, always wearing a tee-shirt and a pair of sneakers and kicking those long, skinny legs of his.

Harry found him in back of the ward office on Broadway.

"Lennie, you been goin' around?"

"Yeah, Harry, so what?"

"You been on the street, I mean, or just hangin' out?"

"Been around. All over. Why you wanna know for?"

"Lookin' for someone."

"Who?"

"Leo. The green-haired guy with the wig."

"Yeah. Know him. A winehead."

"Yeah, him."

"Why you want him for?"

"Got to find him. C'mon, Lennie."

"Got any dough?"

"Nuttin'. Do me a favor. Make it back to ya."

"Sure, Harry. Like you always do, I know. I only heard something. Ain't seen him though."

"What you hear?"

"They say somebody been giving the bums money to light some fires again. Don't know where. Probably on Kenmore in there. Tonight you watch where the trucks go."

"Shit, Lennie. Can't wait that long."

"Then find him yerself. You workin', Harry? You lookin' for stuff?"

"Yeah, I been workin'. Reminds me, you seen Burl and Jimmy around anywhere?"

"I don't know. Yer askin' a lot fer free."

"Yeah, you little shithole. An' I ain't gettin' nuttin'."

"I ought to whup you one, Harry. Across yer smelly mouth, so you'll get the hell outta here."

He headed for Kenmore, for the buildings. He hated this.

69

He wasn't like them louts who haunted these holes. Maybe he should just go back to McMahon and tell him to cram it, take the rap from Marrietta and do some time. But he kept walking, running, across the street in front of a hulking brick brownstone which had once housed six big apartments but was now empty, sheets of plywood nailed over the windows and doors.

In the rear, he saw a loose board over a basement window and knew that they were in this one. Christ, he hated this. He could fall on somebody, or walk in and get shot, or knifed by some crazy spic on dope, no telling what was in these joints. And they smelled worse than anything because the bums pissed in the corners. The cops didn't even go in them; the firemen let them burn.

He pulled away the plywood and lowered himself feet first into the basement. His foot hit; he was sure he'd landed on a rat, a rotten cabbage, something soft he didn't care to look at. The concrete was littered with trash and broken water pipes, the copper fittings stripped by the junkies for scrap. Then Harry saw the rat, about the size of a guinea pig, sitting and gnawing on a box of Quaker Oats. It looked at Harry and didn't move.

He had to get out of here, found the door and climbed over the cans and the bottles to the first floor into a hallway. He kicked open a door and walked into a bare apartment, painted in a light green gloss, hospital green, a picture in a plastic frame of an Irish setter pointing at a pheasant. The room was empty except for a pile of White Castle wrappers and cups in the corner. Harry kicked at the pile and a trio of roaches the size of his toes scuttled up the wall.

It was the same on the second floor, which he got to by stepping up the rubbish-strewn stairs, balancing, walking on glass. He knew the junkies liked to booby-trap the stairs, that they pulled out boards and laid loose linoleum over the top to keep the cops from running up, and he was in no mood to fall through, to rip his leg on a rusty nail or lose his crotch to a splinter-filled beam. He found more bottles, a leftover sofa with stuffing ripped out of it and huge stains on what fabric was left. Then up to the next floor, but again nothing and no one but debris. He went higher; the place seemed to air itself out. A front room had a hole in the floor which was charred and strewn with ashes, an impromptu campfire. And in the corner, sitting with his knees pulled up tightly against his chest, a sleeping guru, was a young, dark-haired Puerto Rican, maybe an Indian. His eyes were closed, motionless; Harry wondered if he were dead, then stepped closer and saw the kid's head gently fall then rise again. He decided the kid was sleeping, or knocked out, but alive.

In a small back room, he stumbled over a purse before spotting a two-foot pile of handbags stacked in a corner, and the floor littered with papers, tissues, cosmetics, all used and pulled apart, some sanitary napkins. And the open pocketbooks, a haven for a purse snatcher, a place where he came to go through his snatches in solitude.

But in all the rooms, most of which Harry stepped in and stepped out of, not bothering to claw through the trash, the remains of food, the bugs, the bottles, the piles of shit, the rags, he found nothing, no one, no Leo.

Now he was fed up with it, sick of treading lightly through this filth. Not even the bums and junkies had to live like this, this stench, the rats, and Harry began to charge through the building. He would find Leo, the green-haired asshole, and beat it out of him. He didn't care who he came in on, another room, another basement, a dope gallery, a building gutted by fire and smelling of rank, wet charcoal.

He hurried now, climbing the stairs, kicking through the trash, coming upon clumps of bums huddled around a bottle, a couple of junkies heating up their spoons, who waved a knife at him when he opened the door. It was stupid of him to do this, he thought once again, stupid to go through all of this just to keep from taking a fall for Burl and Del Corso. He thought again of going back and turning them in; it flashed

71

across his mind, but he erased it with the image of the two of them posting a quick bond then coming after him and breaking his knees.

From what he knew of the torchings, the bums usually crawled into the basements of the buildings with a pint of wine and a quart of gasoline, drank the wine then splattered the gasoline on the beams and lit it. If they were too drunk to get out, too blitzed to feel the heat, their skeletons were found in the debris, skulls smiling. If they made it out, they stumbled into the street and listened for the screams and shouts from the tenants as they grabbed their belongings, their dogs, their kids, and poured into the streets to wait for the firemen.

Back on Winthrop, he ripped a board away from a wooden two-story covered with graffiti trumpeting the local gang-bangers. He looked around to see if anyone was in sight, it was after six and getting dark, and lowered himself through the opening. About halfway down he struck something solid, but not hard. He patted it with his shoe to get better footing and felt the object move slightly, then give as he put weight on it. He went through anyway, realizing as he threw himself in, using the soft object to push off of and drop into the basement, that he had found someone.

He was sitting against the brick of the foundation, Leo, his long, gray trenchcoat still buttoned, his head lying on his left shoulder. Harry let his eyes adjust to the darkness then went over and shook the pink-eyed wino. Leo stared back at him, his eyes wide open and filmy, not focusing, the pupils not moving, his tongue hanging out of the side of his mouth like a setter's, coated with white, chalky residue. Harry did not have to be told.

He cursed and started banging his fists against Leo's shoulders, shaking the old bum so that his green toupee bobbed slightly, enough to reveal a bare patch of greasy forehead. He continued to thump him, Leo, the sonofabitch had to go and do this on him, in this shithole of a place, with an empty

72

bottle in his pocket and his liver so filled with rotgut that it didn't work anymore, his pants drenched for the last time, innards splayed, and Harry just wanting to get the last bit of worthwhile information the crummy bastard ever possessed. He thumped and punched and cursed until Leo was wavering in front of him, his head knocking, tongue wagging loosely and stupidly, then still when Harry stopped, hearing his own breathing, his own heartbeat, the sounds in his own head.

Then Harry decided that he wasn't beating anything out of anybody. That he was looking at a heap which might just as well have been memory, a presence forgotten. For Leo was colder than the stone he leaned against.

6

He was proud of his body, good legs, a little wiry but strong as hell especially in the thighs, good chest, a chest to be breathed with, taking big gulps of air like he had trained himself to do back in Kentucky, where the air was clearer than the stuff up here, which had a taste to it. But, most of all, his was a chest with hair on it, hair that pushed up over his collar when he wore a tee-shirt, growing the way a man's supposed to grow it, thick, with something to it. Yet his arms were his trademark, thick white biceps he could harden into granite, not chunks but rocks, making the veins bulge. Wasn't anyone could take him arm wrestling no matter how many beers he'd had. And the hands too, hands that could wrap around things, muscle them, grab a woman by the cheeks of her ass and make her scream half out of pain and half out of joy, grab a coal pick, an ax, a jackhammer, and make that damn handle sweat.

He would talk like that if you got him going, Donald Ray Burl would, over Weidemann's beer he drank out of the bottle, tilting it down on his lips like a trumpet. The Weidemann's was usually enough to glaze over whatever was on his mind and send him back to Kentucky, back when he was skinny, but starting to fill out. Mostly he remembered running through the hills, digging the red clay, the things kids did. There were five Burl kids in seven years: Lydia, Rose,

Buddy, Donald Ray, and Dolores, all born of Judy Landrew Burl, beginning when she was sixteen and stopping at twenty-three.

What Donald Ray remembered of Art Burl was how black he always was because he coal-mined like everyone else around. He washed up in the company showers but it never took the dirt out of him, from under his nails, which were black like soot, from the grainy pores of his body, sometimes making his face look, after it had been scraped white with soap, as if it was covered with deep, moldy blackheads.

And Art Burl had those big hands, rough, calluses so heavy and hard they felt as if they weren't skin anymore. When the kids were still small, he used to set his elbow on the table, right hand in the air, and challenge them to arm wrestle.

"C'mon and see if you can whup yer daddy."

And Lydia, Rose, and Buddy, all under six with none of their front teeth missing, ganged up against the rock-hard, immovable arm and tried to push it down against the table. They shrieked with laughter, grunted with childish force, while Art Burl's guffaws echoed through the kitchen, and he tipped a bottle of beer to his mouth with his free hand. Then he would swivel in his chair, still laughing through gaps in his teeth, "Daddy, c'mon so we can win ya!" and held out his arm to Lydia, Rose, and Buddy so they could hold on instead of push, and he raised all three of them in the air until they hung like young possums.

As the years passed, Donald Ray began to realize how small the house actually was, that he slept with his sisters and brothers in one room, Momma and Daddy in another room, and that there were only two rooms left, a toilet outside. The bigger he and Buddy got, the bigger Lydia and Rose did, but it didn't matter except to themselves, so they turned their heads. When Judy Burl wasn't having kids she was out working lumber trucks, toughing up her hands like Art's, the kids out on their own. There was never any money, Art wasn't working a union mine and nobody ever made anything outside a union mine, even in one for that matter, never any socks, no food except beer and beans.

It was Donald Ray who got big, skinny but tall, with big feet and arms that hung down to his knees. He was hungry most of the time and combed the countryside for bottles to redeem for pennies so he could buy potato chips and cupcakes. He went to school with the others but didn't pay too much attention to it, deciding early on that he would work the mines like his daddy, who didn't know much past writing his signature and it didn't seem to hurt him.

In 1956, Art Burl had his leg crushed from the thigh down, not inside the mines, but from his 1953 Oldsmobile when it slipped off a jack mired in slimy red clay with Art beneath the back fender.

Donald Ray moved his arm across the table and pushed four upright but empty Weidemann's into the corner. "Guy was smart but stupid, ya know? Say things to me and Buddy I still remember today. Good sense and he knowed it too. Then he turns around and cranks up a car in the clay. Let the damn thing fall right down there on top of him. Damn near cut his leg off and smashed his knee up so he never did walk good after that." Donald Ray took three of the Weidemann's bottles and lined them up, then balanced the fourth on top to start a pyramid.

With his leg stuck in a cast so large he could hardly move, Art Burl spent most of his time sitting and drinking, grumbling in a light stupor about the house and the kids, complaining to Judy when she came home from the lumber yards until she would explode.

"Why don't you shut your trap? Shut it till you can do something for this here family 'cept sit there and drink the money away."

She circled him and leaned over him and shouted into his face then pulled back when he swung at her.

"Just a no-good hillbilly drunk cause of that stupid automobile out there. Falls on you like the dumbest thing I ever seen in all my livin' days."

Buddy and Donald Ray, now eleven and ten, didn't come in when they heard their parents going at it like that. Lydia and Rose stayed with girlfriends until Judy came and got them and dragged them home. In the afternoons, when Buddy and Donald Ray came home early from school, they would lift Art out of his chair and help him skip on one foot out onto the porch, then hand him his rifle and let him shoot at the squirrels or beer bottles as he rocked back in his chair. With one hand, cradling the butt of the rifle, a .30–06, on his shoulder with his cheek, he squeezed off shots that cracked through the air of the backwoods and shattered the brown glass of the bottles.

Yet, as his leg began to heal, Art Burl's nerves began to crack. Two months passed without him once seeing the darkness or feeling the deep dampness of the mines, three months until the money went and he had to borrow from kin. He began to drink in the morning, sent little Dolores off for another box of shells, and spent afternoons blasting away with the rifle.

On one of them, Buddy and Donald Ray moped home from school, afraid of their Daddy the way he was now, coming up the hill into the familiar noise of breaking glass they thought was beer bottles, only to see that what Art Burl was firing at was not the brown, thin glass of the bottles, but the thick, clear glass of the family's Oldsmobile.

He shot at the windows, side, rear, the front windshield, until they were broken out like ice chipped from a block. He shot sitting back, with one hand holding the rifle, the other pounding the cast of his leg. It was no longer just hard times, a bad break that he would have to put up with until it healed itself; it was now taking what was left of him, strapping him in a chair like a cripple, the doctor saying his knee was mashed into not much more than bone chips swimming in

soup, turning him into someone he and his wife and his kids
didn't know anymore.

"I can tell you right now the sonofabitch weren't never
right after that. Got buggy, I guess. Decided his leg weren't
never goin' to fix up and he weren't never goin' to be the
man he once were." And Donald Ray balanced a fifth bottle
on the pyramid, smiling, the gap from his missing lower front
teeth shiny with spit, working on the sixth Weidemann.

From then on, the years were a blur in Donald Ray's mind.
Art Burl got his cast taken off and went back to the mines.
But he couldn't lift or shove anymore and never really felt
that he was holding his own compared to what the arms and
the backs of the other men were pulling. The leg healed
poorly and left him with a bad limp, one which pushed his
knee inward toward his other knee as he walked. On damp,
cold mornings it ached and stiffened and he clenched his fist
and wanted to smash the joint into the pulp that it already
was. But he got out of bed and limped to work before sunrise,
past the shell of the Oldsmobile, which stood where it had
fallen off the jack, the windows in shards in the clay below.

But if he had drifted away from what he himself once was,
from his peace of mind, his work, he had all but caromed off
from Judy. Unbeknownst to the Burl kids, who slept in a
crunch in the next room, Art and Judy Burl were all but silent
strangers in their bed. With her steel hands she pushed him
off, then turned her back in open, blatant sexual hostility,
declaring to him that his body was as unsatisfying to her as
his temperament, his moods, the whole being of Art Burl.

For a while he tried to spite her, match her loathing with
that of his own, blasting away with the rifle day after day.

"Once she walked right out on the porch while he was
shootin' away and she said, 'Stop shooting that gun, Art 'fore
I beat you with it!' and he turned around right there in his
chair and leveled it at her forehead, never taking that finger
a his off the trigger, and said, 'I could kill you and breathe a
lot easier for it. You think about that when you shoot yer

78

mouth off front of me.' And she said, Christ, my momma was a rough one, she says, 'Don't make me laugh.' That's all. Just 'Don't make me laugh,' and stood there like a statue. I'll be doggone if he didn't move the barrel a hair and then blasted one off right over my momma's shoulder. A real cannon shot, that's how it was. And you know that woman never budged one single inch. Didn't flinch so much as she would if a fly was bitin' her tit."

But it wasn't the gun or the frigidity that finally did it. It wasn't the cool stares that cut the house like clotheslines, or the arguments, or the threats. When Judy Burl packed the belongings from the wooden shack, the clothes and the kids into her sister's '55 Chevrolet Biscayne and headed for Ypsilanti, Michigan, she did it after her daughter Lydia, now sixteen and mature, with broad hips and clean bone lines, a clear-eyed, pasty face, when Lydia padded into her bedroom where Judy lay alone one morning and said simply, "Momma, Daddy tried to take up with me."

Donald Ray's elbow twitched and nudged the end bottle of the pyramid, now complete with six empties, and it crashed down on the table. Donald Ray caught one, the others clanked against the table top as if they were made of steel instead of glass, then two broke into pieces. "What the hell—!" shouted the bartender clear across the tavern. Donald Ray jumped to his feet, a beer bottle in one hand, kicking the chair to the floor as he came up, ready to put the place up for grabs.

In Ypsilanti, Judy Burl rented an apartment on the first floor of a leaning frame house, and she and her kids lay on strange beds with their own Kentucky sheets, all of them on their backs looking up at a ceiling which was alive with footsteps, people walking above you in your own house. Only little Dolores slept, knocked out from the exhaustion of the long ride up. The others, and Judy, were so drained of energy, so beaten from half sleeping in the car, that they tossed and chafed against the sheets, unable to close their eyes.

79

The shock of paved streets and sidewalks, a house lost among houses on a block with only a spattering of trees, and more people than anyone could imagine, was softened by the presence of others from down home. Ypsiltucky, they called it. The Burl kids didn't feel so strange even though they realized that most people in Michigan didn't talk like they did. They played with neighbor kids just as unaccustomed to shoes and socks as they were, beating carved sticks against trees.

Judy Burl held some fears for a time, fear that she wouldn't have anything for her family. She never did back home either, but there was always a feeling that somebody around would help out. And a little money seemed to go further, not like here where some of the prices in some of the stores were stupefying. She also had fear of Art, that he would show up and take the kids, the boys maybe, and make trouble. She could protect herself. But the kids, that was different. She applied for a job with her brother-in-law at the Ford plant and again at Hydromatic, but in waiting for her application to go through, she was hired on in a cafeteria. She brought home $60 a week, as much as she and Art earned between them in Kentucky, but the cost of living in the apartment in Ypsi was twice that of Kentucky, and there was never enough money.

Donald Ray, now thirteen and six feet tall, took slowly to the streets. He didn't care much about Ypsilanti no matter what his momma said. Down home was cleaner and less crowded, good woods and creeks for running, and the old man was around, he wasn't all that bad, around with his gun and the things he taught Buddy and Donald Ray.

He tried to get by in the seventh grade and was told by a snotty, fast-talking teacher that he wasn't smart enough for her class. He tested out, as they called it, to the fourth grade, but it would look stupid for a six-foot kid to be in fourth grade, so they told him to sit in the seventh grade and shut up and try to pick up what he could. They sent notes back home to Judy telling her that he needed special tutoring if he was to continue in school. Buddy got a note just like it, and as the two of them walked in the middle of the street on the way home from school, they smiled the smile they knew between them and ripped the letters to shreds. "That's what Daddy would a done," Donald Ray said.

Donald Ray walked down Argyle, sliding from one edge of the sidewalk to the other from the grease of his seven Weidemann's. He bumped against Jimmy Del Corso, who was holding on to the waist of Barbie Dell, whom he'd met in the tavern. They had left after pushing around tables, flailing at the bartender, then getting chopped on the back of the neck with a whiskey bottle and thrown toward the door.

There was no eighth grade, not in 1960 or 1961. Donald Ray, now weighing 165 pounds, couldn't read many words with more than four letters in them. Spelling got in the way. The lady kept telling him to spell the words the way they sounded but they didn't sound the same when Donald Ray said them. And most every word came back with a red check beside it, until Donald Ray could see red checks in his sleep, a sleep in an apartment that he and his brothers and sisters never liked from the start.

Buddy left in 1963, saying he was going back home to work in the mines with Art. He told Judy that, but Donald Ray knew that Buddy was going traveling. He wanted to go down to Louisiana or Florida and catch alligators. Or at least tussle with them. And, in what he always considered the dumbest decision of his life, Donald Ray said he didn't want to go along.

Two months after Buddy left, Donald Ray and two other boys from the neighborhood, good boys from down home who hated Ypsilanti no matter how much they tried to call it Ypsiltucky, the three of them broke a window in the junior high school building and climbed inside. While a night janitor slept like a hog in the boiler room, the three of them, all faring poorly by day, ripped up every piece of paper, every

book, poured ink out of bottles, paint from jars, threw books
and supplies out of desks, typewriters, paintings, flags, anything they could get their hands on, into a frenzied heap.
Three rooms and a hallway were a shambles, Donald Ray's
the worst, before the three boys from down home eased
themselves out the window and ran back to where they
lived.

It was a month later that Donald Ray told Judy in the
kitchen that he had to leave. "I'm one of them who done it,
Momma. To the school. I can't take it no more."

He left by Greyhound bus for Sunnyside Street in Chicago.
Donald Ray Burl, at seventeen, strong, good hands, a chest
with hair growing in thickly, wiry but powerful legs, soon to
become Uptown's newest citizen.

He would move in with a cousin by the name of Gaylord.

At a restaurant, he sat alone drinking black coffee. Jimmy
and Barbie Dell had gone off to Barbie's, pecking and grab-
bing each other as they went. But Donald Ray, in his booth
with eyes barely focusing beneath his canvas lids, started to
feel his body closing in on him. He needed something up,
something down, maybe a girl; he rubbed his crotch. Then
he spotted a black woman sniffing at a guy in the booth near
the door. A hooker probably, but he'd go for almost anything
now. And niggers weren't that bad for the money. Whores
neither.

He laid his head on the table and fell asleep, a spoon digging into his temple, a heavy heap of hair and muscle. In a
moment he was lost in a sodden sleep which brought him
back to the innocent times, when his eyes opened wider,
adjusted much better to the light.

He remembered coming in on the bus, sitting next to the
window taking in what he could see of Michigan from the
highway, then the tip of Indiana. It was dirty in Kentucky
sometimes, and once when he went to West Virginia he saw
how the sky would cloud from the soot of a utility company,
but it was never like the gray-yellow he saw as the bus drove

through Gary. He could smell the sulfur, no mistaking it, worse than anything from the mines, from the auto plants in Ypsilanti, worse than anything he had smelled before.

He turned to the man sitting next to him. "God-awful, ain't it?" then stopped when he realized that the man was snoring beneath a magazine. Donald Ray didn't read on the trip, not and miss what was going by. The bus droned on, fighting the heavier traffic on the expressways leading into Chicago, and Donald Ray came alive with the skyline. Then downtown Chicago, Donald Ray humming under his breath about buildings taller than anything he'd ever seen before, even most mountains, buildings he couldn't see the top of from the bus as it wound its way into the Clark Street terminal. He caught himself gawking like a kid, inching down in the seat to look at the top of a skyscraper, bumping his head on the glass, then talking to himself, damnit, yer gonna be livin' in this city so you got to act like it ain't nothin'. And he sat back in his seat, closed his mouth and held it rigid, eyes ahead and drawn tightly, like this was no big thing for Donald Ray Burl at age seventeen, looking an easy twenty. He had a number in his pocket for Gaylord Hall, 956½ Sunnyside. He would call it and Gaylord would come on down and give him a proper introduction to Chicago, state of Illinois.

And it was minutes before Gaylord showed up with his '61 Chrysler, its swoop fins, pushbutton drive, a crazy, oblong steering wheel, and dashboard lights that glowed turquoise prettier than anything Donald Ray had ever seen before. And Gaylord, whom Donald Ray had never met, swung out of it in blue jeans and a tee-shirt, a pack of Camels wadded in his sleeve, and started joking and slapping Donald Ray on the back like he was some kind of long-lost friend. Gaylord was skinny and bow-legged then, but working on a nice beer belly, working on it right then with a six-pack in the front seat that the two of them began sucking on as soon as the car doors slammed.

Gaylord kept talking and smiling, showing off a front tooth

83

capped with a thin line of gold, saying that he just picked up the car and what a beaut it was and how he was paying on it by the month. After each sentence he sipped beer and ran it over a chaw of tobacco stuffed inside his cheek, then he turned his head, going forty miles per hour down a city street, and spat out the window. He didn't seem to mind that the wind slapped the juice back against the side of the lime-green Chrysler and streaked it something awful. And Donald Ray, with his earthly belongings stuffed inside a cardboard Clorox bleach box in the back seat, said that the Chrysler was probably the finest automobile he had ever ridden in. Gaylord told him that up here in Chicago, Illinois, you get a job and you can get a car like this easy with a loan from the finance company. Donald Ray said he was going to get himself a job, and Gaylord took a long draught from his third can of beer, swallowed, belched, chewed, spat, then said, "Yeah, there's jobs up here, too."

It wasn't but a few days after he'd arrived in Chicago that he discovered the trains. They were simply the CTA to everyone around, but to Donald Ray, once he climbed the stairs at the Wilson Street station, they were an incredible maze of intrigue, forty cents' worth of adventure above and below the streets. Like a kid he haunted the station, then jumped in the Howard Street trains headed south for the Loop. With his eyes inches from the front window, he sat in the single seat at the head of each train, directly across from the engineer and seeing the same stretch of track, the same blackness in the tunnels, as he was seeing.

For hours each day Donald Ray rode them: the Howard, past Addison and Wrigley Field, then Belmont, then Fullerton, then the most exciting, the most dazzling part of the line: the descent into the underground tube just past the Armitage station. It was like a mouth consuming them all, changing light into shadow and darkness, the sound from a hum into an echoing thunder of vibration and noise. Once beneath the street, he would study the houses as they slowly drifted into the landscape; he was suddenly in the lead of a long, curling missile propelling itself through a hole under the earth, and only he was in control. He twisted with the screeching wheels, the grating and screaming of the steel against steel, he leaned with the twisting of the coach, the leaning, the sudden acceleration which whisked him down the track, too fast, too quickly to really see what was coming, kicking up paper and debris in a whirlwind of motion and speed, all the time keeping his eyes keyed to the signal lights on the sides of the tunnel, the reds that switched amber, then the green which meant full highball throttle for as long and as straight as he could see.

He lived it on every trip, day or night, as if it were his private train in his living room. But this was much better, much more frightening and powerful, something which drilled away at his nerves and his sensations until he felt it in his teeth, his fingertips, the muscles in his legs as he pushed his feet against the floor.

From the Howard he switched to the Ravenswood, the Northwest Side train that angled away from the lake at Fullerton and remained elevated. As the Howard dove beneath the sidewalks at Armitage, the Ravenswood stayed aloft, stopping too often at small stations, curling around the near North Side projects before it hit the Loop and actually looped downtown before heading north again. He rode it only because the seat at the head of the first car put him on the edge of the track, giving him a sense of precariousness, of falling over the edge as the train made its curves, of not being able to slow down, of missing a switch and simply hurtling on and over the tracks and into the back ends of the brick buildings which abutted the line. The Ravenswood also gave him an exquisite sense of what it really meant to keep the trains going, of the spaghetti of tracks and switches, the tangle of conduits, cords, breakers, signals, transformers, and catwalks. And always, standing out in his mind's eye, was the raised third rail, the electrified rail that sent off sparks like Roman candles, that had enough juice to turn a man into bacon, enough juice to send the heavy, overloaded, obese trains scraping down the tracks with fury and commotion and speed.

But the Ravenswood was a slower train, usually a shorter one, and Donald Ray soon tired of the cautious way it leaned around curves and crossed over junctions. He was more at home on the Howard, the A or B trains that ignored risk, gathered speed, six cars, and barreled ass straight north or straight south. There was nothing like a dog race with a Ravenswood on a straightaway, or just full throttle with all green lights on an open stretch of track. And there was nothing better than the descent into the tube, the half-moon cylinder that ate the train up. He imagined that it was like the coal cars that took Art Burl and the others into the mines, but he was sure the coal cars didn't go this fast, and weren't as much fun. Things culminated on return trips, a glorious re-entry into daylight when the train smelled the end of the tunnel from North and Clybourn and headed for Fullerton, brightening, a small incline, then open stick for the blue and the dazzle of the daytime as the heaving, rolling animal came up from underground, coal miners and kids, to begin its cruise in the sunshine.

Donald Ray loved it, from his seat on the first car, riding the trains again and again. It was something he never quite got over, a cheap thrill that got into his blood. He vowed that when he became old enough he would do this every day, with real power and from the real source of the train's energy: the engineer's compartment. In those first few weeks in Chicago, there was nothing in his life he wanted more.

Yet there were other things Donald Ray could not get used to on Sunnyside Street. He couldn't get used to so many people, more than in Ypsilanti, many more, and there had been more in Ypsilanti than ever in Kentucky. Here they were stacked on top of each other in buildings so close you couldn't walk between them except in single file. And there were kids, thousands of kids, everywhere on any block you went down, twenty-four in his own building alone, kids like from down home just running and screaming but with no woods, no grass, no real dirt to soak up their noise.

Donald Ray also couldn't get used to the drinking, more alkies than he had ever seen, and winos, the young ones and old ones, throwing their bottles in the street and on the sidewalks, where the kids broke them into smithereens and stamped them into the dirt along with the bottle tops and cigarette butts. A person couldn't run anywhere barefoot, not up here, or his feet would come up looking like they'd been caught in a sausage grinder.

But, more than anything, Donald Ray couldn't get used to the fact that Gaylord told him he couldn't walk anywhere he wanted to after dark. There was too much of a chance to be jackrolled, too many fools around who'd split your head open to the brain just to go through your pockets. It happened at night down the same streets you lived on during the day, Gaylord said. And Donald Ray remembered how Gaylord had told him to carry a knife, something to equalize things a little. Part of it was colored moving in, Gaylord said, some from a lot of bad Indians living around, mostly drunk like they get, then also the Puerto Ricans with them damn knives, and even some down-home boys a little drunk or shakin' cause they ain't got their pills.

Until he got on his feet, he lived with Gaylord and his wife, Oma, and their four kids. It was a furnished apartment and Donald Ray slept on the living-room sofa, which he didn't mind because he could come in at any time without waking the kids. But they didn't return the favor, getting out of bed at seven in the morning, camping in front of the black-and-white television set which was three feet from Donald Ray's nose, to watch the cartoons and the commercials that pounded away at his sleep.

He got on with Gaylord at a grocery warehouse, working

at $2.25 an hour as a hi-lo helper, never driving the forks himself, but lugging the cartons and the cases to even out the loads. He started at five-thirty in the morning and quit at two if the work was done, sometimes staying as long as six. The work was harder than anything he had ever done in his life, draining him so that he looked like a whipped mongrel at the end of a day, like his father looked when he was still pulling his own in the mines. But the work was good for Donald Ray's body: his chest and his arms began to fill out, lining with ribbons of muscle and tendon. And, on top of it, he brought home a check of more than $75 clear each week, not bad for a boy of not yet eighteen, more money than he had ever seen.

In three months he had a furnished room of his own on Racine, a '55 Chevy convertible, and a girlfriend named Patty Napier, whom he met at a bowling alley. "Life is lookin up for me," he wrote in a postcard to his mother back in Ypsilanti. He added a few more words about how he hated the weather in Chicago, sent his love, signed it "Don."

It was Gaylord who had gotten him the job, and Gaylord, with his wife and four mouths to feed, the payments on the gorgeous Chrysler, who got Donald up at 5 A.M., honking the horn out front or banging on his door, and punched in on time. But on some days Donald Ray wouldn't let Gaylord get him out of the sack, either because of the beer the night before or because he had Patty Napier in. The missed days began to come closer and closer together, until after a while the foreman warned Donald Ray that he was through if he missed work again. Three days later he did and he was. It was followed by jobs lost at a Pepsi-Cola warehouse, a drum factory, a tool-and-die shop, another grocery warehouse, a packing plant.

Usually it was beer that he drowned the latest lost job in, sometimes sex with Patty. But they passed, days passed, years he didn't want to count up after he passed his twenty-first. Patty got pregnant and said it could only be Donald Ray's child. He wrote his mother another postcard and said Patty and he were going down to Tennessee, where Patty had kin, to get married. He stayed fifteen months, long enough for Audrey to be born and for Patty to say she was pregnant again, before he left her and drove back up to Chicago and a room on Clifton.

It was the trip to the clinic that had done it, the first trip he took one morning when he was hungover so bad his head felt like a thick, soggy melon. He hadn't really thought of what he would tell the doctor, maybe a little stomach, certainly his head but not from drinking, no he wouldn't mention that. He would simply say he hurt all over because he worked too hard, too many hours, and then see if the doctor would believe him.

When his number was called, he ambled through the open door and sat down in a small room. A man came in with the white coat and a clipboard of a doctor, and before Donald could say three words, before he had said much at all about his chest or his head or his stomach, the man ripped a sheet of paper off his pad and handed it to him and told him to pay the nurse five dollars on his way out. The paper would be filled on the corner in the Rexall drugstore.

The first packet, and he remembered that one for some reason, had yellows and reds inside. The yellows made him nervous and kept him awake, all night if he wanted, and made him want to eat like crazy. The reds put him to sleep, fuzzing over his mind like a half-dozen Weidemann's but without all the belching and the puking. After a while he downright enjoyed the reds, but looked forward to the yellows.

He took more trips back to the clinic, finally down to a routine, always laying down $5, getting the prescription, filling it next door. He was working at a rubber-salvage plant and the yellows got him to work in the morning, the reds got him through the afternoon. He was grinning lazily from one when he lost the job one day in 1967. But so what, he said

89

to himself, so fucking what, as he drove back to his room.

The next afternoon, after lying in his room most of the day, he slipped down the hall and, with a screwdriver, pried his way into another room. He knew the guy, a lot older than he was, and working daily pay in the hash houses. Donald Ray could take him any time. He rummaged around, through the dirty trousers on the floor, the stack of newspapers, bottles and cans stacked in a closet. There was nothing but the television set, which Donald Ray unplugged and walked off with. In ten minutes he was in a hock shop, then $12.50 richer from the first thing he had ever stolen. From then on it was easy. He smiled to himself, thought about it briefly, but mostly wondered why he hadn't thought about doing this before. It had been easy and the money was as green in his pocket as if he'd wrung it out of a sweat shop with five full hours of his own time. And Donald Ray decided that he had found a job he might just be able to hold on to.

7

There is luck, then there is dumb luck, Donald Ray liked to
say, and he said it as he pinched together the bridge of his
eyebrows. Luck is finding that jewelry salesman, he said to
Jimmy Del Corso, but dumb luck is sending Harry Lum into
the parking lot. He rocked back in his overstuffed chair and
slugged Jimmy, guffawing that low hillbilly horse laugh so
loud that it bounced off the walls and the pipes of his furnished three-room basement flat on Magnolia. He and Jimmy
were sitting and sleeping and piling up the Weidemann empties, watching television, popping whatever they could find
inside the white envelopes on the floor, eating pot pies and
beans Jimmy sent a neighbor kid out after. The two of them
had decided to duck low for a few days, to put my ass on the
shelf until things quit burnin', Donald Ray said.

They hadn't waited long that night, pulled around the rear
of the lot where Jimmy spotted an unmarked squad. Then
Donald Ray thought he saw the jagged beams of a flashlight,
heard shouting from the lot, then added up a fast two-and-
two, having been acquainted with such scenes in his life, and
concluded that Harry had just taken the swiftest, cleanest,
most unexpected fall of his career. And Jimmy quietly slid
the Chevy down a side street and out of the neighborhood.
Donald Ray, with all the smugness of a preacher in a whore-
house, started talking about luck and dumb luck.

The next day, from Lennie the runner, they found out that Harry had gotten out and was on the street, looking, asking questions, in a hurry like wineheads seldom are. And they decided that he had made a deal, one that probably included them, and that the wide ways of Wilson Avenue were no longer inviting. They would have to play their angles. Donald Ray suggested hibernating, they both needed a vacation, gain some weight. Jimmy said he still felt itchy with Deborah being dead, and every murder cop keeping his mug on top of her file. He suggested they take off, hit Michigan, or down south to Florida, but Donald Ray said no, that they weren't even hot yet, and to run would make it look like they had been in the ballgame.

"Anyway," Donald Ray said, and poured the remainder of a beer into his gullet, the bottle two inches over his mouth, "we're in the middle of a genuine streak of good luck."

With the dust-coated metal blinds shut tightly over the half windows that faced the street, there was no way to tell night from day in Donald Ray's place. The overhead bulbs burned constantly, taking more juice than the television, as if daylight was no more than sixty watts at a throw, dangling from a cord. The bed lay in the middle of the room, a roll-away sofa that hadn't been rolled back in a year, no sheets covering the stained, off-purple mattress, an army blanket and a few pieces of Donald Ray's raunchy underwear tangled on top. He sat on it and scratched and sucked beer while the soap operas droned on.

"What we gonna do for money, Burl?" Jimmy finally said. He was trying to roll a quarter over his knuckles like he'd seen in the movies.

"What you down to?"

"About twenty. Which wouldn't bother me if Debbie were around."

"Which she ain't," said Donald Ray.

"I don't get no welfare like you do neither."

"Yer shit out of luck, ain't you? You set yerself up with

some chickie who pays the bills and you clean forget to take precautions."

"Shit. I could go out in an hour and get some shit together. I ain't no welfare leech."

"You talkin' about me?"

"Just talking about myself," Jimmy said. "And I'm sick and tired of this shit of sitting around this dump waiting for the cops and some dumb fuck winehead who never was no threat."

"Shit, just take it easy and go buy yourself a pizza. Put you in wop heaven."

Jimmy scowled and looked off into the corner of the room, feeling the surge of his temper. "You know one of these days that smart-ass hillbilly fuckin' mouth of yours is gonna put you in a trunk somewheres trying to breathe through the holes in your head."

Donald Ray laughed, cackled, enjoying the fuming, bitchy, greasy idiot in the corner, once a wop always a wop. "Yeah, maybe one of these days." He laughed and rolled a Weidemann's across the linoleum. "But not today, prick."

The bottle clunked against the television and spun crazily.

Harry had scrambled out of the rancid basement, using Leo as a toehold, and hurried down the walk, through an alley and back to his room. He talked to himself all the way, cursing the situation, feeling the uncertainties, that he should give it all up, do his time and get out and go back to the priests in the old parish. He would tell them about his life, take the oaths, get off the streets. But it passed and he spat against the sidewalk. What kind of a chump was he to let two punks put him in this hole? Who said he didn't have what it takes to get back in the game, being a thief, like a regular job that you go out and do every day and don't complain? If only his damn stomach wouldn't bite him, and steal his flesh away, his breath, maybe the whole ticket.

In his room he threw his things together in a sheet, the

bottles and pills on top, a can of pennies, the stack of papers he kept in a soiled insurance envelope. He pulled the four gray ends together, tied them with a shoelace, and prepared to hoist it over his shoulder. Then it hit him. He was on the run now, with all of his earthly belongings, his life, that damn word, tossed over his back like some bum on the tracks. He didn't have but the change in his pocket, a few days paid for on the room but which he couldn't afford to use up, the towel tokens lying on the bureau.

"To hell with it all," he said, and swung the pack over his back, the force of it throwing him slightly off balance.

Now he had only one place to go, and he would go there and take the crap he knew would come.

What Donald Ray was interested in more than anything, what swelled in his hard Appalachian head with each passing day, turning itself over and over, was a new plan, a new job. And part of it, he contemplated, thought it out even as he stared at the blur of the television, was to get Jimmy Del Corso, the crummy little chicken shit whose favorite act in life was a pivot-and-run, so fulminating, so itchy, so ready to get the rust off his ass, that he would lunge for Donald Ray's new revolutionary plan in a second. It was just dumb to break ass on weekend jobs, bust-and-run jobs, when real planning, real scheming could lead to something big, something the punk pool-hall hustlers, the pill poppers, himself excluded, wouldn't have a chance of getting up. Planning had saved his ass with the jewelry salesman. It had sent him riding down the road like a mudslide in West Virginia while Harry Lum in his sheer stupidity, no planning in his brain, was left with his pants making love to his ankles.

So that afternoon, as the two of them bitched and complained at one another, Donald Ray finally laid things out. He told Jimmy to clear his empty wop head and listen to something he had decided was foolproof. And the two of them sat over paper bags ripped open and strewn about the lone card table, while Donald Ray scratched a diagram with a pencil. And, for the first time in three and a half days, Jimmy forgot about what was bothering him and paid attention.

That night the two of them chuckled over a pizza, Donald Ray's gift to the wop, and more beer, having sent the neighbor kid out with more money than they trusted him with, and the two of them chewed and laughed and made obscene remarks at the *Dating Game*. Donald Ray also had a fresh supply of Dexamyls, swigged them with beer, and in a moment felt wonderful and gushy, like he wanted to nuzzle Jimmy, then flexed his muscles, talked about trash which Jimmy didn't follow or want to, smiled, snarled, then sat down and snuck up on the bugs. At 9:30, after Woolworth's closed, there was a knock on the door and Jimmy opened it to Barbie Dell.

"Came by to see what you boys were doin'. Thought you were dead," she said, her honey hair ratted and swept back over her ears, then falling loosely over her shoulders.

"Well, hellooo Barbie dooo," Donald Ray crooned from the bed, got up on his knees despite the sinking mattress, flexed a tattooed, hairless right bicep.

"Yeah, yeah, c'mon in," Jimmy said. "Wanna beer? Huh? What's the story?"

Barbie took one look at Donald Ray, one of them down-home boys, straddling the sheets and spilling his beer, and curled up her face. "What's got into him? He's crazy," she said in her twangy soprano, flicking the hair over her shoulder and down her back, throwing her baby-blue Woolworth's smock on the table. She put her hands on her hips and looked around the place.

"How can you all *stand* this pig pen? Can't even see the light of day down here," she said. She took a Weidemann's from Jimmy and wiped off the mouth, then nipped at it.

Jimmy slipped over, crept his hand up the wall and leaned down against her shoulder, interested. Barbie saw him without looking, threw out a wide hip, a nice Kentucky ass, the kind of good looks weaned in the hills, coarsened on Wilson Avenue. She was still slim, with white fleshy legs, the hint of a midriff if she wasn't careful, and a pair of breasts, white, blue-veined tits that popped nipples through her bra, strained, invited, and oiled Jimmy on the spot. She had taken him back to her place from the tavern the other night, but both of them had been too drunk to do anything but flop down on each other, not waking for Barbie's kid girl Amy, who screamed because she was hungry and had a pantsful, Jimmy sleeping with his mouth open. But now he remembered what she had felt like, and she was standing right here.

"I ain't seen you two guys around nowhere. Hey, he's really out of it, ain't he?" she said and watched as Donald Ray fell free-fall backward onto the mattress, the bed bouncing with him, his eyes googled.

"We're hangin' low till things blow over," Jimmy said. "We're gettin' something up, though. Real big. Like down here." He cupped the side of his thigh.

"Oh, well I don't know anything about that," Barbie said. "What's this? Pizza? You save some for me? You meanie."

She grabbed Jimmy's arm and twisted the skin, then picked through the remains of pizza, biting at a crust. "Ain't nothin' here for me."

Jimmy leaned over and bit her on the neck, leaving a patch of beer foam on the spot.

"You stop that unless you mean business," Barbie said, and she swung her hair over her shoulder and squared off at him, pushing out a nyloned leg, peanut-butter smooth and creamy, as Jimmy liked to say it, tapering into her black sneakers. She put her chin into her shoulder, bright blue eye shadow that matched her Woolworth smock, and lips that she could push or pull. She was twenty-three years old, Barbie Dell, and she knew damn well what she had and what she wanted and how she could get it.

"What about him?" she said. "He's sort of cute."

"He's so high he could fuck the moon," Jimmy said, never

taking his eyes off Barbie's legs, the black bikini panties he knew were underneath her skirt.

They left while Donald Ray burrowed his head beneath the pillow, his brain full of faces he couldn't begin to recognize, still going up. Barbie explained that her uncle was sleeping over but it wasn't no big thing because he was out most of the time and didn't pay no attention to things. Jimmy shook his head and looked straight up as he led her out of the building, his crotch leading the way, feeling her, that smooth white skin crashing against his own.

As the two of them stepped up to the sidewalk, turning onto Magnolia in the shadowy light of the street lamp, a solitary figure with a bundle over his shoulder stepped into the gangway of the building on the other side of the block. He was a frail, slight man and he headed for the back stairwell. But Jimmy could not have paid less attention, swinging on the smile and touch and the smell of Barbie Dell. They were on the next block by the time the figure with the bundle over his shoulder made it to the fourth-floor landing.

He rapped on the deck-gray screen door, then stood there like a small boy trying to sell candy to the neighbors. His stomach was bothering him. Then he heard the hard, solid heels, the heavy steps coming over the tile of the kitchen, a light, the dead-bolt lock and a chain snapping, then a voice. "What you want?"

"It's me," he said. Then he listened to the silence, pictured the expression, the suspicion as the door lock clicked free.

She looked at him through the screen. She was a dark figure looming within the blackness of the kitchen, and she saw only his outline in the porch light, skinny and hunched over. There was no sound between them, just cold sizing-up, thoughts bouncing, before she turned and exploded.

"Oh, my God! My God! I'm got troubles enough for more people and now you!" she yelled, a loud, shrill carping that echoed against the linoleum.

97

Then she turned, without unlocking the screen, and tramped through the kitchen toward the light of the dining room. "No, un-uh, no sir! Get outta here, Harry, take off! Oh, my God, I'm not takin' you in, not if the Pope told me to tomorrow I'm not gonna open that door. Un-uh, Harry, no sir!"

She shouted as she walked, picking up things with a fury that added to her shrillness, the clomping of her hard heels rapping the floor boards like a hammer.

He stood there about to object, to put in his two cents, but she was a moving target, barging from room to room, and he could do little but drop his bundle to the porch and stand there.

She was short, no more than three inches over five feet, but built like a truck. She wore a navy work dress which came down over her knees into two bullish calves, a pair of black wool socks and heavy-heeled black shoes. She grabbed a squat black handbag, poked into it with a fistful of stubby, strong fingers, shouting, "You're a lout that broke your mother's heart, yah!" getting madder and madder as she thought about it, then turned and puffed into the bathroom and beat a comb into her gray-black hair, which was pulled back and bobby-pinned into a bun. Her red-cabbage face looked back at her in the mirror, without makeup, just the blood of fifty-five years pulsing rage and scorn and pink into her cheeks. `Cholera! Psiakrew!*" she spat, twisting the words gutturally.

Then she came out of the bathroom, across the kitchen, without tripping the light switch. She was heavy and charging, a beefy chest which barreled out to her stomach, a wide, uncompromising rear end. Without looking at him, she growled, "I'm goin' to work. I gotta go to work." And she swung the door shut, clicked the locks back in place.

He stood there with his mouth ajar, about to fight back, then the wind of the door hit him and he heard only her thumping shoes walking away from him on the other side of it.

98

"Ah, to hell with ya. Who needs ya," he muttered.

Then he kicked his bundle into the corner of the porch and sat on it, pulled his knees up and folded his arms across them. He could wait.

She charged out the front way, pausing only to grab her purse and her lunch of sausage and bread and cheese, then slamming the door and jabbing her keys into the two dead-bolt locks. Down three flights of immaculate stairs, stairs she scrubbed herself with water and vinegar every other week, then she went around front to the entrance of the building and stopped out of habit to pick up the pieces of trash mail on the floor. Most of it was for names long since gone, second-class junk mail or bills, thin and angry looking, with warnings stamped on the envelope. She tossed them all in the trash container outside the door; none of them were her problem, and walked quickly on.

She was Helen Pontek, a hard-headed, hard-working Polish widow, owner of this exhausted six-flat on Magnolia, landlady to a dozen or so crumbs who flopped into her furnished rooms for a week or a year, mostly hillbillies, all of whom paid in advance or were thrown out bodily by Helen herself. It was none of her doing, this Uptown neighborhood, this building which was a place to live and a little money but which was a loathsome albatross around her neck. Her neighborhood was Milwaukee and Damen, where she had grown up, gone to church, all her life, where the Polacks were, the old ones who still knew how to eat, and when to go to church, and how to talk. Or maybe further out on the Northwest Side, that would be all right too, where the younger kids bought houses and sent their kids to Catholic schools, or in Niles or Medinah, where there weren't any neighborhoods but where there weren't any coloreds or Puerto Ricans either.

Here she was alone, only her daughter Ilene in the house, two Polacks in Uptown where they didn't belong, not with all the trash, all the riff-raff who came here, who lived and

99

tore up the place, then took off to wherever they came from. It was all wrong in Chicago, a city where neighborhoods were neighborhoods; you knew yours as the wops, the micks, the Jews, the Krauts, and the coloreds knew theirs, and nobody tried to change the order of things. At least, they didn't once upon a time, until the city started to go to hell, the coloreds and the Puerto Ricans spreading like lice, the politicians giving them what they wanted, and any decent white person with a job and some money got out while he could. Mixing races never worked back then, and it wasn't going to work ever, and those that stayed bought more and heavier locks.

That is what Helen Pontek used to tell her lady friends at the markets and at the church clubs and after mass. All the while she was fighting with a husband who did nothing but drink and watch the Wednesday-night fights, who lost more jobs to the bottle than she could remember, each time tying on a bender to forget, and rapping her across the room when she complained that there was nothing in the house but empties. When the cops found Joe Pontek passed out for good in a piss puddle in front of the house, Helen put on an appropriate wake, lit candles at mass, but kept her eyes dry as dust, not one solitary tear for the louse who left her with bad memories and bills and nary a nickel.

She signed on with the night brigade of scrubwomen who boarded the bus at night and headed into the Loop to clean the office buildings. She wound a babushka around her head like they did, put on pairs of ankle socks, heavy aprons, and heavier shoes, and spent the midnight hours scrubbing floors, dusting desks, dumping ashtrays, emptying wastepaper baskets, and whistling polkas to herself in the din of the lights and the solitude of sleeping high rises. When the sun peeked through the mist of the lake, yawning new life into the drives and walks and the concrete, Helen's back began to ache, her hands rubbed smooth from cleanser. She packed up her cleaning closets, finished the bits of cheese and sausage, and joined the other neighborhood mop-and-pail generals at the bus stops for the ride back to Milwaukee Avenue.

It was a thankless, quiet, but steady job which put bread and sour cream on the table, put clothes on Ilene's back, the wolf out the door. She paid the bills and the taxes on the frame house on Wabansia Street, got along and never missed church, read the *Daily Zgoda*. She would tell her lady friends that all she wanted out of life was to work, to scrub, to clean her house, to make chicken soup and peirogee. But then she would cross herself and shake her head, "But I'm tanks God I'm healthy." Said with a sweep of her thick hands and an obvious flick of contempt for her Joe Pontek, who never thanked God for anything but a bottle of hooch.

The years passed like the sodden, unending mop-and-broom night shifts, always there, always over, not without pain or aches or complaints, always there. In the winter of 1961 she took in her father, who was in his seventies and could hardly see. She resented him for what he had done to his wife, her mother, the streak of Polish male that treated women like swine, so much mule to pick up and clean up and settle things, to serve the food and clean the dishes and shut up. She called him Grampa and set him in front of the television, his nose three inches away from the screen so he could see the images of cowboys and wrestlers and *I Love Lucy*. But Helen hated him for outliving her mother, for making her not so much die but give up, with no kind words, that night, oh how she remembered and would tell everyone someday, how he was angry because there wasn't any dinner on the table and he was hungry and had to be fed.

But if he ever brought her an insult above any other, one that lingered like a blotch of a birthmark, it was the insult, the injustice of the son of Grampa's second wife. It made the bum, and everyone in the neighborhood knew him, her stepbrother, as if he were kin, blood, a person you went to mass with. His name was Harry Lumakowski, and he was always in some kind of trouble, always bringing the cops to the

101

street, running down the alleys. They said he stole cars when the keys were left in them, just drove them around the neighborhood until he lost his nerve, then dumped them in an alley and ran off with the battery, a spare tire, or the cigarette lighter. He was just a no-good kid, Helen's mother used to say; you could see it in his face the way he would look away from you, never with a dime in his pocket, pants ripped at the knee, bald sneakers, and when he got older, a stubble of fuzz around hollow cheeks and a neck laced with pimples. He finally went to jail for the first time at the age of seventeen after he and a grade-school friend ripped the head off a parking meter and relieved it of $6 in pennies. They were caught twenty minutes later when a cop spotted them walking down Division Street with their pockets bulging, Harry straining to keep his trousers up, a thief with his pants full.

And, thanks to her father's marital insanity, Helen became tied to Harry Lumakowski for years while Harry and her father played pool and drank beer, the women cleaning up and leaving for work on time. She never had to find out what Harry was up to, it always got back to her, through the hushed whispers of the ladies across the fence, or on the bus, those who'd seen the police come after him, or collar him for lying on the sidewalk, or riding in a car that wasn't his, or pushing a stolen cement mixer down the street. And she was always Harry Lumakowski's sister, stepsister, she would loudly correct, he ain't no relation of mine, through the years until she was sick of it, of him, of her father and his wretched ways.

When her father died of the gout, almost blind, old and fat with the neighborhood kids treating him like a doddering old man who talked funny and couldn't see past his nose, Helen again did not summon up the tears. She paid her respects, did what was expected of her as a daughter, braced for the bill from the undertaker and cursed when it came. But at the opening of the will, a ceremony Harry Lumakowski saw fit to attend, even to the point of taking a shave and looking as respectable as he could, Helen was relieved to learn that her father, for all of his stupidity, had been very specific about who should get what little he had to leave behind. Harry and a handful of distant relatives got $50 each out of an insurance policy. Helen got the deed to the house on Wabansia and also a title to a rooming house on Magnolia in the Uptown section of Chicago. It was a property Helen never knew existed, and learned of from a lawyer who said her father had taken possession of it through his brother and took in rent through a management outfit without realizing much of a profit.

A few days later, Helen prevailed upon a friend to drive her to Magnolia, an address they had to drive slowly by to find, and picked out the building she now owned from a nondescript row of brown brick buildings. It was a sturdy, imposing structure, with walls thicker than anything in the frame house on Wabansia. But she was Helen Pontek, a Polack from Milwaukee Avenue, and she didn't know the first thing about this place, or the neighborhood, or the people who walked the streets. It was Chicago, Illinois, the only place she had ever lived, but the building, 4422 North Magnolia, with all its silent strangeness, might just as well have been in China.

When the sixties saw Wabansia Street slowly turn Spanish, and Ilene complain that her high school was a jungle that she was afraid of, Helen sold the house for $6,000 and moved all her and Ilene's earthly possessions to the fourth-floor apartment on Magnolia. Ilene took a typist's job in the Loop and Helen changed bus lines in order to meet her mop-and-pail starting time. The building was full of furniture and rents came in. It was only right that she live there and make sure the place wasn't torn apart. She expected the same from every hillbilly family she rented to, weekly, with cash, and a three-day grace period before she'd call some friends from the old neighborhood to throw everybody out. She didn't like to do such things, didn't like to treat people as she herself wouldn't like to be treated, still going to mass at St. John

Cantius, but nobody lived in this neighborhood for more than a week without learning what it took. Every kindness you showed scratched you, every piece of credit came out of your skin. Until Helen had a reputation, a rooming house that kept its tenants as long as they wanted to go by the rules, with shoes and soiled underwear and hot plates on the sidewalks if Monday's rent wasn't paid by Thursday.

So Harry, stepbrother Harry, sat there in a huddle in the corner of the back-porch landing, dozing off against the night sounds, finally sleeping soundly against his elbows when midnight passed. He was startled awake by sirens, crunching, curious noises in the alley, but then settled into his uncomfortableness, finally stretching out on the porch boards and using his bundle as a pillow. He didn't dream of anything, occasionally felt his stomach, his bones against the wood, that he was on the downside looking up once again.

At a quarter of six she jerked the back door open and stared at him through the screen. The morning light showed how skinny he really was, with that bloated rotgut belly, like a thousand no good Polacks she'd seen on the streets in her day. This one her stepbrother, Harry Lumakowski, calling himself Lum with that stupid tattoo on his hand, as stupid as most things he did, sleeping on her back porch as if it were the lobby of a flophouse.

"Harry!" she barked. She kicked her shoe against the bottom of the screen. "Harry!"

He awoke suddenly and sat up, looking through the screen, the gentle light of morning not registering with him.

"C'mon, Harry."

He tasted his mouth and tried to swallow, rubbed the back of his hand across his lips. He looked into the screen, the figure standing there in the dress, the apron, the heavy arms.

"C'mon, Helen," he groaned. "C'mon. It's me, Harry."

104

8

The forty-eight hours had passed, the golden time when the heat of a crime still glows, the victim a fresh, haunting stare in the minds of the killer, the witness, the cop. But that time had passed into the fleshy part of the week. Nobody had made any mistakes, no one panicked, no one felt the pang of conscience to tell everything and get some sleep that night. It happened in the murder of Deborah Cortez, quickly, as if from the moment the crowd broke up at the scene in the alley the crime, the corpse, no longer mattered. Only John McMahon kept it alive, there on his clipboard in his attaché case, talking about the angles of it to Gene Farber, his partner, as the two of them drove through the streets of Uptown and the North Side, knocking on doors and trying to pin the fear, the viciousness of the crime on those who didn't have very good answers.

It went on for two days, those forty-eight hours, and they learned everything and nothing about Deborah Cortez. They heard the name of Jimmy Del Corso, "Corso," "the Wop," even the "Kid," a hundred times, too much, too conveniently, like a pass-the-buck routine that had infected everyone. And they knew Del Corso, McMahon had him brought in almost immediately, but also gave him a pass, out of instinct, knowing too much about him, what he was into, what he was capable of, and not being convinced, after studying murder for years, that he was the man they wanted.

Farber was down on Del Corso from the beginning. He considered the Italian to be a petty, temper-tantrumed pooch who liked knives, saying that if he got one solid lead on the prick he'd run him in and book him and sweat it out in court. But McMahon disagreed, seeing the killer as a lot more than Del Corso, someone who not only plunged a knife into her three deep times, but who was mad enough, wild enough, insane enough to throw her out a window from five floors up. Del Corso, in McMahon's mind, was too much of a punk to do that, living off Deborah Cortez like a leech, like a kid, going back to her for money when he was down, bitching at her for his ego, violating her at will, cuffing her around, then stroking her like a puppy and telling her that she was the greatest and he really loved her. If he'd hit her too hard, he'd make it up to her, McMahon reasoned; if he hurt her, even stabbed her, he'd bring her to the emergency room then stand outside with tears in his big Italian eyes, telling himself that he'd lost his head and that it would never happen again. And maybe he could kill her, McMahon was too close to Uptown to rule it out, kill her in a fit of rage and rejection and chaos, but he didn't think Jimmy Del Corso could throw the corpse which was his chick, his meal ticket, his ego out the window. Not the dago prick, the kid who had sat in his office a few nights earlier and grumbled like a punk instead of a killer.

They finally took the case down to Armitage and Sheffield into the Latin neighborhood that lined Halsted Street and the Howard el tracks. There they found Deborah's mother, a sister, and an aunt. The family spoke in broken English, sometimes feinting and squeezing in a quick, muffled exchange between them in Spanish. But they said little. They stared at the two homicide cops with the dour, deep Latin countenances which radiated uncertainty and distrust. Deborah had gone away a few years back, rarely returned, and never told them anything, they said. They knew she was

106

seeing a man, that she was living with him though they were not married. Mrs. Cortez said that she prayed for her daughter at mass every day, attended novenas for her, but that her prayers weren't enough. She knew something like this would happen. Girls like Deborah wouldn't make it in this country. Then she rocked and remained expressionless. McMahon and Farber said thanks, noticed the plastic frame around the 3-D picture of Jesus on the wall, the sprig of plastic flowers, and left.

The break was Harry Lum, a deal that would crack something open if Harry was doing more than playing around. Yet McMahon had his doubts, strong misgivings as he talked with Harry in the front seat of his car that night, that Harry was on a string, in over his head on a rap, and finking in hopes of getting off. McMahon would wait and see, play all the cards, track Uptown and its Harry Lums and Jimmy Del Corsos until somebody ratted, or double-dealt, or simply sold out to the highest bidder.

The next day the lieutenant took them off the Cortez case and put them on a tavern shoot-out. The new case was still hot, with suspects, names, witnesses, a twist away from an arrest. Deborah Cortez was placed next in the pile, her face, the form of her body in the alley becoming more and more remote. McMahon would not work overtime on it, nor let it percolate beneath his exterior like some cases inevitably did. He'd stay with it, stay on top, recheck some of the witnesses, haunt the Greek night clerk, but the case of Deborah Cortez was no lulu, and now no longer current. He believed he knew in his mind how she had been killed, but he really wasn't sure what kind of person did it and for what reason. She was the type of girl who made a lot of friends, a lot of customers, a lot of contacts. Hundreds of men had drilled her, fantasized as she hovered between their legs, been shamed by her, faced guilt, frustration, misgiving, anger, yet always paid her. She could have been stabbed by any one of them, or by none of them. She was a page 37 murder as far as the public was concerned, McMahon realized that too. She was a person who found herself in places more prudent individuals wouldn't be, especially on that Sunday night. He would not forget her, not drop her, not relegate her to the heap of files and reports that buried him every day, but he also would not be taken with her, obsessed or driven like some phony television cop. He had a lot of murders to solve, more almost every day, each with that golden 48 hours. Deborah Cortez, the curvy hooker from Puerto Rico who never made it past her twenty-first birthday, would nuzzle the coolness of the ground for some time before McMahon or any other murder cop would clamp a pair of cuffs around the wrists of her killer. If, indeed, they ever would.

She closed the screen door and left it unlocked without saying a word. It was a struggle for Helen, a fight not to stand there and let Harry have it for all the years, all the wrongs, all the lies, the tricks, the unhappiness he had brought into her life. She could dress him down and up again, in Polish curses and epithets that were untranslatable and much more appropriately disgusting than anything she could come up with in English. But it was six o'clock in the morning, a clear, crisp day that she would only see half of, and she was dead tired from her shift downtown. She headed for her room, still wearing her work uniform, the socks, the babushka around her hair, and closed the bedroom door behind her.

Her clothes came off in a rush, thrown against a chair, then a worn night shirt. She sat on the creaking double bed, the white muslin spread, and crossed herself at the sight of the statue of the Infant of Prague on her bureau. From her chest her hands went to her temples, rubbing them as if she could draw the tightness and the tiredness out, closing her eyes and sighing.

"Oh, boy," she said, then pulled back the spread into a folded pile at the foot of the bed and lay down for the day's six hours of sleep.

Harry had followed her inside but stopped at the kitchen. He plunked his wrinkled, soiled bundle of belongings down on a vinyl-seated chair. The house was quiet except for the ticking of the clock on the stove, kitchen-quiet like on Sunday afternoons in the old neighborhood. He noticed a squat portable radio on the shelf then went to turn it on, maybe the ballgame, but then realized from the oven clock that it was only six, that the birds were awake but hardly anything else. He rubbed the clinkers out of his eyes and locked the screen, then decided to leave the door open because he sort of liked the noise of the morning.

He could try to go back to sleep on the couch in the living room, no, he wouldn't try that just yet. The kitchen was far enough, the refrigerator, and suddenly he felt his stomach, the cardboard taste in his mouth, and he longed for a bottle, a quart, even to drink it out of a glass amidst the yellow wallpaper and the curtains of a kitchen like this. He opened the refrigerator door, spotted a gallon of skimmed milk, eggs, cottage cheese, white butcher's paper which meant cheese or sliced ham or kielbasa or blood sausage. Unwrapping it, nervous at the noise he made, he found that it was sliced baloney, a stack of it three inches thick. With his fingers, the nails black from where he'd been, he grabbed four slices off the top then rewrapped the pile and placed it back on the shelf. He chomped into the baloney with two big bites, the taste filling his mouth, and he looked for a drink. At the tap he saw a plastic glass, filled it, and sat down to his feast. It wouldn't have tasted so good if it wasn't that he had not had a slab of real Polish meat in months, maybe years. The baloney eased into his stomach, gently, without a sound, as soundlessly as Helen had unlatched the screen door and let him in. And he enjoyed it, sitting at a table in a respectable house like this one. He rested his head on his hand, heard the birds, wondered about the Cubs and what they were up to, and closed his eyes. In a moment his head slid onto the table, his right arm stretched out before him like a staff, and he drifted off.

In the bedroom, with the door shut tightly, Helen slept deeply, totally, as only a member of the midnight shift could sleep.

"You look horrible, worse 'n ever, and I don't even wanna know why. I know why. I know what you do without you even tellin' me. I hear stories, I hear things I don't even wanna tell. But I don't say nothing. I just lock it away 'n' don't say nothing."

Helen talked as she moved about the kitchen from the refrigerator to the sink fixing her breakfast. She rushed her words, amplified in a carping singsong, her expression as rigid as the cucumber she cut into. The high ceiling of the kitchen bounced the sentences together, added a slight echo, then poured them onto Harry as he sat at the table, taking it, his hands folded.

"I see you at the door last night and I think to myself, 'Oh, my God, it's him again.' As if I don't got enough to do what with goin' to work every night, scrubbin' up those halls and pickin' up those offices and thinkin' all the time that it's thanks to God and Jesus that I'm healthy and not like Mrs. Pevovar who was always red in the face when she come to work and just the other night she's bendin' over her trash barrel and if her heart didn't give out on her right there, takin' her right there so the poor thing died with herself half in the barrel and half out. Takes the three of us ladies to get her out and we was cryin' and the tears runnin' down our faces like babies. Yah, Harry, yah, but you wouldn't know about them kinds of things. No, un-uh, like you are, sittin' there."

She came over to the table with a plate of baloney and cheese, set a bowl of cucumbers and tomatoes in front of Harry and her own place, then returned to the stove for a pot of coffee and a loaf of bread.

"You don't got to tell me that you're on it. Uh-uh, I been

110

around the bottle all my life and I can see. You better believe it. I can see what it's doin' to ya. That boozin'. I ain't blind."

She picked up a slice of cucumber with her fingers and nibbled at it, then pulled back her chair and sat down. Harry began to jab at the cukes and tomatoes with a fork, still holding his tongue.

"Oh, I don't know," Helen sighed. "Why'd ja come here for? Whattaya want from me?"

Harry poked at his cucumbers, chewed them and sucked at the vinegar she had splashed on them.

"Nuttin'. I just needed a place to stay for a night and if you can't come to your sister then what's this world comin' to? Answer me that," he said.

"Oh, boy, now listen to that and listen to him. Sister, huh? Since when did I ever get to be your sister? Never, that's when. Never as long as I walk on the earth. You remember that. You remember that good 'cause I didn't have to open up no door for you, Harry. I did it because I'm stupid, so stupid I can't see straight."

She picked up a slab of baloney and pinched out a piece from the center, still using her fingers.

"And you better believe you only needed a place for the night. I run a rooming house here, buster. You wanna stay, that's fine. Just sign in on the book over there and pay every Monday like the rest. But just right now I ain't got nuttin'. That's the way I go around here."

"I get paid tomorrow—"

"Paid? That what I hear you say? You get paid? That what you callin' welfare? I know, Harry, don't think I don't hear things. And I know you ain't been workin' nowhere, just loafin' and walkin' the streets like a bum. Yeah, I know. And you gettin' paid—well, if you can take that nigger money and call it gettin' paid then you're a lot lower sunk than I thought you were."

"I'm entitled to that money," Harry said. The hag was getting on him now, bringing back the times when he lis-

111

tened to the same kind of song and dance in the old neighborhood, where the women complained until they drove the
men clean away. They ran to the nearest faraway place they
could find, if for no other reason but to get back their hearing, regain a little peace of mind. And Helen was one of the
best, goading her husband to the grave, hounding him, on his
back like a monkey. Then Harry's stepfather, old Stash
Mikulicz, who couldn't see the red side of a barn from a foot
and a half but still got the brunt of Helen's mouth, yapping,
complaining, throwing tantrums then sending him to hell
and back.

"I'm entitled to what I get. I got me an ulcer now from
being outta work. Sometimes I wake up and my head pounds
like a jackhammer. And how am I gonna hold down a job
with that? I should get it. I'd work if I could. I'd be out there
workin'..." The steam of his words sent his fork into the piles
of cheese slices. Helen followed it all the way, realizing that
he was digging in.

She picked up another slice of cucumber with her fingers
then wiped them on her housecoat. It was noon; she had a
little time to eat and straighten herself up before she started
on the building.

"I don't know, Harry. Every time I see you I got to explain
it for ya. Lay it out like you was some kind of three-year-old
and I was your ma. That stomach problem of yours, uh-huh,
sure, ulcers like I'm the Blessed Virgin. You been drinkin'
again, Harry. Drinkin' all time to where your stomach can't
take it. Next you'll be laid up with the gout, in the hospital,
all because of drinkin'. I seen it. I seen it because it's the way
the family went. Like a plague. Oh, how it broke my heart
to see Pa layin' there in the old neighborhood with his pants
all wet and the kids laughin' at him. And Ma, he broke her
heart, oh, you better believe it, she went out there and
picked him up and washed him and said her prayers. But I
could cry just to tell you how she was a broken woman because of him. And who goes first? She does, as if I ain't got

enough troubles with the lout I married. That Joe was worse than Pa, worse in every way, and lots a times I had the two of them to put up with. The two of them always sluggin' down highballs and beers, callin' in the street crews to toss a few, goin' to weddings and wakes and gettin' so drunk they got into fights, then the police had to cart 'em all down to the station.

"Yah, don't tell me about ulcers, Harry. Ain't no ulcer in this world could stand to live in that belly of yours what with all the booze. Boozin' it up is what that ulcer is, you better believe it. And sure, your head, you complain about it. Who wouldn't with what you put it through, I hear the stories. I live with 'em. It still hurts me. Yup, yup. You're still family, that's what I tell myself but I shouldn't be doin' it. No sir, I should say to hell with ya and forget about ya. If I had one brain in my head that's what I would be doin'. But no, here you are eatin' my food."

"I tol' ya, I'll pay ya. I'm just in a stretch of bad luck is all. Won't be long till I get back on my feet again. That's right," he said, shaking his head and chewing. The coffee was strong but good, better than any he'd had in months.

"Tell me now, tell me the truth. You in trouble again? The police gonna come to my door askin' about ya? What about that, Harry? Tell me the truth, so help me, or I'll throw ya out. I can't have you around with Ilene and her friends when something like that's going on. I don't say nothing, Harry, but I know. I know when the ladies start to talk. Don't think it doesn't get around."

"Them women don't know nothin'," he said. "To hell with 'em. I ain't runnin' from nobody, no cops, nothing. They ain't got nothin' on me."

"You always say that. Always. Sometimes I think you'd go to church and say that same thing even if the police were outside waiting for you. You said it to your ma, sure, I know, said even while you was hidin' the junk you stole under the beds and in the closets. And how she cried and cried when

113

the police came and got ya. All the time and searching her house like she was the criminal, a teef like you, you better believe it. And it broke her heart. I remember when they laid her out and all the ladies in the neighborhood came to church, how they cried for what you done to her. How good she looked laid out, but she died of a broken heart. I know that, don't ask me, but I know that. You better believe it."

She stopped and rubbed her face. Her eyes were moist, overflowing from the thoughts of the old neighborhood, the funerals, the times. She took out a hanky and wound it through her chunky fingers, dabbing at her eyes.

Harry pushed his fork and plate away. "Ah, ya don't know a word about what yer sayin'," he said. Then he stopped, thinking he wouldn't try to fight it. When Helen got wound up, when she threw herself back into the old street, back to the markets on Damen and Milwaukee, the women who washed and gossiped and cried in church, there was no fighting her, no reasoning to be thrown in.

"How's Ilene? How she doin'?"

"She's all right. I don't see her much, what with her workin' downtown during the day and me at night. Mrs. Sladowski does her office. Says it's nice and that Ilene keeps a good desk. Ilene told her where it was and now she gives it a little extra goin'-over. But I don't worry about her. She's a good kid. Makin' pretty good money and goin' to church wit' me regular.

"God only gave me one child but that was a good one. I don't complain. I worry about her in this neighborhood 'cause you don't know who's gonna be around. Like things around here. What with this neighborhood, nothin' but junk. A lot of junk around here. It's goin' to pot and don't nobody care one bit. I keep the building up and it's all I can do. But don't think nobody cares. Un-uh. Got to throw more people out than I thought I ever could. And breakin' windows. John Popovich from the bakery in the old neighborhood helps me when we got to evict. He's a big guy and they don't mess with

114

him like they try me. But I don't know. It's no good. More trouble than it's worth."

She pushed her chair away and cleared off the plates, leaving only the coffee. She walked into her bedroom and in a few moments was back dressed in a house dress and an apron, which covered her from her neck to her knees. She would give the building a going-over as she had the office buildings only hours before, an unending ritual of cleaning and emptying and sweeping.

"What's in that sack you brought with you? It's filthy, just filthy."

"Just a few of my things. I moved out of my place."

She bent down and opened the doors beneath the sink. "Don't think you're movin' in here."

She grabbed a pair of bottles and a brush, then walked through the dining room and into the hallway.

From where he sat he could hear her rustling with pails and mops, getting her tools together. He didn't say anything, just gazed at the pink paint of the kitchen, the pots of plants in the window, the white porcelain of the kitchen sink. He'd grown up in a kitchen like this.

For the rest of the afternoon, while Helen huffed from floor to floor, polishing the woodwork, sweeping and vacuuming the halls, Harry stayed in the kitchen, occasionally wandering out onto the back porch and watching the alley. Despite the coffee and the food, he could feel his stomach again, the nerves, the shakes, the thirst which hung far back in his throat but fought for higher ground. He needed a bottle, needed a nip to get him through the day. But he fought the temptation to leave, knew that if he came back with a brown bag it would be the end. Helen would lock the door and never open it. She could take a lot, his sister could, and he knew, he could feel about just how much, just how far he could push her. The lying, the trouble with the cops, all that she could take, as if she was some kind of saint on the torture wheel, and she would keep her mouth shut about it, as if it were her own special load to bear. But the bottle was something different. She had made a crusade out of that, as if it alone threatened her. He knew it was a red flag in front of her face, bringing out a rage which was uncontrollable, violent. She would claw his eyes out before she would let him drink so much as a shot of cooking sherry in her kitchen. It had been that way for years, ever since the old man went, since Joe Pontek, a good guy in his own right, a guy who could hold his booze, knew how to savor it, but a guy who had a stomach made out of crepe paper. Joe Pontek went fast, kicked like a fish in a pool of piss, and Helen never forgave him for it. Now she would forgive no one for it, not for the booze, not for the bottle, not for the pain and the misery she believed it had brought into her already painful and miserable life.

So he bit the bullet of his thirst, toyed with the change in his pocket, a little over a dollar. As the end of the afternoon came, he decided he didn't want to be around when Helen took her next meal. Her schedule was a half day behind everyone else's thanks to her job—she ate breakfast at noon, lunch with Ilene when she got home from work at six, and her dinner was usually picked at from a brown bag with the other cleaning ladies sitting in the small cleaning closets during a break at two in the morning. But Harry decided to tread lightly, not to frost her, stick a nickel in her squawk box over some lousy piece of cube steak and cause an uproar. So he made his way down the back stairs and walked in the shadows of the setting sun down the alley and over to Wilson.

With sixty-nine cents he liberated a pint of white port from the Liberty Bell and poured it home, crouching in a nearby alley behind an army of trash barrels. He had to be careful, had to watch for cops all the time, the two robbery dicks who were probably mad as hell for making the deal with McMahon, and McMahon himself, the shrimpy murder cop who had a lot to learn before he could pull one over Harry. But he knew McMahon would be pissed as well, probably throw away the key this time, so Harry crouched down and out of sight, suddenly bathed in the sour, rotting odors that leaked from the trash cans, a stench all but unbearable if he weren't flooding his system with the fermented Balm of Gilead.

When the bottle was drained, Harry crept out of the alley, shielded by the increasing darkness, and headed for the Ron-Ric. There he ordered a single hamburger with double onions, a nickel extra, and watched the counterman lay the eighth-of-an-inch-thick piece of dilapidated beef scraps on a bun, then smother it with greasy, stringy griddle onions. The onions came alive inside of Harry's mouth, grease draining from his lower lip to his chin, the residue of wine all but extinguished. He put thirty-three cents on the counter, then felt a smack of relief in knowing that, even though he was busted, flat broke, that it didn't matter because he had a place to go to. He wedged a fingerful of Copenhagen inside his lower lip, spat a brown tracer on the sidewalk, and headed for the alley, always looking over his shoulder, toward Helen's flat. And he thought for a second, Harry, count your lucky stars, rattle your old bones in applause, because tomorrow was the day he would meet the mailman for his month's aid check. Count your lucky stars, and he stepped lively.

He found the back screen open and saw Helen at the sink, Ilene sitting at the table looking at him after hearing his steps on the landing. She was a plain, flat-faced girl of nineteen, still wearing a mid-thigh blue dress complete with a bow in front, navy insignia and a flap over her shoulder, as if she had just left an aircraft carrier. Her face was shiny beneath bangs that hung nearly into her eyes.

"Hi," she said as Harry walked in the kitchen. Helen did not turn around.

"Hello there, Ilene. Well, what you been up to?" Harry said. He pulled up a chair.

"Nothin' much. Just workin', I guess," she said. She looked

at him briefly, then wiped a strand of gray-blond hair from her face. "What you been eatin'? Onions? Ooooooo. I can smell 'em."

He dipped his head and was about to describe the hamburger when he saw Helen whirl and shoot him a stare that could have harpooned a whale. He knew that she knew that onion breath was the smoke from the fire of boozing. Plain as the nose on his face. He froze for a moment, then rubbed a hand down across his eyes and mouth and tried to get back his momentum.

"Yeah, the sandwich boy got a little carried away with the roses."

"*Roses.* You call *that* roses?" Ilene whined. She curled her nose, then looked back down at the *Cosmopolitan* she was paging through.

"Say, there, Ilene, you still rootin' for them Cubs, huh? I remember when you and I was just about the best damn Cubs fans in the neighborhood. 'Member that? Boy, how you liked that little infielder, what was his name? The one got killed in the plane."

"Kenny Hubbs and I liked the Cubs just fine until a few weeks ago," Ilene said. "Now they're losing just *aw*-ful. I can't believe it. My girlfriend and I, man, we went to at least twenty-five games this summer. Sittin' in the bleachers. We always got in with the Bleacher Bums. I even bought a yellow hat which means I'm a member in good standing. Joyce did, too."

"Say now, how do ya like that." Harry beamed. "I bet you seen me a hundred times in that crowd and didn't even know it. I sit in centerfield by the scoreboard lots so I can get on the outfielders. Made that Met guy, what's his name, that little colored fella's been killin' us all year, one time I made him drop one. He turned around and tol' me I was the one."

He noticed that Helen had turned around.

The two of them sat there while Helen finished up at the

sink, then went into her room and changed clothes. It was close to nine o'clock, time for her to pull her hair back into a net, wrap it with the trusty babushka, pack her dinner, and head off for the Loop. Ilene finally got up, and after getting a bag of corn chips and a Diet Rite Cola from the cupboard, sat down and turned on *Hawaii Five-O*. She sat on the sofa Harry had slept on the night before. He followed her and sat in an overstuffed chair, which had a pair of doilies on each arm. *Five-O* was Ilene's favorite show. She nibbled on chips, leaving specks of salt on her cheek, and riveted her eyes on the tube.

Harry was soon into the program too, trying to outsmart the con man who was tying Honolulu in knots, then Helen walked in. He saw her out of the side of his eye, then looked over at her when he realized she had paused at the door and was staring at him.

"Stupid, Harry. That's what I am if you really want to know. I'm just too stupid. I mean," and she dragged the word up the scale, "you'd think I would a learned my lesson."

She shook her head back and forth.

"Ilene, you remember to lock up and turn out the lights."

Then she was gone, Ilene never taking her eyes from the screen, Harry watching the slam of the door.

He slept soundly that night, wearing his pants and tee-shirt, not caring that the couch was lumpy and constricting, cool from the shave he took before he turned in. Sometime later he heard the door creak, and through the darkness and the grogginess of his head he could make out Helen returning from work. But he didn't stir, and soon drifted off again. He awoke with the sunlight and the noise of Ilene in the bathroom. He stretched and yawned, his mouth still haunting him after a dry night. He got up and padded into the kitchen and saw that Ilene had put on water to boil.

"Hi," she said as she mixed her instant coffee, then headed

119

back into the bathroom and her makeup. He shook his head, trying to get the feathers out, and let the coffee burn his tongue.

By nine he was sitting on the steps in front of his old rooming house, watching for the mailman. He thought for a minute, then ducked inside the vestibule to avoid the cops. Today was check day; he would take it in person from the carrier and hustle down to the currency exchange. He never missed a check day, was first in line at the welfare office on Lincoln Avenue to bitch when they were late. It was survival, that check, lime-green survival, for him and thousands of others in Uptown, all looking through curtains and down hallways for the carrier, looking with grim passion on the third of each month. And when the carrier turned onto the street, his gray hat perched high atop an Afro that had long since gone out of control, Harry gripped his palms unconsciously like all the others on the block, knowing the good news was on the way.

In a minute he had it, ripped it open to see the same number he'd seen for a year now, discarded the envelope like a corn husk. It was there, $171.05, in one lump with the signatures and seals that he didn't read or pay any attention to. The figure was there. One hundred twenty-five dollars for a furnished room including heat and utilities, no phone. Forty-three dollars and fifty-five cents for living expenses, food, personal essentials, household supplies. And two dollars fifty cents for laundry. He knew the breakdown, had fought with a caseworker over it every month. Each time a new person, a girl in blue jeans or a shaggy-haired homo who didn't know Harry's name and didn't know his case or his condition or how he had to face life on Wilson Avenue every day, the odds. But each new worker did know the figures, gave Harry mountains of guff when he argued he had to have more, even carfare for trips to the clinic, trips he never could prove he made. And always he was sent away with the same figure. "A man's got to live," he'd shout. "I got to have more to be livin' on, I'm a taxpayer and I'm entitled to get it." But each time they'd shoo him away and tell him to make sure he kept track of his address. And, despite his complaints, his moaning, his demands that he had to have more to exist, he awaited the mail carrier each month as if the kid with the Afro was holding free tickets to the Series.

He tucked the check into his pants, deep into the crotch, then checked to see if any punks were shadowing him. On check day everyone had to be careful. And he looked for cops, looking at everything, life becoming that much more perilous. At the currency exchange he scribbled his name on the back and cashed every bit of it. The clerk counted out the bills and Harry grabbed them, looked around, then hustled off into a corner. He put the entire wad in his pants, this time in the rear end between the crack in his ass. A lot of bums put the dough in their shoes, Harry knew that, and when they were jumped the punks would grab the shoes first, knowing right where the dough was stashed. But if they jumped him, they'd have to search where a lot of people didn't want to look.

He stopped at the door of the exchange, looked sideways down the street, saw a clump of kids on the corner, almost wished for a cop car for a silent escort. Then he made his exit, walking straight and hard down Montrose to Broadway, not stopping at the liquor stores or the taverns, not looking up or sideways, heading for Magnolia and the flat. He made it and hopped up the back way into the kitchen. It was ten in the morning and he was home free, $171.05 richer, with a trace of a thirst, sweat beaded along his brow. He bent down in front of Helen's Hotpoint refrigerator and unhooked the panel along the floor. Then, reaching into his pants, feeling the moist but definitely negotiable currency, he peeled off a sawbuck and tucked the rest inside the lip of the panel. Best treasure chest he'd ever used, even stashed a bottle there back in the old house.

Then he stood up and stretched, feeling quite satisfied with

121

himself. Ten dollars in his pocket and more where that came from. He took a step and kicked open the door beneath the sink. The garbage was overflowing. With a sudden inspiration, a gust of good feeling that he had not had in a long time, too many other things on his mind, he pulled the bag out, tucked in the overhanging papers and started down the back with it. On a nice morning like this, he thought, it is only right that a man carry out the trash. He replaced the lid and looked around the rear of Helen's building, his building if he'd played his cards right with the old man. There were a lot of things that needed fixing, things Helen in all her zealous cleaning could not get at. And the thought hit him, another rainbow on this fine morning, that maybe he could find the time to take them on.

When she got up that morning, just before noon, in her bathrobe and hairpins, she started in again.

"Don't think I ain't aware of the fact that you been stickin' around, Harry. Un-huh, no sir. I meant what I said last night. Stupid. That's what I am. But Ilene she says, Take it easy, Ma, maybe Harry's ready to go straight an' make a new life. And I told her, I said, 'Ilene, if you only knew men like I do.' If she only knew, oh, my God, I mean what Joe put me through and then my Pa after he killed Ma, yeah, you better believe it, laid her out just as if he'd a put a knife in her heart. And I remember those things, I put them right away where someday I'll tell what I really think. Don't you think for a minute I won't, Harry."

She poured herself a half cup of coffee, not getting out any food.

"I got money. I got the dough to pay ya for anything you put out for me."

He laid out his ten-dollar bill on the table, smoothing it on the Formica top.

"Nigger money! *Holetta!*"

"You don't think nothin' a takin' it from the bums you put

up here. Every week is the way I hear it."

He shook his head for emphasis and smugly turned away from her, swiveling the chair.

"What I take from my boarders isn't half enough for what they get outta me. This is the only decent place to live in this neighborhood. Cause a me. Look at the dumps around. I'm clean and scrub and pick up every day when some of these dumps you don't see a caretaker around but every winter and once in spring. Filth, that's what they got. Here I keep this place respectable." She wiped the sides of her mouth. She ignored her coffee, too worked up to mind.

"So let me a room. I'll pay ya for it."

"You better believe you will. And you wouldn't be boozin' it up in there alla time neither. I'd see to that."

She realized that she had not responded to what he'd said, that he had all but asked her to forgive him the past and put him up.

"But a room you don't get. Even if I had one to give ya which I don't. Ma always said don't buy or sell to relatives unless you want to see the family go down the drain. Same with me. I don't rent to you, Harry, because you're family and that's a difference with me. I'm stupid, all these years and I ain't learned a thing. Family. You hear that word? It still means a little something to me even if you ain blood. But Pa took you in, rest his soul, and he'd want me to take you in and be nice too. Stupid, that's what I am."

As she talked he scowled at the table top, for a time forgetting his aches, the hauntings of his system, but now the knee bone began to stiffen, his stomach began to growl.

"Lemme stick around. On my honor. I won't bring no trouble if you lemme stick around."

She got up and tossed her coffee into the sink, covering the porcelain with a coat of brown. She was tired. She decided she wasn't hungry.

123

That afternoon he poked around the building. With a coal shovel he lifted a peaked pile of dog manure into the trash, then spotted another, two in the gangway. He grabbed a box half full of trash, old melon rinds and bean cans, and kicked it along the cement running around the side of the building. With a loud scrape of the shovel, he whisked more piles into the box. There were more out front; the neighborhood was alive with them, alive with monstrous dogs that fought off the burglars. And they left their deposits for yards on either side of the building, some squashed, some old and hard. But he got them all, fanatically, scooping them up and home to the box. As he passed the front door he noticed Helen standing in the vestibule washing the glass. She stopped and looked at him about the time he spotted her. She didn't say anything, didn't change her expression. But she saw him.

When he came around back to dump the box she was standing by the barrels. She dangled a key from her finger.

"This is to the cellar. There's a can of window cement down there and some tools to fix the glass that's out in front. That one in the door keeps gettin' broke by them bums who try to break in and steal the mail. They don't know I got the lock that needs a key to get in and a key to get out. So they just bust my window and make it hard on me. Get some glass down to the store on Montrose. Charge it on my name. But nuttin' else."

Then she turned and began sweeping the porch. Harry took the key and ducked into the cellar.

For the rest of the day he scraped and chipped, tossed out pieces of broken glass, repaired sashes, took measurements for new panes. He was slow and fussy, using tools, for once, for the kind of work they were made for, not adapting them for use in his trunk-punching kit, or his home-burglary kit, his vending-machine kit, his mailbox kit. But he managed to replace a few windows, sweep up after himself, and repair some of the molding that had cracked or warped. It wasn't bad, he said to himself, not bad in times like these to be doing

124

honest work, even work that was barely fit for a craftsman like himself. Wasn't bad.

Finally, he set aside his tools, the can of putty, and went up the back stairs for a drink of water. At the kitchen he realized from the clock that it was after six o'clock. Ilene was sitting at her place at the table picking at her nail polish. And he noticed casually, but not without a bell going off in his head, that a third place had been set out. Helen came away from the stove with a plate of stuffed cabbage, and without saying a word to Harry sat at the table. He took a chair, casually, as if he were the man of the house and had been for twenty-three years instead of twenty-three hours, rubbing his hands together at the sight of the steam wiggling up from the cabbage.

Helen looked at him, sideways while nibbling at a piece of brown bread between her fingers. The only sound came from the clink of silverware against plates. Harry thought he noticed Helen shake her head, slowly as if she were scolding herself or talking to herself, then he blotted it out of view with a forkful of food.

As they ate, Ilene moaned about a girl at the office who sat in front of her but wouldn't talk to her, who ate alone and dyed platinum streaks through her brown hair, who wore too much makeup and didn't even know it, and who was always sticking her finger in her ears and nose and doing God-knows-what with it. Helen nodded and asked where the girl came from, if she was Polish. Ilene said she wasn't, then said that she was just dumb and didn't know any better. Then the conversation thudded to a stop and Ilene began biting her fingernails, now stripped of polish. She stared off at the wall in an absent, imperturbable funk. Harry didn't say anything.

Almost immediately Helen began clearing away the plates, gobbling them up and scraping them off. It was just like always, the old meals where Helen always ran things, always shoveling platters of food, directing it around the table, filling up cups, stacks of bread, bowls of gravy, sour cream,

125

talking and chattering and complaining to Ma and Pa and anyone around, complaining about the neighbors or the relatives, the cost of food, the job, the church, then whisking away the food, wiping off the table and pouring more coffee, eating as if it were a goal in life, an event around which all events revolved. And now, with just herself and the flat-faced Ilene, the dim-witted, acned typist who read *Cosmo* and *True Romances* and spent her money on candy and makeup, and Harry, a silent third party, Helen still ran about like a general, but one with a dwindling army, the pace just not the same.

As she scraped off the plates in the sink, the doorbell rang. An odd, unexpected intrusion in a household with few visitors.

"You see who it is, Ilene, and don't let 'em in," Helen said. She did not turn her back, shouting over the running water.

Ilene went off, leaving the front door open. Harry sat at the table drinking what coffee he had left and looking at his arms, picking the dirt from his nails.

"It's for you, Ma," Ilene called from the hall. "It's a couple of policemen."

Harry took the last word with a jolt, straightened in his chair and shot a glance at Helen, who had whirled and was staring at him. They exchanged silent, deadly accusations, threats, the scowls of old times, all coming back into that short distance between them in the kitchen. Harry could read Helen like a book, Helen him, knowing, boiling under her breath, growling out every guttural Polish condemnation she had ever known, again untranslatable, but as clear and distinct to Harry as the eyes in her head. She stomped across the linoleum, the hard, clomping shoes, yelling, "I'll talk to 'em myself! Don't be lettin' 'em in the house, Ilene!"

She shot one last look, then disappeared into the dining room.

"I'm not," Ilene replied. "But they said they wanted to come up."

126

It was the last Harry heard before he bolted up from the chair and went for the door, stopped, thinking they'd be there too, watching the back and ready for him, certain it was McMahon or some dumb robbery cop with a warrant. Then he froze, thought again like a thief, and went for the sink.

With a single motion he opened the doors beneath the sink, pulled out the plastic wastebasket and pushed it into a corner. Then he knelt down and curled himself into a ball he didn't think possible, his chin touching his knees, his spine curved like a pretzel, and shoved himself inside, beneath the sink, pushing his shoulder under and around the U-shape of the drain pipe. He pulled in his left leg, crouching, jabbed by bottles and brushes, then pulled the door closed by a sponge rack on the inside. He sat there in the discomfort of his own contortion, smelling the damp mustiness of the chamber, feeling the heat of his own breath. He sat there with nothing but thoughts of running, of hiding, of going on the lam, thoughts that had plagued him for as long as he could remember. He sat there in a ball of wrinkled skin and bone, his stomach folded in two and pushing up bubbles of gas, the Harry Lum of old, the coward, the thief, the fuck-up who lined the alleys and the gutters and the shadows of the old neighborhood, who shifted and drifted with middle age like a stagnant pocket of air, stumbling, leeching, panhandling, copping. And he would do it again, flop out into the cold air of Chicago's autumn, his fall, and the icy crunch of winter where the warmest thing on earth was a wad of newspaper in your crotch and a bottle of straight rotgut, he would be out in the world of that once again, tilting toward the edge like a rowboat caught in a current, if Helen so much as lifted the lid off his present shelter, if she so much as hinted to the cops that he was theirs for the taking. He shook and moved his head and clunked his skull across the ear on a pipe. The pain was sudden and deep, but he couldn't move a hand, couldn't budge a muscle to rub it.

Then with a slight nudge of his knee he opened the sink

127

door and tried to hear what was going on. He heard voices, then Ilene came into the kitchen and pulled up a chair. Then it was quiet, and he heard Helen speak. She spoke quietly for her, but loud enough so Harry could hear, in a singsong tone that she put on to be nice, like over the phone or after church. Then she stopped and he heard the low rumblings of the cops, two he figured, talking like a roll of an engine, not discernible.

Then Helen again. "I can't say nothin' for sure."

Harry listened intently, as if perking his ears and straining his neck would bring her voice in clearer.

He thought he heard McMahon, maybe Marrietta, the robbery dick.

Then Helen. "Yeah, yeah, I'm tellin' ya," she said. "He bothers me like he bothers yuse guys and I'd like to be rid of him. For good."

A silence, he could feel himself shaking, sweating, the heat and stricture becoming almost unbearable. Suddenly he was hit with the image of him and his Pa cowering in the bathroom years back, when Ma went to the door to stall the cops out looking for bathtub gin. How Pa used to unscrew the gas pipe from the meter and run it right into his cooker, and the kids, with Ma always giving a new story to the cops, shuttling around the neighborhood in their knickers and short pants, their cute smiles, with a bottle tucked under their coats for the uncles. Then Harry heard her, like Ma in the old days.

"I ain't seen him, I keep tellin' ya," she said. She was insistent, the sense of the family and the church in her voice. "If I'd be seein' him I'd a called ya because I don't want no part of the bum. Period. I mean that like that."

She hesitated, a few sounds of low voices, then the door.

"Yeah, all right," she said. Then the door closed.

Harry, in his misery, his crumpled back and sore joints, felt a rush of resurrection. He was home free.

He kicked the door open and tried to pry himself out. He saw her legs, the thick taper of her calves, as he crept out.

"Look at ya there. Like an animal in a cage. *Oj moj Bozé!* Oh, my God! Harry, I don't know why. You're a good-for-nothing and you're always gonna be."

Helen wrung her hands and looked up at the ceiling. Her voice began to rise, the wail and torture of the old times, the old neighborhood, where you had to lie and alibi and cheat for the men, always covering something up.

"Like I'm tellin' lies and God forgive me that I should for the likes of you. I should a known, you better believe it, I should a known that you come here 'cause yer runnin' and in trouble."

She turned and walked toward the table, then sat crookedly on a chair. Ilene looked at her nails. Helen knocked her fists against the sides of her head, battering her brains with the dough of her knuckles.

Harry stood and shook himself out, trying to keep the cramps from setting into his legs, his back, the sides of his neck.

Then Helen looked over at him, looking with the rage and pity and hatred and contempt of a stepsister, of all the times past, of Poland and the stories of sour milk and potatoes, of mass and the unforgiving priests, of the sidewalks and the hard liquor. And she wrinkled her puffy pink face, ran her hands through her hair, her wide dress forming a sloping hammock between her knees.

"Jesus looks down on you, Harry," she said, saying it more in the tone of a warning than a condemnation, "Jesus looks down on you from heaven and he sees what you do and he *cries.*"

She nodded her head up and down, knowing, certain, "He *cries.*"

129

9

It was a beauty, a pearl, a class A, supercharged hell of a job that Donald Ray knew he'd been created for. And it had come up so easily, out of the mouth of his fence, a used-car salesman who laundered his money and his goods, a slippery creep Donald Ray admired because he could come off so smooth, so suit-and-tie, living in the suburbs, cutting grass and paying taxes, and yet he was as dirty as the rest of them, cashing in on hot televisions and stereos, silverware, binoculars, wedding bands, as if the stuff was a church going Chevrolet with low mileage and bucket seats.

"What you got to pull off, Burl, and I'd do it myself if I was in your racket," the salesman said as the two of them huddled businesslike over the engine of one of the lot's junkers. "What you got to pull off is a warehouse job. Right up to the docks, pre-ferably with inside help, someone who can take you past the gates and the locks and all the automated doors and just load you up as if you were a semi backed in and headed for Cincinnati. Because that way you don't have to worry about second-hand crap that's scratched and marked up and don't bring shit. This stuff is mint, right in the boxes, with serial numbers and warranties and little postcards your buyers can send in to make sure they get good service on the shit. The whole ball of wax. Yeah, that's right. Get into something like that and you're operating on the pro level. None of this diddly-ass shit that can get your tail sent to Joliet or blown into Indiana if some stiff finds you in the house and decides to rewire you with his shotgun. No baby, this is the pro way to go, a real score."

Which was music to Donald Ray's ears, ears that had been clipped by cops on every bust in the book. He'd stolen cars, punched trunks, rifled glove compartments, bounced checks, smashed coin machines, boosted, then held up drugstores, snatched purses, burglarized garages, homes, storage sheds, hustled bicycles, dope, stolen car parts, batteries, even sweet-talked old ladies into giving him quarters. He had arrests for theft, petty and grand, burglary, armed robbery, battery, drunkenness, damage to property, possession of burglary tools, and loitering. He was considered a known burglar, an addict, a general ne'er-do-well. He had served time in all the jails, never for very long, but long enough, always got back into things, dodged cops, pulled off some more jobs, missed others. But it was always hand to mouth, never getting any money, drinking or popping what he did get, trying to set something up, too often flopping down to welfare and begging for a check, carfare, something.

But he came across this plan almost by accident, a fluke that laid an egg in his brain. A week after he had had his little conversation with the fence, he and Jimmy took Barbie Dell to a dentist to have a tooth worked on. She said it was killing her; the dentist said it had to be drilled out and filled, that he could only guess how long she'd gone without having her teeth checked. The dentist told her he'd fill the cavity but suggested that she have some of her teeth lined, with gold if she wanted it; he still did that kind of work. Barbie got up out of the chair and went back to where Jimmy and Donald Ray were sitting and asked them brightly, "You boys think I should have silver or gold in my mouth?"

While Jimmy was fumbling with a magazine, looking at the napkin around Barbie Dell's neck, Donald Ray asked the dentist where he got the gold and silver to stick in teeth. The

131

dentist rather matter-of-factly said he got it from a supply house in town, a place that dealt in all kinds of dentist supplies, of which gold and silver were just a part.

"Well, what do you all think?" Barbie Dell repeated.

Jimmy mumbled that he thought silver was good enough and who in hell was going to pay for it anyway.

But Donald Ray, at a time when his brain was not fuzzed with chemicals or hops, started the wheels going and answered vaguely, almost into the thin air, "I think that's pretty doggone interestin'."

And he sat down and looked at the designs in the wallpaper, not seeing any one of them.

That morning, or afternoon since he wasn't sure and didn't care and got no clue from his apartment and its single bulb, Donald Ray sat in his jockey shorts at the card table scratching ragged drawings on brown shopping bags. He used a stubby lead pencil, which was all but dwarfed in the meat of his fist, drawing diagrams and floor plans, intently, his tongue sticking out of the side of his mouth like a second grader bent on connecting numbers and dots. He paid no heed to the fact that he stank with a four-day-old dew of body odor, or that his teeth were covered with film, his breath dry and papery from the chemicals and the beer. What he saw only was a cockeyed sketch with doors and windows and walls. As he drew, the homemade tattoos on his arms quivered with his veins, his chest and arms still hairy and powerful, down-home hulk, still tough and ready for most anything anyone could afford to let out of a cage. And he whistled, whistled through the spaces in his upper teeth, the gap in his lowers, downright content with himself. "Yessiree perty baby," he hummed, still humming.

As he drew, as he schemed and planned and set things up, he was gripped with the thought that maybe this was what he was really suited for, that such a job befitted his intelligence, his sense of organization, his ability to take control.

132

There were a hundred thousand junkie fuck-ups on the street willing to take a dive for a dry-cleaners job, or a drug-store heist, or daytime house jobs with a piece of housewife ass if it happened to get in the way. But not too many guys around could do what he had planned out right before him, which had come from his own head like a mystery movie, the details, the timing, the execution. What he needed was help, and the prick Del Corso was lucky, lucky from the bottom of his wop heart to the tip of his itchy prick, that he had ever strung on with Donald Ray Burl, probably the baddest, mother-fuckingest, ballsiest, meanest thug around. And soon to be rich, oh-you-ain't-lining-those-teeth-for-nothing rich. Rich. There. Rich.

In the low light of her bedroom, with the wind blowing past faded curtains and onto her sprawling Mediterranean double bed with matching dresser and hanging chain lamp, Barbie Dell slept in the coma of physical fatigue, the after-burn of a bout with Jimmy. Jimmy lay next to her, on his back like a floored middleweight, his mouth open like always, breathing through fluttering lips. They slept on a knot of sheets too tangled to smooth out, their juices mixed, through the drone of Barbie's clock radio, which was her alarm and gave her only two hours before she had to be back behind the record counter at Woolworth's. Jimmy was naked to the waist, then his jockey shorts and black socks, the black hair of his legs a blanket of fur against the white sheets. Barbie Dell wore a flimsy pair of cotton shorty pajamas. She had to be careful when they weren't alone, which was now, even as they slept heavy morning sleep, since her Uncle Herbert was passed out on the couch in the living room and Amy Joy, Barbie's one-year-old, was drooling and gurgling in a soggy pamper in the kitchen.

With no one paying the least bit of attention to her giggles and cries, Amy Joy pulled down a box of Sugar Pops from a counter and started tossing handfuls on the linoleum, shoving them about, then plopping them into her mouth with a gooey fist. A little later she toddled into the living room toward Uncle Herbert, an unemployed drywaller who had been asked to stay only a night but had taken up residence on the sofa for the last two weeks. The child weaved and lurched, caught her balance, the box of Sugar Pops in her hands. She looked into the unshaven face of Uncle Herbert, cooed when she felt the rush of his snoring, then laid her hand softly on his chest. She waited for him to do something, to respond, but he slept like a horse, feeling nothing. Amy Joy blew a bubble of spit on her lips. She grabbed some Sugar Pops. The box dropped to the floor and she went down after it, crushing the foil, finally filling both of her hands. She threw one handful on Uncle Herbert's chest and the individual pops trickled off like balsa wood rocks in a landslide. Uncle Herbert still didn't stir. Then she plopped the other handful on his face, a few dropping into the cavern of his mouth, down the chute of his tongue. He choked, spit up, startling the child, then choked again, a mighty, gulping gag which shook him awake. He roared the Sugar Pops out of his mouth like miniature cannon shots, sat up and saw the rest of the sugar-coated avalanche tumble from his chest. With a single stroke of his big arm he swung out after the child and caught her squarely in the chest. The force of his swing, Uncle Herbert being half awake and fully angry, drove the child, the chubby, bow-legged, dirty-faced Amy Joy, tumbling across the room. She rolled and thunked into the hard plaster of the wall.

She wailed like a siren.

The apartment, Uncle Herbert with spittle stringing down the front of his tee-shirt, Barbie Dell and Jimmy, suddenly aware of their conditions, abruptly sprang to life. Barbie Dell grabbed at a bathrobe and charged off into the living room, prepared to raise hell with whatever and whoever had destroyed the peace. Jimmy scratched himself and yawned, too

134

beat out to get upset at the opera of wailing and shouting and cursing in the other room.

For Harry it was penance, daily acts of contrition that he had to make to keep his title to the sofa. It was a bed he sort of liked, now supplemented with a set of sheets and a genuine pillow. It was a feeling that had come over him lately, maybe due to his age, his view of the sunset of life, or maybe his bones and the hollows of his body which kept nagging him, reminding him that he was burnt out, or rotted out, even rusting. But a few years ago he would have taken off rather than put up with Helen's tongue. It was a fact of a lot of men's lives, he was convinced of it, that they didn't leave home but were driven out, left rather than go batty from the old lady. Then, if they kicked, like Helen's Joe Pontek lying spreadeagle in the gutter with nothing but his glutted liver for a cushion, then the women wailed and did snake dances at the wake, but hours later, and forever after, they held a vengeance, a hatred for the man who had the nerve to escape them by so ruthless a ploy as death.

But Harry had a different feeling about it now, as if his ear was hardened to the wrath of Helen. He was still furtively reaching beneath the Hotpoint for his spending money and redeeming it for port at the Liberty Bell, but he was covering his tracks, downing the whole bottle, never, not-on-your-life never sneaking one into the apartment, afterward loading in a heavy charge of Copenhagen to kill the fumes. But, most important, he was getting his ass back to the flat, like a schoolboy, and going about his chores.

It was becoming the place where he lived, where he belonged, where he was counted on to do his part. He had a little money, all the food he could handle, people to talk to. When he'd been down, some days crawling so close to the bricks that he left fingerprints in them, then it killed him to be lonely, to feel only his own presence and not liking himself. No dogs, no friends, no cousins to tell a Polish joke to. And with the solitude came the brokes, no dough, not just lean or short of cash, but with no money, no dollars, no change in his pocket at all. It was the bottom of that barrel that killed him, the sense of scraping, of walking down wide streets and knowing that he couldn't walk into one single store and buy something, not even a candy bar. And it was the bottom that a lot of men never had to put up with, for there are no trees to pick fruit from, no dead brush to use for firewood, no deer nearby to kill for lunch. In the city, in the concrete and the bricks, there are only the vacant lots and the sidewalks, the cops and other bums more broke than he, all telling him that he's done and out of it, that what he is or what he was doesn't make a bit of damn difference.

He ran through that in his head during the next few days. It sent him about his tasks, meek but cheerful, feeling in his gut the old spunk, giving little people—the ragpickers, the garbage men, the neighbor kids—a lot of guff, as if he were back in the bleachers of Wrigley Field, and he longed to get back up there, mouthing off and telling jokes, getting away with catcalls at the pretty girls, heaping abuse on the center-fielders.

He hopped around the building in a soiled butcher's coat he found in the basement. Helen said he could call himself Dr. Fixit because he looked like a doctor and he was fixing things, then she said the coat belonged to a friend of her mother's who worked in a laboratory of some kind but who had died, a fate common to most of Helen's mother's friends. With it wrapped around him and drooping at the knees, Harry took on a horde of small but necessary jobs around the building. He replaced more windows, patched leaks, painted, plastered, even tried to repair a radiator and a balky refrigerator.

As fast as he finished something, Helen had something else in mind. She ran the building like she ran her dinner table, her finger on every crack in the wall, every leaky faucet. She gave Harry her four-inch ring with a good half pound of keys on it and sent him from room to room, apartment to apartment, in search of cracks and warps and loose tile, bad washers, fixtures, broken boards. He was cheap and fairly competent labor, she realized that from staying on his tail. And, though Harry could not detect it from the tone of her voice, she was growing more and more pleased to have him around. As long as he wanted to put on the old lab coat and wave a paint brush or a hammer, he was family.

"If I was a horse you couldn't work me harder," he complained.

"I wouldn't put up with no horse if he was as lazy as you neither," she said, and pointed him to another job.

After a couple of hours of work in the afternoon, usually by two or three, when Helen herself was up and about the building, Harry stopped and plodded around to the rear steps and into the kitchen. Without a word but almost on cue, Helen joined him and heated up the coffeepot. She brought a plate of cookies, or a few cakes, even some jelly-filled *pa'c-zki* bought from a bakery in the old neighborhood.

"Remember how Pa used to eat these things?" Harry said, pushing a piece into his mouth and smearing the red jelly on his chin.

"Oh, you better believe it. He could really put 'em away," Helen said.

She pulled the plate to her and cut into a *pa'czak* with a table knife.

"That old Mrs. Vloscek used to go to the bakery every day and Pa used to shout at her, 'Pick me up a dozen, Stel,' and they'd be gone by the next day," Helen said.

"And that mutt he had, Lucky—"

"Oh, that Lucky, what a dog!" Helen cut in. She said it with enough volume to fill the kitchen. "That mutt used to follow him all over the place 'cuz Pa used to feed him. Didn't have no food on our table and he's feedin' that mutt. You better believe it, feedin' that mutt."

137

"But that Stella Vloscek left them *pa'czki* by the door—"

"Oh, my God! And that dog Lucky got in the doorway by the back and like he used to when Pa weren't home and he seen that bag a *pa'czki*. . . . Oh, my God!"

The last word hit the lip of her cup and rippled the coffee.

"Dat dog was eatin' the paper when Pa caught him. An' he rapped him a good one in the horn. That Lucky wasn't so lucky that day." Harry laughed and chewed and licked his fingers of the gloppy jelly. "He was pretty hot at that Mrs. Vloscek for doin' that too like that."

"Yeah. Yeah," Helen nodded. "She died. Stel Vloscek. She died."

Harry nursed his coffee. Black, strong, but still better than what he was used to in the diners, or the hotel, or the missions. He drank it, though it burned his tongue, with loud, slurping gulps. He stared absently out the back window, still seeing Pa's dog chewing the *pa'czki*, then Pa belting the hound with his bare hand while it kicked and yelped and tried to escape.

"But that Lucky saved Pa a lot of peaches," he finally said.

"Yeah, he did. For what they was worth."

"I remember them kids would sneak down the alley and try to get past Pa 'cuz his eyes weren't no good no more. 'Member that one came on the roof one day," Harry said.

"And Pa wouldn't see him 'cept Lucky started to bark like that," Helen said. "Then he'd take off down the alley shakin' his fist and them kids laughin' and makin' fun a him like that."

"Yeah, but you know them kids they finally got them peaches, know how?"

"Who? From Pa's tree?"

"Yup! I saw 'em one day they snuck up on the roof next door. On Suroski's roof like that 'cuz he had a ladder by that rain barrel. And those kids did it one day when Lucky was sleepin' and anyway I don't think that mutt's hearin' was so good. And they had a fishin' pole—"

138

"Aw c'mon, Harry—!"

"Naw, I seen it, you better believe it. One of them kids he casted it out like that—" Harry threw his hands out in front of him, "—and they hooked a branch and then they reeled it in like a fish on the line. And Pa an' that dog just sit there sleepin' in the sun while them peaches was bein' grabbed.

"Yeah, I seen it myself and I was laughin' so hard I didn't do anything. Pa never knew that he was missin' out on some a the best peaches in the tree."

Harry laughed at the thought of it. His coffee was gone, the plate of *pa'czki* bare. Helen pressed her thumb against it to pick up the crumbs. She licked off her fingers and thumb, noisily, satisfied.

The two of them sat in silence, in the humming of the refrigerator and the clicking kitchen noises of the afternoon. Harry was dwarfed by his white coat, but clean-shaven, and beginning to gain weight. The food coated his stomach, and though he felt the ever-present urge for a pint, the need for a bottle, the irresistible temptation of cracking open a new cap, he could fight it. He could fight it even as he was sitting there talking old times with Helen. For a moment he felt as if he had never been alone and on the street. He felt as if he had never fought the drinker's shakes and scraped for dimes, that his life had always been normal and satisfied like this very moment.

"He was a mean man, Pa was," Helen cut in.

Harry looked up, then lapsed back into the image of Pa, the old man sitting in the backyard watching the peach tree and sleeping in the sun.

"You better believe it. It broke Ma's heart how mean he was to her and to us kids. And my brother Ernie was the worst. How he treated him. It made me sick," she continued.

Harry didn't say anything. Out of the side of his eye he could see Helen's hands, her fingers picking at the cuticles, picking until they bled.

"That time Ernie was helping with the car. Out in the

street like that. And Ernie wasn't twelve years old, I bet ya. And Pa asked for a wrench and Ernie handed him a pliers. Oh, oh, he handed him a pliers while Pa was layin' under the car and when Pa saw it he pushed himself out from under the car and he said, 'Goddamn you, Ernie! I said a wrench!' and he hit Ernie with that pliers and split his head open. Oh, how Ma cried about that. Ernie with a cut in his head that made his hair fulla blood like that. Made Ma sick just to take care of it.

"And Pa, he never said he was wrong or that he should apologize to Ernie. Never."

Helen shook her head and tightened the lines on her face. It was the way she usually got when the stories progressed from the sentimental to the grim.

"Your ma said it was that clout on Ernie's head what killed him so young," Helen said. "After that he started fallin' asleep on the toilet like that. You'd knock and yell 'Ernie! Ernie!' and then open the door and he'd be sittin' there with his pants down and fast asleep. Yeah, always after Pa hit him on the head like that."

Again they were silent, Harry not wishing to add fuel to the fire. He knew the incident Helen was recalling. He could have supplied a dozen like it of his own. From his own family or others in the neighborhood. But he sat and tasted the coffee in his mouth. He scratched his beard.

"Naw, I think it was that goat that killed Ernie," he finally said. "That goat that Dickie Lunsky had in them lots and Ernie tried to ride it that day."

That did it for Helen. She lost her long face and came alive.

"Oh, that goat! That goat was ridin' all over the neighborhood and eatin' everything like that in sight!"

She laughed as she said it. Harry joined in, surprised by his own exuberance.

"Whatever happened to that Dickie Lunsky? He wasn't all there. People used to say he wasn't as smart as the goat," Harry said.

"But you could hear 'em comin' like the delivery trucks. Lunsky and that goat, and Ma used to say, 'I'd like to shoot that goat and eat it for supper.' "

"And Pa'd say, 'You'd have to shoot Dickie Lunsky too, and he'd ruin the meal.' "

Harry bellowed at the quote he'd remembered. It was something the two of them had grown up with and for some reason hadn't talked about for years.

"He died. That Dickie Lunsky died. Right around Ernie. From that water on his head like they said would happen. Yeah, he died," Helen said. Her voice trailed off into a slow up-and-down shaking of her head.

Then, as quickly as the stories came up, the memories, the visions of Pa and Ernie, Ernie, who had died twenty years ago when he was hit by a truck on Damen Avenue, as vivid as the old times came fluttering up, they left. Helen got up and cleared off the table. Harry sat momentarily, then he too got up and went out the back way to return to his job. And, somewhere in the house, Helen was back at hers.

It went that way for a few days, without announcement or invitation, just a natural gravitation toward the kitchen at that time in the afternoon and the coffee and donuts came out. Then it was regular, each day as if it had been a life-long routine instead of one of only a few days. And one day, as Harry was glazing a window and lost track of the time, Helen appeared at his ladder.

"You comin' for coffee?"

He stopped what he was doing and stepped down the ladder. Later he thought to himself how she had said it, as if she expected him—no, as if she looked forward to their coffee time. They talked, sometimes about what was happening then, usually about the old neighborhood, about Ma and Pa and about the neighbors who were dead or simply not heard from anymore. And Harry wondered each night as he lay on the sofa, through his aches and his stomach and the gnawing in his bones from too many rain-soaked, sleet-soaked nights

141

on the pavement, how long it would stay this way. And he wondered whether or not he wanted it to.

He was painting the vestibule that afternoon, dabbing and daubing in his usual nonchalant way. He was brushing on a coat of glossy beige, it was going on easily, so he daydreamed, decided to knock off early tomorrow since the Cubs were coming back into town. They had swooned their way through September; it pained him to pick up a newspaper and go through the sports pages, losing first place and a twelve-game lead to the crummy Mets. Now, with only a dozen games left in the season, they were frantically trying to hold on and catch up, in second place, unbelievably, after blowing it.

He decided he would get out there to Wrigley Field, get after them, maybe sting them back into shape and put in his order for a Series ticket. He saw the Cubs, Billy Williams, Kessinger, Beckert, Fergie Jenkins, in the trail of his paint brush. Then he glanced blankly out the glass of the front door. He saw them, the couple, a greasy blond and her long-haired, short-legged friend, the two of them swaggering noisily, looking at the ground with lazy, contorted grins. Harry dropped his hand and striped his coat with beige, but as he looked he was certain of it: that same shrimpy punk in his purple shirt—Harry couldn't take his eyes off it and almost fell off the ladder—was Jimmy Del Corso.

As the two of them passed the building's doorway, unaware that they were being eyeballed, Harry scuttled backward off his perch. He left the can of paint wide open, still wielding his brush, suddenly feeling his pulse. He opened the front door and peeked out, then he followed the pair, paint brush in hand, his white coat flapping in the wind as he walked.

The pair continued up Magnolia for a block, still weaving, now arm in arm. Harry could hear them snicker and jabber. He walked next to the buildings, shadowing them, looking more suspicious than he could have realized. Then they turned and stepped down a walk toward a side entrance. Harry stepped quickly, saw them go inside, and went hurriedly toward the same door.

"I got the bastards," he said to himself, then he glanced around to see if anyone had heard him.

He saw that they had gone through an entranceway to another corridor, just below ground level, which led to a basement area. Three doors on either side, built there, he knew, so the landlord could jam in still more flats and gouge more rents. He crept up to the door, listened, heard nothing, then was drawn to a sound of cackling laughter.

He stood at the door and listened, stooping, his ear pressed to the wood. At first it was nothing but a woman's giggling. Then a few taunting words from a male voice, one that he was certain sounded like that of Del Corso. But then he heard it, unmistakably, from a corner of a room just to the left of the door.

"Don't you two peckerhead lovebirds start screwin' while I'm here or yul be throwed out bare ass!"

He didn't listen any longer. It was the hillbilly's voice. None other. Hustling toward the sidewalk, almost running in the rush of his sudden discovery, Harry took off back to the building. Now he had them. Now he had something going for him.

10

He was fat, with curly red hair that bobbed around his head like that of Harpo Marx, a giggle that punctuated his almost nonstop tenor voice. Were he not behind his desk and leaning back in a chair so that he could prop his pudgy legs on a typewriter stand, George Duffy would have been just as at home over a backyard fence. His gab was incessant, his stories, the gossip, the cheesy rumors, the foul stories, the scuttlebutt that ran up and down the streets of Uptown.

McMahon had known him almost from the beginning of his detective tour, the little fat guy who sought out cops and whispered to them in corners, talking out of the side of his mouth, just over the collar, as if things were constantly brewing. Or Duffy ambushed district commanders and neighborhood-relations sergeants at community meetings, slapping them on the back and making jokes, laughing with his head thrown back and his tenor voice squeezed into a wheezing, whistling, uncontrollable guffaw.

He was the Mayor's man so he could get away with it. He was the unseen, unknown administrative aide in the Mayor's Office of Information and Inquiry who worked in a stuffy office doing City Hall's necessary dirty work. It was George Duffy people went to if they couldn't bribe the alderman or the committeeman or the precinct captain or the ward heeler. It was George Duffy they went to if they couldn't squeeze hard enough, or play proper politics. And George would laugh and giggle and make deals in his own mysterious little ways, with telephone calls and visits and huddled meetings that consisted of whispers and grunts and a few nods of important heads.

"So we do what we can do," he'd tell everybody. "In our own little way, of course."

McMahon found himself drawn to Duffy, wondering as always if the fat little Irishman was thirty or forty or somewhere in between, because George knew Uptown like the back of his hand. Duffy roamed Uptown and made peace with problems, trying to keep the lid on so the people in the Hall wouldn't have to take the heat, trying to save face and keep the place out of the papers, to show the troublemakers and the do-gooders who tried to work outside of the machine that they couldn't do anything, couldn't fix a pipe, turn on a fire hydrant, replace a street light, clean a gutter, or kill a rat without George Duffy's permission and his sanction after he'd gone through the channels that only George Duffy could traverse.

"We do what we can do," he'd repeat, giggling and shaking the red curls on his ears, the layers of fat pushing over his belt. "Hizzoner would appreciate it.

"Why does a good copper like yourself come up here to George Duffy?" he asked, then leaned forward and took a pack of Larks from McMahon. "No, don't answer that, Johnny. I like to talk to you coppers."

"I've been runnin' down this one on the Puerto Rican girl at the Vicklen."

"The chickie who went sailing out the window, right?" Duffy said. He raised his voice when he said it, as if to giggle though keeping a straight face.

"Yup. So besides coming up to touch you for a smoke—you probably owe me a pack now, Duffy . . ."

"C'mon, c'mon, I don't steal from coppers."

"Yeah, bullshit. I wondered what you heard. We ain't got

145

much ourselves. Street's drying up on us. Nothin'."

"Yeah, yeah, yeah. I know you been hittin' this one hard. I got the calls. Yeah, yeah, I got the calls. From the hotel guy. Hot. He was hot on account of how you were leanin' on him. Gettin' pissed nowadays, John?"

"Son of a bitch. I'd like to tie his ass in knots. Ram something up so far—"

"Hey, hey, hey, watch it here, heh, heh, heh. Jees-us Lord, Johnny, yer gettin' nasty," Duffy said. He smiled and drew heavily on his cigarette, grimaced as if he didn't like the taste, then swung his feet with a grunt off the desk. "I ain't heard much about that thing, John, not much at all. Doesn't seem to be even too many people pissed off about it. And I hear things, too. But not on this one."

"I told ya, the street can dry up. It can go dust on ya."

"Yeaaaaa . . ." Duffy twanged, nasally. "But ya got to milk it. Ya got to put the right smells under the right noses and then play with 'em. They talk to me. They all talk to me. They all make it up those steps and sit where yer sitting now and then Duffy hears it all, Father Duffy hears it all, as I got a wet nurse for an alderman and a jagoff for a committeeman. Which I enjoy like a case a piles.

"Let me tell ya. Let me tell ya how things run up here. Just so you don't get the impression from the papers or all those candy-ass reform politicians that things are changing in this town. My rosy Irish giggy they're changing. I get things done. Yeah, me, mister nobody who the press reporters, all except the good ones, don't write about so much. But, when the nuts start pinchin', when the ol' man gets hot downtown and the thunder strikes, it comes from this office. Them reformers, them two-bit politicians in their store fronts, that Rinsky creep and his initials, them Indians, the pricks at them centers, all them shits wouldn't know where to pick their noses if it weren't for me right here in this office.

"Clout, yeah, clout, most people who talk about it don't know clout from Jackie Kennedy's tits. Like that alderman I

146

got here. The Phantom, I call him. Around election time I'm out there hustling votes for the prick 'cuz the boys downtown say he's their pooch. But in the meantime, between you and me, he don't know which end of his butt to pick. I got to solve his problems—me—and patch up fights when he gets the captains pissed and make phone calls for him and zip his fly and wipe the milk off his mustache. Once, and this is the truth, honest to God, he asked me to call up his mother and apologize 'cuz he didn't buy her a present for her birthday. But listen to this, heh, heh, oh Jesus, this will make your day, this will get ya. The other day he decides ya see that he's gonna get to the bottom of the daily pay halls, right? Like he's gonna expose their so-called abuses like he was some god-damn fruitcake reporter. So he gets together his old paint clothes, some shit that even the bums on Wilson wouldn't wear, and he goes in the halls and looks for work. So one of the owners, see, he calls me. Now them bastards are shits, believe me, but that's another movie, but he calls me and says what's this prick doin' in my hall? And I go down there and sure enough, there he is, lurkin' off in the corner with this stocking cap pulled over his head. I walks over and he sees me and tries to give me the sign that I should shut up and ignore him. All confidential, right? So I do what anyone would do. I said, 'Hey, Frank, what you doin' lookin' for work here? Ain't bein' alderman enough for ya?' Heh, heh, heh, you should a been there. Thought he was gonna piss in his pants. Everybody lookin' at him, boy, was he sore. But what the hell, you tell me, what's the jagoff doin' there stirring up trouble?"

He stopped and quickly brushed ashes off the front of his tie. He was wearing an orange-and-green-flecked shirt that looked like he'd spilled lasagna on it.

"Glad to see you're keepin' the lid on things," McMahon said.

"Ah, I could write a book about that moron. But nobody would read it 'cuz they'd think it was fiction. I think I'd call it, *I Don't Believe No One Could Be That Dumb,* or maybe *Forty-sixth Ward Jagoff."*

"Call it *Duffy's Reader,*" McMahon said.

George turned up his lip and made a face, then rippled a raspberry.

"So what's up, Johnny? Who's killing who out there that I don't know about?" Duffy said.

"You tell me. Whattaya know about the clerk that called ya?"

"Gus? Yeah, guy's name is Koutsos. Greek. He been around. Got a sheet, too, I know that for a fact. I know from experience that there ain't no job like a night clerk at one of them outhouses for attracting ex-cons."

Duffy stopped and waited for McMahon to press him. But McMahon didn't say anything and nodded for Duffy to go on, to ramble and come up with anything that came into his head.

"Bastard's a complainer. Bitch, bitch, bitch about a lot of things. I met him once doing my rounds. You know, passing the hat and making sure all the fences are mended for primary time. You know we get a lot of play from the hotels. All good, conscientious voters living in them flops. You can count on 'em. So anyway, I'm talking to this guy who ordinarily I wouldn't give the time of day to and he starts telling me some of the problems around the place. Like they was his concern and he was some Mr. Shipshape in the ward, right? But I listen because employees of Hizzoner always listen and it takes me about two and a half seconds to figure out that this guy is takin' me and takin' me bad. Duffy smells 'em, Johnny boy, smells 'em like a copper. This guy's into sellin' things, I say. Only I don't come on this so ingeniously. Fact is, he wondered if I was looking for an 'appliance' as he called it. Something for the little lady. Yeah, my mother. Not that he was selling anything out of the hotel, of course not, Mr. Duffy, but that he had friends and sometimes things got tight for even an employee of the city. So right then and there I realize what this prick's up to. I mean, I make my living in Uptown, right? Not in some nursery school. And I'll lay ya two to one that if he's sellin' TVs he's selling junk and broads and you name it. I got a little cop in me. Those pricks are all alike. And that's all I know."

McMahon smiled, a wide, contented expression of genuine amusement. "Duffy, you always amaze me."

"We do the best we can." Duffy chuckled. Then he shoved his fist into his elbow and smiled. "And when we shoves it in we turns the handle and breaks it off."

His soprano giggle echoed through the room as the two of them stood up and scraped chairs across the floor.

"I owe ya a beer," McMahon said.

"I'll take it, too," Duffy laughed.

McMahon laughed to himself, then turned and headed down the steps for the street. Everybody is a politician, everybody a cop, he thought, even to the detriment of a particular hotel clerk.

Harry rolled the alternatives over and over in his head; they were killing him. He hadn't had to think this hard or this long about anything for years. Not having a bottle or a pot to piss in were problems, agonies he didn't relish. But they didn't take thinking past the element of deciding when to turn a corner, or to punch a trunk, grab a purse, or get in line at the Army, the mission, the Model Cities joints. But now he had a two-sided problem that turned his belly inside out.

He had a hook on Donald Ray and Del Corso. He had those two loud-mouthed, pill-popping pricks over a barrel. With a phone call he could turn them in, a tempting possibility in view of what they had done to him on Lincoln Avenue. He knew he could square things with McMahon and the robbery dicks if he went to bat for them, tonight if he felt like it. And those two wouldn't know what hit them, wouldn't know why the cuffs were snaking around their wrists.

But that was only one sure thing, he knew. It was not a hot

one, not something he'd like to do, since he was all too aware that the two of them could get out on bail and then his life wouldn't be so safe, his steps always shrouded by the possibility that he would be cold-cocked with a pipe so hard that he would see the inside of his skull. The risk was like that. No honor codes once someone started to fink. Lives weren't good for thirty minutes past that point, and every thief worth his take knew it.

What Harry really had was an in. He could come down on Burl and Del Corso with a drop that they wouldn't be about to ignore unless they got rid of him for good. And though that was a possibility—it was a cinch that Del Corso had hit people before, and maybe Burl too—he didn't think they would let him have it before they considered the alternatives. And one of them, Harry saw as he lay on Helen's sofa staring at the ceiling, was the alternative of taking him on and putting him to work.

It would be a trio, just like the old days, he said to himself. With Yaras and Caputo and Lum, the three wild bandits of the West Side picking through joints as if they were there for the taking. Back to the money and the expensive booze and the women that paid attention when you showed some cash. Even at Harry's age, he'd unlimber the tool, and a smile broke out on his face. There in the living room of his stepsister, the television going. His eyes were riveted to the ceiling, seeing visions of past and future, and slowly, mysteriously, with a spontaneity that startled him, his hand slipped down on his crotch.

He awoke a few hours later when Ilene clicked off the set. He looked up long enough, his head clearing, to hear her say, "Geez, waste of electricity," and then wander off to her own bedroom.

But he didn't fall back to sleep. He lay there in the dead-of-night silence, the darkness, nagged by the thoughts of the trap he was falling into. It was Helen, always Helen, that loud, tyrannical woman who gushed like a schoolgirl over her dead mother one minute only to turn hard as stone the next. It was Helen who was his past, the family he'd come out of, and it was Helen who always reminded him of it, how he had shamed them. But he was living off her now. The routine and the comfort he'd known in the past few days were due to her and the order she brought to her house. In the middle of Uptown, the no man's land he had drifted to like every other bum and thief and no-account, a place that was like a prison to his mind and his liver, but it was here that Helen persevered and overcame. She could resist the neighborhood with the same iron hand she used to manage the building, with the smell of kielbasa and *kapusta* that hung over her kitchen, the ring of her voice. And she was using that same power over him.

But she'd played it well, not directly stripping him of anything. She'd taken him in and lied to the police, didn't ask for money. The food was there, the coffee, the laundry washed and folded, the sheets he slept on replaced each week. It was as if he was another part of the routine she had chosen to take on. The money he hid beneath the panel of the refrigerator remained there, except for the lumps he took out of it to buy his daily pint. Yet the bulk of it, still more than $150, was still untouched.

He rolled over and buried his face in the pillow, Helen's pillow, with the bleached smell of the pillow case. The stories of Pa and her brother Ernie, of Dickie Lunsky, of the relatives, all of them flooded past him. He hadn't thought about those things when he lived alone. Milwaukee Avenue and the old neighborhood were something that the cops brought up, or an old-timer on the street. It didn't dominate his consciousness like it did Helen's. He wondered if he was going soft.

He was wide awake now. He pulled a leg out from under the blanket and sat up, yawning, reaching for a cigarette. He stood up and headed for the bathroom. All the coffee made him pee a lot. He needed a nip, something to sting his mouth

151

and settle his bones. The clock suddenly struck, three bongs from the corner of the dining room. He stopped and told himself that here it was three in the morning and he couldn't sleep, he needed a drink and he couldn't have one, couldn't nip when he wanted to nip, his stomach growled, and he wondered again if he was being taken.

The next morning, while Helen was sleeping, he pulled a fin from beneath the refrigerator and went down to the Liberty Bell. But, instead of downing the pint in the alley, he left it unopened and walked directly back to the building. In the basement, he slipped it into a space he'd made in a paint cabinet. Now, he thought to himself, it was there and that was all there was to it. To hell with her.

He went back to his project of painting the sashes and window frames. It was a job Helen said she wanted to finish before winter. She said it as matter-of-factly as she said most things, and Harry didn't catch it until that afternoon. She'd said, "Before winter," but said it with him in mind, as if he was going to be around, of course he was going to be around, and he had better get it done "before winter." "She ain't got no right to tell me what I do before winter," he said out loud to himself. He stepped defiantly down the ladder and headed for the cellar. He found the bag of elderberry wine and cracked it, drinking long, noisy gulps of the wine, as if the blatancy of doing it right there was enough to put Helen in her place. He consciously wished she would walk in on him. He would keep on drinking, long, satisfied, the wine going down like milk, then he suddenly coughed and spat up a mouthful. He had taken too much of it in, clogged his windpipe. Staggering, he put the bottle down heavily on the bench and doubled over in his coughing fit. He hadn't realized that during the last few days he hadn't drunk this much wine so fast, and he was stunned at how hard it hit him.

He left a quarter of the bottle intact and returned to his ladder. Though it wasn't enough booze to really faze him, he missed the first step and caught himself on the rails. He blamed it on Helen, stepped on her, then went on up.

At lunch she scurried about the kitchen. She was still in her bathrobe and her hair was pinned up in back. When Harry sat down she looked at him and her face came alive.

"You should see what I got to show you," she said. Then she left the room for the dining room.

From there she began to talk. "All that jabbering about Pa and Ernie made me look for somethin'."

She returned with an envelope in her hand. "Look at this right here, Harry."

She bent over him and laid the envelope on the table.

"That's at the wedding. Back when Pa met yer Ma and they was married."

It was a black-and-white photograph taken thirty-five years before at the parlor wedding. The two families stood like soldiers, stiff, unsmiling, with only the bridal couple showing any signs of life. Harry was in his twenties, young, lean, with dark hair slicked back, and tough Polish lines to his face. Helen was off to the left of the picture, behind Harry's mother yet looking very much like her. Helen too was thin and dark-haired, with no trace of the sass and back-talk she was known for, or the squealing energy of her polka dancing, a kicker, as Pa used to call her.

"Oh, look at me there. I was so skinny. Now I'm a tub a lard, you betcha," she said. "But look here, Harry. Look at this one."

She pulled out another photo, a smaller one and older, tinged with the brown of the aging paper. "Dat's me at first communion. Look at there."

The two of them stared at the portrait, at the white lace of Helen's dress, her white stockings and white shoes, the long veil that hung to her knees.

"Only seven years old and I was a beautiful little girl," she said. "Ma always tol' me dat."

Harry didn't reply. He tried to see himself in the same picture. He could remember the day fifty some years back when he was dressed in a starched collar and pressed pants. He made first communion with all the rest of the kids, at St. John Cantius, a procession of giggling, elbowing kids each trying to bob his head and get a look at his folks. He saw it all in the portrait of Helen, unsmiling and rigid with flowers and candles as props, in the gray and brown hues of years back.

"Yeah, that's what it was like all right like that," he said.

"Uh-huh," she agreed, the two of them lost in the memories and the sentiment. "Those were the days all right."

Again there was a long silence. Then Harry looked inside his coffee cup and got up from the table.

"Back on the job," he said, and went out the back door.

In the basement he washed away any trace of his lunch with the last of the wine. He went out to the trash cans and dug beneath the garbage before tossing the bottle inside. Then he went back to his ladder and his windows.

"Hey, Lennie! Get yer ass over here."

McMahon had spotted him on Winthrop, pedaling his fat-wheeled delivery bike the opposite direction from traffic. Cars swerving to miss sunken, craterous manhole covers missed Lennie by inches, honking as they swung past him, not seeing in their rear-view mirrors that he shot his left hand in the air with every horn, shooting them a straight, defiant finger. His basket was empty; he was pedaling dead time until he could get back to Wilson. The wind flipped his oily hair past his ears. It pinned his "Here Comes Da Judge" tee-shirt against his chest so that his ribs and his nipples could be traced.

"What ya want?"

"You. For the time being."

"I'm busy so make it quick. I got things to do."

"Quit with the jagoff routines, Lennie, or we'll junk that crate of yours and talk to ya down to the station."

Lennie bent over and leaned in the window on McMahon's

side, his bike still in traffic. His face was framed by the window, inches from McMahon's and all the more noticeably pockmarked and scarred, the short, half-inch scars from knives and knuckles. He didn't look at McMahon or at Farber, only stared at the dashboard.

"What ya carrying, Lennie?" Farber said. He turned and sat sideways on the front seat.

"Nuttin'. Had a delivery on Lawrence."

"One of them kind of deliveries, Lennie? For your junkie friends?" Farber said.

"Huh?" Lennie said, his head down, his forearms pressed against the door.

"All right, all right, enough shit," McMahon said. "We're looking for the guy who killed the girl in the hotel. Nothing else. That's why we stopped you."

"What girl?"

"The girl thrown out the window."

"Yeah. I heared about her."

"What else ya hear?"

"Nuttin'. I don't hear nuttin'." He leaned back and pulled his head up, shot a glance up Winthrop then leaned down once again, eyes still screwed to the dash.

"Look," McMahon said. He looked straight ahead at the vague outline of the buildings and trees along Winthrop. "We need a little help on a killer. We ain't trying to get you on anything else and we don't care about anything else. You help us and we don't forget you. We can be nice to have around in case a tire blows on this two-wheeler of yours."

Lennie said nothing. A shift of wind brought in the odors that lingered in the open spaces under his arms. At this time of the afternoon he should have been sitting behind a desk in the ninth grade. But he had never made it past the seventh, then had become so incorrigible, a regular guest at the Foster Avenue station's juvenile office, that nobody even tried to keep him in school. Though he was quick and intelligent, he could barely read or write and was all but stymied

155

at the challenge of putting a coherent sentence down on paper.

"We know you get around, Lennie," Farber said. "Tell us what ya hear, that's all."

"Nuttin'," he said.

"Okay. I'll get specific," McMahon said. "Whattaya know about the night clerk at the Vicklen? Guy named Gus?"

At that Lennie shifted his weight on his arms. McMahon thought he detected a reaction, a response however slight, however hesitant. Lennie leaned up again, still holding his balance on the seat of his bike, one foot on the street, and he mined his pockets with his hands. Pulling out a pack of cheap cherry-flavored gum, he began to unwrap a stick, then another, letting the thin foil papers fly off down the street. He stuffed three sticks into his mouth. McMahon saw him and shook his head, his hand brushing his forehead. He'd seen hundreds of suspects start chain smoking or chew their nails or itch or pick at scabs or stuff food in their mouths when the questions got close to home. Now Lennie, the punk kid of fourteen, was already sweating out the game.

"C'mon, c'mon," McMahon said rapid-fire. "We ain't got all day."

"I don't know nuttin' about what you guys are talkin' about," Lennie shot back.

"What?" McMahon said. Lennie had blurted his last statement outside the window.

"I don't know a *thang!*" Lennie said. He rolled the words through the slimy ball of gum and saliva rolling through his mouth.

The two detectives said nothing, trying to use the silence, to hang on it. McMahon finally shot a glance at Farber and saw a look of resignation on his face. Lennie was clamming and they knew it. That was all there was to it for the time being.

"Okay, Lennie," McMahon said. "On your way."

"Just remember that we know what you do for a living,"

156

Farber said. As he said it he got a quick but fleeting glance from Lennie as he pulled his head out of the window. It seemed impossible that the kid was only fourteen.

"Thanks a million," McMahon said.

In a moment Lennie was back in traffic, standing and pumping the creaking pedals, the metal of a fender scraping against a tire. Seconds later the detectives' car pulled out and accelerated up Winthrop. As it did, Lennie, without turning his head or changing the rigid expression on his face, shot his left hand into the air and flashed, long and tall like a flagstick, his middle finger.

11

Donald Ray was seldom meticulous about anything. It went against his nature to think too much about any one thing at any one time. Art Burl used to tell him back in the hills, when they went after birds and squirrels, that when you were ready to do something you should do it, do it as hard as you could, then think about it later. That agreed with Donald Ray. It got him into trouble, but it was a way of getting through life that most people couldn't handle, and he could, so what the hell. When he hit drugstores or corner markets, he usually hit them with no more preparation than a few rides past the places, maybe a stroll inside to buy a pack of gum, then around closing time he and whoever was with him would go in, one take the door, the other pull a gun at the register and scoop out the cash. It was quick and easy, ready to do something and then doing it, and minutes later, with cash in a paper bag, it was done.

But this time was different, he told himself that, no cheap-ass drugstore hit, no bump and run. This was an inside plan, and he would take his time about it, plan, take precautions, set it up just right. It wasn't Fort Knox, and he wasn't planning on gold bullion, but it was a medical-supply house, a big one, and that meant dentists, and somewhere a safe where they kept the gold and the silver destined to go into the mouths of people all over Chicago. Only if Donald Ray got his way, if his intricate shopping-bag maps held true, that silver and gold would be detoured from the warm fingers of sweet-talking dentists into the hot hands of cool-walking Mr. Burl. He chortled at the thought of it, then bore down, preparation.

For two nights he lurked in the alley, a diagonal alley running behind North Clark, shielded from the light and any passing cars by the cluster of trash barrels he'd pulled around him like a fort. He sat until dawn, taking only the liberty of a few cigarettes, an occasional upper to keep him awake, watching and taking copious notes. The next night he stayed inside the trash-can blind for a few hours then pulled himself up a utility pole and onto a roof. He hid behind a two-foot-high brick wall, peering over into the alley and even onto Clark Street. And, through the hours of waiting and watching, he got an idea of the pulse of the area, the sounds of the neighborhood, what lights went on, where people walked, dogs, cops, and anything else that moved.

The next day he walked in the front door of the building and was met by a secretary at a switchboard. He asked a question about false teeth, pointed to the gap in his lowers. She smiled and said that they didn't do anything like that, that the business was wholesale only and that he would have to go to a dentist. Then he tried his second ploy, one to buy him a little sightseeing time, and asked her if they had any information, any kind of booklet that could tell him about false teeth, especially for a person with his problem. He put on his best delivery, using the right phrases and greasing a smooth, persuasive tone to his voice. It was good enough for the girl, and she got out from behind her desk and went to ask. As soon as she left, Donald Ray peered into the office behind her glass door, mapping out the partitions, the doorways, then spotted a sign over a distant cubicle. It was printed in large red block letters, two long words he couldn't read, then two he could: KEEP OUT. He clicked the shutter in his mind, congratulated himself for yet another master

159

stroke, then smiled nicely at the girl when she returned and told him she just couldn't come up with anything.

"Well, thanks for everything and anything," he said. Then, pointing to the shiny gap in his lowers, he joked, "This here tunnel is startin' to cut in on my good looks."

The girl smiled and gently turned her eyes upward. Donald Ray raised a paw and waved as he left. That was part of the planning and it was a damn good part, he said to himself, again smelling the bouquet he had presented in his own honor for his own considerable talents.

That night he and Jimmy made their way down to Halsted Street in Jimmy's Chevrolet. It was two in the morning. They turned west at Webster and into an alley next to a boiler-repair company. It was a big, nondescript brick building with overhead doors in front which let out rumbling trucks in the morning and took them back in at night. But Donald Ray and Jimmy were interested in the steel door in back. Jimmy parked the Chevy in a corner near a garage, and the two of them crept quickly down the alley, with nothing but the wind and the swish of the traffic along Halsted to cover them. But they were alone, no one walking or watching, nobody cruising. They went to the door with a crowbar and a set of screwdrivers. They drove the tools into the frame, bending, using all the force they could muster to bend the door and the frame and get at the lock. With remarkably little noise, they got at the mechanism, pried it and it snapped open. They were quickly inside, the door closing behind them.

In the shadows of a single night light hanging from a balcony, they made their way through the building, around the trucks, looking over and under the benches. Donald Ray had marked down exactly what they were after, what they would settle for. He walked right past the office, paying no attention to it or the fact that the glass door was unlocked. Jimmy headed for a workbench and found a heavy-duty crowbar, a pair of metal shears, then, looking further, he found a case with a power drill inside. He couldn't carry them all together and settled for the drill. He signaled to Donald Ray and left, closing the door soundlessly, stepping quickly down the alley to the Chevy, which had its trunk unlocked and waiting. In seconds he was back inside the building and hefting the crowbar and the shears.

Donald Ray still hadn't found what he was after. He opened a panel on one of the trucks, saw a flashlight and used it to probe through the shelves and the tools. Finally he spotted what he wanted in the bed of the truck: a set of tanks and a torch, a supply of welding punks, a striker. He grabbed the handle and hoisted the torch up and out, setting it down by Jimmy and motioning him to take it out. He knew they were almost home, smiled about his planning, his increasingly superb execution. Then in a corner he found another torch, the one he was looking for, an acetylene outfit with four-foot-tall tanks. He'd learned how to use these babies from a con in the state pen. He grabbed it by the handles of its push truck, grimaced at the squeaking, grating noise its iron wheels made on the cement. He stopped at the door and looked at the torch's brass nozzle, perfect, a head that could cut through anything.

In a minute Jimmy was backing the car down the alley. He jumped out, leaving the motor on, and the two of them lifted the torch into the trunk. It barely fit and pushed the car's frame down at least three inches. But it was in and the trunk lid slammed. In a single surge of acceleration, the car was down the alley and off into the street. Donald Ray and Jimmy sat and said nothing, businesslike, off after a successful foray.

As the days passed, Harry got lazier, no longer all that excited about preserving Helen's building. His working turned into puttering; things he could get done in ten minutes took him an hour. Sometimes he just sat at his bench in the cellar and stared, leaned his head against a pipe, and drifted off. He awakened always to Helen, not scolding or

161

shouting, but intentionally kicking over a trash barrel or dropping a shovel. The clanging noise shook him and he hopped back to whatever it was he was doing. But he began to resent her, like a mother getting after him, a wife, a force that gnawed at him.

To shake it, to take his mind off things, he went down and bought a bottle. But he told himself he wouldn't hide it anymore. He wasn't going to act like some shit-pantsed school kid sneaking a cigarette behind the garage. So he kept the pint in his coat pocket and nipped at it when he felt like it.

If he hadn't eaten much, it would bring a fuzz down on him, a glaze on the edge of the world. He would take the steps on his ladder one at a time, slowly, making each one talk to him while his hands wrung the side rails and his chest hugged the upper rungs. Sometimes, when he got to the top, the second or even as high as the third floor, he would stand and weave and hold on, for long minutes, not swinging a paint brush or a putty knife, just holding on and considering it the toughest job in the world.

But the fuzz didn't obscure the shadow that he saw at every corner. It was Helen, always Helen, dogging him and checking up. At first he thought he was imagining it, like some kind of hen-pecked paranoia that automatically went along with his cushy new arrangement with life. But, as the days came and went, he found more and more signs of her heavy hand. He saw brush marks over his, touching up on even the smallest paint jobs. He found repairs that were altered, or changed, glass that was rewashed and repolished. Once he even left a small pile of dirt in a place where he had swept, and an hour later he returned to find it gone.

He told himself that he wouldn't pay any attention to it, but he was fooling himself. It bothered the hell out of him. That after all these years he still had to be responsible to someone. Still, she never said anything, she never told him he was doing a rotten job, or a good one for that matter. She didn't prod him or remind him or nag him. She was just always there, always making sure the finishing touch was not his but hers.

If there was anything that Harry could do well it was replacing windows. He'd learned glazing from his father and it was something he took an old-fashioned pride in. Once the glass was in, and in Helen's building there was always a supply of shattered panes, he tapped in the minute steel tacks and then prepared the putty. He used putty that he bought from the hardware by the pound, not the prepackaged crap. He rolled it and warmed it in his palm, then packed it into the window like a dentist packing a tooth.

But the real secret to glazing a window was in the putty knife, in smoothing the blade over the soft compound and leaving it as clean as marble. To do it Harry slapped the knife against his tongue, wet it good like his pa always did, and ran it over the gray dough. The putty glistened beneath his touch, smooth as the glass he looked through, perfect and spotless. When he finished with a window, with the technique he knew to be flawless, passed from father to son, he tucked the knife in his back pocket and took a moment to admire the work. He'd stack it against any professional piece of glazing done in town.

But one day, a day after he'd finished replacing three windows on the rear of the first floor, he absorbed the last straw. Stopping to check his work, he noticed it immediately. It pissed him off more than anything else she had done—for she had checked each window, testing the putty, then pressing it with her fingers. She went around the entire window, each one of the three, until the putty was a continuous path of thumbprints in gray.

When he saw it he could hardly keep control. He kicked the dirt and spat, cursing loud and long, obscenities that made no sense, garbled in his anger. Finally he stripped off his work coat and hurled it against the cellar door. This was the final blow from a woman who wanted not only his backbone but his soul. She would not stop until she had him clubbed into something and someone he himself didn't even know. If for no other reason than to exact the servitude she felt was hers for all the years he'd disgraced her. She would kill him the way Polish women always killed their men. Like Joe Pontek, and now Harry Lum. She would keep it up, keep putting the thumbprints in his neck until he was bowed and stoop-shouldered and meek like a dog. She would keep it up until he broke or until she drove him back into the gutter and into his hooch, opting for the pain of the bottle over the humiliation of his spirit.

He jumbled all of those thoughts into his head as he stalked down the alley. Nothing alive could keep him from tying one on right now.

He didn't come back for dinner. Instead he walked, fueled with one pint and the bulge of another on his waist. He walked down to Montrose then turned west along the cemetery. Sober, though nicely fogged, he could step a straight line and hold his head up. He was clean-shaven, wearing clean clothes, feeling perfectly respectable. Suddenly he thought of the Cubs and turned for Wrigley Field. But they were out of town; when he needed them most they were in Philadelphia. But he kept walking south, down Clark, and finally decided he would wash a few beers down in the bars around the ballpark.

By ten he headed back to the building. He had taken six trips to the john since he'd started drinking and his mind was totally fudged. Weaving, clinging to the stop signs and parking meters for support, he fought his way up Sheffield Avenue. He vaguely knew the way, and though it took him long minutes to read the street signs he was standing under, he slowly paced off the blocks until he got to Montrose, then over to Magnolia. It took him almost two hours, but finally the outline of Helen's building was in front of him. He made his way around to the rear, fumbling with the keys as he went. It was another fight to make it up the back stairs. Each step seemed to appear then pull back again like some kind

164

of smart-assed escalator. But finally he was on the third-floor landing and jabbing at the keyhole. His key made short pecking sounds against the lock, a slot that seemed to him about as large as a sliver, and he jabbed at it like a woozy fighter poking at an imaginary foe.

Suddenly the door jerked open and he was blinded by the light of the kitchen. It was Ilene. She stood there in her bathrobe.

"Aw, yer really drunk," she whined.

Harry took a step and stumbled across the threshold. Ilene caught him by the arm.

"If Ma were here she'd really kill ya."

He groaned and pulled for the dining room. She held him up and walked him clumsily through the kitchen, the two of them tripping awkwardly, until he collapsed on his sofa.

"Boy, are you polluted," Ilene said. She stood there waiting for some kind of response but was answered only by rasping, wet snores, and the odor of Harry's breath as it steamed off his lips.

"Ugh," Ilene said, then went to her room.

He awoke sometime later because of the pain in his back, a sharp, throbbing ache that made him feel like he was sleeping on a rock. He rolled over and reached behind him, only to find that the rock was actually his bottle. It was half empty from what he could tell in the darkness; at least he could hear what he thought was half the hooch sloshing around inside. He pulled his head up against the back cushions of the sofa and tried to unscrew the cap. It was never too late for a goodnight nip. But, as he unscrewed the top, he lost interest, his hands fell into slow motion, and he flopped down into a dead-out sleep.

The bottle slipped from his hand onto the floor, clunking against the carpet. It lay there with the cap almost but not quite off. The blood-red wine pushed against the cap and seeped slowly through it. It dripped into the carpet slowly, like an intravenous transfusion, dripping to the uneven cadence of Harry's snore in a slowly widening crimson circle into Helen's coral-colored carpeting. Above it, in an intoxicated coma, Harry slept, knocked out, his brain sodden and soaked.

Donald Ray had decided on the exact night and the exact time. He tested out his tools, the tanks, the torches. Everything was set. Then he went out to do one last thing; a friend owed him a favor, and that favor now meant transportation. In an hour, maybe two, he told Jimmy, he'd have things together and they would iron out the details.

Less than forty-five minutes later he returned to the apartment. He came up short at the door when he heard the giggling and squealing inside. Cursing under his breath he jammed the key into the door and barged in. Barbie Dell was sitting up on his bed, her feet crossed in front of her like an Indian, naked to the waist. She jumped and covered her chest with her hands at the sight of Donald Ray. Jimmy was lying on the bed, his shirt and shoes still on, but with his pants pulled down and the bare cheeks of his ass smiling.

"What is this shit, for cryin' out loud!?" Donald Ray roared. He stomped around the bed and kicked the corner of it. The bed jerked and Barbie Dell went for the straps of her bra. She pulled it up then realized it was on backward, the cups jutting from her back. Jimmy scrambled off the bed and pulled up his pants.

"Leave this place for a minute and you two are whorin' after each other," Donald Ray shouted. He spat into the sink. "And I gave you something to do, Corso! Somethin' besides getting your fingers stunk up."

He took two quick steps toward Jimmy and clenched his fist, poised to belt him. Jimmy jumped and scrambled, then put his fists up in defense. But Donald slowed, dropped his hand, raised it menacingly.

"Don't you hit him!" Barbie Dell screamed. She had her

bra on straight and stood up on her knees. "Stop it!"

Jimmy swiveled around the bed, his eyes flashing, his mouth a tight hole of hissing anticipation.

"Get the fuck out and do what I tol' ya," Donald Ray yelled, standing his ground, glowering.

Jimmy wiped his mouth, then went for the door and was out.

That apartment was suddenly quiet. Barbie Dell looked over at Donald Ray, then she sat back to the squeaking of the bed springs. Her hair was mussed, some of the ratted clumps poking wildly up from her head, the long brown-blond tresses hanging over her shoulder on her chest. It contrasted noticeably with her pointed white bra, cups which compacted her tits and pushed them up and out.

"Think yer perty tough, don't ya?" she said. She made no move to button up.

"Punks," said Donald Ray. "I can handle punks."

"You down-home boys think you can take on anything," she said.

"That's right. Anything."

"Couldn't handle me."

She sat back on her ankles, spreading her knees and giving Donald Ray a shot of white crotch framed against her thighs.

He pushed away from the wall, around the bed toward the john, crossing in front and to the side of her as he went. She followed him, her hands on her hips. When he got alongside of her he stopped and with a single motion reached down and tried to goose her, shoving his hand down the shaft of her thighs. She grabbed his forearm, squeezing it and pinching into the hair with her nails, all the while with her eyes on him, the two of them staring each other down, grunting, forcing and pushing. He felt the smooth warmth of her thigh, white and Appalachian, a thigh that was made to be draped around necks, marshmallow soft. She pinched, then with a sudden shove, pushed his hand away.

167

He laughed, rubbed the marks on his arms.

Then she changed her expression, suddenly, like a shade drawing closed.

"You want it?" she said.

"If I did, I'd have it," he said. He went into the bathroom and, without closing the door, he pissed noisily.

"You couldn't never!" she screamed. She angrily searched for her blouse. "Couldn't never if you tried! Not some dumb stupid hillbilly like you! . . ."

She yelled and stammered and tried to come up with a put-down mean enough, bad enough. Then he closed the bathroom door and she stopped, settled down and felt foolish, beaten and breathing hard. She smoothed her hair with her hands, then got off the bed and went to the mirror on the wall and began furiously ripping a comb through the glittering, snarled hive. She hated men, as sure as her name was Barbie Dell she hated them.

"Get up! Get up, Harry, so help me before I hit ya wit' this!" she hollered.

She hollered over him and kicked him in the ankle, a hard, stinging blow that landed on the bone, and he jerked himself awake. Helen had his wine bottle in one hand and a sponge in the other. She was a picture of rage, her puffy, Polish face pink, almost contorted.

"Oh my God! Jesus, Mary—! Why I gotta live wit' this kinda stuff after all these years—! Harry, c'mon, get up and look at what you done! I clean and scrub and clean and keep a decent house here and you got to put me to shame by bringin' in yer booze!"

She bent down and got on all fours. He tried to clear his head long enough to see what she was raving about. He looked down and saw the stain, a puddle of purple, and realized where it had come from. His head felt like a melon and he had a killer case of cotton mouth. But it was secondary to the raging stepsister who stooped in front of him and prepared, for all practical purposes, to kill him.

"You bring it on yerself!" she said, now talking into the rug as she scrubbed but with enough volume to fill the room. "You got everything you want and you got to spoil it. Like I said to the priest, he ain't a fit man for nobody but maybe that's all done now. But no, I'm sittin' here cleanin' up yer booze outta my rug. Your ma bought me this rug for anniversary and if she could see it now, it'd break her heart. She'd cry. You better believe it, Harry, she'd look down on all of this right now and she'd cry!"

Harry blew out his lips like a horse. He felt a belch coming, prodded it but couldn't make it surface, then shook his head until he saw fireflies. He felt as bad as he'd ever felt, a drunk that had low-bridged him like nothing before.

"Ah, let her cry," he finally said, Helen's words finally sinking in.

"What? What you say? You got the gall to talk to me like that about me and your ma after what you done? Look here. Look at this rug. And where am I gonna go to get it clean? That stain there, it's gonna remind me for the rest of my life what you done. And how stupid I was to ever let you in this house again.

"'Cuz face it, Harry, you ain't never happy unless yer lickin' it up. A soak, nothin' but a soak. You better believe it. You always gotta be boozin' and drinkin' before you can be happy. You don't go to mass no more, you don't gotta job, sometimes you get up and you don't even take a shave and I gotta sit here and look at ya."

"So who's tellin' ya to look at me, then?" he replied. He sat up on the couch and spread his legs. His misery, the size of his head put him in no mood to take what she was dishing out.

"Who's tellin' me to look at ya? I mean he's askin' me who's tellin' me to look at him. Oh, my God! Yer eatin' here and sleepin' here and gettin' yer laundry done for nothin' and yer askin' me like that. And now look at this down here. *Oj moj Bozé!*"

She got up and went into the kitchen, marching and swinging her arms. She hadn't even taken off her work clothes yet, hadn't even gotten to her bedroom when she spotted the stain on the rug. She returned with a pan of more soapy water and again began scrubbing.

"What's gonna happen to me? Huh? I ask myself what's gonna happen to me. Like Ma, yep, like Ma."

"Ah, yer killin' yerself," Harry said. He was feeling for a fight. "You wouldn't be happy if you wasn't."

"Me? Me?! You can sit there like that after what you did and you can say things to me like that?

"Well, I'll tell ya, Harry, I'll tell ya what you are if ya don't know yerself. Yer a *pijak!* Ya, just like in the old neighborhood. A *pijak* with all that booze. And lookit you. Skinny legs and all. Just the sign. A *pijak* and that's gonna kill ya like it did Pa and Joe."

"Ah, baloney. I'm not bein' no *pijak*. That's up for them lady friends of yers, not me. I can take it and I can leave it."

He got up and headed for the bathroom. He needed a toilet and a slap of cold water.

"That's what you are. Always lickin' it up until one day when I get the phone call that says yer layin' in some gutter," she continued. "And then me I gotta pay the fee to put you away. I'm the only one you got left, Harry, and still yer lickin' it up."

He shut the door and she with it. He looked into the mirror and saw bags under his eyes the size of satchels. It was one thing to wake up to a drunk, it was quite another to wake up to something like Helen. He had to get out. He had to find a place where he could dry out in peace, a place where he wouldn't have to put up with any sound louder than his own breathing.

It was obvious to him. He thought of Burl and Del Corso. They were close, close yet far enough away from what he had let himself slip into around Helen's building. Today, after a

170

morning of coming down and pulling together, he would slip on down to the cellar apartment where he'd heard the familiar voices and he'd make his presence known. That was it. He reached inside the medicine cabinet for the soap, the razor, and decided to take a shave.

He left shortly after. He went straight to the Ron-Ric on Wilson and decided to clear his head with bad coffee. He had money; after Helen had gone to bed for the morning he went to the Hotpoint and liberated the entire stash. He wasn't going to take the chance of Helen finding it, or, in his present precarious state, of not being able to get back into the house to get it.

He thought about that as he walked. It was a bleak, overcast morning once again, the pale days in fall that promised nothing but colder, crummier days ahead. He ran through the hell he'd taken from Helen. It was nothing new, nothing he hadn't heard her say about the old man or Joe her husband or about any stiff on the street who had gotten on the wrong end of the bottle. He remembered how old Joe Pontek took it only when he felt that his eyeballs were looking back at him. Otherwise he'd belt her, like a lot of other men fighting it out on two fronts, and the two of them would go at it toe-to-toe like heavyweights. The advantage in weight and strength was usually offset by the level of drunkenness; the husbands ended up with as many frying-pan welts over their eyes as the women took cracked lips.

This morning was no different, Harry decided. Except for one thing. And it came to him as clear as the nose on his face. Helen had ranted and heaved and fought the foam from coming out of her nose, but she had never told him to get out. No, he was sure of it, through her whole tirade about what a bum he was, how he didn't take a shave, for crying out loud, about how he was some kind of a *pijak*, a *pijak* no less, what the women always called each other whenever they tipped too many, but through the whole ring of baloney she had never said anything about his getting his ass out of her house and out of her sight.

"Jesus Christ in heaven," he said out loud. He felt like the figures on the billboards with lightbulbs over their heads. It was a shock, could only mean that he was in for trouble, a situation with a few too many angles for him. It wasn't good to get too close to your enemies, he was smart enough to know that.

He walked on, faster now, feeling a lot more alert than he had a minute ago. He was convinced that he would make his move this afternoon. Things were getting fishy; he needed a leg up.

He hung around for a while, aware that the cops still wanted him. He had to stay off the street. But by midafternoon he headed down Magnolia for Burl's building.

He knocked with his knuckles. A reply, "Whattaya want?"

He didn't answer, knew it was Burl. He knocked again and had scarcely pulled his hand away when the door jerked open and Donald Ray stood in front of him. Burl was scowling, dressed in a pair of pants and a tee-shirt, his chest and arms as big as ever. A smile oozed across his face.

"Well, kick my ass, the old fuckin' winehead's here."

Harry walked past him into the room. He stood and faced it, breathing hard but holding a firm, determined look on his face.

"Looks like moldy shit got in," Jimmy said from the corner. He was sitting at the card table watching television.

"Yeah, what the fuck you doin' out of the can?" Donald Ray said.

"Huntin' you two," Harry said. "And yuse guys better play it straight wit' me."

It was easy for him to get hot at the sight of them. It hadn't been that long.

"Shut up, winehead, or I'll punch ya out for good," Donald Ray said.

"I could get you guys. I could run yuse up right to the can. Right in the can," Harry said.

"Who said ya didn't already?" Donald Ray said.

"I didn't. I wouldn't be here if I did. Figure that out for yourself if yer so fuckin' smart."

Jimmy pushed away from the table. "We heard you made a deal with the cops for us. That's what we heard."

"I coulda but I didn't. Yer bastards, goddamn sonsabitches. You knew I was headed for a dive in that parkin' lot and you run me up anyway."

"We didn't know nothin'," snapped Donald Ray. "Now shut the fuck up."

"I'm hot right now on account a both of yuse. Got to lay low. Can't smooch down the street like Romeo over here and his girly."

"Yeah?" said Donald Ray. "How hot are ya? Ya promise the cops you'd give 'em us two guys and then find out we wasn't around? That what happened?"

Harry wiped his face with his right hand. "Dumb stupid hick. You don't think past yer nose. If I was as dumb as you I'd never made it past two years old and I'm a lot past that. If I was cozy with the coppers like you think then would I barge in here and tell ya? Maybe to tell ya that the cops was comin'? Or just to talk about the weather or watch that television over there?"

"Why don't you let me throw him out with the garbage?" Jimmy said.

"Shut up. You too, winehead. Call me stupid one more time, if I hear that word 'hick' used on me like that just once again, I'll bash yer teeth so far down yer throat they'll think yer asshole was yer mouth."

He grunted and moved away from the door, opened the refrigerator and cracked a Weidemann's.

"So I don't give a fuck what you told the cops. Yer out instead of in and that's all the better. We was just testin' ya in that motel job. See if you still had anything in ya.

173

"So you passed first grade. Now we got something big goin' and we can use you if we want to. On second thought, I could just throw yer ass out the door or let Jimmy here carve you up for lunch. Take yer choice."

Harry gritted his teeth. He was hot now.

"You'd better do something like that," he said. " 'Cuz if I don't get something out of yuse two I kin go straight to the coppers and spill my guts and do it without a care in the world. I ain't got nothin' to lose. My butt is in a grinder the way it's goin' now."

"We don't have to let you in on nothin', you understand? You a rookie? Or are you playin' by the book rules?" Donald Ray said.

"Cut me in on somethin' or I'll be all over yuse," Harry said.

"Shit. Listen to him," Jimmy grumbled.

Donald Ray turned and smiled, a big goofy smile that usually came from a pill. He grabbed his beer and gulped down most of it.

"Maybe yer lucky," he said to Harry. "Maybe for once in your dumb life yer gettin' lucky."

He left with the old illusions, the old images dancing in his head. He saw the old times, the preparation when he was running with Yaras and Caputo, the way they used to map things out, figure the angles, the timing, and then pull it off like a military drill. He was good then, part of a team that went in then got out, and it could be the same now. He was sure of it, flexing his fingers, trying to regain the feel, get it back, find the confidence that he held somewhere in the pit of his gut that he could do it again and come out big, set for some time. He couldn't shake the glow that charged through him, and suddenly he became aware of where he was going. He had absent-mindedly headed for Helen's. He stopped, thought of checking into a hotel, then stopped and said what the hell. If today was his lucky day he would take advantage

174

of it. If Helen wasn't going to kick him out he wouldn't leave. He'd stay loose and ready and play things as they laid.

He had a secret, a plan; he was now more than just the bum trying to scrape it together. Maybe Donald Ray was onto something, even though Harry didn't trust him, didn't think he had an ounce of the sense that Caputo and Yaras had back then, even if the hillbilly was now sure of himself. Still, Harry was about to be a part of it, like in the old days, when the big guys got in touch and asked him along on important jobs. Now he would shut his trap and wait, work out the details, keep low, and wait. He couldn't believe the surge he felt, the thrill, and he suddenly felt a taste for a bottle. He had bills in his pocket, cut across an alley and walked brazenly in the front door of the Liberty Bell. It was worth a celebration. He was going to pull off a job once again.

12

"I decided you might as well be around here where I kin watch ya. Ya know too much already and who knows when you could stumble down to one of them liquor stores and start runnin' yer mouth off," Donald Ray said.

He'd come up the alley behind Helen's building and grabbed Harry as he lazed around the place. Now they stood in the light of Donald Ray's apartment.

"Who knows when you'd start talkin' and forget about what was in the past and what goes in the future. That's all I need now," Donald Ray said.

Harry wiped his mouth and leaned against the wall. It was a challenge for him to put up with someone like Burl, someone who was always needling, always shooting off his mouth and daring you to do something about it.

"I been in on plans that'd make this one look like small potatoes," he said.

"Oh, yeah?"

"Yeah. Jobs you wouldn't know about less you read up on 'em in the papers," Harry said.

"Nothin' you ever done made the papers 'cept if you went an' exposed yerself on State and Madison." Donald Ray laughed. He grabbed for a bottle of Weidemann's on the table and tipped it home only to find that it was empty.

"Then probably nobody'd see nothin' anyway, especially no balls."

Harry snarled and looked away. He couldn't stand the droopy-eyed hillbilly any more than he could stand lice. So he shut up and folded his arms in front of him. He would do what he was told for the time being, but he wasn't going to like it or enjoy it. Donald Ray went into the bathroom and ran water into the sink. He wet a comb and began flicking it through his hair, first combing it back and around his ears, then combing wet slashes over his forehead. It glistened from the water and rivulets ran down his neck. He continued to comb it and shape it with his left hand, cocking his head to the left as he stared into the mirror.

Harry sat in the other room looking at the ceiling. The lines of pipes were like bars, parallel bars that reminded him of a lot of rooms he would have rather forgotten.

"I got to break out for a little while," Donald Ray said. "If you know what's good for a winehead, you'll stay around and play with yourself. You could even familiarize yerself with them plans on the papers there. You git to know them and you'll see what this job's all about."

With that he pulled open the door and slammed it behind him. Harry didn't move.

He sat on the folding chair against the glossy green wall for long minutes. He could wait out this kind of thing. Finally he got up and grabbed a magazine from the covers of Donald Ray's rollaway. It was a battered copy of *Playboy*, the foldout ripped through the staples and hanging loose. He set the magazine on his lap and pulled out his Copenhagen. With hardly a glance he swept a fingerful from the can and laid it inside his front lower lip. It bit and packed.

He paged through the *Playboy* for a while but it was little more than words and colors. He stared at the tits but didn't really pay much attention to them; he never really paid much attention to the magazine anyway except to stare at it if he found it in the trash or happened to thumb it on a rack in the liquor stores. After a few moments he tossed it back on the bed, exhaled and tried to clear the phlegm from his throat. He closed his eyes and in the midafternoon heat of the apartment drifted off.

He awakened with the slamming of the door.

"What you doin' here?" Barbie Dell said. She stood in front of him, still wearing her Woolworth's smock and chewing on a Snickers.

"Nothin'."

"I kin see that plain," she said.

She thumped her purse on the table and walked over to the refrigerator. With the door open and the light from inside shining dimly on her, she stood and scanned the unexciting contents.

"I swear they exist on beer around here," she said and turned away from it, letting the door swing slowly shut.

"Well, so how you hangin' loose, Grampa?" she said. Her voice was a twangy seesaw, her hair flying around her shoulders.

"Huh?"

"I *said*, what you doin'? Get it?"

"I'm settin' here."

"Yeah, that's groovy. Real groovy. Where's Donald Ray and Jimmy?"

She walked over to the bed and threw the sheets back, then sat down with one leg on the floor, the other pushed onto the bed and drawing her skirt tightly across her knees.

"Burl went out. Didn't say where so I din't ask him. Jimmy I don't know."

"Didn't say where so I didn't ask him," she parroted.

Harry exhaled and spat a speck of Copenhagen off his lip. He looked away and tried to ignore the girl. He didn't like hillbilly women any more than he liked hillbilly men. Most of them were snotty and lippy, like snakes that could talk.

"You know, you look like my Grampaw."

178

"Yup."

"You *do*. Like he was skinny 'cuz he had emphysema as long as I knowed him. He was like death warmed over. Always swallering and chewing even though there weren't nothin' in his mouth."

"What's that supposed to mean?"

"Well, look at you. Yer movin' yer lip like it had some sore on it or like you was suckin' a carmel or somethin'."

Harry felt the Copenhagen in his lip with his tongue, pushing into it and making a lump.

He didn't say anything, didn't really know what to say. Most women made him itchy, made him feel like he couldn't look them in the eye or carry on a normal conversation. So he wished silently that Barbie Dell, whoever she was and whatever she was doing here, would leave him alone.

She got up and walked over to the plastic gold-painted mirror on the wall. Her hands curled up in an oval as she played with the pins in her hair, and because of her position she pulled her white cotton blouse out of her skirt. Her waist was white, skin so smooth and spotless that Harry found himself staring at it.

She looked at him in the mirror.

"Yer in with them, ain't ya?"

He didn't reply.

"You don't have to tell me. I know yer hangin' around here 'cuz a what they're talkin' about doin'. I think it's crazy. I think it's just dumb to think yer gonna get away with somethin' like that. I told Donald Ray and Jimmy too, right to their faces. I said, 'That's the stupidest dumb plan I ever heared of.' But they don't care. Donald Ray thinks he's robbin' Fort Knox and it's gettin' worse in his head every day. Jimmy he just don't care. He'll do anything. I know that."

She stopped and bit into a bobby pin. She had pulled her hair into a hive over her head with just the longest strands falling down her back.

She turned with her hands still over her head. "What I'd

179

like to know is what yer doin' with it. Yer an old man. You shouldn't be out robbin' and stealin' where you could git killed or shot. You ever think about that?"

Harry rubbed his chin like a man contemplating a shave. "I'm not so old that I don't know what's goin' on. And maybe if you ever thought about it a little you'd know that maybe I was asked to come in."

"Not the way they talk you wasn't."

"Well, you better believe it," he said.

"Yeah, okay, but it still don't make no sense. I don't mean them. Them—they'd do anything. 'Cuz they're just wild like boys back down home that'll do anything if you rile 'em enough. Even Jimmy, he ain't like Donald Ray in a lot of things, but you'd think he was growed up in Kentucky the way he just jumps into anything. He's Italian, ya know, and them Italians I was always told were real secret about things. Like on television. But not him. He's just like some dumb hillbilly who carries a gun under his seat and drinks liquor. And he's Italian.

"But you. Well, that's somethin' else all over again. I mean it when I told ya you look like my Grampaw did. And he wouldn't catch hisself dead doin' something dumb and stupid like what they got planned. Really. I ain't kiddin' now."

"So whatta you care," Harry said.

She finished with her hair and brushed the strands off her blouse. Then she tucked it into her skirt, pulled up her panty hose, and went back to the refrigerator. She opened it and grabbed a beer.

"Look," she said. "I may not look so smart but then I ain't the dumbest thing around neither. I got a kid and a husband who I ain't seen or heard from for three years and I been back an' forth 'tween Georgia and Chicago eight times since I was eighteen. You don't go through all somethin' like that without knowin' somethin'."

"So why don't you know enough to be gettin' away from those two?" Harry said.

180

"That's just what I was gonna ask you," Barbie Dell said. She snapped the top off her can of Weidemann's and tossed it into the sink.

"Yeah, well I got my reasons," Harry said.

"Yeah, and Carter's got liver pills."

"Sure, okay."

"I mean, gee, who ain't got reasons? Who ain't got reasons just to dive off the Empire State Building. But yer an old man who could be my Grampaw and I bet you even got grandkids of yer own and all you kin say is 'I got my reasons.' So when you go to jail like Donald Ray and Jimmy been to a lotta times then you gonna say I still got my reasons?"

She was talking faster now, lippier, sitting on the bed with her legs pulled under her and her skirt hiked up to her crotch.

"I been in the can before."

"Yeah," she said. "I guess you have."

Then she looked at him. "You wanna beer?"

He shook his head. As soon as he did it he had second thoughts. He was going dry.

"Yer a nice-lookin' girlie," Harry said. "What's yer story about all this? I mean, if yer so smart about life and yer gonna be criticizing like this then why are ya sittin' there lookin' at me?"

"Ya know, yer right. Yer damn right for an old creep. You probably seen a lot in life like I have. I come from Commerford, Georgia, and that ain't even on the map. So I'm a hillbilly and big deal, everyone says. I'll tell ya my mother she's about forty now and she looks as old as you. I don't even know how old you are. But my momma see she's got brown lung. Yeah. They ain't nobody around who knows nothin' about that 'cept the people in Georgia who's got it. She works in them sewin' mills makin' sleeves and pockets for shirts. My aunt she worked in the Kotex factory and that was just as bad.

"Was both of them had to work eight or ten hours a day. Momma over them sewin' machines makin' them damn

181

sleeves and things. And the dust in them factories is brown from the material and it ain't got nowhere to go but in yer lungs. And all day it's like that. With no breaks or no lunch 'cuz my momma always said you was too worried about makin' the quota to take off.

"But that dust was just as thick as the coal-minin' dust and my momma's doctor said she was dyin' from it. Bet you didn't know that. Bet a lot of people don't, but I do. And when I see what my momma's dyin' for I know it's for nothin'.

"So the first thing she tells me back in Georgia was to get out and go where you could get a job somewhere away from them mills. So my cousin she went to Over the Rhine, that's in Cincinnati. Bet you didn't know that either. Nothin' but solid hillbillies. And they're chasin' rats worse an we got here. But Laura got me on workin' in a restaurant, which I didn't mind so much. And that's how I got my husband. Got him with the blue plate special, he always said. And I lost him just as fast. He wasn't worth the ring he gave me. Just a mean old boy who got in my pants a little too long.

"But that Terry taught me so much I threw it all away with another no-good ol' man that took me up here. Chicago was where the jobs was, he said, and I followed him even though I had Amy just a few months old. That's me for ya, just up and go and bye, bye, see ya later alligator.

"And ever since then it's been livin' in dumps like Clifton Street, where the rats just run around at night and the kids, I never seen anything like it up here, the kids are so mean and ugly they just break things, bottles, and things, and hang from the fire escapes, and get in all sorts of trouble. And to top it off here in Chicago I never been called so many names before. Like 'hillbilly' is all right if it comes from the right person, but I been called 'hillbilly' and 'hick' so many times by such as the officers of the police that I'm sick of it. And I kin get nasty when they call me names.

"Like the police here. They're awful. I seen a lot of rough ones down home that could flat out a boy with a club, but down there it was sort of a game. You know, you got what was comin' to ya when you got it and sometimes you got away with it. But up here they's all just mean and nasty even to the women. I seen a woman punched in the stomach up here in my neighborhood, yep, by cops while they were laughin'. I seen it."

She stopped and put her beer to her lips, then drank long, consecutive swallows as if it were soda pop.

"You sure jabber a lot," Harry said.

" 'Cuz I know a lot. Don't got no education but I know a lot. Workin' all yer life makes you a lot more smart than you ever were. I can take care of myself, that's one thing I know."

"So why you hangin' around? answer me that. I'll tell you something, if I was yer age I wouldn't be hangin' around here. No sir, you better believe it," he said.

"That's what I asked you in the first place. If I was your age I'd be eatin' cake and ice cream in some old-age home instead of out robbin' and stealin' like yer gonna do if you ain't doin' it now. Old man like you."

Harry shook his head and scraped a low rattle across his throat. He forgot for a moment that he had planned to ignore the girl, to let her talk on without him. "I ain't that old, for the first thing, girlie, and for the reason number two, I do pretty good at bein' a thief."

"Oh, yeah, I can see that. Like that's some fancy outfit yer wearin' and I sure like the shine on the Cadillac of yers out front," Barbie sassed.

"But I know what yer doin', I ain' that dumb," she went on. "If my pa was here he'd probably be volunteerin' to drive or some damn thing. Just 'cuz he ain't got nothin' better to do.

"And that's like me. I kin take 'em or leave 'em. Like that Jimmy. He makes me sick sometimes the way he orders me around. Maybe he treated his kind of women like that but he don't do that to me. But I still come around 'cuz I don't much care. They got beer and they're somebody to talk to. Even sit in a bar with on Friday night, and they keep a lot of creeps away that you wouldn't want to talk to on a deserted island someplace.

" 'Cuz I got a kid, ya see, and I got this shitty job at the five-and-dime store and I also got some dumb uncle who's usin' my place for a hotel. So I come around here to get away once in a while."

She stopped when she heard noise from outside, the sound of footsteps, and the two of them expected Donald Ray or Jimmy to walk in. But the steps passed. The room was silent once again.

"I'll tell ya, yer gonna get in trouble with them two. What's yer name, Harry or somethin'? Well, listen, Harry or somethin', you listen 'cuz yer gonna get in trouble like they're gonna. I seen it a thousand times and it's just a matter of a few days. God, the way Jimmy acts I'm surprised he ain't dead already. He says he been shot up, and I believe that. But up here in this neighborhood ain't hardly nobody who ain't been shot up or stabbed or something. You ever seen so many scars in yer life? Now look at you, you ain't got no scars. Unless you got 'em buried in yer wrinkles. I never thought of that.

"So I don't care what you wanna do. It's your party. I'm just glad I'm smart enough to know better. And I am. I can take it or leave it. Just once in a while I feel like I want someone to have a beer with or make a hamburger for. Just once in a while. Guess that's my only weakness."

"Yeah, that's good," Harry said. He decided not to listen to her. He tried to tell himself that she was a woman and like all the rest.

"I kin see yer all impressed," Barbie said.

Just then the door opened and Donald Ray walked in.

"Christ, if I'd knowed you was comin' I'd a baked ya a cake," he said.

"Who'd eat it?" Barbie Dell said.

"Good, the bitch is here," Donald Ray replied.

"That's me," she said.

Donald Ray looked over at Harry. "Hope you kept your hands to home bein' alone with Jimmy's woman, winehead. Don't want you two mixin' it up on my time."

He laughed and shot a sarcastic glance at Barbie Dell.

"Chuck you too, Farley," she said.

"Don't you wish," Donald Ray said. Then he disappeared into the bathroom.

13

He chose a Thursday night. By 1 A.M. the three of them were in the front seat of the red van driving west through Uptown over to Clark Street. Donald Ray drove this time, making certain that nothing went wrong. Over his shoulder, in the dark of the enclosed van, lay his arsenal of tools: the torches, crowbars, screwdrivers, chisels, hammers, picks, the heavy-duty drill, an extension cord, three flashlights. They were equipped to the teeth, Donald Ray's mind whirring and clicking, Jimmy quiet and moody, his head bobbing with the bouncing of the van, and Harry, keen-eyed, alert, the red skin of his eye sockets glistening, so excited that his blood pressure rocketed, his mouth parched.

Now he was ready to do it, Donald Ray thought, not just some half-baked moonshine of a plan like Art Burl would have thought up. Now, in the presence of equipment, the planning, the diagrams in his mind, now he was ready. As he drove, alert and a little jumpy from nerves and Dexamyls he'd popped for good measure, Donald Ray saw himself as a G-man leading his troops on a mission, a specialist, Mission Impossible. Im-fucking-possible, he thought, until I make it fucking possible. Yeah. And he wheeled the van through traffic.

Harry stared straight ahead, thinking about what they'd set up, seeing his role in it. He would concentrate and come

186

through this time, dependable, a trait you couldn't find much of nowadays, he would be so dependable they'd never plan another job without him. Those were good thoughts, painless visions. He tried not to think of the days that had just passed, the waiting time around Helen's flat when he was restless and edgy. He'd thrown away his paint brush but went out and bought another when he realized he had to finish the job or things would look suspicious. But he slept later and wore the laboratory coat less. He didn't feel so good, he told Helen, the stomach, the legs, anything, anything to shake the illusion within himself that he was some kind of handyman. He had a job going now, and he'd be damned if he would spend his time painting and fighting with a building that was older and more beat out than he was.

Two afternoons in a row he hopped a train down to Wrigley Field. As usual he sat in the middle of the centerfield bleachers, alone in a small opening in the stands if he could find one, savoring the sun and an occasional nip from the bottle of burgundy he'd tucked in his pants. The Cubs were miserable, in a tailspin that even Harry couldn't shake them out of. Durocher, that damn Durocher, and Harry stood up and cursed him every time Leo came out of the dugout, made furious changes and substitutions, but nothing worked. As the afternoons passed, the Cubs faded. Harry ran his wine over his tongue and between his teeth, sitting back and opening his shirt to expose his bony white chest to the September sun. It dawned on him, as he took a swig, that the Cubs fell further and further behind as his bottle became more and more empty. If he gave up wine, he joked, maybe they'd win. But he'd try other things first.

Late in the game his vendor hit him, but Harry brushed him off.

"But you're lettin' me down!" the vendor complained.

"Yeah, yeah, I'm busy," Harry said.

"You lookin' real busy sittin' there," the vendor said turning his back. "And meanwhile I ain't sellin' but peanuts."

187

"Yeah, peanuts, hit me on some peanuts," Harry yelled.

"Ain't got none," the vendor shot back and went on down below.

"Whoever heard of a peanut man wit' no peanuts," Harry laughed.

Later he strolled home, gamboling down Sheffield Avenue without a care, no longer concerned about the cops or the detectives who just a short time ago were a nightmare for him. He was untouchable now, though later, in the grips of sobriety, he cursed himself for being stupid and lackadaisical, that this was the worst time to let up, in the down period before a job he should keep low, stay low, and wait. So he grabbed his lab coat and found jobs in the deepest, darkest corners of the building, working at them to pass the time.

Now, as he rode with his two accomplices, shotgun in a vehicle that was loaded with more tools than he'd seen in one place for a single job, he tried to shove those thoughts out of his mind. He didn't care that Helen had begun to look at him in different ways, in that relentless, knowing way that seemed to sear right through him. He tried to look away and dodge her when he thought that she might be onto his new bit, that the front he had put on since he'd arrived—working and eating and sleeping like a responsible human being— that that facade had been shattered. He thought of getting his old room back, of getting out of her hair and out from the line of fire of her Polish anger, her I-told-you-so's, her flaming questions which pinned him and marked him and splayed him as if he were a guilty husband with lipstick on his neck and cheap perfume mixing with the beer on his collar.

Yet, during the past few days, since he'd been clued in on the plan, not a word had passed between them. She never accused him or threatened him, never scolded or attacked. But those stares, those glances that could raise goose pimples on his arms, gave him the unmistakable impression that she knew, that she was onto him, that his face, his actions, his attitude were an open book. Then he scowled and ignored it, gave excuses and tried to shove it out of his mind. Like now, in the truck, pulling into an alley, he decided that he was once again Harry Lum, thief, and the rest of the shit was out of the picture. Helen was just an old bag who didn't mean anything to him.

The building before them was a century-old brick two-story, one of many that had been remodeled or given a face lift to conform to the twentieth century and its new tenants. The wide bay windows that had once been in front were now bricked in and replaced with small windows eight feet above the sidewalk. The new panes were shatterproof and lined with an alarm system's electronic tape. The van parked in the rear, next to the one-story addition that extended almost to the alley. In seconds Jimmy was standing on top of the van and screwing out the building's outdoor floodlights. He used his hanky, quickly, and the side of the building suddenly went dark. He then motioned to Donald Ray and made his way over to the alarm box on the side near the roof. It had been installed there like a school bell, seemingly out of reach and invulnerable until Jimmy snipped the wires leading to it. He was quick again, with his dark hair and olive complexion, his black and purple shirt, a shadow against the dark sky.

As Jimmy moved, Donald Ray and Harry separated, Harry to the alley as a lookout, Donald Ray into the rear of the van, where he readied the tools they needed to jimmy the back door. Donald Ray looked up momentarily when he heard Jimmy thump down on the van's roof, waited a second, then moved toward the back doors when he saw them open. Jimmy stood in the alley, his head moving from side to side in search of anyone or anything. Harry was doing the same on the other side of the building, ready to hustle them all back into the van if a car came, a midnight drifter out for a stroll, or a yapping dog. At the first sign of an intruder, he would close the doors, and wait things out, hoping the van would look like nothing but a company vehicle parked and locked outside.

In moments Donald Ray and Jimmy were working on the door, Donald Ray with the huge crowbar they'd swiped from the boiler outfit, Jimmy with a small, sharper bar. It was also a metal door, but with a tougher lock than the one they'd snapped the other night. They pried and grunted until the door began to give, the frame crumpling from the pressure. Soon they had opened a gaping seam, the lock still holding but with less and less resistance, until Donald Ray finally leaned back, hissed and put his weight into the bar, using his foot, and muscling for all the leverage he could get, when the door gave, freeing the lock and allowing Jimmy to pull the door open.

Donald Ray stood huffing and sweating, the crowbar heavy in his hands. Jimmy instinctively looked up at the alarm mechanism on the door. He heard it click when he pulled the door open, and though it wasn't necessary, he pulled a pair of wire clippers from his back pocket and snipped the connection. Donald Ray followed him inside, but not before he'd snapped his fingers at Harry to call him over to his new lookout position. Harry hustled over, looking into Donald Ray's face and seeing only concentration, the three of them not having exchanged a word since they'd arrived.

Harry stood by the door and waited, watching, listening. He'd objected to this. He'd complained to Donald Ray that he wasn't no damn watchdog, that Donald Ray could hire some kid to do that. But Donald Ray insisted, pacifying Harry with the promise to call him in for help if they couldn't get inside the offices. Harry felt quite confident that that would be the case, because, apart from brute strength, he didn't think Donald Ray or Jimmy had the brains to get inside a medicine cabinet.

Jimmy and Donald Ray paused and caught themselves once inside the building. It was pitch black inside, no night light, no windows. Jimmy clicked on his flashlight, then the two of them made their way toward the front. They went around a delivery van, a truck like their own but newer, then around a stack of cartons, some barrels, a commercial trash container. Their footsteps echoed through the building, light scrapes against the concrete. Jimmy kept the flashlight beam low and trained on the cement ahead of them. For all his faults, his temper, his bitchiness, his wandering attention span, once inside a building in the dead of night, Jimmy Del Corso was silently efficient. He made no mistakes, seemingly thriving on the stale air and the crackling tension of a burglary. Donald Ray, on the other hand, was nervous and clumsy, anxious to get things over with, to remember the details and get past the problems. He was on Jimmy's heels now, biting his lip in anticipation of what lay ahead.

When they reached the wall where the garage met the main building, Jimmy shone his light slowly across the cinder blocks in search of the door. A four-step stairs went up to a small loading-dock area, but his light, the circle of yellow in the blackness, found nothing more—no door—no matter how hard he looked, how many times he shone the light back and forth. The two of them stood there, dumbfounded, momentarily stunned by what they hadn't found.

"What in hell—!" Donald Ray snapped. He grabbed the light and flashed it impatiently across the wall.

"I don't believe this shit," Jimmy said.

Donald Ray spotted a side door, but it led out to a walkway which led out to Clark Street. At the loading dock—and he trained his light to make sure—he could make out an outline of new bricks forming the lines of a doorway. What was once the entrance to the main building was now a wall of brick, flat, uncompromising brick. They had broken into nothing more than a garage, a storage area, not what Donald Ray had thought was the rear section of the main offices. He stood there realizing his error, feeling the teeth in his mouth.

"This goddamn shack is just settin' here!" Donald Ray

191

wailed. "They went and cut it off from the inside!"

"You sure you made this place?" Jimmy snapped.

"Fuck right I did," answered Donald Ray. "But I weren't never inside back here."

"Shit. What the hell we gonna do?" Jimmy growled.

"We're gettin' in there if we got to blow the damn place up."

Donald Ray turned and went back toward the van, taking the light with him, leaving Jimmy in the darkness. He got to the door and Harry whipped around, looking for some sign, something. The two of them then saw the headlights of a car against a building across the alley. They dove to the pavement and scrambled toward the front of the van. Crouching, breathing hard, hoping on hopes that it wasn't a squad car making rounds, they watched and waited as the lights approached, the sound of tires against the brick of the alley. But it was just a car, a single unspectacular car that continued on through the alley and across a side street into the next alley.

Donald Ray got up and went into the van. He grabbed a chisel and a couple of hammers.

"Hey, thought this was a torch job," Harry whispered.

"Ain't no more," Donald Ray said. "Got a goddamn wall to get through."

Disobeying the plan, Harry followed Donald Ray back into the garage. This was bad, he thought, this kind of thing was all wrong for what they had worked out. You couldn't punch your way into a place like this. But he thought it instead of saying it, and shortly Donald Ray was on his knees with a hammer and chisel. He delivered a solid whack to the head of it, the sound thundered though the garage, then he hit it again.

"No!" Harry objected. He slapped his hand heavily on Donald Ray's shoulder. "Don't do it. This ain't no good. Let's beat it."

Donald Ray snapped his head up. "Get back outside, winehead, fore I bust ya one!"

192

He turned and smashed the chisel again, driving it into the mortar joint. He nodded angrily at Jimmy and Jimmy picked up a chisel and began working away. Harry retreated through the darkness, grumbling and cursing and shaking his head in dread. The ringing blows of the two hammers were deafening, shattering the calm of the garage, bringing visions of swift judgment to Harry's mind. He scrambled for the door, feeling his way from the slight amount of light let in through the doorway. Once outside he closed it roughly against the frame, shutting the sound within the garage. He leaned against the outside wall, again feeling his own heart-beat, his breathing, knowing that the job was botched this way, but aware that he couldn't hear much of the pounding from where he stood. But he didn't like it, knew the vibrations would carry, sound: brazen, foreign sound in the night. He knew it alone was the greatest enemy of the burglar. And Jimmy and Donald Ray, the idiots, were courting the enemy at its worst.

It seemed like hours that he stood there waiting, watching the ends of the alley, the dark windows of second-floor apartments. But nothing stirred. He heard only the monotonous thumping of the hammers inside, like painful jabs, and he ached trying to silence them. Yaras and Caputo wouldn't have done it this way, he thought; they would have regrouped and taken off. A broken plan was no plan at all, they always said, and Donald Ray's plan was to cut through the doors with his torches, quietly and quickly, without sound or distraction, until they were picking among the offices, propositioning the safe. Now the two of them were clobbering chisels for all they're worth, ringing through the night, and Harry, his nerves frayed like the ends of a flag, could hardly stand it.

After a few more minutes Harry crept back inside. He stumbled hurriedly toward the noise and the faint trace of light. When he got to it he couldn't believe his eyes. In back of Donald Ray was a pile of bricks at least two foot tall, and a hole in the wall the size of a crawl space.

"Fuckin' A—!" Jimmy said, poking his head near the opening. He shone the light at it so Donald Ray could take a look.

"This place is some goddamn fort!" Donald Ray said.

Harry realized suddenly what they were talking about. After going through a double layer of brick, one complete outside and one inner wall, they had hit yet another wall of cinder block. It stared back at them like the wall of a safe.

"We must be tappin' right into the supply vault," Donald Ray said. "They must a set it up like that. Otherwise they'd have a door goin' out to this damn place."

Nobody answered him. Jimmy was dragging on the ground from exhaustion. Donald Ray himself was drenched in sweat. They had battered through the wall like miners, and now they felt the pains, the third wall still to get through, and bigger and thicker.

"I can't hit this fuckin' thing no more," Jimmy said.

"C'mon, pansy ass," Donald Ray complained. And he reached inside and took a roundhouse swing at his chisel. But the angle of the tool, his exhaustion, and the force with which he swung made him miss the mark, and he drove the hammer into the back of his hand in a glancing, excruciating blow. He dropped the chisel and snapped the hand to his face; it quivered and shook in front of him, some of the skin broken and beginning to purple.

"Jeee-sus!" he breathed, clenching his teeth and sucking in his breath. The pain suddenly overcame the shock, the numbing instant of the blow. He stumbled backward and sat down on the concrete, squeezing his fist and cursing, fighting the pain, the burn, the anger of it all.

"Oh, Jeee-sus damn, geez, my God, fuckin—" he stuttered. His lips quivered.

For a moment the three of them were stunned and silent, frustrated like children, feeling the despair of a job that was now floundering and reeling out of control. They were shaken out of it, unexpectedly enough, by Jimmy, who suddenly bent down to the hole and began piling up bricks in front of it.

"Got a way that's gonna be quicker than anything," he growled. He stacked the bricks in a straight pile, flush against the inner wall and leading out into the garage.

"What the fuck—?!" Donald Ray spat.

"Seen it in the movies. We're gonna bust our way into the joint," Jimmy said. "Hey, Lum, check for keys in the truck there."

Harry did as he was told, reaching inside the company's van and locating the dangling key ring.

"Yup," he said.

Then Jimmy got up, clapping the dust off his hands, and got into the front seat. He started the van, revving the motor so that it thundered within the expanse of the garage, then shifted it with a chinking sound into first gear. He eased it forward to the pile of bricks, left it idling and hopped out to take a look at the bumper.

"All right. Good as shit. Now here's your chance, gramps," Jimmy said. He suddenly assumed an air of command, an authority he lacked when Donald Ray was bitching and going red in the ears. "Jam it in gear and ram the fuck out of the pile. We'll shove the bastards into the next county if we got to."

Harry winced in surprise at Jimmy's order. He couldn't believe what he'd heard.

"C'mon!" Jimmy yelled and jerked Harry's arm toward the van.

Harry stumbled and tried to object, but in the blur of what was happening, the rumbling of the van's engine, the dust, the darkness, and the adrenalin of a job in the night, he didn't think past what he had been told. Suddenly he was sliding into the front seat of the truck, fumbling for the gear shift.

He didn't see Donald Ray, holding his fist to his cheek, hurry toward the rear door of the building and take up the lookout post. He only saw the slow-motion hand signal of

195

Jimmy, raised above his head and waving, then a swift wave, and Harry tromped down on the gas pedal. The van lurched ahead, bashing into the bricks, jolting at the impact and sending Harry over the steering wheel. It crushed against his gut, and stopped his forehead a hair away from the windshield. The motor stalled. Jimmy bent down and stood up again, nodding his head up and down, giving the signal for Harry to do it again.

"Take it easy, fuckhead!" he yelled. Harry barely heard him. He was still stunned by the collision, the noise of the gunning motor, the roar, and the deafening crunch of the bumper. He couldn't see that the bumper of the van had been smashed into the frame, but had driven the bricks into the hole and cracked the mortar of the inner wall. He could only concentrate on doing it again. Suddenly he had the van running, in reverse then in first gear.

Wham! It exploded against the wall like a thunderclap; the stars, the lightning bugs swarmed in Harry's skull. Jimmy's hand kept on waving, urging him on. The van was suddenly moving again, again heading toward the flat face of the brick as if it were the open road. Harry could see nothing else. He tromped his foot against the pedal, worked the shift, leaned on the steering wheel.

He followed one blast with another, shifting the truck as fast as he could, ramming the wall like a piston. The garage shook with the impact, vibrated with the sound and the crunch of brick and mortar, the dust swirling, Jimmy yelling. In moments it was a giant, uncontrollable battering ram, the squealing tires on cement, the smell of burning rubber, the grind of the transmission, the smack of steel on concrete. Harry drove it, aimed it, punished it, now lost in the flurry of what he was doing, unaware of where he was or what was accounting for the explosions in his head, the jarring of his nerves.

The truck continued to ram the wall, crumbling the bricks,

Jimmy watching but giving no sign of whether or not they were getting through or simply shaking the foundation to its base. And finally Harry didn't see Jimmy at all, didn't see anything. He was lost in the sound and the crunching motion. He didn't see Donald Ray motioning furiously from the back of the garage, he didn't realize that Donald Ray had seen lights flick on in apartments all around the alley. He didn't even see Jimmy slide by the side of the van and sprint across the garage toward Donald Ray.

With Harry busting the van furiously against the wall, shaking the building until it shook the very ground they stood on, Jimmy and Donald Ray emerged from the garage only to see a pair of headlights cut into the nearest side street. They both dove beneath their own van when the headlights flashed into the alley, heard the squeal of tires and the skipping of stones, and knew the cops were descending.

The cruiser jerked to a halt in front of them, idling at an angle to the rear entrance of the garage. The two officers emerged, one with his gun drawn, the other madly tugging at his leather holster. They ran into the dark hole of the open rear door, toward the crashing, jolting, unceasing sounds inside. Jimmy and Donald Ray could smell the polish on the cops' shoes, see their faces in the lineup.

"Run for it!" Donald Ray said, and the two of them struggled from under the van like moles, Donald Ray forgetting the pain in his hand, and in seconds they bolted across the alley and over a fence separating the adjoining yard. Their tails weren't out of sight a second before another cruiser cut a swath of light in the alley, its engine groaning, the thumping, throbbing garage now under siege.

They came at Harry from two directions, edging along the sides of the garage, feeling their way with one hand, the other outstretched and pointing revolvers at the front windows of the van. The only light came from the flashlights which had been dropped to the floor and were shooting beams of white ice up the side of the brick. The van's head-lights were smashed out, lost in the dust and the swirl and the deafening noise.

Suddenly the cop on the left side of the building reached the van, crept closer, his movement a silent film of stealth, lost in the sound of the truck, the van that Harry was now a part of, going through the motions; reverse, brake, shift, first, gas, slam!; reverse, brake, shift, first, gas, slam!; reverse. The cop leveled his gun at the window, twelve inches from Harry's left ear.

Harry saw it, the blue-gray barrel, the hole, frightening him beyond belief, freezing his sense once again, and he fell against the steering wheel, the van lurching into gear and stalling.

Then all was silent, silent in the falling dust and the echo, the running footsteps of patrolmen coming up from the rear. A beam of a flashlight illumined Harry as he lay across the wheel, half-conscious, trying to fight through the haze and the gray and the ghosts in his head, realizing that it was suddenly over. He didn't move. He shut his eyes like a child and uttered a low, inaudible groan.

The front of the company's van was smashed from the collisions, twisted and beaten in, the bumper bent into the grille. One of the cops ran his flashlight over the pile of bricks, a pile of rubble and broken stone. He bent down and looked into the hole. The inner wall had been broken through, pushing cinder block into the office on the other side and toppling a heavy steel cabinet. Papers and office equipment were strewn everywhere.

More cops came up from behind, all with flashlights, the garage suddenly a sea of jagged light and jabbering.

One of the two original officers at the scene straightened up after looking at the hole and jammed his revolver back into its holster. "Do you believe this!?" he said to nobody in particular. He kicked a chisel.

His partner opened the door on Harry's side and pulled

198

him out of the front seat. Harry stumbled against the cop and stood like a drunk against the van. Outside of the click of the cuffs and the bite of the steel into his wrists as they were pinned behind his back, he felt nothing.

The cackle of police radios rasped through the air, the hum of idling engines, more uniforms. Harry was pushed through it, his head down and bobbing against his collarbone, shoved toward a paddy wagon. The door shut on him like a lid on a coffin, closing him in once again, in blackness and solitude. He became one with the bare metal bench he was sitting on.

Inside the garage a half-dozen cops inspected the hole in the wall.

"Woke up every damn neighbor on the block," a patrolman said.

"It's class. These jagoffs just don't got it no more. Look at this."

A sergeant, crooking his neck and talking into his shoulder radio, joined the crowd. He coughed at the dust. Suddenly someone tripped a light and the entire garage was illuminated. It showed the extent of the destruction, like a collision on the freeway, a twisted truck caught in a rock slide.

"Jesus," said the sergeant. "Now I seen everything."

14

McMahon looked across his desk from the cradle of his hands, his elbows propped on the paperwork in front of him. He looked but said nothing. It was after 4 A.M. in the Damen Avenue station, the forlorn time when the office lights burned brightly but only a trickle of detectives came and went. But now McMahon was cutting through the hum of the lights and the weight of his own tiredness and concentrating on the thin frame that sat hunched over in the chair beside his desk.

"So, Harry," he said slowly. He could faintly hear the clacking of the typewriters from the floor below, where the burglary dicks were completing their reports on the episode they had just interrupted. "So whattaya think, huh?"

Harry sat in the middle of the wooden chair, his head down, his hands cuffed and lying harmlessly across his lap.

"It wasn't but a couple of weeks ago that you were here in this room. Right here. And the officer in charge told me the story, laid it all out for me." McMahon dropped his hand from his cheek and reached for a burning cigarette. He blew the smoke sideways out of his mouth.

"So I think to myself that there's got to be a lot more to the thing than what's on the surface. I see a guy like yourself and I figure a few things that might make sense. Now correct me if I'm wrong here, Harry. I think here's a guy who is down on his ass but maybe not out. Here's a guy who knows this town, from the old neighborhood. I respect that. I grew up in the same thing and I understand. So I think maybe here's a guy that could be my uncle if I was Polish, or a guy that could a been a fella on the block, or maybe someone running the precinct."

He paused, his speech soft and moderated, like a counselor or a preacher in the privacy of his chambers.

"And I look at your sheet and you got a lot of strikes. So who ain't? So maybe you've hit hard times that nobody but yourself knows about. It says that you're fifty-seven years old, which strikes me as a nice age if you're comfortable and a pretty rotten one if you're not.

"But then I add up all these things and a lot of others and the one point that sticks out is that I get the feeling that in spite of a lot of things you're not dumb. A guy can't knock around the old neighborhood and make his living around town and not learn a few things along the way. So maybe it ain't enough to qualify you for a Ph.D., but then there's a lot of knowledge not in the books. I know that too, Harry."

He stopped once again but Harry did not stir. He made no effort to lift his head or look into McMahon's face. His spine curved in the chair like a spoon. They had taken him in the wagon quietly and unceremoniously to the Damen Avenue station. He'd been led through the parking lot, up the steps, then formally booked into the arrest ledger. He had answered the questions with a low mumbling, hardly enough to be heard, once trying to lift his hand and show the desk sergeant the name marked across his fist. When the sergeant had asked if he wanted to make a phone call he shrugged, thought for a second about Helen or maybe the sheeny lawyer he used to know, but then he shook his head and waited for the detectives to take him up the stairs. His mind had been a blank of resignation, he thought of nothing, saw and heard only what went on before his nose. He was an automaton who would do, as he had done so many times before in his life, what he was told.

"So I talk to you and all those things fall in place for me in my mind," McMahon went on. "But most of all, you tell me that you can help me with a murder. You can help me do my job. So we talk and we work out something. No big deal or nothing, but something that you and I can handle. I respect you and you respect me, I know that, or so that's what I was telling myself.

"You know, for all the shit that you read or that you see on television, this business ain't that special. We don't go around making big deals. We don't go around bargaining and playing like bookies to get our pinches. We talk to people like I talked to you and we made an arrangement, no big deal, just an arrangement between us that we can handle. You got out of the car and I decided to sit tight and wait. I've always got things to do and I can wait."

McMahon lifted his elbows off the desk and reclined in his chair. The metal squeaked, he swiveled and looked sideways at Harry.

"So tell me where we went wrong."

Harry had heard him, though he didn't lift his head. He knew what the murder cop wanted. He didn't care anymore. He'd tell everything he knew. The cuffs were on his wrists; they might just as well have been around his neck.

"Yeah," he said, then asked for a cigarette. McMahon placed it in Harry's lips and lit it. Harry dragged then lifted his hands in front of his face, his fingers fanning out from the cuffs like a bouquet, and replaced the cigarette in the side of his mouth. With it dangling precariously as he talked, inhaling and exhaling the smoke with no regard for the ashes which fell like snow on his pants, he began to tell about green-haired Leo. He didn't leave out a detail.

McMahon listened then pushed away from his desk. "Who put you up to the first job?"

"Guy named Burl and this kid Del Corso."

McMahon's eyes lifted slightly at the names. He recalled the sight of the sullen, dark-eyed punk who had sat in the chair Harry was now in.

"So whattaya know about these two?"

Harry looked up at the homicide detective for the first time.

"Nothin.' They're just thieves like me," he said. Then he told McMahon the details of the first job, releasing the information as if it were a relief to tell it, to let someone else in the world know what they had done to him. He didn't think about the consequences, whether or not McMahon would use what he was saying against him, whether it would put him in jail. He only knew that he was going to get Burl and Del Corso. He'd had it with them, and he felt no responsibility to live up to any phony code of honor. The facts behind the supply-house job came pouring out, where they got the tools, how they set it up, what they were after. Harry left nothing out, nothing that he knew or that he had been told. And, strangely enough, it felt good, if just for an instant, that he could nail the bastards for what they'd done to him. Even if he'd never told a cop this much info in his life, Harry was doing it now, with a cigarette, in handcuffs, in the middle of the night, shortly before he would be led off to a cell.

McMahon listened to every word. He was aware that Harry was spilling his guts, that he had been pushed to the limit. And, from being a cop as long as he had been, he knew this was a prime time, a chance to milk another set of eyes and ears for all they were worth.

"So who killed the Puerto Rican girl? Del Corso? He do it?"

"Ahhh, I dunno," Harry groused. "He's a punk. Always fightin' and shootin' off his mouth. He could do anything and probably done it. But they ain't never said nothing about it while I was with 'em."

"So I'm right back where I started, right, Harry?"

"If you say so."

"Well, I went out on a string because I got to solve a murder. You go back on the street and come back here tonight with cuffs and a new pinch and still I'm left with a fart in a hailstorm. No closer, no farther away than when I started," McMahon said.

Harry shrugged his shoulders. His cigarette was burning into his fingers.

"At least tell me something. Who'd those two hang in with? What broads? Something."

Harry shook his head, stared at the floor.

"What'd they do with their stuff? How about a fence?"

"Yeah, I can tell ya that."

"Well?"

"Burl had some guy, some car salesman on Western by the cemetery. He set up this job."

"Who? You got a name?"

"Naw."

"Okay. What else?"

"Del Corso, I ain't sure. He talked about some hotel guy."

"Yeah?"

"Some guy workin' nights in a hotel. That's what he talked about. I ain't got no name on that either."

"That it?"

"Yup."

There was silence between the two of them, long moments. It was an amiable impasse. McMahon clicked the connections in his mind and scoured his memory for the sights, the people he could fit behind what Harry had just told him. Harry sat with his head down. He dropped the cigarette to the tile floor, where it burned itself out.

"You know you'll probably go up for this one," McMahon finally said.

Harry didn't respond.

"You got anyone to bat for ya? Anyone to at least go bail?"

Harry looked up and for a moment was jarred from his funk. He considered the possibilities.

204

"Let me at least make a phone call for ya," McMahon said.

"Suit yourself," Harry said.

For twenty minutes they'd scrambled like rabbits through the alleys and the backyards. Ducking behind bushes and watching for headlights, the squeal of tires that meant a cruiser, they ran uncertain of whether or not they had been seen or if Harry Lum would talk. A thousand things had blown up in their faces but they thought only of escaping with their skins. They finally angled over toward Foster Avenue and were relieved to see the light and relative activity of the main street. In the neighborhoods and side streets they would attract attention for merely being there at three o'-clock in the morning. On Foster, they could walk and catch their breath and try to look like they had no secrets. They finally found a twenty-four-hour laundromat and waited there until a bus came. By paying forty cents each they were delivered from the scene and deposited back in Uptown.

Donald Ray thought immediately about the possibility of tracing the van. With a good investigation it could lead the cops right to him. And the tools and torches inside would be linked with the boiler-company burglary. It was a bum situation, a hole that Donald Ray had dug around himself. He thought about it and cursed the fact as he sat in the seat of the empty bus. Jimmy beside him kept rubbing his mouth; he smelled of perspiration. Suddenly Donald Ray's hand began to throb, the hand he had clobbered with the sledgehammer. He raised it and saw that it was becoming purple and swollen. He'd broken a bone, on top of the whole mess, a plan blown to bits, two separate raps hanging over his head, on top of all that, he'd broken his fucking hand.

From the bus they walked over to the one place that they could safely stay: Barbie Dell's. She was the only person in the world who could deliver them, the only person the police and God himself didn't have a lead on. Jimmy leaned on her doorbell, then punched it in a cadence, on again, off again.

205

"C'mon, bitch," Jimmy growled and punched the buzzer.

Finally a light went on on the third floor and Barbie Dell's head poked out of the window.

"Who in hell's down there?!" she screamed. She was leaning sideways, her hair in curlers, Amy Joy yelping on her hip.

"Open up! It's us," Jimmy yelled.

They heard the window slam shut, then a few minutes later the door to the front foyer opened and Barbie stepped down. She had on a bathrobe, open in front and offering a clean view of her white skin, her black panties.

"Damnit! What's goin' on!" she sputtered. "Get me outta bed an' wake up the child. C'mon, Jimmy, you tell me."

Her high-pitched voice whined through the hallway. Jimmy stepped in front of her and went for the stairway. Donald Ray waited and followed Barbie Dell up the stairs.

"We ran into some trouble. We got to stay here tonight until we can figure things out," Jimmy said.

"God! Lookit yer hand!" Barbie said to Donald Ray. "You got to get that doctored. It's awful!"

"Yer damn right," Donald Ray muttered.

The three of them trudged up the steps and went into the apartment, where Amy Joy was sitting on the living room floor. She had stopped crying and was playing with a fork and a tin of a leftover pot pie.

"Someone tell me what in hell this is all about. Why in tarnation I got to get up in the middle of the night for you two? C'mon, Jimmy!"

Barbie stood in the middle of the room with her hands on her hips. She was unconcerned about her open housecoat, or the tangle of her hair. Donald Ray looked at her, then he thought to himself that she was getting fat. Just like a lot of hillbilly women who drop a kid, then drop their tits, their gut, their ass.

Jimmy ignored her and walked straight for the bathroom. His disappearance was followed by the sound of rushing water, the flush of the toilet.

206

"We ran into a whole shitload of bad luck tonight," Donald Ray said.

"You stealin' again?"

"Tryin' to," Donald Ray answered. He tried to clench his bad fist but couldn't. The pain shot into his wrist and up his arm. "Lately we can't seem to boost a candy bar from Walgreen's."

"Put you in jail if you keep tryin'."

"They gotta catch me first."

He sat down on Uncle Herbert's couch, vacant for the past two nights because Uncle Herbert hadn't been heard from. One of his tee-shirts lay wadded between the cushions. Donald Ray spread his knees and sat forward examining his wounded mitt, gingerly squeezing it with his good hand. Barbie Dell knelt before him and pulled his good hand away. She took the wrist of his other hand and turned it to the light.

"Oh, gee whiz, it's really awful!" she said.

"Yer tellin' me."

"How'd ya git it?"

"Hit it with a hammer."

"A hammer?" she squealed. "What you doin' with a hammer?"

"It's a long story you don't want to know about."

"Sounds stupid."

"Why don't you just shut up and do something useful? Get me a beer if you got one."

"I ain't." She rocked back on her knees and put her hands on her hips. "That all you can think about is beer when yer hand is achin' like that?"

"Damn thing could be sliced clean off and I'd still need a beer."

She got up and went into the kitchen.

In the light and the quiet of the room Donald Ray looked over to where Barbie Dell's kid was sitting. The child looked up and laughed, gurgled, then threw the pie tin in the air.

"Here," Barbie Dell said when she returned.

"What the hell is that?"

"Tomato juice. All I got 'cept water."

Donald Ray scowled, then took the glass, raised his bad hand from his shirt pocket then stopped. He exhaled and wedged the glass of juice between his knees and with his good hand dug a small packet out of his pocket. He popped a red.

"Oh, I see now," said Barbie Dell, her face a washed-out blanket of exhaustion and impatience.

Donald Ray leaned back and closed his eyes, eyes itchy and wide, waiting for the red to seep through his blood and his brain and take him down. He didn't want to think or bitch or run through the catastrophe of the night. He just wanted to go under and lose himself in the only way he really felt comfortable. If he were lucky, if it hit, his head would be submerged and he would drift under. He felt Barbie Dell's hand on his thigh. Opening his eyes just enough to see the angle of her form, he saw her lift his hand and poke it gently. He grunted.

"I think you broke a bone. It's blue, Donald Ray," she said.

"Still be there in the morning. Fuck it," he said. He closed his eyes and felt for the blackness.

Soon she was winding a white gauze wrapping around the fist. The pain shot pins up the arm.

"Shit."

"Shut up."

He sat up and bit into his lip. If a bone was broken he was feeling it now. Barbie Dell's fingers gripped the hand like a vise. The gauze tightened the area, increased the pain. It brought Donald Ray awake again, but he resisted his urge to stop her. Instead he reached over with his good hand and snaked it inside her robe. He quickly found a hanging, warm breast and felt for the nipple.

"Oh, you sonofabitch!" Barbie Dell said and pulled her shoulder back.

Donald Ray grinned and stared at her, looking right into

her eyes, her wide, fiery Appalachian eyes, her down-home hill eyes. She stared back and ran her tongue quickly over her mouth, then smoothed her hair, trying to do something with her hands but hit him.

"I don't know why I pay attention to you, you shithead," she snapped.

Donald Ray kept his smile plastered across his face, a smile oiled with the sludge that was now in his blood, the chemical starting to take hold.

"Yer just awful, and I don't know why I even let you in here." She pulled her robe belt tight and got up on her feet, still looking at him.

"With Jimmy in the next room in my bed and my child right there in front of you," she said.

Donald Ray leaned back once again. He eyed Amy Joy on the floor. "The kid don't mind. She likes me," he said. "Come on over here, ya little piss pants."

Then his eyes closed slowly but solidly, his smile lazed off into a chin that drooped then dropped.

Barbie Dell went over and with one arm swooped up Amy Joy. She went into the kitchen and clanked around long enough to fill up a bottle with tomato juice, stick it in Amy Joy's mouth, and then deposit the kid in her crib. Seconds later the springs of her bed creaked, and Barbie slid, nude to her panties, next to Jimmy, who was snoring, immovable, out cold.

Donald Ray kicked a foot out before him and conked out sitting back on the couch. His foot flopped on its side and hit the half-filled juice glass. A blood-red river wound its way over the linoleum toward the living-room rug.

About ten minutes passed before the doorway to Barbie Dell's bedroom was lightened by her white form, her cream-colored, panty-striped body as it padded across the floor toward the couch. She took Donald Ray's shoulders and pushed them until he fell onto the couch, his head hitting Uncle Herbert's makeshift pillow. Then she lifted his knees, his feet, and stretched him out the length of the sofa. He was jarred into semi-consciousness.

"What you doin'?" he mumbled, the words catching on his lips. He had no idea what or who it was, or where he was.

Then he felt the sensations running up his chest, a spider, a hand, a handful of fingernails crawling crazily up his chest, his chest now shirtless and exposed, his hair being nipped and caught in the nails. He opened his eyes as far as he could, if only a slight crack, and realized that Barbie Dell was lying next to him, half on top of him, one leg entwined around his, her crotch molded around his hip. He tried to respond, to orient himself, then he jumped at the sudden pain on his neck, a pain intense but short, then tickling, then exciting, and realized she had bit him.

"What you doin'?"

Then he got his right arm free, the arm with his good hand, and felt the hollow of her back, the sloping valley terraced with light cat hair, her butt bone, the elastic of her panties. Then she was out of his hold and on top of him, high, straddling him like a kid winning a wrestling match, and he suddenly lost himself in the soft, crashing flesh of her breasts as she bent over him and ran them over his face. He opened his mouth and tried to nip them, to suck the nipples, but she wouldn't pause long enough for him to do anything but be the shore for the waves, and he reached forward and cupped his hand beneath the soft, moist, exuding slope of her crotch.

He thought he heard her moan, then thought it might have been himself, and suddenly he was lost in what she was doing to him, squatting between his legs and pulling out everything he owned beneath his shorts.

"What you doin'?" he repeated, this time pushing it, groaning it.

"Shut up," she said, the words shooting up his belly.

He jumped at her touch, her tongue, and his left hand impulsively jumped from his side and hit the side of the couch. The broken bone, the swollen, simmering flesh exploded in pain, opened his eyes into saucers and sent out a gasp from his throat. But it was a gasp mingled in the pleasure of what was going on below, with increasing tempo and unrelieved sensation, a caressing and laving so intense, so wonderful that it smothered the pain, smothered the glaze of the chemicals in his blood, and awakened him to the reality of the room and himself to where he wanted to reach out and kick out and clutch in pain or joy, suffering and ecstasy. He didn't know which.

For long minutes he sat there in front of McMahon's desk, sitting with his spine curved, his head down. He closed his eyes but he did not sleep, instead just shut the world out. When McMahon got up and left the room he left Harry alone, a single figure among a sea of desks and tables and bulletin boards, in bright fluorescent light but black in his own solitude. The handcuffs remained around his wrists.

At a quarter of five McMahon came back up the stairs and gently shook Harry's shoulder.

"You want a cup of coffee? A sandwich or something?"

Harry shook his head, still facing the floor.

"Well, look. I got to go out so let's go down to the lockup."

It was not odd for him to be treating a prisoner like this, to be concerned if not considerate of his comfort. But McMahon felt even more now, something genuine for the slight frame that sat before him, the slender almost fragile old man that he led through the office and down the stairs. Still, there was other work to do, a partner who waited in the car, and McMahon was anxious to get back on the shift.

At the lockup Harry walked inside the cell without being told and sat down on the steel cot. The door remained open while the lockup attendant marked his clipboard. He wore the department's off-street uniform, a navy-blue work shirt and pants with a single white patch noting Chicago Police, a visored baseball cap. He walked over and nodded at Harry, then swung the door shut. In another cell two women slept sitting in opposite corners, and the third cell held a black man who lay on his back, the steel springs etching a design in his white shirt, smoke curling up from his mouth and a hand with a cigarette. The lockup smelled of disinfectant and concrete, a cold, clammy repository for the night's catch until the Central Detention wagon showed up in the morning.

"Weren't you here a while back?" the lockup man said to Harry. He spoke over a wet cigar wedged and unlit in the side of his mouth. "Gettin' ta know ya better 'an my wife."

Harry heard him but did not look up or respond. He suddenly was aware of the cuffs being off his wrists, taken off before he'd entered the cell, and he felt for a cigarette. He looked around and realized where he was, knew where he was as if he'd lived here all his life. This side of the bars was his life, a reality that no longer struck him suddenly but instead became a part of him, as casually as the sun went behind the clouds. A few hours ago he was free and ambitious, a part of a household, addressed by his first name, free to sneak up to the Hotpoint and liberate a fin for a bottle, to drink it in his own peace of mind. Now he was sodden and trampled, contained by bars that were unremitting and unresponsive, totally unfree. And all he could do was lean back against the concrete block and feel for a cigarette.

It was late and quiet in the lockup, the smell of ammonia, the jagged light from bulbs covered by wire muzzles. The lockup man leaned against Harry's cell door, sideways, looking blankly down the row of cells. Then he turned and looked in on Harry.

"Yeah. Gettin' ta know ya better 'an my wife," he said.

Harry was startled suddenly by a banging, rattling noise around him. He jerked his head up and faced the lockup man, who was rapping a clipboard between the bars.

"All right, rise and shine! The early bird gets the worm!" he yelled.

212

It was morning, time to go downtown.

The lockup man continued down the row, beating his clipboard and shouting over his cigar. Some of the prisoners bitched back at him, sullen with exhaustion and heavy heads. The racket echoed off the walls and the floor. Harry shook himself and stood up.

"C'mon, c'mon! This ain't breakfast in bed!"

The two black women stretched and moaned in the cell next to him. They were bleary yet madeup, black hookers trussed in girdles and panty stockings that fought their midriffs, high swirling wigs sitting heavily on their heads. They glowered through the bars.

Harry's door opened.

"All right, straight out back now and don't shit around or it's cuffs for all ya."

He walked outside the cell door and stood still, waiting, something he would now learn to do again, still waiting.

"C'mon, ya want me to carry ya to the truck!?"

Harry turned and followed the concrete, the steps to two men standing outside the large blue-and-white Central Detention van backed up to the back of the station house.

He stepped up and in, then sat down in the new smell, the oppressive closeness of the wagon; he suddenly sensed his insides, how crummy he felt. It hit quickly, the shakes, the thirst, the dry stench of morning after he'd slept on steel and concrete in his clothes. He longed for a drink, for a shave like he'd taken for the past couple of weeks in Helen's place, for a cigarette, for something to cover the seams in his mouth.

The others followed him, stepping up and sitting next to him along the steel benches on each side of the trailer. They did not look at each other, no eyes meeting, but brooded in their own early-morning discomfort. It was a fetid mixture of body smells and breath, of empty stomachs and habits that needed attending to. Six of them all together, herded into the truck like the cattle they'd become. They sat in silence with

213

the truck's doors open while the lockup men had a cigarette with the boys from C.D.

Finally, absently, they closed the heavy doors and buttoned up the wagon as if it were a beef locker. The truck pulled away and the heads inside felt the motion of it, ignored it, swayed with it.

Sometime later the truck pulled up behind the Criminal Courts Building at Twenty-sixth and California; the doors were opened to waiting bailiffs. The procession was slow and moody; Harry finally stood up and was the last to step down from the van. He was hungry now, itchy from his own smell, his mouth dry and foul. He walked down a narrow corridor. The building was ancient and crowded, with felony courts and lockups on each floor. Harry knew it as well as any building in his life. He saw it always on the downside, after a pinch, usually a botched job like the night before. Those walking in single file before him also knew the place, its faded paint, its high ceilings, the heat in the summer, the dry heat of red-hot radiators in the winter. Never comfortable, never sane, never anything but a layover between one jail and the next. Those who were lucky had friends, lawyers, or relatives who were interested enough or concerned enough or guilty or rich enough to put up bail. The rest just sat and waited, cultivating joneses from habits or the d.t.s or simple hunger. And now Harry was among them, waiting in the narrow, stifling rooms for court to begin, for his name to be called, for the short procedure that would identify him and his number and then send him back to jail. And jail, in Cook County, Chicago, Illinois, was the universal hole created and sustained and populated by people like himself. It was the single reason why he tried to shut off his brain, why he refused to think thoughts about wine, or the Cubs, or jobs, or Helen, or Uptown, the old neighborhood, the cops, his wine, anything. It was the single reason why he settled into a stuporous funk which blanketed his consciousness like a drunk. He sat like a zombie, walked like a zombie, raised his fist, the L-U-M, when asked, then stared at the floor like a zombie, the walking dead, Harry Lum, in prison again and feeling every bit of it, not feeling any of it.

Then he said it, a slight sound that came from deep inside of him. "War-*nek*-e."

McMahon phoned at six-thirty, when Harry said Helen would be home. She answered and listened, McMahon recited the brief facts of Harry's arrest, and she replied only with a curse in Polish. It ground out of her throat in a guttural roll, *"Psiakrew."*

For two hours she ranted in solitude, in the morning light of her kitchen. She shook with anger, cursing herself for letting it happen. She tried to decide if she should leave him there, leave him to rot in his own wretchedness. He was only a stepbrother, and not worthy of that, or her. Pounding her fist on the table, at times shaking, she fretted and worried over what she should do. He was family, the ladies would tell her that, the priest would tell her that, even if he was a bum and a drunk and a good-for-nothing. Then she wondered why God had burdened her life like this, why he had put Harry around her neck when all she wanted was to get by and live in peace.

Her face was puffy with the strain. She had bitten the nails on her fingers until they bled. The officer had told her where Harry would be arraigned, and suddenly in the midst of her anguish and her misery she began to pity herself. Harry's arrest was another trial for her and she would meet her trials with sorrow and self-pity, believing that it was part of the price to pay for being a woman, for being Polish in a day when that didn't count for very much, for being the last of a family which had been shattered and broken and separated by death and the bottle. Harry was just another part of it, so was this building, this load of responsibility in this God-forsaken neighborhood. She would face her life and her trials, keep her medals pinned to her brassière strap, her scapulars,

215

her rosary in her purse. She would trudge off to mass, to Thursday-night novenas, and she would look up into the face of Jesus on the altar and in the glass, and she would cry. Helen would cry until the tears ran down her cheeks and onto her sweater.

But right now she took note of the time and tried to figure out how to get way out to Twenty-sixth and California, the Criminal Courts Building. If nothing else, she would get one last look at Harry and it would be enough for her to tell him what she really felt.

Moments later she was on Sheridan waiting for the Number 17 bus.

A half hour later, the granite block of the Criminal Courts Building loomed in front of her. Clutching a piece of paper on which she had written a court branch number, the number the detective had been careful to give her, she started up the steps. She was there on time, she was always on time.

The sun shone on her back as she went. It seemed that mornings filled with tasks like this one were always nice, maddeningly nice.

15

When Donald Ray awoke she was gone. He shook his head and rubbed his eyes and realized that his fly was open, the flaps of his pants laid back and exposing him to the world. Quickly buttoning up he was jolted once again by his hand, now swollen and unwieldy beneath the gauze Barbie Dell had wrapped around it. He examined it, then thought of her, how she had bitched at him and clawed at him then come out and taken him for a juice ride as sweet and as dedicated as any he'd taken with any floozie on the block. The little hillbilly bitch, he thought, the type he knew back home with pants as wet and willing as an ice-cream bar in ninety degrees. They'd hate you and spit at you all as a buildup to doing what she did last night, right under the nose of Jimmy, who was so dumb he'd slept right through it, while she rode him, Donald Ray, and milked and clutched and oozed so much satisfaction as to sound downright illegal. But now she was gone, only Donald Ray's small smug smile and the mingled odors of his underwear, the scratches on his chest to testify to her earnest, vengeful, ovulating presence.

Standing up he walked through the dried stream of tomato juice and went into the kitchen. He felt lousy, dried out and hung over. In the refrigerator he found nothing but jars of baby food, Velveeta cheese, and a package of hot dogs. He grabbed a couple of the wieners, searched for a beer and settled for the half-empty can of tomato juice. He turned around and found Barbie Dell standing against the doorway, her bathrobe tightly drawn around her.

"Mornin', tiger," he said.

"Shut up," she said and went over to make coffee.

He stuffed the raw dogs down and washed them with the juice, tastes he could hardly stomach. Relieving himself in the bathroom, his stomach churning as he stood there, he didn't bother to close the door, didn't bother to look at her. It was after nine and his hand hurt like hell. In minutes he was down the steps and into the street, without saying a word or making much noise, Barbie Dell standing there with her bleached, tangled hair a swirl of confusion on her shoulders. She drank black coffee and waited for Amy Joy to start to cry.

At the health clinic they told him he should go to a hospital and have the hand set, that he had more than likely broken the bone and that it should be attended to properly. He told them to wrap it and set it themselves, that that was good enough for him. The doctor shook his head and said the best he could do would be to wrap it similar to a cast, that it would hurt, and that Donald Ray was crazy if he didn't have plaster put on it. Donald Ray said he was crazy and that he didn't have the time. He walked out with his hand rebound and hurting like a bitch, throbbing as if some out-of-control acid were boring away at the insides of his fist. He couldn't clench it or rub it or caress it into calming down, but he'd prevailed on the doctor to give him some pills for the pain, always pills for the pain, wherever it was, and they took his five dollars, his green card, and gave him the packet. Now he popped a red and a yellow, a gray-red, hoping one or all would take the electricity away and set him free. He felt the rush, the jolt to his brain, walked, then swerved like a drunk, and realized that he was ascending, pushing out his flaps, the jive in his fist shooting drill shocks, pinching and exploding inside him until he was rising in spite of himself, his shoes losing touch with the concrete.

Then, in the slosh of swirling pain and confusion, his head half screwed on, Donald Ray began to run his good hand through his pockets, feeling along his breast and his ass for the bulge of his wallet and the wad of his cash. He barely remembered the bungle of the night before, the light and the echoes of the job, and it seemed like weeks, years ago, something nagging at his subconscious and pissing him off. He felt his pockets, his left hand throbbed, then he realized the one thing that brought reality crashing around his ears like a cold-cocking in a gangway: he was broke. The clinic had taken his last fin, taken his last refuge, and now he needed money, needed it badly and right now. He decided to get on with it, carried by a momentum surging through his blood and his brain, stronger than his hill savvy, his common sense, his logic, what Art Burl would have done, a surge that decided in a second that he would get back to his room and get what he needed to get him some dough. He didn't consider the cops, didn't care about the cops, didn't care that they were the logical obstacles between him and the freedom of the city. He walked the streets, pointed himself in the direction, exhaled like a moose starting out across the plains, his body still strong, still layered with sinew and gristle and a toughness built in and not easily eased out. The morning was clear, autumn, and he would do what was in front of him, getting on back to the room and going to his strength.

He walked down Kenmore over to Montrose, then over to Magnolia. As he moved, taking big though uneven strides, in his black Levi's and white socks, his pointed leather shoes that turned up at the toes, his white on white shirt beneath a black, stretched-at-the-elbows Banlon sweater, his stringy hair that still lay on top of his head in waves thanks to an early-morning comb job, he didn't realize that his very mug was in the process of being put in the upper left-hand corner of the next day's Chicago Police Department Daily Bulletin. The squad car that passed him without notice this morning would tomorrow have his portrait on top of the pile on the

219

clipboard on the front seat. It would be headlined "Wanted for Burglary Investigation," then Donald Ray's mug shots, the ones he'd taken with his eyes wide to disguise the droop, a few months back on a stolen auto bust that never stuck. "Donald Ray Burl" it would read, "Arrest Number I.R. 789665, Alias: Donald Burlstrom, Don Gates, Fred Gates; Last Known Address, 4628 N. Kenmore Avenue." And it would go on to profile him like the light-heavyweight that he was: "Male, white, 26, 5-foot-11 inches, 175 pounds, muscular build, medium complexion, blue eyes, brown hair." Then it would talk about how he was wanted to connection with the attempted burglary on Clark Street two nights before, and how he had violated his probation and how he was a known narcotics addict who hung around Wilson and Kenmore. It was a pretty complete sheet. And thousands of cops would read it and slip it lightly into their minds before they would move on and out into the streets.

But Donald Ray would be totally unaware of it, totally unaware that it had a lot to do with the present state of his head, his burning hand, his cravings, and the fact that he was penniless and growing itchy, desperate. This morning he walked in the relative safety of his anonymity, tomorrow less so, a matter of pure fate, whether or not some rookie, or some wizened uniformed patrolman would spot him and casually put his mug together with that on the bulletin, or if a bur- glary dick got lucky enough, if they dogged his flat, his shadow, or if for one instant Donald Ray's luck washed out; then they'd take him. Now he didn't know and didn't give a shit. He rammed the key into his lock, back to his flat without a hassle, for the last time because the place was hot, and over to the wall behind the refrigerator.

With a grunt, a shove of his shoulder, his good hand and his legs, he pushed the heavy old refrigerator away and exposed a hole in the plaster, lathe board cut away forming an oblong hole, and he reached in, scattering the crawling life in the wall, and felt the cold assurance, the lines, the weight of his

220

Titan FIE automatic. Now, damnit, he was ready to go out and get him some trouble, most of all to get him some money. The gun slid into his pants, under his sweater, a built-in nest, and he was out the door.

All the planning of the felony Donald Ray Burl was about to commit took place as he walked out of his flat for the last time, up the steps onto the sidewalk. The scene of the crime would be the first convenient spot, the victim the first logical individual who would happen to come into view, the timing directly dependent on who was around. Donald Ray was ready, his gun was in his belt, and he was broke. To him, in Uptown, living the existence he did, in extreme financial straits, bankruptcy so blatant and so immediate that it could only be translated into the state of being solidly, unequivocally, flat-out broke, the chemicals loitering in his brain and the pain in his hand serving as catalysts, to Donald Ray it was reason enough to commit what he was going to commit right at that very moment.

He headed down an alley, walking slowly but directly for the parking lot of the Hi-Lo Market on Broadway. He didn't know, but he had a suspicion that at this time of the morning that might be the place, might be the spot where he could pull it off and do it in a hurry. He didn't consider the merits of what he was doing, whether it was the kind of job that befitted a person like himself, a thief of his stature, whether it was a comedown from the seemingly fool-proof scheme he had built his world around just yesterday. He didn't muse over the fact that had the job been pulled off he would have been delivered from penny-ante, high-risk scores like this one. That was all crap that would drive him crazy if he let it, nonsense that was best pissed and moaned over a beer, over many beers and plenty of shitface. Now he would do what he had to do and think about things later.

He walked toward the back entrance of the wide asphalt lot shielded by the trash containers and a semi-trailer backed into a loading dock. There were a few cars in the lot, but generally little activity, a wide, littered, but sleepy spot that he could use for his own, an open ground, bump and take off. He walked cautiously, lurked, then before him, coming from the opposite direction down the alley, he spotted her. She was middle-aged and portly, her purse wound around her forearm, walking quickly because she knew where she was. She spotted him almost at the time that he eyeballed her, she glanced up, then down, then quickened her pace and headed for the opening which led into the parking lot. He walked toward her, both coming at each other down the alley, both hurrying for different reasons.

Donald Ray knew that it wasn't even a contest. His strides outdistanced hers, easily, with menacing sureness that transformed him into something much different than he actually was. For in the moment, in the split-second, when the woman realized what was happening, she saw a figure who was not Donald Ray Burl, not the ambling, overgrown boy from the hills who used to tag along with his brother and yelp when his daddy winged squirrels, not the muscled hillbilly who loved to drink beer and tell raccoon stories about down home, the arm-wrestling champ of Wilson Avenue. She saw none of that, not even his face, his blue eyes, his clean, sturdy bone lines; for this nameless, faceless woman who was on her way for some coffee cake and a quart of skimmed milk, a can of soup and some Kleenex, saw only the form and the outline of what she knew to be crime and violence and fear in her small, unobtrusive life.

Donald Ray came closer, only about six feet away now, and he suddenly saw the woman look up at him as she tried to slip past. But he didn't see a face, or a human being, or anything that lived and breathed like he himself did. He saw only a figure and the position of the piece of cheap vinyl hanging from her arm. In a second the woman was next to him, no higher than his armpit, and he pivoted on the sand of the alley and pushed her. She screamed and tried to retain her balance, sending her arms out, the purse swinging. But the force of the push sent her against the fence adjoining the parking lot and she tripped and fell. In the confused, awkward motion, a shout working its way from her throat, Donald Ray ripped at her sweater and her dress, scraping the flabby skin on her arms and yanking the purse away. He pulled it, snapped it off her arm with a force that sent her falling clumsily to the pavement, her hip bone cracking with the fall, her purse no longer a part of her.

With a jump he was off and running, down the alley then through a gangway and onto a side street. He flipped the purse under his sweater, walked swiftly, the frenzy of motion injecting a spurt of reality into his mind, clearing his head, and he suddenly realized that he had just pulled off a snatch and now he had to finish it off. He found a submerged basement entrance near the alley, drawing cover from the cans and the overhead porch. Riffling through the handbag, through the wadded tissue and letters, he finally found a tattered change purse. He unclipped it and found the bills, three fins and a couple of singles, plus some change, fifty, seventy-five, eighty-three cents. That was it, and he wadded it and shoved it into his pocket, not a half-million bucks worth of gold and silver fillings, but seventeen dollars and eighty-three cents. More money than he'd awakened with this morning.

Wasting little time he took off his sweater, thinking that the police might be cruising and looking for a dark-on-dark suspect, then hopped out of his hideaway, leaving the purse open and scattered on the steps behind him. It was time to take off, put some distance between him and the parking lot, between him and the only finger that could accuse, and get him something to eat. He had done it, feeling the pistol in his waist that he hadn't been forced to use, which was good on jobs like this. Quick and painless, petty, a fact that he was still aware of and which kept the smile from his face, but he had done it, and on mornings like this, his hand, the circumstances, just doing things was something.

She sat and waited on a bench in a room filled mostly with blacks. It was stuffy and filled with smoke despite the fact that smoking wasn't permitted. When a chesty, white-shirted bailiff came in he loudly and gruffly announced that all cigarettes had to be extinguished. A host of butts dropped from fingers beneath the benches, onto the floor where they were stamped into a smear of soot and tobacco.

Helen crossed her legs and talked to no one. She did not take off her coat or her babushka. She only rolled and crumpled the sheet of paper on which she had written the branch number given her by the detective. But she was here now, in the courtroom with the lime-green paint and the high ceilings, the crowd, the lists tacked to the sideboards, the bailiffs calling out names in monotones. Finally everyone stood up at the sight of a black-robed judge. He was old and hidden behind a pair of horn-rimmed glasses, barely acknowledging the presence of anyone else in the room but the court clerk, who was feeding him documents like hay to a horse. The activity went on noisily, without any obvious order, with people walking back and forth in front of the bench, names being called, conferences with the judge and men in suits who carried briefcases. Occasionally it stopped long enough for everyone to witness a semblance of a trial. Two groups stood across from each other, shielded by the men in suits with sheaves of papers in their hands. The judge took off his glasses and looked down at the faces in front of him, a discussion followed, the judge asked some questions, then abruptly everyone turned and marched toward the back of the courtroom, the last person being a young Mexican with fearful eyes and a handkerchief wound around his neck.

It made no sense to Helen. She couldn't hear what was being said and she didn't know what was going on. She had tried to look at the lists but when she got to them she didn't see a name that even came close to Harry's. But she was too intimidated to ask, too confused and resentful finally of the very fact that she was there.

It went on for an hour, now fifteen minutes before eleven, and Helen felt the exhaustion creeping into her body. She had been up all night working and this kind of strain wasn't good for her. She knew that, and she held it against Harry, blaming him for the discomfort she was feeling, the stuffiness, the disgusting parade of people around her, the odors, the money and time it took to take a bus, two buses, and even get to this hole.

Then she heard his name, barked across the room by the clerk as the other names had been, only this one was what she had been waiting for. She pushed and leaned her way into the aisle, stepping on feet and kicking shins to get up to the front. She walked past a bailiff, up to the bench though she was the only one there. The judge looked at her, then lifted up his glasses as he spoke.

"And who are you, madam?"

"I'm Mrs. Helen Pontek and the sister of the man you been callin'."

The judge looked down at this papers. From the right side of the room the bailiff emerged, stepped aside, and Harry walked in front of him. He walked with his head down, the cuffs around his wrists and hands dangling in front of him. Then he raised his head and saw Helen. His eyes immediately fell without a sense of recognition, without emotion. He was tired and totally worn out, as she was; his back ached, his throat ached, his stomach was twisting like a shoestring. He didn't fight it to summon any measure of emotion for her, any feeling of gratitude or shame. He could only look down and try to hear what he had to hear. He was being pushed and pulled, at this time living in the hollow of his brain and the precipice of his aching body, and he simply couldn't push or pull back.

The judge read off a list of numbers then translated them into something that said Harry had been arrested and

225

charged with damage to property and attempted burglary.

He asked Harry if he had a lawyer.

Harry shook his head.

"Kindly look up at the bench when you answer, sir," the judge said. He spoke in the tone of a teacher reprimanding a pupil.

Helen looked across at Harry, staring at him as if she expected him to do something besides stand like a nitwit.

"Do you wish to retain a lawyer or should the court appoint one for you?"

Harry again shook his head.

"What does that mean?"

"How much does it cost for a lawyer?" Helen interrupted, loudly so that the bailiffs glared at her.

"It's not a matter of how much it costs, madam," the judge said. "It's a matter here of whether or not the defendant has counsel or if the court should appoint one."

"We can get a lawyer," Helen said.

"All right. Continue the case until November 22. To be present with counsel. Bail set at five thousand dollars."

Suddenly the bailiff put his arm under Harry's shoulder and led him off, the clerk announced another name, another number. Helen was left standing alone in front of the bench and a judge who was no longer looking at her.

"What now? What do I do?"

The judge looked up. "Talk to the clerk of the court, madam."

A heavy-set clerk came over and led her toward the tables at the side of the bench. Helen went though she had no idea what was happening.

"Bail's been set at five thousand. Post one-tenth of that, five hundred," the bailiff said.

"What? What's this about some five thousand dollars? Who's gonna be payin' five thousand dollars and for what?" she said in a rage, her voice booming throughout the room

226

and causing the judge to pause and look at her, the clerks to grimace at the disturbance.

Finally one of the women sitting at the table, a woman also dressed in the white uniform of the court clerks, got up and took Helen out of the courtroom into the hall. She tried to calm her down, tried to get her to pay attention and keep from pointing at the courtroom and the judge. Then the woman said something in Polish. Helen shut up and listened to her.

"Look," the woman said. She had short, light brown hair clipped around her ears. "The judge just arraigned your husband. . . ."

"Not my husband! No husband a mine! Dat's my stepbrother, that's all he is and all he ever will be!"

"Okay, okay. Yer stepbrother then. He was just arraigned on an arrest for burglary and breakin' and enterin'. That's a felony and the judge has got to be holding the prisoner until you can bail him out."

"Why didn't he say that? That's the five thousand dollars? Who's got that kind of money?"

"That's what bail he set but you don't have to pay all of it. You got to put up just five hunnerd if you want him out of jail."

"Five hunnert?"

Helen's mouth remained open as the words came out. She looked into the face of the woman.

"You Popolski, dear?" she said.

"Yeah. Mantuszak."

"That's nice," Helen said.

The woman closed her eyes and shook her head wearily. "Yeah, well, that's the story if you want him out of jail."

"Then what? Goin' to court like for drinkin'?"

"Yep, when everyone's done givin' continuances."

"What's that?"

"That's when they postpone the trial for something. Takes

227

about a year to go through sometimes."

"A year?"

"Sometimes more."

"And what happens to Harry all that time?"

"He's in jail unless you get him out."

"So if they let him off after a year then what?"

"Then he spent a year in jail for nothin'."

"Yeah?"

"Yup. Happens a lot."

"Well, that's where the bum belongs."

"Dat's all right too, but I thought I should tell ya what's goin' on on account a yer Polish and all."

"That's nice of you. Yer a sweet girl," Helen said. "So you say I got to put up that five hunnert or he stays in jail a year for nothin'?"

"It's up to you. I got to get back on the job."

"Yeah, tanks a lot."

"You all right now?"

"Yeah, tank you, I'm all right."

Then she was alone, having come all the way she had for the few minutes in front of the judge to hear what she had heard. Harry had not so much as looked at her for more than two seconds, standing there as if he were laying on the sidewalk in front of the house in the old neighborhood, like Pa or Joe, just looking and saying nothing and causing all the trouble in the world. Helen looked at the door where the woman had gone, then she looked down the hall. It was deserted, and she realized that in this huge echoing corridor she was standing all alone.

From the courtroom Harry went back into the tank to wait out the roster. He had no idea of the time, of what day it was, of where and when his future would unfold in anything but a routine of lines and commands, of decisions made for him. Then, with the others, he was herded out of the room down the back stairs, given the rough warnings about escape at-

228

tempts, then led to the cellblock. He knew he would have to steel himself into a whole new posture of survival, in jail, the hole, the place no animal would opt for. Now it would be home as the streets had been, like his room, the lunacy of Uptown. For everything that had been a part of his life on the street, that which drove him to drink, or to steal, to rifle the pants of unconscious winos, to panhandle, to protect himself, to lie, to cajole, to pander—all of that would come to play in prison. Only now it would be concentrated, contained within walls with so-called guards and power structures, but just as rampant and uncontrolled, just as powerful and corrupt, as criminal as it had been on the outside.

He sat and tried to think of nothing else but how to protect himself. He was back in prison, the reality was returning to him.

16

With ten dollars of the money he got a furnished room at the
Endicott Hotel, a third-floor dump on Lawrence Avenue.
Lawrence was north of where he usually hung out, just
enough of a change of scenery to give him an edge, to convince him of his freedom and his immunity from the cops.
His room had a sink, a cot, and a tile floor. The john was down
the hall next to a large clammy shower room which smelled
of Lysol yet remained a home for the chunkiest silverfish
he'd ever seen. His payment in advance provided him with
two towel tokens and a change of sheets. As he reclined on
the cot he whistled out loud to himself. "Home is where yer
ass is, Burl," he said. Then he tried to spit the length of the
room into the basin, but came up short.

As he lay there, he began to talk to himself again. He
absent-mindedly reached his hand over to the table next to
the bed. His fingers groped for an instant, then it dawned on
him that he was reaching for a radio that wasn't there. This
room didn't even have a radio, his was still in his old apartment, and now there was no way for him to get to his world
of WJJD. Those were the call letters to Roy Acuff, Ernest
Tubbs, Bobby Bare, and Loretta Lynn, the country and western sound that was salve to his soul, the twangy background
to his life no matter where he'd been, in the hills, Ypsilanti,
or Uptown.

It hit him almost the second he put his foot out of his cousin Gaylord's Chrysler, his first glimpse of Uptown and Chicago, that the guitars and the dobros of country and western, his sound, seeped out of open screens and doorways, from dashboards and landings, out of not just an apartment here and there, but from each one, every room, every place on the block where people ate and slept and fought. From it he knew this place would be home, or could be. He was convinced of it on Sunday afternoons in the spring when cars lining Clifton Street being washed, or those jacked up on steel milk crates being worked over by a good old boy with a beer and a crescent wrench, poured out nothing but WJJD, country music for Chicagoland, wailing and whining, stroking dogs and breaking hearts.

He remembered how he'd become obsessed with it, a crazy fan of the stars and the hits. He began to buy records even though he didn't have a phonograph. Finally he bought a used mahogany-cased 1957 Columbia hi-fi from a second-hand store. But it worked, with a stylus as heavy as a hammer and a turntable covered with felt, damn right it worked. And Donald began playing his 45s and his stereo albums, even though his set couldn't negotiate stereo any better than a Victrola could have, and his corner of Gaylord's house became one more source of the droning country sound.

The record player moved him from humming into singing, an urge to perform and outcroon Bobby Bare, his favorite, or Johnny Cash. Once, while helping Gaylord change the shocks on the Chrysler, he hopped up on the hood and helped Bobby belt out the words to "I Wanna Go Home." He loved himself, sang right through a holler from Gaylord to hand him a pliers, and then smiled in extreme satisfaction when he looked down to see a three-year-old runny-nosed kid clapping and turning around in circles. It was enough to send Donald Ray into the next number, a Marty Robbins, much to the delight of a stray hound, which howled and nipped at the shoulders of the whirling kid.

When Donald Ray was finished, and while he was fielding the catcalls of a handful of unappreciative neighbors down the block, he slapped his chest and urged the hound to jump up on the hood with him. "C'mon, dawg! C'mon, boy!" he begged and slapped and pulled and made faces until the mutt paid attention and poised its hind legs. At a final command the dog sprang and cleared the hood. It yelped and nipped and jumped at Donald Ray, who laughed and batted its ears. "Good old dawg! Good old egg, you are, jumpin' like a good old dawg!" And suddenly the hound took another leap at Donald Ray's eyes, excited and overjuiced, and Donald Ray yelled "Hey!" then grabbed the mutt around the ribs and held it to him. He started hollering with Tammy Wynette and the dog began to howl with him, slobbering all over his face, ear-splitting yelps, like dogs Donald Ray saw on the *Johnny Carson Show*.

It was a commotion and drew the neighbor kids, who began laughing and mimicking the dog, howling and adding to the racket. Gaylord pulled his head from beneath the car and gawked. Three other men working on their heaps threw down their tools and walked over. They were not amused, were hung over and irritable, and they wanted little more than to shut everybody, but mostly Donald Ray and his singing mutt, up.

Donald Ray could remember it well, see it all, how they first bitched at him and he lipped back. Words led to threats, fingers pointed, menacingly, until one of the men came over and yanked Donald Ray's foot enough to send him flipping off Gaylord's hood. The rest was haymakers and uppercuts, wild scuffling and kicking with Donald Ray in the middle. It ended with three paddy wagons and enough cops to settle a full-scale riot. The cops hustled everyone into the wagons and down to the Foster Avenue station. A few hours later, with most everyone sick of being robbed of their Sunday afternoon, they became anxious to be quiet and take back their insults. The cops let them out the back way, without

232

pressing charges. But by the time Donald Ray got back to Clifton Street, back to Gaylord, who had done nothing during the entire melee but hide beneath the Chrysler, the wonderful singing dog was gone. Donald Ray never saw it again, not even when he sang from the hood again, or crooned off the back porch.

It all came back to him, those scenes of the early times, good times compared to now. His life, he thought, seemed to be nothing but looking back at times that seemed better. Yet when he thought even further, he remembered that back then he didn't think things were all that great. And he wondered if there ever had been a time in his life when he thought things were good, and that they really were.

Now he knew only that he was down and hustling. He looked at his watch, felt his gut, and decided it was time to go out once again, to regroup and figure out how he could dig himself out of the hole. He would have to go it alone. Del Corso was done, too hot and too dumb to risk staying around. And now that Barbie Dell had gotten a piece of him, there was no telling when she would hold it over his head, bleed him for it to Jimmy or anyone else who came between him and her.

He thought about taking off back home. Most hillbillies did that when they got into trouble. They just begged, or stole the nearest Pontiac Bonneville, gassed it with super premium, and lead-footed it back down home, where the hills would take them in. There they'd move in with an aunt or a momma or a wife and wait, maybe get a job and live for a few years, all the time not answering mail and hoping that the marshal didn't come up the road with some fucker in a shirt and tie and extradition papers. So many of the down-home boys shuttled back and forth that they called both Chicago and West Virginia home; just a matter of which one you happened to be resting your ass and your carburetors in at the time.

But that took effort of the kind Donald Ray wasn't inter-

233

ested in at the moment. He could dodge the cops, grow some hair on his face or lose a little weight, anything to keep on ice. It was better that than giving up and getting on down into the grime and the sweat of back home. Plus the fact that as far as he knew only Art Burl was there. Momma and the sisters had stayed in Ypsi; he couldn't go there either. Buddy was God knows where if he even was still alive. But Art, the old man, was in bad times, all of his cookies gone, according to a cousin who came to Chicago and had seen Art only last year. Art was getting old and crazy, the cousin had told Donald, and probably would greet him with a shotgun blast before he even bothered to make sure it was really his own boy.

Donald Ray would stay. Take his chances. He was good at that. Now he just needed money. Always needed money. There was something about his pockets that just didn't feel right without it. It would drive him to do what he had to do: to go out again and get cash the quickest, most efficient way he knew how. It didn't matter who got in the way now, or what, or if he had to use the revolver that dug into the soft flesh of his belly. It didn't have a lot to do with thought or logic or planning or strategy. Now things were tight and times were bad. Donald Ray was down and holed up in a cracker box of a room in a bug-ridden hotel. He'd go out and pop the first slug of cash he could find.

He sat across the cell from Harry, looking out into the block as he talked. He was a burly man in his late forties; it was hard for Harry to tell. He wore his hair in a brush cut that was steel gray and clipped so close around his ears that it looked like a cap. The rolls of fat bunched together on the back of his neck. He talked in a gruff, bass voice much like every heavy, every bouncer, every overweight slob Harry had ever met.

"This guy didn't even have to try on my old lady, prolly not," he said. "She'd fall for the paper boy if he waited around for a tip. So I proves it for myself by comin' home a little early on her square-dance nights and watchin' her and this guy say their little goodnights in the car. She musta stayed out there at least twenty minutes with him; right there in the front seat. And I knew she was leanin' over and moonin' him and gigglin' like she does when she's tight at weddings. But this time I knows she wasn't tight.

"So I put a stop to it. Ended it once and for all. I keep a shotgun in my trunk durin' bird season. And I got shells and everything, so I'm ready. I'm thinkin' all the time what I'm gonna do when I sees 'em. And funny thing, it was pretty easy. I got my gun out just like I was takin' target practice. I wasn't even mad, ya know what I mean? And I come from the back way, through the kitchen like I was some kind of madman. And there the two of 'em are in the bedroom already. This guy standin' there in his boxer shorts and my old lady in some outfit I ain't never seen before. And before I know it I'm squeezin' off shells. Shot him right in the boxer shorts. Yeah, right in the keesters. And then I lets her have it. They say she's still alive in surgery but she sure as hell don't deserve it. My lawyer says he kin get me off on temporary insanity. Which is sure as hell what I was except for when I shot the guy. Ain't no insanity could shoot like that. Right in the boxer shorts. He was standin' there right in his boxer shorts."

Then he stopped. The cell suddenly dominated the two of them in the midst of their silence. The guy looked over at Harry half expecting some kind of response.

"Maybe he wanted to box," Harry said quietly. Then he looked away.

"Jesus," the guy replied.

Harry stared out into the space of the cell block, the dark gray tiers of the jail. He looked up at his cellmate and thought he saw glistening pouches around the guy's eyes, as if he had told his story and was glad it was out. He wouldn't be around for long, Harry knew. He wasn't a con. So Harry said to hell

235

with him; he had problems of his own. The story was forgotten, who could believe it anyway, and Harry settled back to think his own thoughts, to keep his head from plaguing him with doubts or regrets about where he was. He waited for someone to give a command, for a bell to ring. This was prison and he wouldn't have to make his own decisions, wouldn't have to face his own will. He began to feel his stomach once again, the lining beginning to curl in revolt, the juices mixing and coming up short. He needed money and he needed a contact, the old pecking order of jails that he knew well, because the two meant a bottle whenever he needed one. All it would take was balls and ambition, a little cunning, some dough in the right palm, and the booze was his as if he'd laid the price of a pint down on the counter. There wasn't anything he couldn't get on the inside, and he knew this as well as he knew anything about prison, that he couldn't get on the outside. It simply went through different channels, came from different sources, but ended up in the same spot, the same gut.

He settled into the realization, turned it over in his mind, considering the possibilities, the risks, even in a rat hole like the Cook County Jail, and gradually, subtly, reassuringly for the first time in as long as he could remember, Harry began to feel his confidence.

For most of that night and the following day Helen turned it over. She complained to Ilene at dinner, ranting about Harry, about how he was a plague on the family, a yoke around her shoulders, a lout true to the ilk that had gone before him. She paced back and forth in front of the kitchen sink, screeching in a caterwaul that Ilene had grown accustomed to in such times. She scolded and berated him, "He's walkin' into that courtroom trial and here's his own stepsister standin' there, his own family, and he don't even so much as say somethin' to me. Nuttin'!" as if he were sitting at the table, like an incorrigible child, taking it.

236

Ilene didn't answer or object, she didn't try to interject a comment or calm her mother down. She just paged through her *Mademoiselle* and stared blankly at the pages, Helen's tirade an accompaniment to her reading. If Helen asked a question, she answered it herself. If she wanted assurance that her views on the moral stature of Harry were accurate, she quickly gave it to herself. Hers was a sustained, prolonged soliloquy that needed Ilene as an audience so that it would not bounce off the walls, so Helen would be able to convince herself that someone else indeed felt as she did even if Ilene didn't appear moved by the situation. Finally she shut her magazine and looked up at Helen.

"Aw, Ma," she said, "why don't ya take it easy for a while?" Then she went into the bathroom.

The next morning after work Helen went to St. John Cantius in the old neighborhood and knelt through the morning mass, then lingered while she kneaded her rosary and prayed for herself and her trials. Soon the tears began to well, then overflowed into rivulets that streamed down her cheeks, and which she didn't try to blot or wipe away. She didn't know how many times she had been driven to this, to get calluses on her knees and talk to Jesus about her troubles. There were other ladies like herself kneeling in the massive stone tabernacle, and all probably with similar woes, the same cares to bring to the church and throw up to the altar, their hands crisscrossing their chests over and over again, their heads bowed in solemn, unwavering consternation. If they were anything at all like Helen they felt themselves more alive here than anywhere else, feeding their souls with solid doses of self-pity and solace, crying like children at a drowning, weaving and shaking and mumbling prayers which became litanies of almost hypnotic power, putting in coins and lighting candles, genuflecting at the Blessed Virgin, praying before the saints.

Helen finally got up and went to the confessional, where she whispered her stories in Polish. It was not so much her own confession as it was that of Harry, of what he had done, how he had destroyed the family's name, how he had caused Helen tears and sleepless nights, now in jail and wallowing in his own disrespect, his own lack of respectability for a man his age. Helen poured it out much as she had to Ilene the night before. She chewed off the adjectives, cautioned herself against swearing, especially here in this place, but spared no idioms of abuse when she described him.

The priest replied, almost imperceptibly, that Helen should forgive those who had trespassed against her, chiding her for being so impatient and so demanding, then he said she should love her brother as Jesus loved her. She thanked the priest and went out to say her ritual number of Hail Marys. Then she lit a candle, genuflected still another time. With slow but definite steps she walked down the concrete walkway and headed for Milwaukee Avenue. Though she had gone through the motions, purged herself in the church of her youth, Helen had really known all along what she was finally going to do. She had brought her savings passbook along as evidence. Twenty minutes later she walked out of the Savings and Loan Association, where she had kept her money for forty years. She stuffed the envelope into the bottom of her purse, clutched it to her with the tenacity of an animal guarding his newly captured prey. In the envelope, in clean twenty-dollar bills, was five hundred dollars.

Harry was in the dinner hall, scooping home vegetable soup, when a guard came up to him and tapped his shoulder. He followed as the guard led him through the normal cell doors and out toward the office where Harry had been admitted earlier.

"You been sprung," the guard said.

"Whaaaa—?" Harry mouthed, then ran to keep up.

In the next few moments he was given his valuables in a manila envelope and told to sign a paper saying that he was who he said he was and that everything the Cook County Jail had taken from him had been returned. Harry scribbled on the lines where the officer pointed and then was directed toward a door. He opened it, walked, then another, all unlocked, until he was in the lobby of the jailhouse. He was face to face with Helen. She stood with her hands at her sides.

"Let's go," she said.

He followed her.

17

For days Jimmy Del Corso slept through the mornings and most of the afternoons, waking only to push Barbie Dell's brat off his chest and roll over again. Barbie went off to her job at Woolworth's before ten, leaving her kid and Jimmy to fight it out together, hardly a contest because Jimmy preferred to stay in bed and didn't care what Amy Joy got into as long as she didn't toddle into the bedroom. In late afternoons, Jimmy plodded into the kitchen, wearing only his jockey shorts, his hair a straggly explosion of curls, and rummaged through the refrigerator. He ate raw hot dogs and half a head of lettuce, then cursed the icebox for lacking beer, pizza, pickles, and other essentials.

It went on until Barbie came home one night on her dinner hour to change Amy Joy's pants and feed her. Jimmy began his harangue.

"Oh, I see," she cut him off. "Yer thinkin' a makin' this yer permanent home, right, buster? Maybe even a little maid service?"

"You got it, toots."

"And maybe I could hurry home and fix some fried chicken and french fries."

"Nice. Super. Grade-A."

"And maybe bake you a big chocolate cake."

She pulled the words, whining them with a heavy down-home accent and sarcastic singsong, all the while shoving spoonfuls of food into Amy Joy's mouth, and smiling serenely.

"Good. Good. That's just super-fuckin' good. When you startin'?" he said. He stood against the counter top wearing a pair of trousers but barefoot and shirtless.

"Well, think agin, you loafer!" She scowled.

He jerked up and pushed the steel and Formica table with his hand, knocking the jar of baby food onto the floor, where it bounced and splattered strained plums on the tile.

"Look, bitch!" he shouted. "I don't need none of yer god-damned lip and I ain't takin' it!"

Barbie stood up quickly, bumping the table herself, and leaned forward toward him. Her face was a pasty mixture of defiance and scorn, eyes narrow, her thin, hillbilly lips tight on her teeth.

"Yeah, well, that's about all you ain't takin'. 'Cuz yer freeloadin' in my house and on my food and on my rent check, buster. So don't git to thinkin' you can treat me like all them other whores you hang around with. Don't think it for one solitary second!"

He raised his hand and swung at her, but she raised hers to meet it and the two slapped fists. She managed to grab Jimmy's and throw it back at him.

"That neither!" she shouted. Her voice now pitched, cutting with a temper that had been defined and honed many times over. "I ain't takin' it from you no more. You'll have the tussle of yer life if you try an' hit me around!"

She sat down heavily and grabbed Amy Joy's hand so roughly that the child jumped and began to whimper. Then Barbie reached across the floor for the bottle of plums and shoved another spoonful into the child's surprised mouth.

Jimmy got up and pushed the table once again, trying to make noise, or vent his rage, or show some measure of the anger he felt but that he had been forced to eat.

"Fuck you!" he growled. He was about to kick the door when he realized he was barefoot. "Fuck you, you fuckin'

241

hillbilly bitch! Fuck!" he ranted and disappeared into the bedroom.

He was more furious than ever now, and he grabbed the blanket from the bed and threw it on the floor. He would get her, he'd fix her, he'd show her that she couldn't shit on him like that, to his face, and get away with it. No woman could.

With a leap he charged through the bedroom door and went for the kitchen. He caught her just as she stood up. With one hand he spun her around; she tripped awkwardly in her surprise, but only for a second until she could see what was happening, and she moved to meet it. But he had the momentum and managed to push her again, backward until her back thumped against the door of the refrigerator. Then he moved in; though he was scarcely taller, though he was skinnier, with bones and thin twines of muscle where she was thick and solid, he managed to pin her. He dug in with a raised knee against her thigh and his hands on her arms.

"You stop it, Jimmy! You stop it or I'll let you have it!" she screamed. Her cries set off Amy Joy into a pitched, petrified wail.

"I'll stop it until I got you yellin' for more," he grunted. His face was tight against hers, his heavy, black-rooted beard, the curly chaos of his hair, breath sour and stagnant. "I'll make ya scream that yer sorry for that fat lip of yours and sorry that you ever even thought anything bad about me."

She pushed and hissed at him, the kitchen alive with the screaming of Amy Joy and the scuffling and kicking, the hollow clopping against the metal of the refrigerator door. Suddenly she caught him leaning the wrong way and with a thrust she pushed him from her.

"You ain't the man, un-huh, you ain't even half the man who could make me say I'm sorry about anything! You or that Italian thing a yers you think is so tremendous. Well, it ain't an' I had better," she screamed.

Jimmy stood in the center of the kitchen, half bent, not sure whether to charge her or hit her or what.

"You ain't had shit," he sneered.

"That ain't the point, Jimmy, and you better get this through your thick head from now on. I can get anything or anyone I want. I done it so I know it. I don't *need* anyone, 'specially you. I know that for a fact."

Jimmy wiped his mouth with the back of his hand. He was getting whomped. She stood in front of him, an immovable, unmanageable bitch.

"Yeah, then go ahead, see what you scrape up. Nobody I know would say it's worth the time."

"Ain't what Don said."

"Don who?"

"Don Burl, for your information."

"You fucked with Burl?"

"Sometime, anytime, all the time."

He began to redden, the blood pushing against the veins in his neck.

"Son of a bitch!" he yelled.

He came at her with his fist clenched and shaking inches away from his face. She pushed out her hands to fend him off, but he stopped, his fist still raised and shaking, his mouth a circle once again, blowing spit in quick, angry gasps.

"Yer hicks, dumb hillbilly hicks and I shoulda known," he sputtered. "I'll kill him when I see him. I'd kill you too without thinking twice about it. I will too as soon—"

"You ain't killin' nobody," she snarled. "Now get the hell outta here!"

He held himself, his fist still clenched and shaking, then he went for the bedroom.

He grabbed the handle of the top drawer of the dresser and pulled it, scattering underwear and nylon stockings and jewelry. He kicked a few pieces up in the air, still out of control, but then he heard them fall harmlessly, and stupidly. He waited for her to respond, to stomp into the room and begin it all over again. But he didn't hear her, only the sound of his own spitting and his own breaths. He knew he had taken a beating and that it was time to get out.

Without washing or shaving or combing his hair, still reek-
ing with the smells he'd slept in for two days, he pulled on
his cuffed plaid pants and his black-and-purple knit shirt, his
pointed black leather shoes. He'd get them, maybe not today
or tomorrow, but someday, sometime when they weren't
looking and not expecting the kid from the corner to come
at them. He'd show Burl that he couldn't get away with what
he'd done, screwing his woman right under his nose, taking
him, the two of them smug and cocky about it as if they
belonged to some exclusive hillbilly club that the rest of the
world couldn't crack. But he'd get them, get Burl. As soon as
he could get up and out, time to regroup, to find him another
place and get him some money.

From the bus stop they walked down Sheridan Road toward the building. Helen walked heavily, with short steps,
the purse she always carried with her dangling from her
elbow. It was getting cold, a damp, wet cold that dug in and
bit, a prelude to winter. Harry bowed his head from the gale
of it, tucking his chin into his neck and walking, walking just
a half-step behind Helen, with his hands in his pockets.

"Look at you like that. In the clink and I got to come and
git ya out. My good money that I worked and scrubbed for,
that I saved every week by pennies, yeah, Harry, pennies,
but you wouldn't know what that was all about."

She talked into herself, with her voice low but steady,
buffeted by the wind to where it trailed out behind her and
he could barely hear. But she kept on, in the wind and the
sounds of the street, the gathering dusk, the heaviness that
hung over them as they walked.

"So I ask myself what am I doin' this for? And I ask Jesus,
and I ask the priest, and I pray, and I ask them but I don't
tell nobody. I just keep it locked up inside as if there was
somethin' there. I keep askin' myself that. Just like Pa, it all
runs the same, you better believe it. How many times didn't

Ma put the house in hock or the car or one time she pawned her wedding band, yep, the wedding band that Jesus Christ gave her she sold just to get Pa out of the clink. And here I am wit' you. After all these years and Ma in the grave from what he done to her. And here I am walkin' the streets with a bum like you, Harry. I don't know what to do in that court-house, what kind of money they say they're needin'. I shoulda called up the jail keeper and told him to throw away the key. You better believe it. Yeah, throw it away, mister, and keep him there for good."

She stopped as the rolling moan of a police siren inter-rupted, then the rushing motion of the charging blue-and-white squad car as it hesitated at a stop sign then accelerated. Neither of them looked up at it.

"So why didn't ya?" he suddenly said. His voice was buried in his shirt but loud enough so that she was aware that he had said something.

"Listen to you. Stay in jail like a criminal. Like half your life. In the clink for this or that. The first time losing your job and me and your ma beggin' the boss to keep ya on and give ya a chance to straighten up. Then after that no jobs, nobody gonna hire a guy wit' a record. And I would have to go to work alla time and look at the ladies. They talk, don't think I don't know they talk, and when you was taken in that time I saw Mrs. Kosciusko and she was looking at me funny like. Yeah, don't think I don't know that they're talkin' about things. I know, and sometimes it hurts me like a knife in my heart."

He mumbled his thoughts. "Put up all that dough 'cuz some women who don't know shit from shinola are talkin'?"

"You don't know the half of it, Harry," she went on, ignor-ing the words from him, then turning the corner with the building in sight. "I keep it locked up inside of me and I don't tell no one. I don't even tell the priest what's inside of me. But someday. Someday. You just wait."

"Five bills. That what it was? Five hunnerd to spring me?"

She turned and headed down the sidewalk to the rear. He followed mechanically, not walking just moving, like a well-trained pet that knows the route. They climbed the back steps in silence. Only at the porch Harry paused and looked out into the alley, the slanting lights and the trees barren and nagged by the unrelenting wind.

"Five bills," he repeated.

He followed her into the kitchen. She switched on the light. She went into a small pantry where she kept canned goods and cleaning tools and came out with a Jewel Food Stores shopping bag. Walking past him, slipping her coat from her arms as she went, she started in again.

"I work and scrub and clean up every night and this is what I get," she said. Still, her voice was mild and almost conversational, not the usual pitched ranting colored with Polish and reverberating off the walls like the roar of an evangelist. Now she spoke as if she were reciting, absently, a litany of reproof.

"I never should a opened that door over there, Harry. Never. So I was stupid and thinking that things could change 'cuz we're gettin' older now. I think for a while that maybe you ain't the Harry that was my stepbrother from the old neighborhood. But I shoulda known. You better believe it. Now I got troubles I never dreamed about."

She left the kitchen and went into the bathroom. He could hear her open the medicine chest and clink bottles around. Then a thud, another, and he realized that she was dropping things into the shopping bag.

"Ma used to talk to me about things," she said, her voice slightly louder from the bathroom. "She used to say that things didn't never change for her. She always said, 'Now, Helen, you remember, once a rat always a rat.' She'd say, 'Once a soak always a soak.' Then she'd point out some of them old men on the corners, some of them like Mr. Wojda who sat on them chairs by the trees and played cards and told stories. All us kids used to like them old men but not Ma. She'd say, 'That Stanley Wojda was a mean man, a *mean*

246

man, Helen, and don't you ever forget it.'

"So I kept the same thing in my head about Pa. He was gettin' old and watchin' wrestlin' and everyone was treatin' him good and callin' him Grampa even though they weren't in the family. And they used to say to me, 'What a nice old man yer Pa is,' and I'd smile and say, 'Yep,' but you better believe I never forgot. I never forgot that he was a mean man, how he used to treat Ma, how he stole from her and told her lies and how he hit her when he was drunk which was alla time. I never forgot how he hit Ernie and how he whipped them dogs, just hit them dogs until they was squealin' and barkin' and half dead. I never forgot that 'cuz Ma told me not to. Not even when Pa was old and couldn't hardly see no more. That's what yer memory will do to ya. Yep, ya start to think about the old times and how it was in the old neighborhood and you start to forget, you start to forget how rough it was and how much them people used to hurt each other. Sure, it was better than it is today, I ain't sayin' it ain't, but it still wasn't no good. Just the things we want to remember about how good the food was and the weddings and goin' ta church. And we don't remember how we used to cry. How Ma used to cry. That's what yer memory does to ya."

She walked out of the bathroom into the living room, switching on a lamp and the overhead light as she went. Harry leaned against the kitchen counter, not wanting to go at it with her, not sure what his next move would be. He went over to the tap and got a glass of water.

She soon returned to the kitchen. Her coat was off, the bag in her hands. Harry turned with the glass in his hand and realized that she was holding his belongings. There in the Jewel bag, unceremoniously packed, was everything he called his own. Helen put the bag on the table and went over to the refrigerator. Bending down, with the pleats of her work dress drawing tightly against her back and her rear end, she felt around the space beneath the icebox, the space Harry had used to store his stash.

247

"Yeah, that's 'cuz I remember. That was the same place Pa used to hide his pay he was holdin' back so he could go on boozin' and not let Ma know. But she knew. She knew alla time 'cuz she tol' me. I knew it too on you, Harry, like a book plain and simple. And you thought you was gettin' away with somethin'. Gettin' away with somethin' 'cuz I'm too stupid to figure things out. After all these years, Harry, with what Pa did and then Joe, yeah, he had his hiding places too, and now you."

She stood up and brushed herself off.

"Now I tell myself not to get upset anymore. And the priest he tells me to love everybody and forget about the bad. But no, Harry, I got to remember. Like Ma. So now I'm rememberin' good."

She went to the table and grabbed the bag, then turned and opened the back door. With one hand she held the door open, the bag in the other. She looked over at Harry, Helen Pontek, his stepsister, with her puffed cheeks and her mouth drawn tightly closed, her thick stocky hands, the ever-present work dress.

Harry put the glass on the sink and walked for the door. He could see what she wanted out of him. He wouldn't argue.

"I'll pay ya that money back, Helen. Five hunnerd for the bail bond. I'll pay ya."

He took the bag from her and walked out onto the porch. She closed the screen behind him and he heard the click of the latch.

"You'll get the money from me," he said.

She paused as she was about to close the door. Her face was solid, expressionless, her eyes open and unwavering.

"Okay, Harry," she said. "I'm not talkin' about it no more."

Then she closed the door. He stood alone on the landing, his shadow long in the light of the porch bulb. Again he heard the click of the dead-bolt lock, and her heavy walk against the kitchen floor.

The Jewel bag was heavy in his hand, a couple of shirts and

a pair of pants, underwear he had picked up recently. Suddenly he felt the wind, the outdoors, and the absence of the warm kitchen smell. He went for the steps, then stopped, and slowly he sat down in the corner of the porch, his back to the railing. He pulled his knees up.

With a little food, a couple of beers to wash out the tubes, and another packet of pills. Donald Ray went back out into the street. He was edgy, restless, driven by the momentum he'd gained from the earlier score, pushed by the frustration of knowing that he'd taken big risks, a job in which a living human being had seen his face but which he'd come away from with peanuts, only enough dough to keep him in cigarettes. He could still feel the jabbing of the gun in his belt, a presence which reminded him, nagged at him, as if to say that since it was there it should be used.

So by early evening he made his way up Broadway, keeping his eyes open, contemplating his next move. Once again he walked without knowing his mug was on the day's Police Bulletin, that almost every police car that idly passed him could have nabbed him if the patrolmen had taken the effort to do their homework. But in his ignorance, his notoriety, Donald Ray walked and schemed and prepared himself for his next felony. He was going now, a lone wolf in the full moon, "Yer a one-man crime wave, Burl," he chuckled once again, one job already and a second, whatever it would be, on the way. It was a desperate, uncomplicated, unavoidable reality, this night like any other in Uptown.

He walked slowly, self-contained, almost lost in his own thoughts as sparse as they were, his hands in his pockets. The street was noisy and alive, if for no other reason than because of the neon from the bars and the pay halls, the angular lights of cars and the overhead street lights. But the sidewalk, the wide uneven sidewalk that was so much a part of Broadway, was surprisingly empty, almost devoid of the usual parade of faces that aimlessly patrolled it. Now it was just Donald Ray

249

Burl, alone, on the prowl, looking for trouble and not finding much of it.

He crossed Windsor and caught her almost out of the corner of his eye. She was on the opposite side of the street, a woman in a coat and carrying a shopping bag, apparently waiting for the southbound Broadway bus. She waited and stared down at the street, scolding the bus for not appearing, with a scowling, thin-eyed frown across her face. In a second she was fixed in Donald Ray's mind, impulsively, without thought or decision, as if today was his day to encounter defenseless women in opportune spots. Here was another, right now, standing alone on a street that for some reason was suddenly quiet and deserted, and he jaywalked across Broadway, taking long steps and closing in.

She did not turn toward him as he crossed Broadway or as he came closer to where she stood. She remained with her back to him, staring intently up Broadway toward Wilson, trying to pry the bus from the distance. Short, round, almost shapeless except for the bag that hung from her hands, she stood as an open target for him. This would be easier than the other, he thought, but only a fleeting thought, for he was seeing nothing more than the sprint that he would need to turn the corner at Wilson and disappear into the no man's land on Clifton across to Racine. It was a single, unsullied bullet of an impulse: he was suddenly no further away than ten yards from the woman, the shape, and he could see the outline of a black handbag stuffed in the top of her shopping bag. On the glide he would pluck it out and take off, he thought, closing in, she not even turning at the sound of his steps, perhaps deaf, or hard of hearing, one of those thick-necked Slavic women who worked the laundries and took late buses home without fear or timidity, and suddenly was on top of her, reaching out, the act.

He shot his hand out at the black form of the purse and suddenly the woman turned. In one motion he grabbed the handbag and some of the paper from the bag. It ripped loudly as he pulled, a quick jerk, and he could see the woman's right arm coming around, swinging like the boom of a crane, together with a burst of a shout. But he had the purse and a step and out of the side of his eye he saw the bag rip, the woman's arm jerk upward and rip it even more so that the contents—packages, bags, objects—cascaded out and over the walk. But any sound was lost in her bellow, a loud baritone shout that rang through the street.

"Thief! Thief! Help me! Hurry! Help! Hellllllp!" she roared, with such force that it startled even Donald Ray, drilling him like an alarm bell in a deserted alley.

Suddenly he pulled up, whirled, for no reason he could think of other than the impulse that his legs seemed to shoot to his brain, and he pulled his gun from his belt. He faced the woman and waved it at her, like a baton, a signal, a flare, anything but a gun, for he realized that he wasn't pointing it.

"Shut yer mouth!" he yelled, still stumbling with his momentum, the gun a flag in front of his own face.

"Nooooooo!" the woman yelled, louder now, like a hand siren gaining power. "Hellllllp!! Get me, thief!!!!"

He turned and ran, again running, this time with the fear that had gripped him before, a wild, uncontrollable push from his legs and his stomach and his lungs. He thought he heard the woman yell "Gun!" was sure he heard the squeal of tires, the flash of lights, and he ran even harder, saw the approach of the el station and hit it.

As he disappeared into the station, what he thought he had heard to be squealing tires was actually that: a blue-and-white squad car hurtling around the corner of Windsor and shooting down the opposite side of Broadway toward the woman. In the quiet and the moment of stillness after the snatch, they had heard the woman's screams, two patrolmen, and their adrenalin sprung them into action.

251

She waved and motioned at them frantically. The squad car stopped long enough for a door to open and an officer to stick his head out.

"What? Which way!?" he barked at the woman.

"He robbed me with a gun!!! A gun!!! Over there on the el!!!" she screamed and the car spun off, squealing tires and sending dust and stones across the pavement.

In a few strides Donald Ray leaped past the station attendant's window, hurdling the turnstile, and with giant steps he climbed the stairs leading to the platform. As he went up he heard the train roar in, north or southbound, he didn't care, for Wilson Avenue's platform lay in the middle of the tracks and took trains from both ways. He slowed at the top, stuffing the handbag into his shirt, and in two steps he was on the train, the coachman routinely sticking his head out the window to see if he had to let on or let off any more passengers. Then the doors closed, quickly, as if Donald Ray had been working the controls himself. The train was in motion, oblivious of the commotion which raged just below it, the ticket taker trying to sound the alarm buzzer, the buzzer for a jumper, her missed fare, the sudden presence of the officers storming the station in pursuit.

As Donald Ray had just done, one officer ran past the teller's window then squeezed by the turnstile, overloaded with too much equipment to jump it. With lumbering steps he made it to the platform in time to see the train gaining speed, a good thirty yards from the platform, heading for the straightaway dead south.

He cursed, then stopped and backtracked down to his partner.

"Get on the radio!" he yelled. "We'll get him at Addison."

The squad shot down Montrose over to Sheridan, then right down Sheffield toward the stop. They could see the outline of the train on the tracks, between the buildings, traveling quickly and totally unimpeded, even as they dodged and bounced and swiveled through the congestion of the streets.

Donald Ray headed for the back of the car, past a black kid who was sleeping with his head propped against a window. No one in the car took notice of him, of the bulge in his shirt, of his breathing, the sweat which was pouring down the sides of his face. He sat down in a heap, welcoming the noise and lurching of the elevated train, another of the trains he still had a soft spot for, that intrigued him and held a constant lure for him. Now it was his haven, his hideout amidst the fury that went on in the street. He rummaged through the purse, found the billfold almost immediately, and suddenly he turned and began to wrestle with the latches on the window. With nobody around to see him, the motorman far away and the conductor leaning his head out the window two cars down, Donald Ray tossed the purse out into the blackness which raced by him. He didn't even see it fall.

Then for a moment he sat, sinking his body into the seat, exhausted temporarily, facing north as the train traveled south, but luxuriously wrapped in his clattering safety, a refuge from whatever or whoever was chasing him. He would ride it, riding as he had always loved to do, until he sank into the reality of being a rider instead of a refugee. Then his thoughts of complacency left him; he looked out the window to see if he could spot any cops, to see where he was and plan where he would get off. If he was right about what he thought he heard, the cops might have been behind him, might be waiting for him if they were quick enough and interested enough to go after the pinch. So he would not let up, he cocked his head, felt the revolver in his belt, now stuffed next to the billfold he'd just lifted. The lights of a station approached.

"Addison," he said to himself.

From his days of riding the trains he knew the stops as if they were grade-school multiplication tables drilled into his

253

head. He glanced up at the train's roller, read "A," and realized smugly that the train would pause, the engineer checking his lights and easing off on the throttle, at the approach of the station, but only that, for the "A" train highballed from Wilson to Belmont, fourteen long blocks of unimpeded straightaway, and it would roar past the Addison stop as if it were a hick town on the run of the Broadway Limited.

As Donald Ray gauged the Addison approach, the squad car lurched around the corner of Sheffield onto Addison, in front of the gates to Wrigley Field, and blew out a last burst of speed before squealing to a halt beneath the station. It was met almost head-on by another squad coming down Addison from Halsted, and the four patrolmen suddenly converged on each other and scrambled for the steps leading to the platform. As they huffed toward the upper level, they felt the vibration of the train passing, hoped it was a northbound, then the lead officer emerged on the platform and once again kicked himself for his mistake. The "A" train, Donald Ray Burl in the fourth car near the rear, flew on by.

In his own cubicle of safety, Donald Ray looked around him, once again checking on who was in the car, if anyone was watching him. Besides the sleeping kid he spotted two Puerto Ricans sitting by the far door. They were jabbering to each other in Spanish, trying to shout above the noise, and Donald Ray was certain they took no notice of him. Then, for the first time since the snatch, he was curious about what he'd gotten. He went for the billfold in his shirt, then stopped, thinking that now wasn't the time. He'd look through it somewhere alone; that would be no problem. Now he had to make sure that his escape was total, that the cops at Broadway weren't dogging him. He was almost sure they weren't, or wouldn't because he knew what cops thought about the shit in Uptown, and he knew how hard they chased, how far they pushed on the cheap stuff. In a way it made the street grabs almost safer, more of a sure thing than a store robbery or a burglary since no detective would come around trying to piece things together. If you could make your grab and run, do it and do it when it had to be done, then you were almost one hundred percent in the clear as soon as you ducked out of sight. It was hard work, the takes often pitiful, but it had its advantages.

Lost in his thoughts, he was momentarily surprised when the train slowed for the Belmont stop. He wasn't in the clear yet, they could be here, waiting, and he prepared to spring into another car. Then the doors methodically opened, held, then closed again. With a lurch, a halting spurt of power, the train moved again, and he sat back.

Moments later he sensed the Fullerton approach, the wide bed of tracks where the Ravenswood line merged and headed into the last main North Side stop. Then he saw it too, saw it like no human being without his edge, without his discriminating vision could, a blur of mars light bobbing on a building below, fuzz blue, on Fullerton, then a shirt, a cop on the platform. Suddenly he was caught in the panic of it once again, that they were there for him. The train lurched, decelerated, and Donald Ray instinctively knew that the engineer had braked for a signal, something out of the routine, and he was sure the cops were stopping the train.

He got up quickly and dashed for an aisle seat near the door. His head darted from side to side, checking his safety valves, his routes, the people on the car who could help him or who could dig his grave. Then it hit him that if the cops came on board they would spot him like a patch of neon, him with a gun in his belt, the billfold in his gut, sweat and grime and quick breaths and guilt oozing from him. He would have to make a break. His head jerked forward as the train slowed, slowing, then swiveled out to take in the contour of the platform, and suddenly the train was still. He glanced quickly out the windows, then he heard the jingling, the telltale noise of cop.

He knew he had no choice. Suddenly he was on the platform and running, hurtling around the dividing posts, the

255

rain shelters. The cop saw only a leg and a pivot. Then he took chase.

"Hey! There he goes!" he shouted and ran down the platform in pursuit.

The other officer heard him and jumped quickly out of the train, almost bumping into his partner as he charged down the boards.

Donald Ray saw nothing but tracks and darkness and space in front of him. He heard the cops, heard them running, his own steps, and suddenly he made his decision. With a single leap he jumped from the platform onto the tracks. He hurdled the rails, seeing the third rail like a beacon, knowing he had to jump it and stay clear of it above all else. With three leaps he was on the catwalk between the tracks, the boardwalk used by repair crews. He ran with giant strides, his hard leather shoes clomping on the boards.

Both of the cops stopped at the end of the platform, straining to stop their momentum. Then one of them jumped heavily onto the tracks, clunking down on the wooden ties like a barrel.

"Get 'im at Armitage!" he yelled and took off in a half sprint, half jog down the tracks. He too eyed the electrified third rail as if it were a rattlesnake ready to strike.

His partner clomped across the platform toward the steps. Then he stopped to shout at two more blue shirts that had hustled into sight.

"The guy's on the tracks! Get 'im at Armitage!" he shouted. He stopped to collect his breath when he realized that the two officers he'd shouted at understood and were charging back to their squad.

The cop leaned heavily against an iron post on the platform, breathing hard and loud and feeling the blood rush to his head. He was overweight and beet-red in the face.

"Jesus!" he gasped.

Donald Ray saw nothing but track in front of him, nothing but the steel gray arteries that crisscrossed and wound over each other like eels. He saw the lumps of switches and fuse boxes, transformers and junctions, jumped them, dodged them, caught the red lights that flew past his head and the wind that he was sucking into his chest. Suddenly he spotted the Armitage station, the lights curling over the platform. He could jump up on it and hustle down and out, free once again, anything to get off the tracks. It was a couple of hundred yards away, four blocks from Fullerton, and he ran for it as if it were his life's goal, deliverance from the jungle of wood and steel and electricity that surrounded him in this no man's land, the bed he loved so when he was sitting in the lead of a car but that had suddenly been transformed into a deadly field through which he had to run, a field laced with death so brutal and burning, voltage that would melt the roof of his skull if it hit him, a field mined with traps and devices that he knew nothing about and yet over which he was stepping as if they were rocks in a creek bed.

The lights of the station came nearer, suddenly like floodlamps. They were all that mattered, all he saw. Then, just as quickly, just as totally, he spotted the deadly blue specter below. He sank with it, as if he'd been shot. It was the cops and they would be coming up even as he would take his first steps down. Just as quickly as the station had loomed as his ace it had faded beyond hope, and he reached for whatever reserve he could summon to make it past the lights, to spring past the station and beyond.

He went to his legs, legs which ached and strained because they had not been pushed like this in years, his lungs heaving and clawing at his throat. Then a single eye came out of the pit that he'd always loved, the opening of the tunnel where the trains went underground. The eye that came for him was that of a northbound "B" train hitting the semidarkness of the night after the pitch of the tunnel. Suddenly the horn rang out, the high-pitched squeal that reminded him of an animal call, a deer, or an elk, though he'd never really heard either one. It startled him, then angered him, and he kept

257

charging, kept going for the pit that was now pushing up the eye, the snaking train, horn squealing.

Then it rushed by him. The wind and the motion pushed him, as if trying to send him off his course and into the maze of rails. He fought it and kept his balance, now out of the glare of the station's lights. He slowed, by necessity because he was almost dead from fatigue, and looked back. Through the fifty yards to the station he spotted officers coming up the steps and hustling onto the platform. He crouched and kept moving, heard a voice, a stampede of footsteps. He stumbled ahead, bending over and moving like an aching dog, still aware of the rails and the possibility that one bad step, a trip, a twisted foot, could fry him.

Then he felt the earth sag, the decline, and suddenly he was being taken by his own weight, his own inertia, into the hole. Now, for the first time in his life, without the protection of a subway car or the glass in front of his face, or even the thin veneer of his fantasies, he was truly in the tunnel, the exciting half-moon tube that would swallow him as it always did the roaring cars. He felt the gravel beneath his feet, saw the angles of the fences, the backs of the houses; he was falling, flailing, stumbling almost drunkenly. Yet he was now strangely elated, awed by what he was slipping into, and gradually he was consumed by the darkness, chilled by the clammy cool of underground.

Immediately he headed for the wall, and the small concrete walkway that hugged the side of the tunnel. He jumped toward it, hopping with awkward, exaggerated, and painful leaps over the rails. Suddenly he was at the ledge, feeling the concrete and pulling himself up to the walk. He sat on it and panted like a racehorse.

He jerked his head up and stared into the wide, lighted expanse of the tunnel's entrance. He was only about ten yards into the cover of darkness, hidden from those outside, but able to see any figure that crossed the horizon of the tracks and began the descent into the tube. He thought at first only of running some more, of getting together what strength he could muster and going deeper into the pit. But then the possibilities hit him. If the cops didn't take after him on foot, and he expected to see them lumbering into view any second now, perhaps they would take a train after him, riding it like an armored tank into the tunnel. Their guns would be poking out of the windows like howitzers on turrets, he was sure of that, the car going ever so slowly, ready to crack off a volley of potshots at the first thing that moved, be it a rat with a tail, or a rat with a tee-shirt and a hillbilly twang.

He got up and started moving, walking, lurching against the rounded sides of the tunnel in an attempt to look backward and forward. If he fell off the walk he'd be gone. If he didn't watch his rear they'd be on him and lay a shot in his back as easy as if he were the outlined figure at the end of the shooting range. He kept going, every ten yards coming under the bare lightbulbs that hugged the tunnel.

Then he saw them. Two figures, bobbing up and down in what looked like a slow run, suddenly coming into the light of the tunnel's mouth and beginning their descent. He could see the outline of their hats, the heavy waists, and he knew what they were and why they were coming. He increased his pace, the mouth of the tunnel suddenly becoming smaller, the distant light fading until he was totally inside the tube. He could only go one way, he could only rely on the safety of the two-foot-wide ledge of concrete that was his runway.

Suddenly an eye hit him and he froze, a northbound train. Its horn sounded, an engineer who saw him and was no doubt startled, but who could only slow and honk and then move the train on in a gust of wind and noise and sparks. Then lights hit him from the rear, a southbound train, coming on him as if it was going to sideswipe him, the margin looking that close, and send him splattering against the sides of the tunnel like an inky bug on a windshield. It came on him, down on him, drilling into his brain, and suddenly he felt all the fear and momentary helplessness that he was sure people felt just before death. He didn't see anything but the train. He caught his breath and saw only what it was going to do to him. Slapping his palms against the wall, his back flat against it and hugging it, Donald Ray froze and moaned and envisioned a .38-caliber service revolver poised from a window and aimed at his neck. He lost track of it all in the sudden explosion of sound as the train rushed by him, the motion and wind strafing him, his mind popping like no high he'd ever known, waiting for something to happen.

Then it was by him. He shuddered at the relief, and suddenly he realized that he was shaking uncontrollably. He was afraid as he had never been before and he could do nothing in those long seconds but tremble. It cracked through him. He saw his home in Kentucky, his mother and Art Burl. He suddenly thought of how old he was and that his life was immediately bunched into this one solitary, clammy place. He wanted to give up and give in, to collapse and get as far away as possible from the pain he'd just realized. He was breathing hard and bobbing his head, a motion which clapped his teeth together and brought him back to the present. He shook himself and looked out at the light of the entrance. They were there and closing.

He took off once again toward the darkness. Now he was off; he turned momentarily and saw the bouncing, running figures. In an instant he pulled out his revolver and cracked off a shot. It surprised him with the sound, a round, echoing carom of a shot that seemed to lose itself in the black of the tunnel after its initial burst. He paused for a moment, crouching, trying to see what he had brought on with the shot.

"Shit," he said out loud. "Why'd I do that for?"

And he turned and ran.

The two cops were running clumsily when they heard the crack. Though they were straining to see where they were running, aware of the tunnel and the noises that came from behind and below them, they instinctively knew the sound of gunfire, and they stopped dead, both crouching and struggling for their revolvers. They were only about twenty-five yards from the mouth of the tunnel, painfully vulnerable in the dim light of the outside.

"Bastard does have a gun," one of them grunted. He motioned toward the side of the tracks and the two of them gingerly stepped laterally across the tracks.

"Jesus, I hate this shit," the second officer said.

The two of them hopped the rails, jangling the equipment which hung heavily on their belts. They were shirt-sleeved and sweating large patches of navy into their light-blue uniforms. Then the first officer abruptly stopped and stepped back into the middle of the tracks. He lifted his revolver and pulled off three shots, aiming them not into the center of the tunnel but at the sides. They pinged off the concrete, echoing and rolling through the darkness.

With each shot the cop smiled and gauged the carom, the crazy path the bullets would take once they kissed the curvature of the tunnel.

"Let the jagoff play with those for a while," he said, then pulled himself clumsily up onto the ledge.

Donald Ray was sure now; he'd heard the crack of gunfire. Now it was for keeps. The cops could spend all night flushing him out; they were like that when they got pissed off. So, hell, he could stay in the hole as long as they could, slipping from one side to the other, hiding behind the partitions and blind spots to keep out of sight. The next station was North and Clybourn, six long and dank blocks from Armitage, a strip of dead track that offered him little if anything of an escape.

Slowly, gradually, he felt himself lapsing into a walk. He jerked loose the cheap wallet that had become a jabbing presence in his gut. He walked over to a single tunnel light and held the wallet up to it. In a change pouch, rolled up into tight cylinders, were two bills, one a twenty, one a fifty. Donald Ray couldn't believe it, couldn't believe that on a crummy grab like that off of a beefy laundry bag he'd gotten seventy bucks. It was more than he'd gotten in all of his last few jobs combined. And he had it here in this hole, with cops on his ass. He unraveled the bills, smoothed them with his fingers and creased them lengthwise. He'd stolen seventy bucks and now he'd hang on to it. And for a moment, with a sudden surge of down-home piss and spit, he felt like Art Burl, training his sight on something in the woods, seeing through the darkness and pinching the cheeks of the two scrawny, tow-headed kids by his heels, a bitching, slugging lout of a guy who could hold his own and hold it well.

He was running again, pushing himself into an awkward, offbalance trot to stay away from the raised juice rail, but in so doing bumping and scraping his shoulder against the concrete. The more he ran, the more his head filled with a sense of escape, that he could not stay down here much longer. He couldn't wait for them to close in on him, to flush him out like a mole from both sides and from both ends. There wasn't time to plan his moves or gather energy. As he ran he wondered whether or not he should somehow get across to the northbound track and head back for Armitage, or if he should push for North and Clybourn. Both plans were chock-full of unknowns, damnably complex at a time when he wanted things to be simple. He wondered about the cops, about the guns they were carrying—he could see himself in the sights of their shotguns, or their sniper rifles, the trigger-happy bastards with more fire power than an artillery squadron, bored and happy to have a chance to ventilate some hillbilly —then it hit him, even as the breath poured from him and his jogging continued ceaselessly, that he had not an idea of how many were chasing him, or where they were right now, or even, and this shot through him like hope to a drowning man, if they were still on him at all.

Then he saw the station, suddenly breaking the dim gray-yellow of the tunnel with a blaze of white light. It was a stage, an open arena of fluorescent lights and ceramic tiles, and it beckoned him even as it momentarily scared his guts into his throat.

He pulled up and stopped. He hugged the wall and tried to bend down and out of sight. But he realized he had nowhere to go, nothing to crouch behind. Then he heard a muted jingling sound from the rear.

They were coming, damnit; he couldn't keep the visions of an ambush from crowding in. He could hear the explosions, see the bullets spinning in midair as they came for him.

He moved forward. He still saw nothing on the track and not a person on the platform. He was sure now that they were waiting for him. Then out of the corner of his eye he caught a new beam of light. It came on him only yards before the station opened up to him. He saw that the light was coming through a walkway, about a yard wide, that led through the dividing wall between the tracks to the northbound tracks and the opposite platform. He ran for it, suddenly caught in the blaze of light that was the station. Reaching inside his belt, going for it for the first time with any sense of mission or need, he took out his Titan and held it tightly.

He glanced back and forth at the stretch of platform. Then he saw blue. A uniformed patrolman across the tracks, his gun out and leveled in front of him, coolly stared into the mouth of the tunnel. Donald Ray shot at him, a wild, impulsive shot he'd neither aimed nor sighted. The explosion rang in his ears, and he saw only the first motions of the officer as the cop whirled and shot back at where he thought the gunfire had come from.

With a leap Donald Ray pulled himself up on the platform. He turned left, then right, and he saw the single exit. He began running, sprinting once again down the concrete runway that was the vacant platform. The exit sign poked out from the white ceramic walls, ahead of him, his beacon of escape.

Shots cracked behind him, but they were lost in the fury of his running, then more, two shots, he was sure of it, and he turned, almost losing his balance and scuffing the heels of his shoes on the cement, and fired once down the platform. He saw nothing but the whirling, dizzying lights before he reached out for the wall and pulled himself around the corner of the exit. Ahead of him was a long stairway, three flights in all, and he began taking the steps three at a time. He was panting loudly, the muscles in his legs aching, and he grabbed at the shining white tiles as if to make them pull him up.

He attacked the final flight. He tasted the blood in his throat, fought the thinness in his head, his body about to collapse. But he saw the light from the circular stationhouse. It meant the street, and maybe he had made it.

He turned at the stairs and saw white, the white of a haze he couldn't distinguish, a white that was part of his mind and part of his surroundings. For the North-Clybourn station was a hexagonal building bordering each corner of a diagonal intersection, each wall white with 1920s tile, opening to a large lobby and three entrances, but more importantly, three exits.

With a lunge, a weaving, offbalance gallop, he pulled himself, reaching for air and an imaginary railing, up to the level of the street. He was inside the station, a single, enclosed ticket booth in its center, railings and turnstiles winding around it, and then the exit turnstile. He eyed only the doors leading out, straight out. He saw no one and nothing, not the plain-clothes detectives who darted into each of the side entrances. Instead he pushed his Kentucky body, every juice in his gut, every tendon, every muscle he could feel, toward the low brass railing that ran in front of the booth and was the one thing separating him from the open lobby and the open doors.

He went for it like a sprinter going for the tape. He didn't hear the shouts, didn't see the blues and the greens of the dicks, didn't see the steel of their automatics. But with a final effort, one lunge for freedom and escape from the clutches of the subway tunnel, he went for the railing. With a lateral motion he pawed at it with his free but smashed hand, sending the other, his gun hand, shooting outward, and prepared to lift himself up and over and out.

As he hit it, as he felt the cool of the smooth brass, he pushed up and his feet left the ground. Up, his body leaning and pushing over, when the explosions filled the building. Cracking, deafening, rolling in the cool of the ceramic and the cement until they hit him, a cold-cocking like he'd gotten once before on Wilson Avenue from an Indian and the blunt end of a quart bottle of beer. He saw a curtain close over his mind, a dizzy, lazy, comfortable curtain of black, like the black of a Kentucky pool, the spring water, the breath of down home. He lost hold of the rail; in midflight his left foot dropped and caught on the bar. He was falling, flying, felt himself drifting then sinking. He wanted to say something, to smooth it out, to square things, but then he couldn't, couldn't summon the reserves from his strong Kentucky self, couldn't because of the burning in his head and chest.

The body hit the terrazzo floor a virtual dead weight. It had caught four slugs, three in the chest, one just beneath the eye, all cutting swaths through vital organs. It was a matter of seconds, perhaps less, until the heaving, tensed, desperate mass of adult torso was nothing more than a carcass. It lay in a pile, bunched against the brass railing. A pool of blood began to well by the mouth, a fragment of a tooth.

Slowly, as if they were unsure of just how still the corpse was, six members of the East Chicago Avenue task force stepped slowly into the middle of the station. None of them knew what or who it was that they had just picked out of the air. They only saw the blood, the heap of hair, and knew that they had got him.

McMahon could no longer give the Deborah Cortez case much of his time. It was sixth or seventh on the pile now, beneath more shootings, stabbings, most of them in Uptown, and most recently a case of a Filipino who sat down in his bathtub with his bills, his unemployment, his bad English, and a gallon of gasoline, pouring the latter over himself, and lighting it. Each case, regardless of how routine or how bizarre, with or without a suspect, produced mountains of reports, hours of paperwork that the detectives had to complete after each shift.

It was now up to a lieutenant if McMahon was to continue on with the Cortez case. Either that or McMahon's own curiosity and his own overtime. His partner didn't push him much on it, for Farber was convinced in his own mind that the answer to the whole thing was probably contained solely in the hotel night clerk, the bastard Greek whom they could smell all the way back to the station but who moaned and complained that he was the cleanest thing out of Greece since Plato.

Still, McMahon kept his ears open and hit some of his informants, his I.O.U.s for information, anything they might have heard, anything on the Greek, or the Vicklen Hotel, or both.

It was Farber who took the message. A burglary dick he had once worked with called him with a hunch, and in a few minutes Farber and McMahon were headed for the Vicklen Hotel. It was early afternoon, and as the two of them walked through the lobby they simultaneously looked over to the clerk's desk. They spotted a different person behind it, not the Greek, but that was to be expected, given the Greek's hours. Still, the two of them looked anyway, checking, two murder cops constantly checking.

In an open third-floor room they met the burglary dick, a Puerto Rican, one of the few Spanish detectives on the force, named Rojas. He was standing in the corner of the flat's living room, a lime-green room with lavender furniture that had been pushed and maneuvered out of place to the point that the apartment was in shambles.

"Hey, Gene," Rojas said as he looked over. His olive complexion complemented his impeccably trimmed black hair. He wore dark tailored suits and shirts with high collars, ties held in place with tacks and jewelry that thrived on his hands.

"Over here," he said. He motioned them over to where he was talking to a thin, blond-haired man of about thirty-five. The man was frail but tanned and clean-shaven, dressed in Levi's with a crease on each pant leg and a bright-colored print shirt with two buttons open. To the detectives he spelled fruitcake, his place and its furniture, the man's soft, measured, cautious tones.

"This guy's been taken for about everything that worked in the place," Rojas said.

The blond man looked up suspiciously at McMahon and Farber, then looked down once again and revealed a smoldering cigarette cupped in his right hand. He puffed it quickly, then blew out the smoke without inhaling.

"You know, all the stuff, stereo, jewelry, television. Somebody with a key most likely, from the looks of the door and what we've come up with," Rojas said. "But there's something else Mr. Harris told me that I thought you might wanna hear. I'll describe it myself if you don't mind."

He looked at Harris. "I don't mind," the man said. He again puffed at his cigarette.

"Our man at the desk is on this. You know, the clerk on the graveyard shift? Greek guy that we've pinched a lot of times on hot goods, a little fence work, the usual, you know. Anyone takes a room here for more than a week and he gets a discount so long as he buys a piece of equipment from the Greek. Like Mr. Harris here, bought himself a nice Sony, now dearly departed, but he got a good price on it, right?"

267

"So the Greek is selling shit to people here. So what. Hot stuff, right?" Farber said.

"Yep, but we knew that. We knew it goes on all over this place and in damn near every joint in the neighborhood. But we don't do much unless we get someone with a beef who'll go to bat for us. Christ, some of this crap comes right out of the boxcars and still has a warranty on it. And the Greek all the time keeps saying to me, 'Go ahead, here's the keys. Check the place.' He knows he's cool with this merchandise."

Rojas paused for a minute. He noticed that Mr. Harris was fidgeting, growing impatient with the dicks.

"C'mon, let's go outside," Rojas said.

McMahon and Farber followed him.

"The bastard sells to the fruits, see," Rojas said. "And he leans on them so they don't say nothing. But I'll tell you right now every piece of furniture in this hotel is probably hot."

"So why us?" McMahon said.

"Yeah, sorry I'm takin' so long," Rojas said. "See, this Harris guy in there is dirty himself. Got a few pinches for copping, things like that, hangs around. Now he's been ripped off by one of his fruit friends, see, and he's furious so he calls us. He's leaving town, picking up and going, so he's decided to bag a few of his buddies. The Greek's one, the guy who stole his stuff is another.

"In the middle of it all he casually tells me that he didn't get his radio from the Greek. He bought it from a prostitute working the building. A little Puerto Rican girl named Debbie. Said she was selling stuff from her room and he bought it to help her out on her rent. You got it?"

Farber hit it first. "Christ, so that's it. Same girl is thrown out the window."

"That's how I see it," said Rojas.

"And the Greek did the throwing," said McMahon.

"Yep. Perfect for him," Rojas cut in. "It's one thing to mess around doing pussy but it's another to take business from the man in charge."

"So where does it leave you?" asked Farber.

Rojas pulled his chin up from out of his collar. "I think I can lean on the fruit to stay in town and go to court on the Greek. Small shit, but with some work we can trace the sets to him and maybe go to the judge with a possession and illegal sale. It ain't much, but this guy's pretty good. But maybe you got a murder case, huh?"

Rojas smiled. His teeth were white and polished, crowning his good looks.

"First break on it so far," said Farber.

"One of my people," Rojas said; again he smiled, now with a trace of sarcasm. "I hope you guys remember that for me."

Farber nodded at the Spanish dick; McMahon smiled at Rojas' humor, his style.

They decided to drive to the Greek's house on the Northwest Side. If they were lucky they'd catch him in bed and maybe groggy enough to let down his defenses. Farber drove; McMahon thumbed through the cases on the clipboard. It was unending, like a nonstop melodrama, except that it was real, played out in professional form by real people, and him, a cop, picking away at the pile as if he alone were able to make order out of it. Even if he didn't think about it that way, even if he didn't let the specifics of the job of solving murders get on him like that, saddle him with the responsibility of putting reason behind them, or cohesion, or even a semblance of sanity, he still thumbed through them, like an operator negotiating the telephone directory, a mailman pacing through his route. That, and no more.

"Whatta we got?" Farber said, interrupting McMahon's concentration.

"The Greek? What can we say? Lot of shit around his collar but nothing that will make a State's Attorney do somersaults," McMahon said.

"So no case unless he talks."

McMahon laughed. "Yeah, and this guy's gonna talk like Big Tuna's gonna turn in his relatives."

269

Farber didn't reply. Then he spoke if only to verbalize his own thoughts.

"But we got him. Case or no case, this guy threw the broad out the window sure as I'm sitting here. You know it, I know it—" Farber stopped short.

"So . . ." McMahon added, his head was again in his clipboard, his mind re-enacting other murders of other days, other persons, other ways.

"So we ain't got shit," Farber said.

He said it as they passed Lawrence and Western, the neon of Greek restaurants and a different neighborhood.

The house was a two-story frame, an unspectacular building in the middle of the block. They pushed a doorbell twice and the door was opened by a boy of about fifteen wearing blue jeans and a sweatshirt.

"He ain't here," the boy said, but only as Farber walked by him into the living room.

They didn't bother to show badges or explain themselves. They blankly stepped on newspapers and dirty clothes, talked above the television. Farber opened doors, closets, a bathroom, then he walked into a side bedroom.

"You got a search warrant?" the boy yelled behind them.

"You been watchin' too much television, kid," McMahon said.

Farber switched on the light in the bedroom and saw the disheveled bed. He walked over to it and felt the mattress. As he expected, it was warm.

McMahon went into the kitchen.

"C'mon, Gene," he called. He said it as soon as he spotted the open rear door.

The two of them went out into the backyard, Farber into a small aluminum-sided garage. He found the door locked, then headed back into the house to get the keys. He met the kid in the kitchen. The boy was eating from a box of dry cereal.

"I tol' ya he wasn't here," the kid said.

In the rear yard, Farber satisfied himself that the Greek wasn't in the garage. He went out the door and gave a quick check to the alley. As he came around the bushes he heard a noise from a trash barrel. He grabbed at his revolver.

In the alley he saw him. The Greek turned quickly with nothing but a cover to one of the barrels in his hands. He was wearing a pair of pants with the belt loose and the fly open, slippers on his feet, and his pajama top.

"All right, we got ya," Farber said. He released his hold on his pistol and went for the Greek.

The Greek turned and flipped the cover loudly on the barrel.

"You ain't got shit, copper," he said.

The streets were the same, the endless paths of concrete and curbs that started out logically and sanely, but somehow always curved or veered or gave in to dead ends or through-ways that turned toward Broadway, then up to Wilson. It was that way now for Harry, walking with his Jewel shopping bag, walking and thinking, even if the thoughts stumbled and lurched through his mind, thoughts about what he was going to do. He still had some money, around a hundred bucks stashed in different places on his body. It was still the best insulation against the cold and the wind that raked him as he walked. Dough was still the best defense against a wind that would get worse, not better, with November, weather that would turn unforgiving, for at least four more months in Uptown. As he walked, digging with his fingers into the paper sack, he knew very well that, should he and his money become parted, the cold and the chill would become predatory, scraping at the skin on his ankles and the bones over his heart.

But for now the money was enough to get him some food, some coffee, a pillow, and finally, some wine. That took his mind off his body, his aches, the aging which came at him from his stomach and then his nerves. He knew too well what

271

it was like to cough so much that you couldn't hold a cigarette. Those things came, like blizzards that had to be ridden out, yet as he walked down Magnolia, turning onto Wilson, he decided not to fret about what he wasn't feeling now.

He saw Helen at the door, standing there like she had always done, like some kind of statue to women as Harry had always known them, women who took care of things to the point where they ran them, and then they threw you out. Yet, as he felt the bag he was carrying, as he cursed the cold that crept over his collar, he couldn't summon the anger or the resentment or even the sense of betrayal to condemn Helen, or to spit at her in the concrete, or to carry on about what she had done to him only minutes ago. She was family and she did what she had to do. He did what he had to do. He was Harry Lum, and who in hell knew what that meant. He didn't. Not anymore, not with his stomach going on him, and the raps over his head, the scores that had been blown, the weather, the bag in his hand.

He came up on a tavern, an illuminated Hamm's sign, and he turned to go in. Then he stopped, as if someone had touched his arm, his eye taken suddenly by the red newspaper box on the corner. In its window he read the black ink of yesterday's headline. It went simply, "And Counting . . ." and Harry bent down to see that they were referring to the season, the Cubs, another drive gone sour. They were in the last series of the year.

He reached into his pockets for change but had none. From his shirt pocket he took out a dollar bill and walked into the bar. It was quiet and dark, a television going in a corner of the ceiling and the half-dozen barflies watching it and saying nothing.

"Change? What's change?" the bartender said.

"Change for a shot an' a beer," Harry said.

"That's what I thought ya said," the bartender replied.

He set up Harry and Harry downed both glasses standing up, the booze hitting his neck with a slap, then going down.

272

He picked up the change and went out for the newspaper. It was a routine article about the Cubs, how they had lost yesterday and done it before a handful of people on a dreary day. The game meant nothing except that it was slowly coming to an end, another season made for other teams, the Series a far-off phenomenon for other cities, cities with sunshine and green grass instead of wind and cold.

Harry read the article like he read all the others, slowly, turning over the names, figuring the distance the Cubs had fallen behind, eight and a half games out, third place after a great start and promise of taking it all, of bleachers full of squealing, chanting, obnoxious fans, and Harry Lum mugging and yelling and swigging Old Style in the middle of them all.

He read the article like he read them as a kid. There was something about the end of ball season, a feeling that came at no other time but maybe at funerals, as if something genuine had been taken from him, the scoreboard empty, the bleachers cold and useless. He tossed the paper into the trash bin, without reading its inside, and began walking again. Now he walked, at seven o'clock at night on Wilson Avenue, not as a man who would have to fight it out on the streets with his wine and his winos, the cops, muggers, the kids, the rain and the ice, but as Harry Lum, the greatest fan Lon Warneke, old Arkansas Humming Bird, ever had, and as Harry Lum who had been betrayed by a season that was up and ending on him.

"Damn Cubs," he muttered. He went west on Wilson, mouthing all the way the reasons why they'd blown it, the games in Cincinnati, Durocher, the crummy relief pitchers, all the times they'd blown it, talking to himself, scolding, clenching his free hand and slapping it against his leg.

He crossed Wilson and headed for the Liberty Bell. The shot and beer had made him thirsty, growled in the stomach, sent fingers reaching back up his esophagus and into his throat, where they scraped his tongue. There were more

273

men on the street now, wearing the long coats someone had given them, huddling and hunching their shoulders, looking up with faces that looked like the tops of cans that had been ripped open, eyes buried in the sockets, lips that hung and flapped for saliva.

One of them fell away from the wall and came at Harry. He stumbled and lifted his arm, his hand cupped, up toward Harry.

"Hey, buddy . . ." the bum began.

"Ah, lay off," Harry barked and walked past him.

He saw that the bum had taken him for something other than one of them. Maybe it was his walk, his clothes that had been pressed and washed, a fullness to his face that hadn't been there three weeks ago. Whatever it was, whatever made the wino hit him for a dime, Harry took it as a sure signal that he himself wasn't a bum, wasn't a bum ass on the curb, and he rolled the thought over his mind as he crossed another street and headed for his bottle of white port.

He paid for it with another dollar from his shirt pocket. The pint sank into his crotch, his jacket pulled over it, cover for a friend, another bottle that was life when it was there and death when it wasn't.

Out of the store, he scanned the sidewalk and headed for the barren lots of Clifton Street, where he could pour home the port in peace. Then he would think about things, about the night and where he would sleep, but the doubt, the sodden fatalism of a flop escaped him because he had some money, and as long as he had it he could put himself up with something decent, something with toilets that flushed and radiators that worked. Then he would see about things, maybe grab some stones, find Frank Tulka the booster and move some of his stuff, get some tools and punch trunks. He had a bottle and he had his wits, savvy bred on Milwaukee Avenue and smoothed, refined through the years. He was a thief. Harry Lum, a thief, and he knew that counted for something.

274

He walked watching his flanks, checking his rear and the uncertain sidewalk, the vacant no man's land of Clifton and Racine and its mud, cars, the bottles. It was the open spaces that worried him, the shadows, each beam of light that came from cars on the street. Then, feeling one coming on him from the rear, he tightened up, visualizing the money on him and the bottle in his waist. But the car passed, a white Chevy, slowing, and Harry watched as it seemed to linger, now driving toward Montrose and losing its taillights in the dark, but angling toward the curb.

He kept walking, kept eying the car that had stopped now, maybe a hundred yards ahead of him, its lights still on, motor still running. The familiarity of it didn't hit him; he didn't place it or make connections. He just wanted to walk and find his spot where he could sit down out of the wind and pop the cap on his port. He thought of cutting across the lot, but he kept going, nearing the Chevy.

Then he heard its motor come alive and the press of its tires against the pavement. The car swung left and cut across Clifton, baring its side, stopped when it couldn't make the U-turn, reversed, and then with sudden acceleration came toward him. Harry saw nothing but headlights, the bright beams flooding him and blinding him as the car swerved across Clifton into the opposite lane, close to the sidewalk. Shielding his face with his bag, Harry tried to think in seconds whether he should run or hit the ground or what.

The engine came down on him, its groaning, straining roar, until it was only yards away, still with the blinding blaze of light and noise. Then a head poked out of the driver's window, a dark head with hair greasy and glinting in the white and the light. As quick as it appeared it went back inside, but not before Harry saw it and registered the face. The punk dago, Jimmy Del Corso. Harry started to run. He turned and cut into the darkness of the lot, the hidden gullies, the rocks and cables, but he ran with uneven steps on legs that didn't run often or well.

He stumbled as the blast cracked the air. He lost his balance, nearly fell, his arms flailing and the shopping bag flying from his fingers. It was a shot, a pistol crack as definite and cutting in the night as anything he knew. And he felt it, the lash on his left shoulder, the sting first hot then numb, and he reached up with his hand, still running, still awkward and tripping through the muddle of debris beneath his feet. He braced for another, that this was what it was like to die in a field with his back to his enemy and nothing in front of him but darkness and space and darkness. But he didn't hear it, didn't hear a second blast or anything but the boring drone of an engine. He looked back as he ran, and through a vision jumping and wobbly, the brace of the night air pushing through his lungs, and he saw the two crimson taillights traveling away from him, the light and the car, the explosions and the suddenness of Jimmy Del Corso now gone, swallowed by the blankness of the vacant lot and the empty street.

Harry slowed to a stumble, a walk. He saw the forms of buildings on the west side of Racine. He felt his shoulder once again, pulled his hand away and saw that it was smudged with a dark paste. It was wetness from his shoulder. He put his fingers quickly to his mouth and tasted it, blood, the rancid, stinging taste of his own blood. His hand covered his shoulder again, and he walked on, to Montrose and around a corner to a filling station. It was closed, its driveways blocked with parked cars, but in the rear Harry sought out a row of trailers. If it had been winter, with an inch of ice and zero temperatures, he would have had no chance, for the trailers would have been locked to keep out the bums who used them as motel rooms, with newspapers to keep out the cold and walls to piss against. But now they were still open, leaning on their hitches and open, and Harry headed for the biggest one.

With one hand he unlatched the door, leaving blood prints on the handle, and climbed in. It closed behind him, shutting in blackness that engulfed him, and he sat in a corner and began to probe his shoulder. The material of his jacket had been ripped open by the bullet, a crease that lacerated the skin, and because of the burning that now descended into his arm, the sting that came whenever he touched it, he was sure it had hit the bone. Pulling the bottle from his waist, unscrewing the cap with his teeth, he gingerly poured some port into his right hand and patted the wine into the wound. It stung, biting into the shoulder, thinning the blood, wine with wine. And Harry sat there, breathing heavily through his mouth, having been shot at, tracked then escaping and now hiding out, but it was him, Harry Lum, thief, too excited to drink his port, too excited to do anything but dab it on his wound, too excited, and he shook himself and knew, dead certain, that this was nothing but good, his shoulder, that he was once again into something.